WHERE THE SILVER RIVER ENDS

Anna Quon

Invisible Publishing

Halifax & Prince Edward County

Library and Archives Canada Cataloguing in Publication

Title: Where the silver river ends : a novel / Anna Quon.
Names: Quon, Anna, 1968- author.
Identifiers: Canadiana (print) 20210357851 | Canadiana (ebook) 2021035786X | ISBN 9781988784878 (softcover) | ISBN 9781988784915 (HTML)
Classification: LCC PS8633.U65 W44 2022 | DDC C813/.6—dc23

Edited by Stephanie Domet
Cover and interior design by Megan Fildes
Typeset in Laurentian
With thanks to type designer Rod McDonald

Invisible Publishing is committed to protecting our natural environment. As part of our efforts, both the cover and interior of this book are printed on acid-free 100% post-consumer recycled fibres.

Printed and bound in Canada.

Invisible Publishing | Halifax & Prince Edward County
www.invisiblepublishing.com

Published with the generous assistance of the Canada Council for the Arts, the Ontario Arts Council, and the Government of Canada.

To my ancestors. To the future.

Let's pledge—beyond human ties—to be friends,
And meet where the Silver River ends.

Li Bai, translated by Vikram Seth,
from "Drinking Alone with the Moon"

CHAPTER 1

Joan's hand hovered in the air, poised in front of the white-board. She turned to face the serious-looking Hungarian businessmen and women, stolid government clerks, a sole retired professor. The last was the only one who smiled at her. Even though he looked nothing like her father, there was something—the tweed jacket, maybe? Joan began to tremble. What was she doing here, so far from home? And now—she was about to leave again.

Joan turned back to the board to hide her face from her students, who rustled behind her, copying words into their notebooks. "If I had_____I would_____."

If I had known I was leaving, she thought, I would have said goodbye. To whom? To these people? She barely knew them. If I'd said goodbye, I would have trembled like an aspen. If I'd trembled like an aspen, you would have known all it took was a puff of wind to shake me. If you'd known, you might have turned into a puff of wind, a puff of smoke, and followed me like the scent of wine and cigarettes.

The students were silent, waiting. Joan fingered the marker. There was ink on her hands. A couple men glow-ered at her. She heard them thinking, as they rearranged themselves in their seats, that their employers had sent them here to practise English with this Canadian, this ama-teur, and here she stood, awkward as a newborn fawn. The women, their hair frosted and deadened under the over-head fluorescents, rolled their eyes.

Joan put the marker on the ledge. Her voice shaky, she turned to the professor, who was smiling. Expectantly, she thought.

"If I—for example, if I had a million dollars," she said, "I would...?" She nodded to him. He looked amused. "It's from a song," Joan said. "A Canadian song."

There was shuffling and muted comments. The professor spoke, in a clear, sonorous voice.

"If I had a million dollars, I would give a quarter to the church, a quarter to the university, and with the rest I would buy a little boat to sail to the Mediterranean," he said. Joan gazed at him, taken aback by his self-assurance. Someone snorted. The professor looked unperturbed. "Miss Simpson, if I may ask. If you had a million dollars, what would you do?"

Joan had thought about that question the night before, and she had no idea. The class was humming now. She heard the words Mercedes-Benz and Monte Carlo, and giddy laughter from the women. The talk of money had roused the class. The professor still gazed at her, waiting for her answer.

I would go to China, Joan thought. The idea surprised her. I would go to the village where my grandparents lived, open the gate to their house, and knock on their door. Other people lived there now. I would give them a bag of oranges and they would invite me in and offer me tea. I would tell them why I was there. Why would I be there? Joan didn't know. Just to look, maybe...to see the place where the river of her family began. Then she would leave and find a hotel room where she could sleep for a long time, she thought. Eat Chinese takeout, if there was such a thing in China. And watch television, in a language she didn't understand.

"I would go to China," Joan said. "Where my mother's family came from."

The professor nodded, pleased. A woman with long nails that clicked around the glass of tea she always brought to class from the café next door piped up.

"Shanghai?" she asked.

Joan shook her head. "No." But she didn't even know the name of her grandfather's village. Her cheeks burned. She would have to ask her mother. Would she know? These days her mother too had long nails, blond streaks in her hair. She looked like a different person, ever since she and Joan's father, a Yorkshireman who had transplanted himself to Nova Scotia thirty-five years ago for the love of the delicate Chinese Canadian girl Joan's mother had been, had divorced.

When she looked at the professor, Joan felt her father's sharp blue eyes on her. They hadn't always been so critical, but had been made so by the disappointments of life: the bewildering unhappiness of his wife, and his only daughter, Joan's, incomprehensible lack of progress. What would he think of her leaving this job, as she had all her others? Would it be more painful to him to know she had quit work again than to hear what Tibor had done to her that morning? Her father's face creased with both irritation and concern. Joan brushed the thought away. She did not need her parents at this moment. She needed time to gather her thoughts.

Joan's class ignored her and, chatting loudly in Hungarian, was on the verge of chaos. What would Madame B. think? Joan clapped her hands loudly, and they looked at her with vague interest. She mustered her courage.

"Your assignment is to interview a classmate. To ask them what they would do if they had a million dollars, and to write their answers using this phrase." Some of the students turned to one another, confused. The professor stood up and explained in Hungarian what Joan had asked of them. They began to pair off, turning their desks toward one another.

"English, please!" the professor called out pleasantly, but they ignored him. He was the only student left without a partner. He glanced over at Joan, who smiled apologetically.

"I'm sorry...I must..." Joan waved her hand at the desk. Cheerful and undeterred, the professor sat down to interview himself.

What Joan needed, she thought as she pretended to do paperwork at her desk, was to take the train, that very afternoon, from Budapest to Bratislava, far away from Tibor and the unthinkable thing he had done. Bratislava, the capital of neighbouring Slovakia, was cheaper than Vienna, and still comfortably, stolidly, grimly Eastern European. In Canada, she had felt like a misfit, a failure even; here, if she was a misfit, there was a good reason for it—her foreignness was a given, not a source of mystification. It would be the same in Bratislava. Joan had filed the city away in her mind as a possible place to visit, or look for work—or escape to if necessary. And escape was what she needed now.

"Don't worry, Joan," Tibor had said when Joan arrived in Budapest. "You speak English. It is good. But Hungary is my country. I help you." He had called her his friend, and to his social circle, he introduced her as his Canadian sister, his mother's Canadian daughter. Tibor's male acquaintances, thick, unsmiling men, barely seemed to tolerate him, and regarded her with suspicion. Canadian? They thought his mother was dead. The few women he knew, their hair dyed flaming red or bleached like driftwood, their cheeks and noses plastered with makeup to hide the porous, drinker's skin, were openly hostile to her. Only the birdlike Madame B., who owned the small, shabby storefront language school where Joan worked as an English conversation teacher, treated her with something like cordiality.

While her students told one another what they'd do if they came into money, Joan jotted notes about what she must do to leave Budapest behind. The bank—rent money for Tibor. The train station, where she would buy a ticket and store her suitcases. One large and one small, they held all she owned in the world—her clothes and toiletries, a few books, including her orange-covered journal, which she'd kept for years without writing in it. A small photo of her mother and father laughing together before they were married. They looked so young and happy, their eyes shining blindly from the shadows of the pub doorway they were stepping out of.

Joan didn't want anything Tibor had given her, not even the copy of an old photo, in a beautiful silver frame, of the man he thought of as his father, Josef, and his mother, Edna, on their wedding day. In black and white, Edna's dark eyes looked soulful and pensive, and her hand smoothed the front of her dress, as though to brush away what grew inside her belly. Edna had been Joan's dearest friend in Canada before she died. Edna had practically raised her. Joan's eyes blurred.

She brushed her hand over her face, as though she was tired, so the students wouldn't see her expression. But they were too busy grilling one another about their imaginary, new-found wealth, to notice her.

"Don't worry, Joan," Tibor had said. When she'd arrived, exhausted, in Budapest four years earlier, she was grateful to Tibor for finding her a room in a flat not far from his own. She shared it with two working women in their twenties who were rarely home. Tibor had also secured a job for her at the language school owned by Madame B. Unsure how things worked in this new place, unsure of anything, Joan mindlessly accepted everything. She was doing this for Edna, after all. The details hardly mattered.

How easily she'd fallen into the routine of sleeping late each day, heading to the school for afternoon classes, then buying her groceries at several small shops each evening on the way back to her room. Ignoring the bewildering array of experiences a relatively young woman in a foreign city might choose from, she'd holed herself up at night with a radio Tibor had loaned her and books pilfered from the shelves of the language school.

On the weekend sometimes, Tibor would ring the bell to her flat.

"Joan? Come have coffee!" he commanded. Lonely and thankful, she always agreed, but the uneasy feeling she was beholden to someone she barely knew, a man almost twice her age, persisted. Afterward, when she returned to her room, a strange fatigue fell over her, as though she'd undergone rigorous physical exercise, and she would usually take a nap.

Often at these meetings, they would talk about his work— Tibor had a job at the bank as some sort of clerk—and a variety of characters Joan had trouble keeping straight. Like an elder brother, he gave his advice freely.

"Don't walk alone at night in Budapest," he warned. "Don't drink in taverns." She gawked at him. She barely drank alcohol at all and would never have thought to venture into one of the dark, hole-in-the-wall establishments by herself. "Call me if you want to go to the cinema. Do you like your flatmates? Do you miss your parents?" He was insistent on asking questions, but, Joan soon detected, the answers were not so important to him. When he looked at her, he seemed to see someone else looking back at him through her eyes. Edna perhaps? The same way she, when she looked at him, searched his face for any sign of his mother. Edna was always between them, a longing that could not be quenched.

Joan remembered herself. For a few more minutes, she was a language school teacher, in front of her students, in the heart of Budapest. The class had quieted but was now restless, waiting for instructions. Joan forced herself to stand. This was the last time she would teach them. Amid the exclamations, the scoffing, the general excitement roused by imagining what a million dollars could mean, Joan recorded the luxuries and pleasures her students would purchase on the whiteboard. There were bottles of aged whisky and high-priced cars, cruises and spa vacations, homes in the country. The professor maintained his original answer but added, "I would give some money to my children. They are all doing well but perhaps they will help take care of me in my old age." He looked amused at the idea, as though he, a healthy middle-aged man with an esteemed position at the university, might never grow old.

Joan looked at her watch. It was time to say goodbye. She told them she would be leaving Budapest and that this would be her last class with them. They looked at her with mild curiosity; the professor, with disappointment and concern. While the other students filed out, still buoyant with the idea of money, he hung back. Joan gathered her things.

"Where will you go?" he asked.

Joan shrugged. Suddenly, Bratislava seemed very far away.

He put out his hand to shake hers.

"Thank you for the English lessons," he said. Yes, his eyes were the same blue as her father's—her father, who was at this moment, she imagined, in flight above Mexico or Central America, the jet that carried him slipping a bank of cloud into the sky's eternal sea.

Joan's suitcases made a smooth rolling noise down the darkened hall to Madame B.'s office. She knew she would have to wait—Madame B. ran the school by herself and was always buried in paperwork. Joan sat in the outer office, on the high-backed, maroon benches where she had waited so many times for her paycheque. Madame B., on the phone, waved her thin hand at Joan through the window that separated them. Though she was only in her forties, small, bony, and elegantly coiffed, Madame B.'s thin shoulders bowed with osteoporosis—or maybe it was simply the job that had made her old before her time.

Joan leaned back into the seat, trying to think what she would say. When she'd woken up this morning she'd had no idea she'd be leaving the country. But if, when she first moved to Tibor's flat from her bed-sitting room, she'd known what would happen, she would have fled Budapest then instead. She would have avoided this complicated grief at losing someone she once thought might be like family. Like home.

Three weeks earlier, Tibor had offered her refuge. The bedsit he'd initially helped her find, where she shared a one-burner hot plate and a bathroom with a dour waitress and an icy but impeccably clean shop clerk, was adequate— until the landlord evicted them in order to rent out the place to tourists. The waitress screamed in the landlord's face that she wasn't going anywhere, but the shop clerk poured red paint all over the bathroom, clogging the sink and rendering the toilet unusable. Joan, anxiety fluttering in her throat like a bird, quickly pulled together her two suitcases and left for Tibor's.

Though she'd lived only a kilometre away from him for almost four years, Joan felt awkward at first. Tibor was exuberant to have Joan as his roommate and insisted on treating her like a guest, refusing to let her wash dishes or do other chores. She realized he was lonely, living for so many years as a bachelor. He'd never married, perhaps because he spent a lot of time helping his father, Josef, on his farm, or perhaps because of Josef's bitterness about his own marriage, which had ended when Edna left him and Tibor, still a toddler, without a word in the middle of the night so long ago. Though Tibor harboured no ill will toward his mother—she remained a dreamy, romantic figure in his mind—he had probably been left marriage-shy by his upbringing, without even knowing it.

Joan shifted in her seat. Madame B. languidly waved her pen as she listened to the person on the other end of the phone—or perhaps now she was on hold? She rolled her eyes at Joan as though her conversation partner was droning on too long.

Joan liked Tibor well enough—at least, she had convinced herself that she did—and the warmth with which he welcomed her to live in his flat was almost alarming. Some evenings, when she would've liked to retire to her bedroom, he insisted on hearing the same stories again and again of her growing up near Edna, the teenage mother who'd abandoned him and fled Hungary.

"I remember her," he said, nodding dreamily, his thick fingers crooked around the stem of a wineglass. "Curly dark hair."

Joan found herself slipping inside Tibor's head as he pictured a young Edna turning slightly to scoop her purse off the table by the farmhouse door of the main room, Josef snoring in their makeshift bed by the fireplace. A dark-eyed toddler in his crib, he watched her leave; Edna turned her whole rosy-cheeked face toward him, smiling lovingly as she said goodbye. But Joan always believed Edna had left in a hurry, never looking back.

The Edna Joan loved had been fierce, stout, and buxom, and yet coquettish as a schoolgirl. For twenty years, she'd lived with and kept house for the Jamiesons, an elderly couple whose bungalow stood next to the one owned by Joan's family in Dartmouth, Nova Scotia. Edna was also Joan's after-school caregiver for many years, practically raising her while both Joan's parents worked. Master of the kitchen, a staunch but earthy Catholic, Edna was feared and yet dismissed by her Anglo-Protestant neighbours—and lonely. How lonely she must have been, Joan thought. Edna had no friends besides Joan's own mother, who was half Edna's age and would visit Edna when she was bored, or when she wanted to smoke and drink Edna's gin, which was stashed under the kitchen sink at the Jamiesons' bungalow. Their house was a muted, stifling place but nevertheless the setting of many of Joan's happiest memories.

Edna was the reason Joan had come to Budapest. She was the only person Joan missed, with a burning in her throat as though she had drunk something hard. Edna, who had left her the letter to give to Josef, the husband she had abandoned sixty years ago.

"How are you, Joan?"

Madame B. stood in the door of her office, her puffy lipsticked lips pulled into a smile to greet Joan. She regarded the suitcases with interest. "Are you going away for the weekend?" she asked, her voice high-pitched and nasal, as she ushered Joan to the seat facing her desk.

"No, I—I'm sorry, Madame," Joan said, "but I will not be able to teach here any longer. I have had…an emergency and will need to leave Budapest this evening."

Behind her glasses, Madame's heavily made-up eyes narrowed. Joan felt a pang. She had always felt there was something real behind Madame's elaborate and showy formality. But now she was shut out. Madame nodded coolly.

"I am sorry to put you in this difficult position. I really must leave Budapest."

Joan realized she must sound secretive and suspect, but she didn't have the will or energy to make up a death in the family or love affair gone wrong. Madame B., softening, seemed to imagine it for her.

"You are young," she said, with an exaggerated sigh. Joan didn't feel young—she was in her mid-thirties—but she lowered her eyes. "Among the young, drama and crises are something absolutely normal. Thank you," Madame said, holding her head high and her bony hand out to take Joan's. "I wish you well. Where will you go?"

Joan knew she could say any city in the world and it wouldn't matter. Madame's eyes had already shifted to the pile of papers on her desk. Joan wasn't about to tell her or anyone connected to Tibor that she was headed to Bratislava. Slovakia was a country she knew little about, but one she had a tenuous connection to through her mother's boyfriend, David Song. His first wife had been a fierce Slovak woman, as out of place in Dartmouth as Edna had been. The Danube ran through Bratislava as it did Budapest, and that was somehow comforting to Joan. Maybe there would be the same wild swans, or their cousins, floating by in the rose-coloured evening there.

"I am going north," Joan said. Madame B.'s eyebrows arched. Joan knew it was not the usual thing to say, but she also knew Madame, with all her experience of foreign teachers, had developed a tolerance, indulgent and almost motherly, of the vagaries of North American young people. Even the older ones, she had once told Joan at the staff Christmas party, her lips loosened slightly by the festive punch—even the rarer middle-aged and senior citizens— had a childish impetuousness about them. North? That could mean a thousand different things. Perhaps, Joan thought, Madame B. would take it as Joan meant it—a way of saying she should not ask.

Madame B. was the one person in Budapest she considered anything like a friend, now that Tibor was not one. Joan was desperate not to lose her last tie to this place. It was as though she needed one friendly face to say goodbye to, so it wouldn't feel like she was only fleeing this city. Edna had started here, among these cobblestones. Joan didn't want to leave without knowing she could come back.

Madame B.'s smile softened. Joan's relief and gratitude flooded through her and she heard her own heart beating against her chest.

"Safe travels," Madame sang in her nasal soprano, which to Joan, in that moment, carried with it hope and a kind of magical promise.

Joan took her bags to the station. Next to the lockers was a place to leave luggage behind a counter, where a man with slicked-back black hair was arguing with a woman in a sweater and flimsy summer dress over bags she had supposedly left but had lost the ticket for.

"My whole life is in there!" the woman wailed in Hungarian, tottering on her red high-heeled sandals.

The man said a few curt words to her.

"Fattyú!" she spat at him. Bastard.

Joan, stashing her things in a locker with a grimy and battered metal door, felt as though she'd been stung by a bee. How recently she had said that very word to Tibor. The man barked viciously back, as the woman sniffed, her nose in the air, and turned on her heel, pulling a small, flowered suitcase on wheels behind her. Joan imagined its larger sister, waiting forlornly in the room behind the counter. A life abandoned.

Joan headed for the bank. The teller, a man in his fifties, was a colleague of Tibor's. He nodded to Joan in recognition when she asked to withdraw the equivalent of a week's rent, then added, "I would like to withdraw the balance in Slovak koruny and American dollars." American money was good everywhere, and Joan did not know how long she would stay in Bratislava.

The teller leered at her. "Give my greetings to Tibor," he said in Hungarian, pushing the bills toward her under the glass. His teeth were like baby teeth, with large spaces between each one. She took the money, stiffly and without saying a word, and left. She felt his eyes on her as she pushed open the heavy, ornate door of the bank and let it close smoothly behind her.

Joan walked back to Tibor's flat along the river, where the shadows of the trees lengthened and deepened. The very last cricket of long-gone summer creaked somewhere among the tall, ornamental grass. It was October, harvest time, Halloween. She thought about stopping, of simply blending into the shadows so she could escape the eyes of passersby. It was the kind of thought she hadn't had for many months. She brushed it aside and walked more quickly, her stiff-soled flats clicking on the Danube promenade's stone surface.

It was in this same river that Tibor had scattered Edna's ashes from the bridge near his flat when he brought them home from Canada. And so, just as she had once left Budapest by river, so many years ago, Edna had left again, running down to the sea. Now it was Joan's turn. When she got to Bratislava, she would be upriver from that bridge. Edna would not be there, mingling with the water, clinging to the stones like chimney soot or car exhaust. But the Danube, Joan realized, would always be a path back to the city that held Edna at birth, and again at death, like a still-beating heart.

Joan wanted to hang on to that thought. She stopped, gazing blindly across the river's wide expanse. The last time she had left Budapest was only a couple weeks previous. Not long after Joan decided to stay with Tibor, he insisted on taking her in his dusty old beater of a car to visit his father in the country. Joan had last seen Josef when she first arrived from Canada, bewildered with grief over Edna's death; the day she had placed Edna's letter in his hands, the letter Edna had written when she was beginning to lose her faculties, some time before she died—the letter that explained why she had abandoned her husband and baby son so many years before, and asked for forgiveness. Edna had waited till she was gone, till Joan could not refuse the letter and the money the envelope contained, to ask Joan from beyond the grave to travel to Hungary to deliver this missive to Tibor's father. She waited, Joan knew, till Josef would not be able to respond to her, to refuse her apology, to renounce the love he'd once had for her and throw it in her face. Edna was fierce and Edna was brave, but she was not brave or fierce enough to face that. Joan had been happy for a second trip out of the city. In Tibor's rickety Trabant, they left the cobblestoned centre of Budapest, past dwindling high-rises and small shops, and spent twenty minutes on the highway. It seemed to Joan, clutching the edge of her seat, that the car would fall apart each time Tibor shifted gears. Finally he took an exit that circled around a grove of tall and slender poplars into bare fields. Birds trilled; blond grasses at the edge of the ditch that lined the highway rustled in the breeze. Tibor, who had almost been shouting in distracted English and Hungarian above the sound of the engine all the way from the centre of Budapest, quieted. His pale blue eyes took on a faraway look, and Joan relaxed into her seat, gazing out at the huge electrical towers that crossed the fields, connected to each other by wires that dipped and swooped.

Josef raised his hand to greet them at the door. He had become a knitting needle of a man. Sitting at the kitchen table in the dusty farmhouse, he kept his hands wrapped around a mug of tea while Tibor, animated by an energy Joan assumed to be love, kept up the little conversation between the three of them. Josef, stiff, grey stubble outlining his gaunt cheeks, stared at Joan from under wild eyebrows. She was Edna's friend, after all, party to his dead wife's treachery and anguish, shame and defiance, and the terrible knowledge of why Edna had left him. Joan wasn't sure if she read in Josef's weathered face outrage, a flicker of sadness, or a plea for forgiveness. It seemed the shadow of all three passed in succession over his features. Eventually, he turned away and she glimpsed the fine cheekbones and aquiline profile of the young man he had been when Edna knew him, so different from Tibor's blunted thickness.

On the way home from the farm, Tibor was quiet. Joan, saved by the loudness of the engine, did not feel she had to make conversation, and almost fell asleep. When they reached the lane beside Tibor's flat, she was roused by the car coming to a halt and the sudden silence. Against the tick of the cooling engine, Tibor said only, "My father is old." He held the car keys limply in his lap. As he got out of the car, slowly pushing himself upright from sitting with the help of the door frame, Joan noticed his bent back and realized that Tibor too was passing out of middle age into that crumbling space before decrepitude.

Josef died in his sleep two days after their visit. Perhaps, Joan thought painfully, it was too much for Josef to hear that the bearer of Edna's fateful letter (which had simultaneously destroyed his world and made sense of it) had moved into Tibor's flat. She was, Joan imagined, too close, too familiar, too agonizing. Did Josef fear she would tell Tibor about the letter? Writing in Hungarian in a spidery hand, Edna had pleaded, accused, and confessed. Joan thought it must have shattered the bitter shell around Josef's heart to hear Edna say Tibor was not his son. That Josef's own father had raped Edna in a haze of drunkenness, as she lay, stunned into silence, in the same bedroom where Josef's sisters slept. Four years ago, sitting at his kitchen table while Tibor excused himself to the outhouse, Josef had briefly crumpled under the news. As far as she knew, Josef had never told Tibor about the letter and Joan did not feel it was a story Edna would want her to share with her only son.

After Josef died, Tibor sat in his kitchen and drank for three days. His brow was heavy and dark. The empty bottles, smudged and dusty-looking, gathered beside the sink. He didn't seem to notice when Joan came and went. Sometimes he would sleep, his head on his arms, and sometimes when she thought he was asleep he would shout suddenly, a single word that disintegrated into a slurry of mumbling, sobs, then snores. The smell was terrible.

Joan took a deep breath and began to walk again along the Danube. The river too smelled today, faintly, of something unpleasant. Joan had been preparing herself since morning to return to the flat, but what would she find when she arrived? Tibor had been on the floor when she'd left for school, still drunk and sobbing, while she made coffee and gathered her things.

She paused again at the last familiar riverside bench, only a few hundred metres from the flat. The clouds had strung themselves across the sky like a white caravan crossing a blue desert. A cool breeze skittered over the silvery surface of the river. The Danube was a working river, with barges and garbage scows alongside yachts and commercial cruising vessels, all silhouetted against the water. They were small compared to the broad span of the river, but something about their presence felt ominous—they were like sunspots, patches of skin that darkened and would not heal.

Somewhere in him, Tibor must know about the secret in Edna's letter. In his drunken grief he had called out to Josef to forgive him for...what?

Joan shifted uncomfortably on the bench.

There was one regrettable moment in which she let down her guard. When she'd heard Tibor cry out, her heart beat fast, with a kind of recognition, and a river undammed inside her. Finally, she'd found the node of affection for Tibor she could pin, cautiously, to her own heart. The compassion she felt for Tibor in that moment was born of a shared feeling that they'd both been disappointments to their fathers.

Joan cringed. She'd wished she could share with Tibor that she understood him better now. He had been defeated by Josef's death. It was as though he'd turned his pockets inside out and found them empty. His eyes were mournful and beseeching, his mouth frowned sloppily, he stumbled when he walked, even when he was sober. But she was also on the alert. Something was ticking inside her, and it told her of coming catastrophe.

After three days of drinking, Tibor did not touch alcohol for a long, dry week, and things seemed to return to almost normal. Despite her aversion to domesticity, she bought flowers from the grocery store and stuck them in a jar on the kitchen table. When Tibor came home that evening he didn't seem to notice them, but the next morning the jar was moved to a table by a window in the living room, whether so they could have more sunlight or to get them out of the way, Joan didn't know. She baked an apple custard cake, something she knew Tibor liked. When she put a slice on a plate with a fork and set it in front of him, he stared at it and then at her. Joan crumbled. She sat down across the table from him.

"I am so sorry you lost your father, Tibor," she said. His face had a grey pallor and she thought he might faint, but instead his hand shot out to hold hers. Startled, and without even thinking, she withdrew it.

She could forgive him. It was an awkward moment, to be sure, but she knew it was a mistake, that he regretted it. But Tibor began to drink again in the evenings, and barely spoke to her. She could see him struggling again, but this time he did not cry out or even mumble drunkenly. He was quiet, as though steeling his resolve. When he finished drinking for the evening, he lurched to his bed without even removing his shoes, which clumped leadenly over the hall tiles. Joan sat in her own bed, her lesson planner on her lap, listening. She got the feeling that he was lying in bed, listening for her at the same time.

Joan stood up. There were more people on the promenade, hurrying home from work. She pulled her fleece up around her neck. Summer had stretched itself as far as it could but autumn was demanding its due. Joan began walking the last few hundred metres to the flat, the thing she had tried to avoid thinking of rising in her consciousness like a loaf of bread.

That morning, Joan had woken gradually to the sun already sitting, squat and toadlike, on her bedroom floor. What time was it? Her watch said ten. There was no sound from Tibor's room, so he too must have slept in. He was taking a long weekend to go to the farm again, where there was much to be done before he could sell it. Joan knew he was dreading the sale. He had grown up there, and no doubt the farm held many memories both joyful and painful. Tibor had asked Joan to go with him, but thankfully she had her afternoons at the language school as an excuse not to.

She pulled her father's old cardigan around her. She would make coffee, and what kind of breakfast for Tibor's hangover? She couldn't remember, and an old anxiety crept over her.

Tibor was sitting at the kitchen table already, in his underwear, a wine bottle half empty in one hand. It was too late for her to back into her room. He looked up at her with glassy eyes.

"Come, sit," he said, his voice thick and smelling harshly of drink.

Joan's heart sank. Tibor grinned sloppily at her and tried to get up.

"I make breakfast," he said, leaning on his knuckles on the table and walking himself sideways toward the stove. She was reminded of a great ape, and giggled nervously. It sounded more like a hiccup. Encouraged, Tibor grabbed a spatula and began waving it around. He cracked eggs into the cold frying pan and swished them, glancing over at Joan and grinning. Joan tried to smile back. Tibor had forgotten to light the gas.

When he realized a minute later, he began to laugh and cough, clutching his stomach as though to hold in his intestines. Joan couldn't help it. Pity and disgust were all she felt. He made a show of turning on the element, and the blue flame, like a halo, circled the ring under the pan.

Joan wanted coffee. She smelled it from the next flat over, but the coffee pot on the stove was cold. But she wasn't desperate enough to approach Tibor. Instead, she pulled the breadboard across the table, where she sat and began to carefully cut thin slices of rye bread off a dark loaf. It seemed dusty, Joan thought, and a slice of onion clung to the knife, but she was determined to brush it off as normal. Normal to wake up on a Thursday to find your housemate drunk and half dressed. Normal to feel a shadow come over you in the middle of a sunny morning.

The eggs were burning. Tibor was trying to arrange paper napkins on a tray. Joan felt panic rise in her.

"Tibor," she finally said. When he was sober, Tibor had a feminine touch when it came to domestic matters, but drunk, his hands seemed big and clumsy. He swore volubly and attempted to recover.

"Eggs," he remarked. She nodded. He divided the browned mass onto two plates, set one down, and brought the second to her end of the table with a flourish.

"Thank you," she said.

He squeezed her shoulders and gave her a sloppy kiss on the cheek. She ducked her head slightly. He nuzzled her neck with his nose, then squeezed her breasts.

Joan froze for a matter of seconds. His hands were dry and warm, and it almost felt like he was shining apples against her shirt, but his breath was hot. She lurched sideways. Her chair tipped over. Tibor stumbled backward and sat down heavily on the floor, his head bouncing off a wooden chest. Edna's, Joan remembered. He gazed around, eyes unfocused.

Joan leaned against the table, breathing hard, as though she had been running. Rigid with anger.

"Bastard," she said quietly. He didn't seem to hear. Louder this time. "Fattyú."

He turned his head and put up a hand as though to shield himself from a blow.

It was the first time she had used that word, one she

heard on the streets among the young and aimless, drunks, and Tibor's friends. She regretted its black and venomous power, but at least it was out of her and couldn't poison her. Tibor scrunched his eyes closed and began to wail, both hands over his ears.

Joan felt Edna watching her. Pitying her. She trembled with anger, but a weak feeling overcame her. To prevent herself from crying, she moved to the stove and began to open cupboard doors and bang them shut again, making a pot of coffee. Tibor was lying on his side on the floor, sobbing quietly. When it was ready, she put a cup of coffee on the floor next to his head, and sat at the kitchen table for a minute, watching him to make sure he would not try anything else. She knew she would leave that day for Bratislava, a city merely a couple hundred kilometres but a whole country away, an escape hatch she'd held somewhere in her mind, ever since she had arrived in Hungary and felt the uncomfortable weight of Tibor's friendship bear down on her. Bratislava. Relief flooded through her, a river as wide as the Danube.

As Joan approached Tibor's flat, a little knot of anxiety tightened in her stomach—but she no longer needed to suck on cough drops until they numbed her tongue, her whole head, and calmed the fluttering inside her. She'd found a way to cup it in her hands, to contain and soothe it. That was what moving halfway around the world had done. She could ignore the knot, at least for the moment.

The gate to the flat swung open on rusty hinges. Tibor was home, Joan could tell. The flat was dark, but the radio played in the living room, on the other side of the door. She put her key in the lock, but it too swung open with the pressure. As if every pretense of a separation between inside and out had been discarded.

Tibor sat on the chesterfield. Pale, dishevelled, grey stubble covering his chin, still half drunk. Joan thought he must have been drinking all day. He didn't look up at her until she stepped into the flat, leaving the door ajar, and even then he didn't seem to recognize her.

"Goodbye," Joan said. Her hand raised in farewell, this was a moment she had anticipated since leaving the flat earlier that day. "I am leaving the key here. I will not be back." She spoke loudly, deliberately, as she placed the rent money on the table with the key on top of it.

Tibor blinked slowly, trying to focus, but it was no use.

Joan closed the door behind her, deflated. She had wanted him to say something so she could spit out her anger and disgust, but instead she felt only a demoralizing pity. Shame. Why had she returned? She had needed to see his face, to fix in her mind what she was leaving. And, cruel though it was, for him to know that, like Edna, she was abandoning him.

Walking slowly back to the station, Joan only looked over her shoulder twice to make sure he wasn't following her. She didn't expect him to, but it was almost an obligation to imagine he might.

She bought a limp sandwich at the canteen and a bottled soft drink, swallowing them down as she sat on a bench in the dim light, waiting for the train. Eating felt like a necessity after a day without food, but one she could barely tolerate.

Tibor would be sobering up by now. Sitting at the kitchen table, shoulders hunched, nursing a mug of coffee. He would run his hands both ways through his unwashed hair. Eventually it would dawn on him that she had gone. His stomach would ache for what he'd done. Regret, shame, and bitter disappointment. She felt it as though it were her own. Perhaps it was her own.

The train would be here soon. On her way to the locker, Joan realized the city hadn't exactly been a home to her. She felt like a tadpole in a bucket of pond water, waiting to be carried somewhere else. But it had been a container for her grieving over many things: Edna's death, her parents' breakup, her life as yet undefined.

There was a note taped to the locker that held Joan's bags. The page of a notebook. Could Tibor have known somehow? She felt her heart beat against the roof of her mouth. But no, it was some sort of student art project, she realized. The note was in English and read like one of her classroom exercises—a fill-in-the-blank.

"When the train leaves, I leave behind..." There were instructions at the bottom of the paper. She was supposed to write something, to start a list that other people would add to.

I leave behind... Joan wasn't exactly sure what or who, besides Tibor. And yet. She felt the mute tug of a child's hand and dark eyes looking up at her from a pale face. Whose child? Not hers. Joan didn't know what to make of this thought. She filed it away in the mental box where she kept other impenetrable notions and visions that came to her.

Joan stood on the platform as the train pulled up and weary commuters began to get on. It was four or five hours to Bratislava by train, not far. Joan arranged her bags in an empty compartment and stood in the train's narrow passageway, leaning against the sill of the open window. When the train began to move, the still air started to brush past her like an animal, slow to rouse. Soon, though, the cool wind whipped her hair across her face as she flew past dark trees and power lines, stars slowly rising from the glow of the horizon.

How strange it was that she, a hapless Canadian, was on a train rushing through the dark countryside of a foreign land to yet another place she knew almost nothing about. How had she arrived at this moment? It was as though luck were a magical wind that blew her from one corner to the next, good, bad, or indifferent. Mostly good—or for good. Even Tibor, as awful a connection as he had proved to be, had pushed her to the next point in her journey. Joan pulled her hand over her forehead as though to wipe away his memory.

Her life was organized by small coincidences, which, like the gears of a watch, were all turning together to move her forward to wherever she was supposed to go to next. Was everyone's life like this? Joan didn't know. Some certainly struggled more than others. Edna, for example, who worked hard her whole life and then died alone at a nursing home. It seared Joan's heart. Joan had ardently wished Edna was her own mother, instead of the distracted, dissatisfied Gillian, but Edna had struggled as long as Joan had known her, for money, for acceptance, and with her secrets.

Still, Edna represented happiness and plenty. As the train sped away from Budapest, Joan felt a longing for Edna, who had strutted to church with a long peacock feather in her cap, made mountains of poppyseed cake, and sewed Joan dresses made from pretty cotton prints covered in flowers and cherries and birds. Edna, who greeted her after school with a soft, powdery kiss on each cheek, and sat her down at the kitchen table for a tall glass of milk and whatever cake she had recently baked. Edna, who dabbed at her eyes after watching a particularly stunning episode of *General Hospital*, and gathered Joan into her deep bosom when she fell on the concrete walk and skinned her knees. Edna, who had stars in her eyes when Ricky brought the paper to the Jamiesons' door.

"You like?" she asked sixteen-year-old Joan, who flushed with annoyance and mortification. "Ricky's teeth are perfect. His smile is perfect. He look like movie star!" Edna dreamily opined. "Next time, you go to door. Give him poppyseed cake." She was forever trying to push her young paperboy and her young friend toward one another.

Ricky must have struggled too, Joan thought. He'd gone from skipping school and smoking pot to running his own business. Now he was a reliable friend, left behind, though he was in Dartmouth, while Joan continued to drift like seaweed in the current of other people's lives. The thing that made the difference, she thought with some shame, was money. Her parents, comfortably middle class, had not let her go hungry or homeless. Money was the grease that oiled the gears of the watch of her life, that allowed her to wander without much direction or thought. And it was Edna's money, hard-earned and saved, that had brought her to Budapest in the first place.

But now Joan had chosen something else, a destination her old friend had not intended for her. Bratislava, a convenient way station en route to—where? It was a whole other country. A whole new language—but English was her currency, good in almost any country. Joan knew she was lucky to have been born with English in her mouth, a proverbial silver spoon. She might not make a doctor's salary, but people needed what she had to offer. Lawyers, businesspeople, students, and teachers had a thirst that could not be quenched. It didn't seem to matter that she didn't have a university degree. That, in fact, she was not as well educated as some of her students' teenage sons and daughters. She spoke slowly and clearly, with a barely discernible accent, and knew proper grammar, even if she didn't always know why it was correct. That was enough to be an English conversation teacher, even though conversation had never been her personal forte.

Joan spoke into the dark rush of wind past her face, releasing all the Hungarian she knew. The words slipped away as though carried by a current, back in the direction from which she'd come. From now on it would be Slovak, a mildly enemy language to Tibor's Hungarian friends. They had told her how the Hungarians who visited Slovakia were treated as second-class citizens, regarded with suspicion, veiled hostility, and outright contempt. Some had been beaten.

"As if we were no better than Cigányok," one woman with quivering jowls had sputtered. "Gypsies," Joan had learned over her four years in Hungary, was a derogatory term for Roma people, one that she, like most people she'd known in Canada, had used without knowing. Were the Roma so despised that even Tibor's ragged band of "friends" looked down upon them?

As if on cue, a Romani mother with a baby brushed past Joan on the train—hips swaying, peaceful and relaxed, as though she were strolling in a garden. Joan caught a whiff of her own foreignness. It was she who was the intruder here, the stilted stranger, but the Romani woman had not guarded herself or her child. She had walked by her as if Joan were not even there, though her jeans brushed Joan's leg and the charms on her gold bracelet, tinkling softly as she passed, seemed meant to announce her presence to the world.

A few young Slovaks who had clearly been drinking boarded the train with a German shepherd at one of the small-town stops. Joan retreated to the cabin where her suitcases sat and shut the door. There was no escape route now, and her breath fluttered in her chest. She could hear loud voices, but it was not long before they quieted, and Joan thought they must have fallen asleep. She felt herself nodding off, but jerked awake as the train's brakes squealed at the next town. When the train started moving again, she heard the call for the next stop, in the conductor's bored-sounding voice: "Bratislava."

Joan stood up, unbalanced. Her luggage steadied her. She headed down the narrow passageway, swaying uncertainly with the train's motion. A couple cabins away, the young Slovak men were sprawled asleep, while the German shepherd, its dirty coat uncared for and its large head and ears perked attentively, peered at her. There were food wrappers and bottles scattered across the floor and seats, and the young men were arranged haphazardly, their scrawny limbs flung everywhere, their faces grey and open-mouthed.

A couple people disembarked the train before Joan. The Roma woman and her baby were nowhere to be seen. Perhaps they'd gotten off at a previous stop, Joan thought. She hoped so, and that the drunken young men had not seen them before they fell asleep. Joan had been careful in Budapest not to be out alone in the dark. Here too, in yet another strange city, she felt a jagged danger.

She hesitated before descending the steps to the platform. Though anchored for the moment by her luggage, Joan felt a dizzying sensation, like she was spiralling downward into the watery depths of a river she could not name.

CHAPTER 2

Joan pushed her wheeled suitcases before her down the steps, the smaller balanced on top of the larger. There was a steep drop to the ground from the last stair and she nearly fell. In the dark on the platform, someone laughed gruffly and seemed to curse her in a sing-song rhyme she did not understand. A drunk man, his jacket swaying as he lurched forward. Joan's heart beat fast, but he kept going, his legs barely holding him upright.

Joan's suitcase wheels rasped behind her. She moved tentatively along the platform, unsure of her footing and of where she would go to spend the night. And she was hungry, her stomach like a sea anemone, opening and closing to grasp something that wasn't there.

A young man leaned in the shadow of the station, tall and thin with hair as black and slick as oil. Joan stiffened, then forced herself to slow down. He gestured to her with an open palm. A gold chain hung on his thin wrist. Roma, Joan thought.

"Speak English?" he asked. Joan nodded. He had a toothy grin that, nevertheless, she thought, looked calculated. "You need hotel tonight?" Joan hesitated, then nodded once. "I know one. Not dear. Also clean. Come."

He began to walk away. Joan stood rooted to the spot. He sighed an exaggerated sigh.

"Here is brochure," he said, pulling a rumpled pamphlet from his pocket. Clearly he had only one. He made sure he held it when she put out her hand to look at it. Hotel Svatopluk, it said. There was a garish colour photo of a tan stucco building with baroque decoration, window boxes of red geraniums, in front of which Slovak folk dancers danced, apparently joyfully, in traditional costume.

Joan waved him off. "No, thank you," she said.

The young man's face fell. "Please," he said. "My brothers and sisters have had nothing to eat today."

Joan peered at him. His face was so perfectly sad that she almost smiled at his skilful act. Then he turned toward her and she was startled to notice a little scar at the corner of his mouth, which gave the left corner of his lips a permanent downward turn.

"Where is the hotel?" she asked.

He brightened. "Come," he said, waving her forward. His legs were long and he walked quickly. "It is not far."

Joan was breathing hard and she felt shin splints forming. "What's your name?" she called out, to make him stop.

He turned and when he saw her twenty feet behind him, out of breath, he strode back to her. "My name is Milan." He hesitated, then added, "Milan Holub."

Joan felt surprised and grateful. To give your full name to a stranger was a powerful thing. She wanted to trust him. And yet... "My name is Jenny," she said. "I am from Canada."

"My sister's English name is Jenny!" he said, and straightened. "She works for tourism. She is travel agent. In America. She helped me get this job!"

Smiling incredulously, Joan shook her head, as if to say, What a wonder!

Milan offered his hand to take her suitcases. Joan pulled back, involuntarily.

"Sorry," Milan said, and shrugged. "Come." He gestured ahead of him. "Just to the corner." And Joan saw the tan-coloured stucco building, and imagined the remnants of geraniums in its window boxes, straight ahead of them in the dark.

Joan allowed Milan to drag her suitcases up the few stone steps, wheels clattering loudly. He buzzed the intercom and was greeted on the other end by a sleepy voice. The door opened slightly. Milan pushed against it, and they entered a dimly lit passageway with a dark wooden counter backed by an office. An old woman wearing a house dress, her hair piled on her head in a bun, shuffled toward them, paperwork in hand.

"Dobrý vecêčer, Pani," he said, sweeping his hand toward Joan. This is Jenny, she imagined him saying. She is from Canada. She'd like a room, if you please.

The old woman, her face haughty and bored, fingered the paperwork.

"For how long do you want the room?" Milan asked.

Joan shrugged and shook her head, noticing the old woman's impatience. "One night?" she asked.

"If you take the room for two or three nights, it is cheaper," he said, adding in a confidential tone, "And you make the pani very happy." The woman looked at him, her brow knitted in anger. Milan smiled ingratiatingly at her.

"Two nights then," Joan conceded. "How much?"

Milan radiated glee. When the old woman shook her fingers at him, indicating how many koruny it would be, he shook his head and spoke softly, almost in a purr.

The woman was clearly accustomed to this. She listened and nodded but her face remained grim.

"Nie," she said, when he proposed a number.

His gestures grew more animated but his voice became even more soothing and reasonable. Finally, almost in disgust, the woman waved her hand at him and nodded. He beamed at her, his teeth flashing white in the lamplight.

Milan dragged Joan's bags behind him up the concrete staircase. It had been a grand hotel at some point in history, but now it was shadowy and dilapidated, only dimly lit by a few sconces. Milan nodded to a couple of the doors, which each opened a crack at the sound of his voice.

"Pán Štubûňa, ako sa máte?" he asked respectfully, nodding to the left. "Pani Duliková, dobrý večer."

Joan saw a sliver of each ghostly face, a white nose, straggly silver hair, before the doors closed with a creak. She imagined dusty little apartments, each containing a sole, aging occupant. She thought of the nursing home where Edna had lived her last days, confused and alone. Joan felt her cheeks warm and tears sprout, but she wiped them away with the back of her hand.

"And here," Milan said, stopping in front of a set of double doors, "is your room."

He thrust a large key in the lock and rattled, pushing with his shoulder against the door. It opened into a space so dark there were no distinguishing features, until Milan flipped a switch and six dusty wall sconces at shoulder height sprang to light. Joan looked around and saw a red upholstered divan and other Victorian parlour furniture.

"Mrs. Watterson's room," he said, in a regretful tone. Joan was confused for a moment. Did someone else live here? "Englishwoman. Very proper, very kind. She died two years past."

Milan fingered the fringe of a standing lampshade. "She taught me English. In exchange for I read to her. She was almost blind for one year. I read to her Dickens. And poetry." He shook his head. "We studied Dickens in school. The Communists liked him. I knew the stories... but poetry...Shakespeare!" he whistled. "I don't know why English must be so difficult," he said, eyebrows knit together. "If it is the language of all the world, it must be simpler."

Milan wiped the hair out of his eyes. Joan had taken him to be about twenty because he was so tall, but now she thought it more likely he was only seventeen or eighteen.

Milan went around the room pointing out its features. Joan glimpsed a narrow bed with a corner of the sheet neatly turned down. It reassured her. Milan opened a small cupboard.

"Here is blanket, here is for your clothes-es," he said.

Joan's lips twitched. She had become accustomed to the mix of fairly sophisticated grammatical constructions and humorous mistakes that Eastern European speakers, trained using British textbooks, took as standard English, but it never failed to amuse her.

"The WC," Milan said of an open door. Suddenly Joan realized she hadn't been inside one for a very long time.

"I leave you now," Milan said with a bow. Joan felt half disappointed and half relieved. "But I will see you tomorrow," he added brightly. Tomorrow? Wasn't his job here done? "I show you the breakfast room!" he said.

Joan shook her head. "It's very kind," she said, "But I am sure the lady at the front desk will be able to tell me where it is."

Milan shook his head in return and smiled. "She doesn't speak English," he confided.

Joan had forgotten that she was in another country now. Not even the country where she had grown comfortable being a stranger, but yet another land in which to feel her way, like Mrs. Watterson must have before her.

Joan handed Milan an American five-dollar bill. His eyes widened. She almost regretted her generosity—he grabbed her hand and pumped it so hard she felt off balance. Suddenly he seemed to remember himself, stood up straight, and said with dignity, "Thank you, Miss Jenny."

After Milan closed the door behind him, Joan sat down in the WC. Emptying her bladder felt like crying. There was the same warm relief, the same depleted and yet healed feeling afterward. She sat there for a long time, looking up at the ceiling. There was a single light bulb high above her, faint as an evening star. The walls were a rusty red, and where the wall met the floor was many years' worth of grime, which nothing but scrubbing on hands and knees with a toothbrush could remedy.

In the dimly lit main room, Joan brushed aside the long dusty sheers at the window. The window pane was tall, two metres at least, easy to break and slip through, should she need to escape for some reason. The lights of the city glowed out of the darkness, the harsh Communist-era street lights and the muted lights from flats in old buildings. Somehow it was a known quantity, though she had never been there before. Perhaps it was the alien and yet familiar flavour of Eastern European cities that reassured her she was not just a sightseer, a tourist. That although she was a stranger here, she had come with a purpose greater than pleasure, even if she didn't know yet what that purpose was.

Joan pulled on a nightdress, ate some stale crackers she found in the kitchenette, an alcove with a kettle, hot plate, and small fridge, and then was too tired to brush her teeth. She lay on the little bed, looking up at the ceiling. There was a dimmer switch by her head to turn down the wall sconces, but before she had a chance to reach for it, her own mind's light dimmed, and she was pulled into the dark vortex of sleep. It was the first time since she had come to stay in Tibor's flat that she did not dream with the light, flickering awareness of another person's breathing. The first time since leaving home—the home of her birth, her family home, the place where she grew and grew stunted—that she did not feel she could only follow silently in the wake of someone else's sleeping, ever watchful and ready for flight.

CHAPTER 3

Joan woke to sunlight streaming through the dusty window. She lay still, listening to her own breath. There were muffled sounds from the hall, a door opening, closing, slippers shuffling. Quiet voices murmuring past her door. It was the kind of place that would drive her mother mad, a satisfying thought. There was a kind of stillness, a moated quiet that would seem deadly to someone as restless as Gillian.

Really, she should have let her parents know she had left Budapest—left the country, in fact. She would. But after breakfast. First, she would sit quietly and drink tea with lemon and sugar, imagining she had no connections. No past, like a river, the water always new as it rushed past the places that marked human time.

There was a knock on the door.

Joan drew the sheets around her and didn't answer. Milan's voice called to her.

"Miss, time for breakfast. You must have coffee, no?"

Joan's throat ached. The clock radio beside her bed read half past eight, which she knew was late already. "I am coming," she called. "Thank you."

Joan pulled on her clothes and smoothed her hair. Ragged inside but simply sleepy-looking outside. She opened the door to an empty corridor.

Where was Milan? The deserted hall, ever-lit by dim wall sconces, stretched before her. She set one foot outside her door as if stepping into new-fallen snow.

Milan's head popped out from a door to her left.

"One moment," he said, disappearing.

She stood in the middle of the hall, feeling strangely helpless.

Milan appeared again, as though pulled from a magician's hat. He was wearing a yellow, red, and green vest over a black turtleneck and baggy yellow pants, with a jaunty fedora, slightly too big for him, slipping over one ear. He looked sleepy but flashed a bright smile. An unlit cigarette hung between his fingertips.

"Breakfast. Káva," he moaned. Coffee. Had he waited for her to have breakfast? The kindness startled her.

"Do you live here?" she asked, as they headed down the hall.

He smiled at the floor. "Yes" he said, "with my family." He glanced at her. "Three sisters, two brothers. My mother. My drunken father."

Again, Joan was startled by Milan's openness. Why did he trust her? Joan wondered whether their apartment was bigger than her one room. Five children, a teenager, two parents. She pictured laundry hung from one wall to the other, children napping in corners.

In the lobby, Front Desk Pani, as Joan privately thought of her, was nowhere to be seen.

"She is sleeping," Milan said quietly, pointing to a door to a back room behind the counter. Indeed, Joan could hear the snoring. Surprisingly delicate, each snore ending in a fluttering sigh. Joan wondered if she ever went out, to buy groceries, or go to the bank.

"Downstairs," Milan said, opening a small door next to the front desk, where a jumble of jackets and coats hung on hooks made walking hazardous. Below them, a small staircase curved out of sight, whitewashed and clean. There was no handrail, so Joan clutched the wall with her right hand as they descended. "Careful, Canadian," Milan said, grinning. "Many drunken Slovaks died on these stairs."

The staircase led to a white room, brightly lit by bare overhead bulbs, filled with folding card tables covered in plastic tablecloths. At the end of the room was a canteen, where a few old women dressed in dirty white aprons waddled back and forth.

Milan ambled up to the counter and took two glass mugs. The nearest woman in white, a kerchief perched on top of her grey hair like a Chinese folded napkin, glared at him and shouted, shaking a large spoon at him. He shrank, curling as though to protect his chest. It wasn't until the woman broke into a grin and Milan threw his shoulders back and beamed that Joan realized they were acting out a ritual of affection in the guise of abuse.

The other women turned their backs on the pair as if they didn't care enough to even disapprove. When Milan's server friend smiled, her gold-capped front tooth gleamed. She spooned two large bowls of cream of wheat for Milan and Joan and thrust two jars of jam toward them. Nodding to Joan and smiling, she commented, "Pekná je."

Milan rolled his eyes and replied in a low voice. "She says you're pretty," he confided, grinning. Joan was speechless. "I told her you are as old as my mother."

If it were true, Joan thought, Milan would have been born to a teenager. It could well be the case.

"This is Lena. What is your name, Lena is asking," Milan said. Joan opened her mouth to answer. "Jenny," Milan said proudly. "Ako moja sestra. My sister is called same name."

Joan reddened. "Actually," she said, "my friends—and my family—call me Joan."

Milan looked at her thoughtfully. "Joan," he said finally. Coolly, Joan imagined. "Like Joan of Arc?"

"Yes," Joan replied wretchedly.

"Joan of Arc," he repeated, as though mulling it over. "She was Catholic."

Joan nodded, then shook her head and shrugged. She had no idea what the repercussions of commenting one way or the other might be.

"My family is Catholic. My mother prays to the Virgin every morning. But I," Milan said, puffing out his chest, "I am atheist. In Slovak is same. Ateista."

Lena's face grew sombre, and she shook her head, making the sign of the cross over her ample bust.

Milan grinned. "Lena worries I am a communist. She doesn't like Russians."

It had been a long while since Joan had felt the need to search for a religion. In fact, she had only been mildly troubled by spiritual questions for a brief time. But in a country like Slovakia, she suspected, religion was a way to declare your political allegiance and your patriotism. Thankfully, as a Canadian, her casual ambivalence toward such things would be tolerated, perhaps even expected.

Milan took his bowl of cereal and spooned a generous glob of jam on top, then flooded it with milk. Joan did the same and followed him to the table nearest the stairs. They ate silently. Then Milan said, "This is my favourite dish."

Cream of wheat, Joan thought. Did he consider that a dish? Milan ate steadily, savouring each spoonful, and still finished before she had eaten half of hers. He approached the counter for more, and Lena, clicking her tongue in reprimand, ladled the last of the pot into his bowl. She also thrust some bread rolls into his hands when she saw her colleagues had turned their backs. Milan tucked the bread into the ample pockets of his pants and slipped her the cigarette from behind his ear. It disappeared into the pouch on the front of her apron.

Joan turned quickly in her chair so he wouldn't know she'd watched him. Milan whistled on his way back to his seat, happy, then spooned the cream of wheat into his mouth in record time. He sat back in his chair, resting his hands over his stomach.

"Now you know where is breakfast. I am only bringing new guests here for one time and then I am not permitted, except on Sunday." He crossed himself with a flourish, and Lena clucked her tongue. He grinned at her, then turned to the bowl in front of him. He seemed wistful as he pulled the spoon once more around the inside of it, mourning its emptiness with his eyes.

Joan had the feeling Milan was always hungry. She suspected that he would be a good ally, guide, and even friend. She made a note to buy some fruit and cheese, for herself and a little to share. His perpetual motion might be related to hunger, and she couldn't stand the thought of feeling that way herself. Emptiness and scarcity frightened her.

Milan stood up abruptly, smiled, and bowed. "Miss... Joan." He emphasized her name. She blushed.

"Wait," she said. "Would you... show me the market? And tell me where to find the English schools? I...know nothing. About Bratislava."

"True," he said. "But I must work. You come with me on my—" He struggled for a word. "On my—way."

He must mean his work route, Joan thought. She nodded eagerly.

"Yes," she said, "I can pay you." Milan's face was inscrutable. "With English lessons," Joan added. He was proud, clearly, though the other night, he had begged for his brothers and sisters.

"Maybe you can help me," he said simply. "One day, I dream I go to Canada."

An old anxiety crept up Joan's throat, a reluctance to have anyone depend on her. Feeling weak, she gave a quick nod. What was she getting herself into?

His face was beatific for a moment. Then reality prevailed. Breakfast over, down to business. He rubbed his hands together. "Ideme," he said. We go.

Joan stood up quickly, remembering to smooth her skirt. She had only her purse, and she felt naked without her suitcase, or even a bag for food. But after they'd climbed the whitewashed stairs, on the way past the desk, Pani appeared, looking sleepy and cross, and Milan grabbed a net bag off a nail by the window where hung an assortment of other bags, umbrellas, and a pair of crutches. Below was a pile of shoes, boots, and slippers, emanating a smell of worn leather and the faint stink of feet. They had been sprinkled with some sort of powder to hold the smell in check but it made the mass look like something out of Pompeii, covered in volcanic ash. Or like the new bronze shoe monument she had visited in Budapest that year, in honour of the Jews who were forced to take off their shoes at the edge of the Danube before they were shot, their bodies falling like trees into the great river. It had been covered by the dust of a dry, hot summer.

Joan shuddered. There were children's shoes in the pile. Front Desk Pani, awake now, fixed Joan with her gaze. She turned away. Milan was outside, bounding down the stairs. At the bottom, he looked over his shoulder but didn't see her. She watched him shrug, put his hands in his pockets, and begin to walk away.

"Wait," Joan cried, bursting through the front door of the hotel.

Milan whirled around. "Hurry, Canadian! I can't be late!"

Joan shrank inside herself until she saw he was grinning.

She had to trot to keep up with Milan. "Why is there a pile of shoes by Pani's desk?" she panted.

Milan shrugged. "It has always been there," he said, as though that explained everything.

They wound their way down a couple of narrow side streets lined with buildings of the same vintage as the Hotel Svatopluk and eventually emerged into a cobblestone square. There were a handful of stalls, one with a few withered tomatoes, pale green banana peppers, and radishes. Another had smoked meats, coils of sausages, and hunks of unidentifiable flesh. And the last had loaves of rye and graham flour bread, baguettes and rolls. Joan had just eaten, but the salty, smoky smell of the sausage and the wholesome-scented hollow of a roll ripped open still made her mouth water.

Milan eyed the rolls. "You can buy bread less dear at the bakeshop," he murmured, his eyes darting back and forth over the meats. "And these," he nodded to the sausages, "are not good quality." He smiled and tipped his hat at the meat vendor, who was as ruddy and thick as his own product. The man's eyes narrowed, and he looked away. Joan had the uncomfortable feeling that Milan knew him and that the two of them had an uneasy truce, not even congenial on the surface.

As they walked kitty-corner across the square, Milan noted, "Saturday there are more farmers. More vegetables and fruits. Today it is only for tourists. On our street, near the hotel, there are some small shops, a butcher, a baker, fruit and vegetable, *and*," he said with a flourish, "a cake shop." He began to walk faster. "You can buy chocolates and torte and poppyseed cake and..." His voice trailed off. A group of Slovak youth, about Milan's age, walked toward them down the street. Milan hunched slightly and began to speak in soft, evenly modulated Slovak. With his eyes, he asked her to play along.

The group of youth flowed around and past them like a school of fish, glancing at Joan and Milan with hard and unforgiving faces. Milan stopped as if to look in a shop window where the Slovak flag hung behind a display of potato chips and other snacks, then glanced over his shoulder. The youth passed, their amorphous group flowing over the cobblestones and around the bend.

Milan hunched his shoulders and put his hands in his pockets, preoccupied. Joan felt vulnerable, as though she had just witnessed a crime of some kind.

"Thank you," he said as he kept walking. "I only wanted them to pass. I know them. When I was wearing nice jacket, and tie at my work, they..." He shook his head. "Now, if I dress a little bit crazy, they don't bother me. I am only some Gypsy. This hat," he said, shaking his head. "But no matter, it was my grandfather's."

Joan wanted to ask what had happened between Milan and this group of young men, but she knew that if he told her a terrible story, of being beaten and burned with cigarette butts in some dark corner, she wouldn't sleep later. Her mind would churn away at it till it came out like rancid butter.

They came to an abrupt halt outside a narrow doorway with a small blue sign with white lettering. Joan recognized the words Anglická and Škola. English school. There was also a white image of a jet plane taking off.

"This is English school my sister studied," Milan said proudly. "It is special for tourism English. Here you ask about teaching."

Joan looked doubtfully at the sign. What did she know about tourism?

Milan was about to push open the door when Joan said, "Wait."

He stopped, looking back at her with curiosity.

"I—I am not ready. I don't have my resumé."

His brow crinkled.

"My CV. Curriculum vitae." Joan was quite certain she would not be qualified to teach here. "Can you show me where some other English schools are? Then I will come back later with my CV and try them all."

Milan looked impressed. "Maybe Canadians are—" he struggled to find the word "—maybe you know how to be success more than Slovaks."

Joan shrugged. Milan took her a couple blocks away to a small business school in a dusty yellowed building located next to an abstract art gallery. A few doors away was a gymnázium or high school in a pink-fronted building in Rococo style.

"There also is the university," he said, eyes widening slightly.

Joan nodded and shrugged again. It was doubtful she'd find a job there.

Milan took off the fedora and wiped his brow. "It is time for me to leave you," he said. "I must work. Will you find your way? If you are lost, you must ask, "'Kde je Hotel Svatopluk?'"

Joan nodded, though she felt uncertain. He had helped her enough. He tipped his hat to her with a flourish and bowed, then turned and disappeared around the corner. Joan's hands went limp, and she felt suddenly bereft.

It was not far to the hotel. Joan made her way back along the cobblestones, trying to look unconcerned. There were people everywhere, going somewhere, as in every city. When she stopped at a shop window to examine a display of fruit, with tiny Slovak flags on toothpicks stuck between them, she caught a glimpse of her reflection, her hair wisping out of her ponytail, her dark skirt rumpled. A cashier, an older woman in a tunic-style apron with a mop in her hand, gazed down at her. Whether it was real or not, Joan felt approbation from her, disapproval of a kind that Joan's grandmother was expert at. Severe. Glowering. Joan wondered if it was simply because she was aimless and the woman thought her too old to be aimless. Joan felt it herself. But she knew she was trying, this time, to swim against the current instead of letting it carry her where it would. She straightened her shoulders and continued down the street.

On the way past the tourism English school, young women in uniform and a few young men spilled out onto the street. Milan's sister Jenny would have been among them not so long ago, her dark hair swinging behind her as theirs did. Joan wondered how it came to be that Jenny had found a spot in a college like this one while Milan seemed to have to make his own way in the world. For her, perhaps, like these other young people, their voices bright and ringing in the autumn air, the streets of Bratislava were a way to somewhere else. But for Milan, it seemed, they were both his place of business and his school, the only element he swam in.

Back at the Svatopluk, Joan took several copies of her CV from an envelope in the large suitcase. The CV was out of date—it said she currently worked for Madame B.'s Hungarian language school—but there was nothing she could do about that now. The wall sconces shone faintly between the sunlit windows. Joan left them on, their buzz almost imperceptible.

She retraced her steps, past the tourism language school and the dusty yellow building, to the pink Rococo school. Quaking slightly, she pressed the buzzer and waited. A balding middle-aged man pushed open the imposing wooden doors and stood aside to let her pass. He asked her something in Slovak, and she replied, "I only speak English."

"Ahhh," he said, followed by a stream of Slovak she could not understand. Joan shrugged, apologetic and miserable. "English?" he finally asked. "Teach English?"

"Ano," she said, relieved. Yes.

The man led her to an office at the back of the building, which was quite a bit bigger than it seemed from outside. As she waited at the door, young people in maroon skirts and blazers and pants and dress shirts glanced at her curiously as they passed through the hall. Joan's heart sank. This looked like an elite private gymnázium. Not the kind of place she had hoped to be able to find work, but she had to start somewhere.

The woman in the office beckoned to her to come in. Joan sat on a wooden chair across from the desk.

"How may I help you?" the woman asked, her voice somehow both pleasant and screechy. Joan tried to arrange her face.

"I am an English conversation teacher," she began. The woman's eyebrows drew together. Joan stammered. "I...I am interested in applying to work at your school." The woman silently held out her hand and Joan fumbled for her resumé. It was a single page.

"You work in Hungary?" Joan nodded. The woman's nostrils flared slightly. "You do not mention university. You haven't a degree?" Joan shook her head no. The woman handed back her resumé. "I am afraid I cannot help you.

We have no openings at the moment, and all of our substitute teachers have university degrees."

Joan nodded. She couldn't say a word. It was of course as she expected, but she had not steeled herself for the disappointment.

She walked out into the street and took her time walking to the next school, the one housed in the dusty yellow building. She took a deep breath and threw her shoulders back, then pulled open the glass door. There was a desk like the one at the Hotel Svatopluk—tall, long, and dark, with glass windows and several women sitting behind them. They glanced at her briefly, and she tried to attract their attention with what she hoped was a dazzling smile. One of them, in a bored voice, asked her a question in Slovak. Joan launched breathlessly into an English explanation.

"I am an English conversation teacher. Canadian. Učitelka angličtiny, Kanaďanka." The Slovak words Milan had taught her, which she had not dared attempt at the first school but which she felt she must now, were unfamiliar on her tongue. The women tittered behind long-nailed hands at Joan's awkward speech. Reddening, Joan thrust her resumé through the slot under the glass partition. The woman closest to her retrieved it. Giving it a cursory glance, she asked in a startlingly deep voice, "University?" Joan, tears beginning to gather behind her eyes, shook her head. The woman gave her a half smile and handed back her resumé with what appeared to be genuine regret. But when Joan looked up, the other woman's eyes seemed to glitter with suppressed mirth. Was it her imagination? She took her resumé and hurriedly pushed her way out the glass door. She thought she heard laughter.

The sun, high in the sky, glinted off the cobblestones, and Joan's stomach began to rumble.

What could she do? She walked around the corner, onto the street where the tourism English school, marked by the sign with the jet plane painted on it, waited for her. She didn't have the stomach to face it.

Joan continued back to the hotel, stopping for rolls at the nearby bakeshop, and some soft cheese and wizened yellow apples next door at the grocery. She bought extra to share with Milan, just in case. Joan sat on an ancient wall and ate, her mind trying to work through what had happened that morning. Of course she would need a university degree to teach in Bratislava. In Budapest too she would have needed one, had Tibor not secured her the job with Madame B. She stiffened at the thought of Tibor. Would he again, or possibly still, be sitting in his flat in a drunken stupor?

In the distance, Joan saw Milan in his unmistakable bright-coloured clothing approaching. His head was down and occasionally he seemed to kick an invisible stone out of his way. As he drew closer, Joan lifted a tentative hand in greeting. Milan brightened momentarily and sat beside her on the wall.

"I am no lucky today," Milan said, squinting into the distance. Joan handed him a roll and some cheese. His eyes narrowed, dark and suspicious.

"I ate already," Joan said.

Milan nodded and tore the roll in half, placing the rest of the cheese, a chunk of considerable thickness, between the pieces of bread. He took a large bite, and in a moment the entire thing was gone. Joan turned away to give him privacy, but he was already wiping his mouth with his sleeve. He did not look at her, but she thought he seemed happier.

"Are you lucky today? How with English schools?" he asked.

Joan shook her head and stared at the ground. "I don't have a university degree, Milan. It will be difficult to find a job, even though I worked four years in Budapest as a conversation teacher."

"It is no easy," Milan said. "But you must try."

"I went to two English schools. I think they were laughing at me. I didn't go to the tourism language school. I don't know anything about tourism."

Milan leapt to his feet. "You must try. We go."

Joan shook her head and scowled.

Milan leaned against the wall, hands in pockets. "Okay, Canadian. You don't try. You can go to Canada. Here, in Slovensko, we must try. Or we die." He began to walk away.

Joan, stunned and shame-faced, got up and trailed after him. It was her old habit, hard to break, of following in another's wake—but at least this time it was in the service of her independence. Milan grinned at her over one shoulder.

CHAPTER 4

Milan pushed open the door of the tourism English school and disappeared into the dark interior. Joan followed. A woman who looked like she could be the sister of the woman at the front desk of the Hotel Svatopluk sat at the same kind of high counter surrounded by glass windows. She gazed disdainfully at Milan, who spoke coldly and politely. Joan caught the words učitelka and kanaďanka. Strange how the most important things about her in Budapest and here in Bratislava were so wholly different than the things that defined her in Canada. There she was a daughter, mixed race, a misfit. She didn't try to pretend she was anything else. Here, she needed to seem respectable, professional even— and the coat of respectability was strange and ill-fitting. Perhaps even more than her lack of a university degree, she felt hindered by the evidence of her awkwardness.

Joan felt weak as the woman gave her a dubious once-over. She waved her into the waiting area's faded vinyl chairs.

Milan did not sit down. "I will leave you now." Anxiety rose in her throat. He patted her arm as though he were her elder. "It is good. Talk with the lady." Milan bent toward Joan confidentially. "She knows English well. She only pretends."

Joan wondered why she would pretend. There were many things she did not understand, but Joan felt a presentiment—odd and unfamiliar, because she did not think of herself as a naturally intuitive person—that all would be revealed. Even Milan's unusual life and all the secret filaments extending out from him would unravel themselves in good time. She was glad for this gradual unrolling, because she suspected that all at once might be too much for her.

Milan had shamed her into coming here to this third school to try for a job. What was his interest in her success? Perhaps it was the famous Slovak hospitality she'd heard North American expats in Hungary talk about. But he had also said something that echoed through her now: "We must try, or we die." Why did he care what happened to her, a relative stranger?

Joan gripped her purse on her lap. A door opened and closed, and the woman at the front desk beckoned to her with a stern face.

"The director," she said. "You may go in."

Joan stood quickly, smoothing her skirt. She rapped on the door that had opened and closed, and jumped slightly when a male voice commanded, "Come in."

Joan entered the office, shadowy as a forest, and scented, strangely, with cloves. How did people work without light? A languid plume of smoke rose from the director's cigarette. She could see from his silhouette that he had a square-jowled face, and guessed he was leaving middle age behind. She felt a slight tremor run through her. He looked like Tibor.

The illusion was dispelled when he opened the blinds. She saw a man who was balding, to be sure, but whose remaining hair was a fiery red. His eyes were shrewd and alive, and his smile, though perfunctory, seemed to cover kindness. He was not jowled, after all, but sporting a red beard that was well groomed and greying.

"Yes?" he asked loudly. "What can I do for you?" His accent was not Slovak.

Joan felt her mouth hanging open. The man waved to a chair, impatiently, she thought. His cigarette, she realized, was the source of the pungent clove smell. She coughed, and then she couldn't stop. The director pushed a small bowl of mints on the desk toward her, encouraging her to scoop up a handful.

"I need to replenish the bowl. Please take them all." He stubbed out his cigarette, looking pleased. "So you are not a smoker then?" he asked.

Joan shook her head, unable to speak.

"I am trying to quit. It's very unusual here in Slovakia to be a man my age who doesn't smoke, but my wife is adamant I must." He waved the smoke away. "What's your name?" he asked loudly, leaning toward her, as though he thought her hard of hearing. "Mine's Robbie Burns, if you will believe it." He looked amused. "My dear old da," he said with a lilt. "Couldn't help himself. He loved the old country."

Joan cleared her throat again. "Joan Simpson," she said, clutching her purse.

Burns peered at her through the smoke. Scrutinizing her face, her slanted eyes.

"I'm half Chinese," she said. "My father is English. But I am Canadian."

Robbie Burns sat back. "And I, though I spent my childhood in Scotland, am Slovak," he said. Proud, he thrust his chest out above his round belly.

They sat silently for a moment, then the director put out his hand.

"Your CV?" he asked. "I assume you are here about a job."

Joan had a sinking feeling as she pulled it out of her purse and handed it to him. The single page, listing her work at the nursing home in Canada and the English teaching job in Budapest. The rest before that were failures at best, disasters at worst. Like her attempt to drive a school bus. Joan shuddered.

Burns squinted at her. "Budapest. Beautiful place. What brought you to Bratislava?"

Joan thought for a moment about what to say. She was running away, as Edna had before her, from an untenable situation. "I—wanted a change of scenery." She blushed immediately, realizing how feeble she sounded, but Burns was looking at the paper.

"Says here you taught English conversation for four years at a language school."

"Yes—actually, it is closer to three and a half."

"But I've barely heard you speak."

"What...would you like me to say?"

"Tell me something about yourself."

Joan always hated that question. "I—I had a friend from Hungary. In Nova Scotia. I was working at her nursing home. Then my friend died—and I wanted a change." It felt to Joan that her life had started then, with Edna's death. Before that she'd been floating in amniotic fluid, only half aware.

Burns laughed. "Nové Škótsko," he said. "We are practically cousins then." He cleared his throat and frowned slightly. "You don't have a university degree."

"No," Joan allowed, then spoke words she never imagined possible. "I am, however, a competent teacher and the students like me." It wasn't exactly a lie, but she blushed deeply.

"There now, I am glad to hear it!" Burns grinned broadly. "What have you read lately?"

Joan thought hard. The truth was she hadn't read a good book in a long time. "I've read some Agatha Christie novels, the newspaper, and some grammar texts," she admitted, looking at her hands.

"Fine. You should make a good conversation teacher then. I only need someone for maybe four hours a week." Joan's face fell. "However, if you can do housekeeping, laundry, and cook, my wife and I could use you as an assistant. Next door, where we live."

Joan slowly shook her head. It wasn't perfect, but surely it couldn't really be this easy?

"No?" Burns looked surprised and disappointed.

Joan looked up quickly and nodded. "Yes," she said.

Burns stood and reached out a freckled hand to shake hers. "Alright. I want you to meet my wife and son then." His son? He opened a sliding door that Joan had assumed was a closet. He took a step over the threshold into a small room, lined on all sides with old suits, caps, work clothes, and, below them, flowerpots and gardening tools. He opened another door that led into a hall. A small bell rang in Joan's head. Narnia, she thought.

The hall was an ordinary sort of back passageway, leading to a window overlooking a courtyard on the right. But Burns turned left, past a large kitchen with a gas stove and tall cupboards, to a room where an old woman sat, next to a small, dark-haired boy, on an old sofa, watching a Slovak children's program. He looked up at the sound of his father's footsteps and stared at Joan with dark eyes.

"My boy," Burns said tenderly. "Peter is three, almost four," he said to Joan.

Four years old? He is small for his age, she thought. The boy said nothing but reached out his arms for his father to pick him up. The old woman clucked in Slovak. Peter wrapped his arms around his father's neck and nestled his chin nestled against the man's shoulder.

Burns turned and continued walking toward the sunlit foyer. The old woman attempted to get to her feet. Joan offered an arm, but was waved on by a large, liver-spotted hand. She followed Burns, Peter in his arms staring back at her over his shoulder. There was something unsettling about the boy. So silent, unsmiling. So serious. Burns disappeared to the right before Joan reached the foyer. Sunlight bathed a tiled floor and a staircase leading to the rooms upstairs. She was reminded of a scene from her past, or several scenes, which blended together to give her the sense at this moment of having stood here before. The spell of sunlight never changed, she knew, from one century to the next. Joan was tempted to simply remain there with her eyes closed, but willed herself instead to follow Burns.

He stood with the boy in the crook of his arm, bending over a woman seated in a wheelchair parked on the dark red carpet. She was slender, almost frighteningly so, and the bones of her knees and ankles were knobby as a colt's beneath her leggings. Her head wobbled slightly with a tremor, and Burns used his free hand to gently push the bridge of her glasses up from their precarious perch on the end of her nose. Can she not use her hands? Joan wondered anxiously.

"Miša, to je Joan."

Miša jerked her head in a nod. "Dobrý deň," she said in a voice whose modulation was somewhat erratic. She looked up at Burns, who spoke quietly, perhaps indicating that he thought Joan would make her a decent assistant. Miša looked up at him and nodded, smiling at Joan. Did she speak English? Joan felt the fluttering breath of panic around her heart until Miša chimed, "I am pleased to meet you. Do you like children?"

Joan stood stock-still She didn't know. The trauma flooded back to her, of driving a school bus full of weeping five-year-olds, her near hysterical outburst, and the endless cough drops she had consumed to keep calm. The memory made her stomach weak.

"I don't. I don't like children," Miša said. She reached shakily for her son, her wide grin mischievous. "Only this one." Peter slipped from Burns's arms into her lap.

Joan exhaled. So she is not paralyzed, Joan thought, at least not from the waist up, and she has a sense of humour. The little boy gazed at Joan from where he clung to his mother's neck like a monkey, rubbing his nose against her shoulder. There was not a hint of a smile on his small face.

The Burnses seemed to be waiting for something. Joan tried grinning broadly at the boy. Nothing. How did he come to be so expressionless this early in his young life? Clearly, he was attached to his parents, and Joan couldn't think of what would allow her to climb into his affections. She turned away, turned back, and grinned at him again, but got no reaction. She drew her eyebrows together and puffed her cheeks out. The boy opened his eyes wide and grinned before burying his face in Miša's chest. Burns smiled kindly and Miša's small teeth gleamed.

"She doesn't like children either!" she sang, delighted, stroking her boy's hair.

Burns waved Joan to sit down on a long sofa, while he lowered himself awkwardly into a wooden rocking chair. It must once have been Miša's, Joan thought. It was too narrow for Burns's generous girth.

"So," he said, "Miša needs help with many things. She likes to bake but her hands shake, and it's hard for her to measure ingredients. She likes to write letters but has a hard time holding a pen. And she loves to take care of Peter, but of course she needs help."

Miša mocked him gently. "Of course," she said. "I cannot speak for myself." Burns blushed and hid his eyes with his hand. "My husband. Actually," she said, "I love music, and poetry. I want to practise English. The girls in our school are afraid of me. Because of my big, horrible wheelchair. But you are not afraid, are you?"

Joan shook her head. She was used to wheelchairs, after working in the nursing-home kitchen where Edna had lived the last years of her life.

Miša nodded. "That is good." She looked tired. Burns rose and took Peter from her. "I usually sleep in the afternoon," she said. Joan figured it was now about mid-afternoon. "And sometimes in the morning," Miša added. "Then you will need to look after Peter." Burns nodded. "You will help me in the morning—to bathe and dress, and do exercises."

Joan swallowed. She had never done work like that before.

"That is, eight to nine," said Burns. "During that time I will look after Peter. After that, Pani Marta will care for him and you will be with Miša. You will make lunch and have it with us. In the afternoon you will have a break while Miša sleeps and Peter naps—although you must be prepared for him to wake—and Pani Marta shops and cleans. When she comes home, she will prepare supper and you will care for Peter. Until four. We will pay you for forty hours, and occasionally, if we need your help at an odd time, on the weekend, for example, if I need to go out and Miša is alone with Peter, you will receive extra compensation."

No mention of teaching. A glorified babysitter was what they wanted. But she needed a job.

"Also," Burns said, "we have a small room upstairs that you may use. It is furnished, with a bed and a desk, and a place for clothes. Usually we rent it to a student, but lately—" Burns seemed to debate how to put what came next. He looked at his wife.

"Lately, I need more help," Miša said flatly.

"Okay," Joan said, and made an effort to smile.

Burns gazed at her. "It's not exactly what you thought when you walked in the door of our school," he said kindly.

"Take some time to think about it."

Joan shook her head. "I accept," she said, this time reaching her hand out first to shake his.

Burns put his pipe in his mouth. "Come back Monday for eight," he said around it, nodding goodbye.

Miša took Joan's hand in both of hers. "Peter and Robo and I—we will try not to be cranky early in the morning. When you come." She shook Joan's hand jerkily up and down as though she were using a hand pump.

It must have taken all her energy, Joan thought. She could feel Miša's fluted bones, as delicate as a sparrow's, through the paper-thin skin. Her life force was a slim river snaking through her, from what source Joan couldn't tell. But it seemed to Joan it might soon dry up, as though Miša were a handful of flowers hung upside down from a door frame to dry.

With Peter balanced on one arm, Burns escorted Joan into the foyer. The sun had gone behind a cloud, but it was still warm there and full of light.

"Thank you, Ms. Simpson," he said. The little boy stared at her. She frowned quickly and stuck out her tongue. He smiled and turned away from her, then back to gaze at her from his father's shoulder, dark-eyed and inscrutable.

Joan stepped into the street. No wheelchair could get through the narrow door. She wondered what Miša would do if there was a fire. Joan realized too she had forgotten to check for her own escape route.

The sun was low in the sky. What should she do? Find a phone and call her parents. Buy a map and something for supper and try to find her way around this town. She wanted to locate a church. Not to pray, but so she could sit in a cold pew and look into the dim reaches of a vaulted nave to think.

Joan walked slowly, glutted with newness. Already Bratislava—as symbolized by Milan—had replaced Budapest. The Hungarian capital receded like the tide in her consciousness, as though it were not still a living city, a mere two hundred kilometres away, but somewhere that only existed in her memory. But then Tibor appeared, like a nail she'd stepped on. She still felt for him a mixture of anger and pity. The pity, she realized, was the more bitter and poisonous, but it was as though she had no tools with which to view him except that. Pity was like looking at him and his now-wretched life through the wrong end of a telescope.

Joan wanted to keep her distance from the memory of him. She didn't even want to imagine what he felt or thought about what he'd done, though it might help her have compassion for him. Perhaps because of that, she wanted to put more than the distance between cities between them, to wipe him clean from her memory of Budapest and of Edna.

But Joan couldn't shake Edna's sorrowful gaze, which she recalled when thinking of the past month of her life. As though Joan was somehow to blame, as though she had disappointed her old friend. It was an almost intolerable feeling, so Joan put it away in her mental box, alongside the dark-eyed child who had tugged mutely at her imagination in the Budapest train station. A child that looked much like the Burnses' son, Peter.

In a small grocery store Joan bought a wedge of smoked gouda and a couple of small chocolate bars. Across the street was a post office, where she thought she could buy a map.

"Change money? Telephone?" she asked.

The unsmiling clerk pointed at the map with her finger. "Tu," she said.

Joan felt confused. Her grade-school French was getting in the way. "You?" she said. "Me?" She pointed at herself.

The shop clerk gestured around the store. "Tu." Here.

Joan nodded and quickly drew a little picture of an envelope. "Tu?"

The clerk, impatient but amused, stabbed at the map with her finger. "Tam. Telefon."

Joan drew a small receiver, the universal symbol for a phone. "Tam. Change money." She then drew a dollar sign next to the telephone receiver, indicating the currency exchange counter.

It was not far, the clerk pointed, and beside it on the map was a cross, indicating a church.

Joan nodded. "Ďakujem." She handed the clerk an American five-dollar bill, which disappeared into a pocket on the front of the woman's apron.

The clerk had one more thing to add. "Pozor," she said, pointing to the church.

Joan gathered from signs she had passed on the street where construction was happening, pozor meant "careful" or "danger."

The woman continued, pantomiming an obsequious beggar, her hand out. "Cigáni." Gypsies.

Joan withered. She gave a stiff parting nod and walked out into the street again. The sun and air were expansive, free, and did not judge.

The cathedral was several blocks away. Joan wondered whether Milan might be there, flogging the rooms at the Hotel Svatopluk. Maybe he stayed close to the train stations and bus depots. On Monday she would begin a life of work again, but right now she was free. She would wander around the old town and get the lay of the land, sit on a bench, and watch people—women in their heels trying to cross cobblestone streets, sour-looking old men drinking beer, young people from the gymnázium calling to one another as they made their way from class to cafeteria, their self-assured, worldly tone familiar even though she couldn't understand them. Milan should be among them.

At the main square, Joan was accosted by a couple of dark-eyed, dusk-cheeked children, no older than five or six, eyes pleading, hands outstretched. Joan was both fascinated and repelled by the pity they evoked in her. They were clearly con artists, so accomplished at their task they had forgotten that fact themselves. The children stroked her sleeve and pulled at her jacket with their small hands, which, at the same time, she knew, were feeling for her wallet. She put her hands in her own pockets and pulled out a couple of the apples she had purchased, presenting the children with one each. They looked at the apples dully, as though they didn't know what they were, but took them and hid them among the folds of their clothes and continued to pester her. Helpless and ashamed, Joan waved them away, as she walked toward the currency exchange counter, where a curt, dark-haired man took her American and Hungarian bills and thrust a wad of Slovak koruny under the plexiglass barrier.

At the telephone centre, the international phone operators waited with headphones on. The place was otherwise empty. Joan gave her number to the first operator, a brisk young woman who barely looked at her but thrust a piece of paper under the transparent barrier with a number on it. Joan pulled out the required koruny and slid them under the barrier.

She entered a small closet with a phone, which felt as she thought a confessional must. The operator connected her to an English-speaking operator who rang her mother's number. The familiar sound of its ring made

Joan slightly anxious. Would her mother answer? Gillian lived alone but spent a lot of time with David, who was comfortable picking up the phone when she couldn't. In the small Chinese community in Dartmouth, Nova Scotia, they were among the tiny few who had married outside their race: Gillian to Joan's father, a blue-eyed Englishman also named David, and David Song to a long-haired Slovak woman who died of breast cancer when their daughters were still young. Gillian and the new David, as Joan sometimes thought of him, had perhaps grown less adventurous in their old age and, with no parents left to rebel against, had decided to date another Chinese. The coincidence that she herself had ended up in Slovakia, home of the new David's dead wife, was not lost on Joan.

After a few rings, her mother's voice crackled across the ocean. "Hello?"

"Hi, Mum," Joan said.

"Joan! How are you?"

"I'm in Slovakia. Mum, I just got a new job." Joan knew her mother would be impressed. "At a language school. I will be the personal assistant to the director and his wife." That was stretching the truth only a little. If she were to give herself a job title on her resumé, that's what she would write.

The silence on her mother's end confused her. "Mum? What's wrong?" Joan asked. Her mother's voice had caught in her throat.

"Joan, that's amazing!" Gillian managed to say. "I'm so proud. So proud."

Guilty and pleased, Joan felt her cheeks redden.

"Slovakia," Gillian mused. "How funny! David's wife was from Slovakia. Do you remember their daughter Adriana?"

Vaguely, Joan thought. All the children of Chinese parents in Halifax at least knew of one another, and Joan noticed other mixed-race kids in particular. A certain memory of Adriana stuck out for her. At the annual Chinese Society Christmas party, held in an old school gym, a quiet girl of about ten or eleven had hung back from the other raucous children. Her Caucasian mother's face was angular and wicked-looking, and she wore long curly hair and a sly smile. Joan was several years out of high school by then and noted the disconcerting impatience with which the woman yanked her daughter's hand to drag her away from the wall, the other hand balanced on her own heavily pregnant belly. A year later, Adriana's mother was dying, and the funeral, which Joan attended with her parents and the rest of the Chinese community, was the last time she'd seen Adriana. She'd pitied the girl, but she'd faded from Joan's consciousness. Like so many other names and faces that had slipped silently into the stream of forgotten things.

"She had a kind of breakdown. She stayed in the Nova Scotia Hospital for a bit," Gillian said in a hushed voice. "But now she's...well, she's doing well. A little fragile maybe, but she's kind of tough too. She's so young. Just twenty, I think. In fact, she is planning to go to Slovakia to do some... research. Into her roots."

Joan tasted embarrassment on her mother's behalf. Gillian had never used to use terms like "finding one's roots."

They each waited for the other to say something. Joan cleared her throat. "Does she have somewhere to stay?"

"I don't know. But I doubt it. Do you have a suggestion?"

Joan wanted to say no. She didn't want to get caught up in one of her mother's convoluted romances or in the fragile life of a broken-down girl. But she could help Milan out if she referred Adriana to him.

"I know someone who can help. He helped me find my room at the Hotel Svatopluk in Bratislava..." Joan trailed off.

I know a boy who has trouble getting enough to eat.

Gillian squealed. "That's perfect!" She scribbled down the address and phone number of the hotel and chattered excitedly about how relieved David would be to know Adriana would be looked after. Joan didn't plan on looking after Adriana, but felt it was no use to contradict her mother.

Joan wondered how things like this happened. Gillian's life was so full of drama and minor plotting, so different from her own. To Joan it was as if every day was unmapped, but her mother was constantly trying to wrangle and knead the parts of her life into the shape she desired. Perhaps when Joan was conceived, her mother's machinations had backfired, because she was given a daughter who floated amorphously, as alien to Gillian as moon dust.

"I'll give your contact information to David for Adriana. It will probably thrill her that you're going to be able to show her around."

Joan doubted that, but what good would it do to say anything? Adriana was barely out of teenagehood. Joan pictured the young woman falling over herself laughing, drunk in the stairwell of some apartment building with new-found Slovak friends holding her up by her elbows. She would be lucky if Bratislava wasn't a never-ending hangover. There was something grim about the place. Despite the way the Danube, or the Dunaj as the Slovaks called it, sparkled through Bratislava as it had through Budapest, the city seemed to her dour and thick with melancholy. She realized it might be the cast of her own mood that made it appear so, but a lens dimmed with regret was as real as any other.

Joan waited for her mother to settle, but Gillian was distracted.

"Oh my God, I'll be late for work!" she said, a flurry of activity ensuing on her end of the line.

"Bye, Mum," Joan said. "Tell Dad I called."

Joan figured her mother would tell him if she remembered. They talked to each occasionally, were cordial, but generally, Joan thought, uninterested—a secret barb to her. When she got her first paycheque, and her father was back from his travels, Joan would call him.

Joan left the telephone centre. Back on the cobblestone square, a feeling of helplessness overcame her. What was she doing here? It was as if she were falling through a funnel, from a wide-open world through a dark and narrow place. Surely she would end up somewhere else, somewhere brighter—but how long would it take? And what would her life look like in the end?

The square was brilliant in the sunlight. In the distance, near the cathedral, Joan saw Milan talking to a man in a robe. She recognized Milan's colourful clothing and the hat he was waving around. Warm relief flushed through her. At least she knew one person, someone who, despite his precarious circumstances, had managed to hook her up with a room and a job. Milan looked like he was arguing with the other man, who was tonsured like a monk, his robe tied with a piece of rope. When Milan saw her, he stopped gesturing and thrust his hands in his pockets. The monk turned toward her. She thought, what an ugly mouth. But then his face stretched into a practised, beatific expression as he looked to the heavens and raised his arms. Pigeons floated down to feed on whatever he held in his hands.

Joan stopped at a distance. Milan, done for the moment, walked toward her, his face dark. Behind him, pigeons settled on the ugly-mouthed man's shoulders, and with arms outstretched he turned slowly, gathering an admiring crowd of tourists. Milan looked back over his shoulder, disgusted.

"St. Francis is making good business today. Many koruny," he muttered.

Indeed, Joan noticed that the monk was passing around a basket like a holy busker, collecting donations. For God's creatures, Joan imagined him saying, as he made the sign of the cross over each blessed soul. Later he would take off the robe in the washroom of the cathedral, give a handful of coins to the collection box (for which the priest would smile and dip his head ingratiatingly), and stride across the square with a cigarette hanging from his mouth to catch a bus to the pub near his apartment block.

Was she really such a cynic? Yes, she decided. But it didn't matter. Joan followed Milan across the square, back in the direction of the hotel.

"What were you arguing about?" she asked.

Milan scowled. "Brother Francis should give me koruny. I bring the tourists here to see him and we had agreement. But he is liar." Milan kicked the dust. He stopped and passed his hand over his face.

"I got the job. With the language school." Joan tried to look cheerful. "I'll give you some money when they pay me."

Milan looked at her in wonderment. "You will teach there?" he asked.

Joan shrugged. "There's a little boy. I will take care of him. And help his mother with her—work."

"You are lucky," he said. "It is not easy here to have job."

Joan felt a pang of guilt. "They will let me have a room in their house."

Milan looked confused. "But you won't stay at the hotel?"

It dawned on Joan that Milan probably got a small commission for every night she remained in the Svatopluk. Her face reddened. It was like she was taking money out of the pocket of a poor man.

Milan looked at his feet. "It's good that you will live with a family," he said. "You will be less alone."

Joan was at a loss for words. But there was Adriana's impending arrival. "I have a...friend. She will come to Bratislava soon and she will need a room."

Milan perked up. "I meet her at the station! If you agree," he said.

"Of course," Joan said. Thinking: you are a free agent, and it will save me time.

But Milan cried, "We go together!"

Buoyed by the turn of events, Milan chatted all the way to the hotel. Joan felt relieved, almost giddy, herself. The Danube was bright, only slightly wrinkled by an almost unnoticeable breeze. Joan tried to forget the nature of her new job. She figured it might involve boredom and misery at times, but that didn't frighten her. It was the child's silence and dark, unreadable eyes that tugged an anxious thread.

"When will she come, your friend?" Milan asked as they mounted the hotel steps. Joan shrugged. She had no idea.

Alone in her room, on an old postcard with a photo of the Hotel Svatopluk Joan found in the desk drawer, she wrote, *Dear Ricky*.

There were so many things to tell him about. She knew she couldn't fit them all here. *I am in Bratislava now. I have a new job...* She wanted to be able to tell Ricky, who always listened with mild attention and respect to whatever she had to say, everything. Ricky, to whom Edna, while her mind was still good, had entrusted the letter meant for Joan to give Josef, the husband she'd abandoned, the letter that contained her pain, regret, plea for forgiveness, and was accompanied by the crisp hundreds that allowed Joan to travel to Budapest in the first place.

Joan had never actually sent Ricky a postcard—she was

too wary of the power of such a missive. Clutching Edna's letter to Josef, she had gotten on a plane to Hungary and, like the Edna of her imagination, never looked back. Edna's letter took Joan away from Ricky, and whatever budding affection they had for each other. The same letter proved too much for Josef, who was whittled away by his own heart for nearly four years after reading it—and so, it was also indirectly the source of Tibor's unravelling. Joan wondered whether Edna could have foreseen this chain of events. She imagined her old friend floating down the river of stars that was the Milky Way, looking back in grief at the carnage a single truth had wrought among the people she loved.

Joan knew she would never send the postcard she was writing to Ricky now, but would stick it in the orange notebook with all her other unsent notes to him. But even though he was only her journal personified, she felt she was speaking to the real Ricky, that somehow he would be absorbing the vibration of the words she scribbled on the backs of postcards, even the words she spoke to him in her head. The idea of living with a family was almost more terrifying than coming to Bratislava alone, Joan realized. She imagined Ricky reaching out his hand for hers, to comfort her. As anxious as she was, she did not try to brush the thought away.

Joan slept for the rest of the afternoon. She was dimly aware of the room whirling around her as though she were spinning down though that same dark funnel. What was it? Something to do with the passage of time. Even though the end point of the journey was shrouded in darkness for her, there was an end point, only one. There was no such thing as a tunnel without an end. She might be falling, but she was falling somewhere.

CHAPTER 5

Joan heard a knocking on her door.

"Miss Simpson," someone called to her over the border of sleep.

Joan rubbed her eyes. What time was it? Her watch said six. When she opened the door, Milan bowed low.

"My mother asks you to come to our—home. To eat with us." He sounded almost solemn.

"I am pleased to accept your mother's invitation," Joan said. Milan looked confused for a moment. "Yes, I will eat with you. Thank you to your mother."

"I told her you are Canadian. She wants to know about Canada. But she is good cook," he said apologetically.

Joan picked up the net bag that held the apples, bread, and cheese left over from lunch. "I bought some extra things."

Milan eyed the bag hungrily, then looked away.

"Of course, your mother can save them. For tomorrow, or another time."

Milan looked deflated.

"Or we can have them today, with what she cooked." Joan put her shoes on and followed Milan down the hall. She could smell paprika, onions, and garlic. Pork? It smelled delicious. Milan pushed open the door to his family's rooms. Joan surveyed the scene by the glow of a few scattered lamps. There was a neatly made bed in the corner where two small children of indeterminate age and gender bounced, and a listless girl of about nine sat in her undershirt and panties.

A short woman with a round back tended a stove on the other side of the room. She smiled at Joan uncertainly, her dark eyes flickering and fierce.

"Joan, this is my mother, Mária."

Joan handed her the bag of food, which Mária took quickly and thrust under the counter. The woman then extended her hand to Joan. It was small and brown and weathered. Joan was surprised—she had thought Mária would be in her mid to late thirties, not much older than herself. Maybe she was, but she looked like Milan's grandmother, not his mother. Still, her grip was very strong, almost frighteningly so.

Two more tiny children, fresh from a bath—they were naked except for towels—rushed to leap on the bed. The oldest girl appeared flushed with fever, but they paid no attention to her. Milan's mother brought the child a deep plate of clear broth, from which she took one sip. Mária put the back of her hand to her daughter's forehead. In hushed tones she told the girl to go to the armchair in the corner, where she curled up under a blanket with an enormous red flower and fell asleep. Her cheekbones shone with perspiration, her Roman nose flared slightly, and her black hair fell around her small face. Mária pressed the large gold cross that hung around her neck to the girl's brow, whether to bless or cool her, Joan didn't know. She wished she had a camera. In the dim light she felt as though she was witnessing the end of something—not the child's life but something more ancient, a way of being human that, though elaborate and bright, remained to her impenetrably dark.

"Tata je doma?" Milan asked.

Mária nodded toward the adjoining room, from under the door of which crept a faint smell of stale cigarettes.

Milan sat down at the table and pulled the chair beside him out for Joan to sit on. The children on the bed stopped jumping, as if just noticing her. They stared at Joan with dark, violet-shadowed eyes. They reminded her of Peter. Did all Slovak children have such an unsettling gaze?

Mária dished out small bowls of stew. There was half a large loaf of rye bread on the table, which Milan sliced carefully on an already crumb-covered cutting board. The children swarmed him, grabbing slices.

"Milan, de man!" they cried. Milan dangled the bread in front of them one at a time.

Joan thought she could eat three times as much as she'd been given and still be hungry. She hoped there would be bread left for the adults, but soon realized she didn't have to worry. Mária handed Milan a large plate of flat bread, which he held out to Joan.

"Marikla," he said, smiling,

The door to the adjoining room opened, and a small, wiry man with a grizzled beard stepped through it. He sat at the table without saying a word. His eyes were droopy as a basset hound's. The children gave him a wide berth, clustering at Milan's elbows. Mária silently put a mug of coffee in front of her sour-smelling husband. Joan's stomach flopped delicately. Alcohol and stale cigarettes.

No one introduced Joan to Milan's father. She watched Milan tear his bread into small pieces to soak in the stew and did the same. Mária looked at her with glowing eyes.

"Milan, šmakinel tuke?" Mária asked. Milan murmured his assent. She grabbed his arm and nodded at Joan.

"Taste good?" he asked her between mouthfuls. Joan nodded and, for Mária's benefit, rubbed a circle on her belly and made appreciative noises. The children giggled, and Mária smiled broadly.

"Which part of Canada are you from? How cold is it? What do people do there? Do you have bears where you live? Wolves? Are there Indians? Do Canadians believe in Jesus and the Virgin Mary? Is everyone rich there?" Mária peppered Joan with questions, with Milan patiently translating between mouthfuls of soup and bread. The children listened wide-eyed while Milan's father, bleary and grey, ignored everything but the soup, spooning it mechanically with a shaky hand.

Joan's stomach grumbled, but she answered as fully as possible, elaborating for interest's sake. Yes, there are bears, but not in the city. And yes, there are Indians, and in my home province they are called Mi'kmaq and they do not live in wigwams anymore, they live in houses and apartments like everyone else.

Mária gazed at her, then turned to Milan. "Sar o Roma," she said.

He shrugged apologetically at Joan. "We know nothing about Canada," he said.

Mária stood up, came around the table, and grabbed Joan's bowl, although Joan hadn't finished the stew yet. Disappointed, Joan sat with her spoon poised for nothing.

The children, who had been listening intently to the exchange between Mária and Joan, stopped chewing. Mária began to ladle more stew into Joan's bowl.

"E Gabriela na chal," Mária said, gesturing to the sleeping nine-year-old and shaking her head. Gabriela, the ill girl, wasn't going to eat, so Joan might as well have her share, Milan explained with a shrug. Joan held up a hand in protest.

The spoon in Milan's father's hand clattered to the table and he glowered at Mária. Suddenly he bellowed at the top of his lungs, rose from the table on uncertain legs, and disappeared into the adjoining room.

Stunned, Joan stopped eating too. Mária, who had cowered with her hands over her ears at the sound of her husband's voice, put her palms to her eyes. Milan looked down at his bowl. Mária's hands covered her face, but she wasn't crying. She rubbed her eyes and cheeks as though tired and tried to smile.

"Forgive him. My father is shame there is not more to eat," Milan said.

Joan's heart tightened and panic rose in her throat. Had she caused Mária and this family some harm? She got up from her chair in a rush. Milan didn't look up.

"Please tell your mother, I thank her very much for her hospitality and the delicious food." Joan put her hand in her pocket and took out the mints she'd stashed there from Robbie Burns's desk. She placed them in front of Milan to distribute, but he made no move to reach for them. The other children's small hands snatched them from their places, and the mints vanished as quickly as they had appeared.

Mária sat down and wearily raised her hand. Joan did her best to smile back but she felt her mouth crumbling.

Milan walked her down the hall.

"My father doesn't have job, and he drinks the money from the government. He is—"

Frustrated, Joan thought. Ashamed. She knew there was more Milan could say, if only it would make a difference. But what could it change? She felt for Mária, and the children, and their big-eyed hunger.

"Don't worry," she said, at the door of her room. "Don't think any more about it."

Half smiling, he kissed his hand and waved it in her direction. It surprised her—but perhaps it was a gesture meant to replace an old-fashioned practice of men kissing women's hands. Joan decided it meant nothing more than a handshake, albeit a relieved and gallant one.

She felt like crying and beating the wall with her hands. She was glad she was leaving. She would call her mother again tomorrow and let her know that Adriana Song was welcome to her room, if she could get to Bratislava this weekend. That should light a fire under her, Joan thought.

When she opened the door to her room, she saw an envelope had been pushed under her door. It was a fax, a note sent by her mother to the hotel. All it said was, "Adriana will fly to Vienna tomorrow. Can you meet her at the train station in Bratislava on Sunday? All love to you."

Joan stared at the fax. Gillian must have got on the phone right away after talking to Joan and arranged everything. For once, she and her mother were on the same page about something, though likely for very different reasons. Joan wanted Adriana to replace her in the room for the sake of Milan's commission. What Gillian's motives were, Joan did not know.

Joan sat on her bed. Tomorrow, she figured, she would head to the station to see when the train was coming from Vienna, unless Milan knew. On Sunday, she would bring Adriana to her room in the Hotel Svatopluk, introduce her to Milan, and then pack her own things to take to her new room in Burns's house. She realized she hadn't even asked to see the room, as she'd been so stunned by the speed at which she'd got the job, but it seemed the least of her worries. Tomorrow at breakfast she would tell Milan the good news—that even though Joan would be leaving, Adriana would immediately take her place. Exchanging one Canadian for another—who would even notice? She smiled to herself as sleep drifted over her like fog.

CHAPTER 6
ADRIANA

Below me, the shadow of the plane, encircled by a halo of many colours against the cloud. A talisman, a hopeful sign, as a rainbow always is. I don't want to let it go. Soon it will be night and this bright shadow will disappear, replaced by the blinking lights on the plane's wings.

I've been planning for this trip for several months and had booked my ticket for the new year, but yesterday everything happened so quickly I can barely believe I'm already in the air, floating toward Vienna at jet speed. Gillian called me, and in that breathless way of hers, explained how her daughter Joan was in Slovakia "as we speak" and would love for me to join her. I rolled my eyes a little because Gillian exaggerates, but I felt relief—I'd have someone, even if it's someone I don't know. Joan is a hazy memory to me, stolid, socially awkward, and now a thirty-five-year-old English teacher. Years ago at a dinner party, I remember her sitting with her parents, making her way through a plate heaped with soy sauce chicken wings and rice, while everyone else her age sat together, laughing and talking in the basement rec room. Even then, I understood that kind of isolation, because I engaged in it too. Separation as a means of self-protection.

Gillian also said that she had talked "with David" (my father's name always sounds strange coming from her lips) and that they would pay to change the date of my ticket if I wanted to leave earlier.

"As a gift," Gillian said. "From us to you and Joan." I thanked her. Gillian seemed surprised that I agreed, as though she'd been prepared to try to convince me. But I was ready to go. I'd already moved back to my dad's house from the apartment I'd shared with Jazz, and she was off to do other things. My best friend since high school and she let me go, cool as a cucumber, as my dad always said. But I knew she'd miss me, because she drove me to the airport and squeezed my hand, though she wouldn't come in to see me off because she hates airports as much as she hates hospitals.

My little sister, Beth, who looks so much more like our mother's daughter than I do, also squeezed my hand when I was ready to leave the house.

"Ouch," I said, but she didn't let go. Her eyes were terrified. "Beth, I'm coming back. In about a month. Please, you're hurting me." She released me and seemed to go limp.

"Beth," I said, "I'll bring you a real Slovak doll. Take good care of Dad while I'm away." But I know that Gillian will be around, and that she gets along with Beth without much effort on either of their parts. Maybe that's why Dad is so taken with Gillian. He looks at her with gooey eyes. It's offputting, but I'm glad he's happy.

After the plane took off and we were high in the air, the glinting lakes winking up at me from where they nestled in the forests, I imagined my dad and Gillian and Beth in front of our tiny house, waving up at me, Jazz raising a beer to me from some downtown bar. And I imagined the brick bulk of the hospital, at the edge of the harbour, a reminder of what I hoped to forget. And yet, it was my time in the mental hospital that made me ready for this trip, hungry for it, actually. My father was moved to tears that I wanted to get to know my mother and her family, but really, I just want to put her to rest. My mother is long dead, and I need to bury her.

Also, I want this whole world with its barbs and its glitter, its freshness and its aridity. It's hard to find the right words, but I want everything about it. I'm afraid of that dark dead place that swallowed me up. Like I was in a boat on the River Styx, my mother gently poling our way past the flaming shadows, her face white with terror and regret. But it wasn't her fault. She kept me safe, passing through that barren country. Now it's time for me to release her from that journey and deliver her safely to the other side.

CHAPTER 7

Joan woke early, the sun still low in the east. Her mind felt about in the semi-dark for something familiar. Bratislava. The word tasted metallic in her dry mouth. Saturday. A day to sleep in, laze about in her housecoat and slippers, and read the paper. But if she were to read the paper, she would have to go out and get it herself. She stared up at the ceiling. Would Milan work today? She thought so. Joan lay as though flattened by life—and no wonder. Her world had changed entirely in forty-eight hours.

She slowly sat up and put her feet on the ground. This she could do. First shower, then get breakfast and the paper, and hole up for the rest of the day. Except she would need to speak with Milan about Adriana's arrival. She might need his help to ask about the timing of the Sunday train from Vienna, though she would try to find out herself at the station. And she would have to pay her bill at the front desk, and let Front Desk Pani know she would stay another night. For this too she might need Milan. In Budapest, she had looked to Tibor for help, until she learned enough Hungarian to get by. Thankfully, the time of that particular dependence was past.

Joan got washed and dressed and out the door. As she passed Milan's apartment, she could hear murmuring and the sounds of dishes being washed and children's high-pitched voices. It was still early, before eight, and the Hotel Svatopluk was just waking up. At the front desk, Pani was eating some bread and cheese, and drinking a tiny cup of espresso. Joan approached with her wallet in hand. Front Desk Pani eyed her severely.

"Good morning," Joan said. "I would like to stay one more night."

The woman looked exasperated. "Nehovorím anglicky," she said. I don't speak English. Joan felt helpless.

"Milan," Joan said. Pani nodded. Yes, Joan should wait.

Joan sat on a narrow bench in the dim foyer that smelled faintly of must, across from the white-dusted pile of old shoes. She cleared her throat several times, as though it could rid her of a feeling of helplessness, but it could not. Fearful and irritated, she stood up and looked down the corridor. Milan was nowhere in sight.

Someone approached from the darkness of the hall. It was Mária, a kerchief on her head, a bucket in one hand and a mop in the other. She greeted Joan with glowing eyes. Joan nodded good morning and asked, "Milan?" Mária pointed to the entrance of the Svatopluk. Joan gathered he was out already. His mother blinked her eyes apologetically at Joan, and then in a pleasant stream of Slovak, spoke to Front Desk Pani, who looked angry as she waved Joan off. Still, she pointed to her watch, to the number twelve. Meaning Joan should return at noon, she gathered.

Joan took herself outside onto the cobblestone street. It was not so busy yet, but there were a few people walking with their heads down, as though not quite awake. A man staggered slightly along the centre of the cobblestones. He had probably been at the train station cafeteria for beer when it opened at six. Joan gave him a wide berth and he did not notice her.

She wanted coffee badly. But first she walked to the train station to check schedules. She could not make head or tail out of the plastic-encased yellow lists posted on the platform, so she got in line to speak with the man at the ticket counter. When Joan's turn came, she asked in English the hour of tomorrow's train from Vienna. He glared at her and pointed to the platform's lists. The woman behind Joan pushed in front of her as though she were a mere obstacle, leaving her standing, helpless, in a stream of people.

Deflated, Joan made her way back to the corner grocery. She bought food for the day and for the next. She did not know how late the shops stayed open and imagined they would be closed tomorrow, on Sunday, in so Catholic a country. Joan bought extra for Milan, but she could not carry enough nor afford to feed his whole family. And yet, with a little help from Milan, that is what Mária did, thanks to her bucket and mop and bent back.

Joan wandered the streets of old Bratislava. She passed designer clothing boutiques, tiny fragrance and cosmetic shops, art galleries with prints and etchings for sale, shabby corner stores with high narrow shelves stocked with cookies, potato chips, and stubby glass bottles of beer and soda, and faceless buildings that might house offices or apartments. Somehow none of the places she passed felt like they were open to her. It must, she thought, be her own trepidation. She resolved to find a café, sit down, and, like a tourist, watch the city awaken and unfold.

A couple kilometres or more from the Hotel Svatopluk, Joan began to flag. She saw a café with a small awning over a dark interior. Although it hardly seemed open, she pulled on the door handle and went in. The place didn't look like much but it was clean and fairly spacious. The sleepy-looking barista, a young woman with long curly brown hair, nodded at her.

"Americano?" she asked in a slightly weary tone. Her high nasal pitch reminded Joan of someone—who? An old teacher of hers?

"Nie," Joan answered stiffly, and in stilted Slovak, added, "Prosím, espresso."

The young woman nodded without looking up, turned, and a few moments later pushed a tiny cup on a saucer toward Joan. Joan downed it at the counter and, fortified but somewhat embarrassed, asked again, "Prosím, espresso?"

The barista raised her eyebrows slightly and looked over her shoulder. There were no other customers. She nodded, motioning to a table by the window.

"Sadnite si sem." She also brought Joan a small basket with a couple packages of cookies.

There was a bulletin board on the wall beside the table, covered in newspaper clippings, papers, and posters, some photocopied in black and white. Before she sat down, Joan glanced at the ads for tutors, editors, and language teachers. Surprisingly, she thought, there were ads for overseas English-as-a-foreign-language teachers. Brazil, Saudia Arabia, Russia, China. The last one caught her attention. A language school in Shandong province. A two-year contract, numerous positions teaching English to children in a primary school. Send resumé by mail or email, with photograph, and we will contact you for an interview. It sounded so easy. Could it really be that simple to get a teaching job halfway around the world? But then it had been practically her experience in Budapest—though then, Tibor had helped her.

Joan sat with her back to the job board. There was no one else in the café except for a professorial-looking man with round glasses and greying curly brown hair. He had a tall glass of water beside him and several espresso cups, and was working intently on his laptop. The barista cleared the espresso cups from the man's table. He glanced up at her and a smile flickered briefly across his face. Joan wondered what subject was so absorbing to him that he was spending a Saturday morning holed up in this dingy spot, working as though his life depended on it. She felt a certain envy—she could not remember a time when anything had so engrossed her.

Joan gazed out the window. There were more people about now, and cars. Women with shopping bags, and whose heels tapped the cobblestones loudly as they passed. Young men and women on bicycles, clearly tourists, and a delivery truck, which stopped outside the café and unloaded a dolly full of trays of what looked to be beer bottles. The delivery man wheeled the dolly toward the café door and opened it with some difficulty. The barista hurried to help, and the professor looked up with a frown. He said something, in a mild but clearly displeased tone, to the delivery man, who shrugged and gave the young woman a clipboard to sign. After leaving the trays in the back of the café near the counter, the delivery man nodded to the professor, whose forehead wrinkled as he waved back. So, thought Joan, this professor is not a customer. Perhaps he owned the place.

The barista brought Joan a glass of water and took away the espresso cups.

"Thank you," Joan said without thinking.

The young woman's face was pleasantly apologetic. "Very sorry. The delivery should have come yesterday, but it seems the Café Eureka is not a priority for suppliers." Joan was astonished. The barista's English was perfect.

Joan longed to ask where she had learned it, but she was already on her way back to the counter.

Joan dug in her wallet for a loonie she knew was there. For four years, since first leaving Canada, she had held on to it for luck, but now, somehow, she felt ready to give it up. She placed it on the table next to the empty glass.

Her hand shook slightly. Luck was something she did not put a lot of stock in, and yet—hadn't she had her share? She'd been lucky yesterday to get a job and a room, lucky to meet Milan, lucky to have her parents' somewhat bewildered concern all her adult life, or she would have been not only jobless but homeless and hungry. And yet it was only after meeting Milan that she understood this to be true. It was luck too that had brought Edna into her life. If English was Joan's currency, luck had been her passport into the relationships that had supported and nourished her for as long as she could remember.

The loonie vibrated a few times, then settled. The professor looked up at the sound and seemed to notice Joan for the first time. Joan felt something electric pass through her that left her palms tingling. She nodded to him as she got up to leave. He looked much like her father had, some twenty years ago.

Joan walked slowly back in the direction of the Svatopluk. She felt less on edge, despite the two espressos, and more at home on Bratislava's winding streets. The people she passed were simply caught up in their own lives. No one paid any attention to her. Her invisibility wasn't personal, but she felt like a forgotten specimen in a jar. Normally it was reassuring to Joan to be invisible in this way, but today it gave her nausea. The professor's glance had awakened in her a longing for recognition by another human being.

Halfway to the Svatopluk, Joan realized the nausea was partly hunger, that she was ravenous. She stopped for lunch at a little cafeteria that offered cold salads made from ham and potato and mayonnaise, and rožky, long white rolls that appeared to be a staple food. Avoiding the bottled soft drinks, she asked instead for water, which also came—sparkling—in a bottle. Joan stood at the counter and ate, gazing out the window. On her left, a man, unshaven in a baggy coat, wolfed down his food without lifting his head. On her right, a young mother absent-mindedly pushed a stroller back and forth with one hand while she ate a salad and read a magazine, her sleeping toddler rosy with dreams.

Joan wondered where the woman had bought the magazine. A bookstore perhaps? Maybe a bookstore would also sell English newspapers. Joan wiped her mouth and took herself back into the street.

Surely there must be a bookstore somewhere in the old centre of this city? Before walking too long, she noticed, in the second-storey window of a tall building, a long poster with a whitewashed version of what was meant to be a Roma man, she was sure, books spread between his hands like an accordion. He had a gold ring in his ear, wore a colourful embroidered vest and a feathered cap.

Joan climbed the concrete stairs to a door on the second floor, which opened onto a large room lit by fluorescent lights. Though it was early in the day, there were already a number of customers browsing. Classical music played, slightly more obtrusively than it would have in a Canadian store, Joan noted.

She made her way to the counter, where a young man who looked as though he had stepped out of the 1970s leaned with his chin in hand, flipping through a magazine. It was in English.

"Excuse me," she said. He looked up without changing position. "Do you have any English newspapers?"

He nodded, straightening. "We have the *London Times*, but it is a week old," he said, his accent light and slightly bored-sounding. "We also have Slovak English-language newspaper but they are about *our* news."

Joan nodded. Did she want Slovak news, or did she want news of the West and the rest of the world? It didn't really matter. She wanted newsprint and English.

"We do have *Time* magazine" he said.

Joan looked at the English-language magazines behind the counter. "I'd like a Slovak English paper, and *Time* and *Life*," she said. He did not look at her as he slid them into a plastic bag, his eyes wandering back to his magazine.

Joan went outside to find a bench. Surreptitiously, she sniffed inside the bag of her purchases, put her hand on the warm newspaper, flipped through the magazines but did not read them. Later, she thought, when I get back to the Svatopluk. *Time* and *Life*. It had never before occurred to her how strange and elemental these titles were.

She watched passersby with their bags and bundles and carts. People of all ages seemed to be everywhere. There were even what appeared to be foreign students, African and Asian, who spoke to one another in English, French, Slovak, and other languages. They seemed to recognize her as a fellow foreigner. At least, she felt they looked at her curiously, until she looked away. Was it the way she dressed? Slovak women, with their tinted hair and glossy nails, dressed with considerably more style and panache. They dressed to be noticed, even if the aim was simply to blend in. Joan thought her jeans and T-shirt and nondescript jacket to be unremarkable, but perhaps that was the giveaway. Joan wasn't sure this was the kind of attention she had been craving, but it was something at least. She existed.

When Joan reached the Svatopluk, Milan was sitting on the steps, looking morose. He leapt to his feet when he saw her.

"Canadian! Hurry! I must to train station. I must work!"

Joan flurried. "Can you help me pay my bill with Pani? I

will walk with you to the train station. I have lunch for you."

Milan rolled his eyes and motioned her inside. Speaking to a stone-faced Pani in soft and persuasive Slovak, he negotiated Joan's bill.

"I will stay tonight and tomorrow night also," Joan decided.

Milan sighed. "You must pay same as first night for two more nights."

Joan didn't argue. She handed a fistful of koruny to Milan. Pani slid the glass wall sideways and counted them one by one, and then again.

Milan waved a hand without looking at Joan. "I haven't time to ask better price. Tomorrow. I must go."

"Wait. I will walk with you!" Joan said.

Milan, impatient, waved her away. "You walk too slowly. The train is coming in seven minutes."

Joan, ashamed, shoved a couple rolls, apples, and a bottle of yogourt in a mesh bag in his direction. He hesitated, then took them.

"When does the train from Vienna come in tomorrow?" she shouted after him. Not looking back, he held up his hand, five fingers spread. Five o'clock? She was too tired to follow him, to ask for clarification. Tomorrow.

Joan, several hundred koruny poorer, went down the darkened hall to her room. Occasionally she would see a door open or close, and today a grey-faced old man in his undershirt hugged the wall as he passed her door. Joan said a quiet "Dobrý deň," but didn't understand his rasping reply. Only when she closed the door behind her did she realize it was Milan's father, smelling of cigarettes and resignation.

Joan lay on her stomach and ate, reading her newspaper and magazines in bed, like a teenager. She had even bought a package of potato chips (crisps, they were called on the sign, she supposed in the manner of the British) and a couple of small chocolate bars. Eventually she lifted her head from where it had settled on the empty crisp package and realized she had fallen asleep. Was it surprising that she was so tired? She had left Budapest one day and found a job the next. Tomorrow her life would be turned upside down when her mother's lover's daughter arrived. The next day she would begin work and move to a new home with a family and a strange little boy. It was breathtaking. Time. Life. Joan opened another chocolate bar and reached under the bed for her suitcase. Inside was the orange notebook— her journal, which she had carried across the sea, and which, though she had not written a word in it, had kept her company as a repository for her postcards to Ricky. Now, however, she was starting a new chapter of her life, one that warranted something else. Something more permanent than notes scribbled on ephemera.

Dear Ricky, she began, in black ink. The words that christened the pages of her journal were tentative and still addressed the person who she felt listened best to her. A wisp of longing for familiar things and people rose in her.

Joan didn't know what she should write about first. Adriana? Milan? The Burns family? The professor at the Café Eureka? What actually came out was a surprise to her. *I miss my father.* Her father was a man with a sharp mind for administrative details, and his critical blue eyes surveyed Joan and her usual joblessness with a disappointment that Joan found hard to bear. But she knew he loved her. Not with the bottomless devotion he had shown to Mao in his early years, nor the bowled-over sweetness he'd felt for her mother during their courtship, but with the confused and worried helplessness of a parent whose child is not what he had imagined her to be. Joan had never known what he'd wanted of her. They rarely spoke, but when they did, she felt closer to him than she ever had to Gillian. How are you, Joan? I'm fine, Dad. Do you need money? No, Dad, I'm fine. He would tell her tales of beaches and rainforests and glass-bottom boats from his latest adventure, but she barely heard the words, focused instead on the slightly raspy tenor of his voice, which reminded her of when they used to sit in his study, just the two of them, and he would read to her from one of his books. Then they would say goodbye, and she would feel calm and soothed for a time, until the longing for her father's voice returned.

Joan ate the chocolate bars slowly. All she had for supper was bread and cheese again, but it didn't matter. Her father was somewhere—Mexico? Costa Rica?—and she would eventually talk to him when he returned to Canada. She would tell him, although he never asked in those words, what she had been doing with her life. And for a moment she would feel the lens of his kind heart turned on her, and imagine he really saw her.

CHAPTER 8

"Miss!" Loud knocking on the door. "Miss Joan, now is breakfast time!"

Joan struggled awake. What time was it? Nine. How could she have slept so late? She pulled on her robe and slippers and shuffled to the door, opening it to Milan mid-knock.

"Miss," he said urgently. "Today is Sunday. In honour of the blessed Virgin, we have special breakfast. Palacinky!"

Joan half smiled at Milan's feigned piety.

He pointed to his naked wrist, as though to a watch. "Come. We are late!"

"Wait! I have to dress!" Joan said, Milan rolled his eyes impatiently. She closed the door on him and locked it, then quickly pulled on a sundress that lay on the top of a pile of clothes in her suitcase. When she flung open the door, expecting he might have left, Milan seemed to halt in surprise.

"You look nice, Canadian," he said, grinning. Joan rubbed the sleep from her eyes to cover her blush.

"It's clean," she said.

"Ideme," Milan snorted, looking pleased.

Joan followed Milan down the hall. He was in good spirits, whistling, hands in his pockets. Before they descended the whitewashed staircase to the basement dining hall, he paused. "Pozor," he said. "We cannot eat palacinky if you die on these stairs."

Joan wondered sleepily what palacinky was. Was it really a special day? Her stomach felt hollow.

Milan's favourite kitchen worker, Lena, was not there. In her place was a short, stony-faced matron serving what looked to be crepes.

"Sunday," he said solemnly. "God's day."

She handed him a plate with two steaming crepes, and he crossed himself, despite his self-proclaimed atheism. The woman glared at his outrageous hypocrisy. With obvious relish he placed a dollop of sour cream on each crepe, topped by a heaping spoonful of cherry jam.

"My favourite," he said, just as he had said about the cream of wheat on Friday.

Joan followed suit with her palacinky. They looked insubstantial rolled up on her plate. She followed Milan to an empty table in the middle of the dining hall. A couple hungover-looking men sat, each alone in a far corner of the room, drinking coffee. Tibor.

Milan smacked his lips, clearly enjoying each mouthful. Joan ate slowly, and when he was finished Milan eyed her remaining crepe. Joan thought about giving it to him, but knew she would need every bite of it.

"Milan, I have news," Joan said, as she finished the last of the crepe. Milan hid his disappointment well. "My Canadian friend will come to Bratislava. Today." Milan was clearly startled. "I do not know how she arranged it so quickly, but I am to meet Adriana at the train station. Did you tell me yesterday the train from Vienna arrives at five o'clock?"

Milan fingered his fork, looking slightly confused. He had only just downed a cup of espresso. "There are several," he said.

Joan frowned. She didn't want to call her mother to ask, so she would wait at the station for the first train, and if Adriana wasn't on it, for the second, then the third. She would bring a book.

"I will wait with you," Milan said. "Today I am free." Joan gazed at him, and Milan shrugged and grinned. "It is work on God's day, but...I am atheist. I will help your friend talk to Pani upstairs."

After breakfast, Joan changed clothes again into something suitable for the late fall weather, and she and Milan walked to the station. They sat on a bench on the platform. The first train would not come from Vienna for an hour.

"We must practise English," Milan said. He hunched over, elbows on knees, hands dangling between them, and squinted into the sunlight. "What is our lesson today, teacher?" he asked.

"Let's just talk," Joan said.

Milan nodded. "What is our subject?"

"Why don't you tell me about your work?" Joan asked. She wanted to know how Milan earned enough to survive, what he did when he wasn't arguing with St. Francis of Assisi in the church square.

Milan waved his hand and looked away. "It is nothing," he said dismissively. "It is not work. It is...trash." Milan frowned. "I need another work. But there are not so many jobs for Roma. Not good jobs. I want to do business. I tried," he said. "My mother cleans Hotel Svatopluk. She works too hard. But she also makes good food. I wanted sell in the market. My sister give me money, and I buy meat and potato, onion. But the butcher—you remember? At the market. He sold to me meat of poor quality. Some was bad. We must throw away half. Half! I sold everything my mother made, but there was not enough profit. To buy more food for the next week. And so...that opportunity is lost."

Milan's face was red with anger. He lurched forward, exasperated, but his hands remained limp and helpless. What could he do? Joan thought. Her face reddened in sympathy.

"For everyone. It is hard. But for Roma..." He shook his head. "Mrs. Watterson, she who lived in your room—she tell me, be proud you are Roma. Learn English, it will help you in life. She spoke English like the Queen." He shook his head with a regretful smile. "But she was a little bit wrong. It helps, yes. And I am proud," he said matter-of-factly. "But so was my father, before time. In my country, there is nothing for Roma."

Joan looked down at her feet. So recently she had thought the same thing about herself, but it was obvious that, unlike Joan, Milan had no easy escape route.

"My sister Jenny wants help us. But all she can is send a little money. And is not enough to go to school and learn tourism. I haven't enough koruny for college. Her husband," he said derisively, "is American tourist. He came here to teach English and drink beer. In America he is also like tourist. But he doesn't teach there. Only drinks."

Joan watched Milan in silence, his chin cupped in his hands. A moment ago, he had told her he had no future, but now he seemed to forget his despair as he surveyed the people hurrying in both directions across the platform. His eyes flickered. Joan imagined he must be sizing them up as potential business, though it was not always apparent to her why some of them were more worthy of his attention than others.

"See that lady?" he asked, nodding slightly toward a tired-looking woman in neat but drab business attire. She was pulling an overnight case behind her and carrying a worn briefcase. Joan nodded. "She is from Morava. She doesn't like Roma. It is pity because she come to city every week and need to stay at hotel." He smiled as she hurried past and tipped his hat. She fixed him with an icy stare, then turned her head away, imperious. Milan turned to Joan and grinned, but there was a slight twist to his mouth.

Milan spent the next hour commenting on passersby and their potential as customers. Joan was alternately amused and horrified. This one was a commuter from the town of Nitra two hours northeast each day, both ways. He had read almost every book in the Nitra library en route. Sometimes he needed a bed for the night. That woman lived in Austria but visited her grandmother each weekend in Bratislava, taking back cheap liquor with her. This one was a drug dealer, a prostitute, a con man. Milan seemed to have gained his knowledge not mostly from business dealings but from snippets of conversations overheard on the phone or at the ticket counter, receipts and business cards accidentally dropped. Joan was fascinated. Milan was like a crow, collecting little shiny bits and pieces to decorate the nest of his brain.

Milan gazed across the platform at the busy stream of people who were passing in both directions. A young woman, with black hair and slanted eyes, stood looking tired and lost. That's Adriana, Joan thought, rising slowly and brushing invisible dust from her lap. She was about as Joan remembered—slender, slightly cowed-looking, but much taller, taller now than Joan. Milan surveyed her critically. Joan noticed Adriana was wearing an almost nondescript blue outfit, unremarkable except that something about it flagged it as expensive. Did she look like the kind of person who would mock someone like Milan?

Adriana caught sight of Joan and, her face almost collapsing with relief, trotted toward them, pulling a suitcase behind her. Milan, self-conscious now, prepared himself, taking off his cap to wipe the hair across his forehead.

Joan offered her hand. Adriana pumped it hard.

"Thank you for meeting me, thank you," she said. Her voice pitched high, exhausted, edged with hysteria. "I don't know what I would have done." Joan didn't either. She'd been lucky to run into Milan on her own arrival.

He hung back, slightly hunched.

"This is—my friend, Milan," Joan said. It was the first time she had used the word *friend* in relation to Milan, and it put Adriana visibly at ease. It seemed to help Milan relax too. Adriana's hair, shiny and straight, swung forward as she reached out an earnest hand to shake his. She was like a bird: nervous, drab, but glossy-throated.

Milan seemed shy as he shook her hand. "Milan Holub," he said.

The pearls around Adriana's neck bobbed. Her whole outfit was matronly and ill-fitting, though she was, Joan realized, only two or three years older than Milan. Joan longed to give the pearls a firm tug to see them spill from their broken string and roll across the platform. Milan too looked at the pearls, and it seemed to Joan he blushed. Was he thinking about how many koruny they were worth? Or how they looked against Adriana's slim neck?

They walked together toward the Svatopluk, Joan chattering nervously about arrangements. Adriana could have her room when Joan left in the morning, but for that evening they would share the room. Joan thought she must be able to get another cot set up in there, if they were charming to Front Desk Pani—Pani Svatoplukova, as Joan suddenly thought to call her. The woman had never offered Joan her real name, and Joan had not dared to ask. She almost thought of the woman as being married to the hotel, so Pani Svatoplukova was a fitting moniker.

Milan, glumly ensconced in his own thoughts, kept his eyes on his feet. Adriana was pale as a spent rain cloud. Had she been crying on the train? Joan quickly explained the breakfast routine, where to find the telephone office, groceries, and bakery. So much had happened, and she realized she had learned a great deal in so short a time that she felt almost proud of herself. But her chatter, echoing around her as if she was walking solo through an abandoned warehouse, was essentially empty.

When they reached the Svatopluk, they paused at the front doors. Joan turned to Milan expectantly, but he was scuffing at a blob of chewing gum on the step with the toe of his boot. Adriana said nothing.

"Wait here," Joan commanded. She had bolstered her own self-confidence by rattling off her knowledge of Bratislava and was feeling strangely maternal toward Adriana. "I will ask the woman at the front desk about a cot."

Joan entered the dimly lit hallway. Pani Svatoplukova was in the back office, the blue light from her television glowing. Even at midday, it was like midnight in there. Joan rang the bell. The woman emerged, her eyes bleary from watching the soaps in the dark. When she saw Joan, her face became a mask. Joan felt her confidence wither but proceeded anyway.

"Dobrý deň, Pani, ako sa máte?"

Pani Svatoplukova's eyes flickered, surprised that Joan knew a few Slovak words, and her mouth softened slightly. "Dobrý deň," she returned crisply.

Joan, stumbling between Slovak and English, tried to explain that her friend, her kamarátka from Canada, was here; that she would like to take over her room from tomorrow, Monday, Pondelok, but was there a small bed, a cot (Joan drew a picture of something resembling a bed) that she could sleep on in Joan's suite till then? Pani looked doubtful. She will pay extra, Joan explained, drawing a hand offering dollar signs. Pani nodded, pleased. Joan felt pleased too that she had managed to communicate something relatively complex to so critical an audience.

When Joan returned outside to share the good news with Adriana and Milan, she found them in conversation.

"It's not that easy," Adriana was saying in a clipped soprano. "In Canada, it's hard for young people to find decent jobs too. Especially in Nova Scotia," she said. "You have to know someone."

Milan nodded earnestly. "But there, Roma looks like any foreigner," he said. "Canadians don't say, this one is Roma, shut the door."

Joan was astounded that Milan had so quickly revealed to the young woman that he was Roma. Perhaps telling Joan at the train station had been a turning point for him.

Adriana thought for a moment. "It's true," she allowed. "I've never even met a Roma before. If I hadn't asked, I would have thought you were—" She considered for a moment. "Italian? Or Spanish?"

Milan puffed out his chest. "I am Roma," he said with bravado. "No football player."

Adriana shook her head and smiled. "No da Vinci or Picasso either, I take it?" she said.

Milan looked confused, then blushed. "Roma was survive many centuries here. We haven't time to make cathedrals or flying machines or paintings. No. We survive. It's good, I think?" he proposed coolly.

"Of course," Adriana said, blushing. "And Gyp—Roma people's music is famous all over the world."

Milan looked pleased. "In Canada? You know Rómska music?"

Adriana nodded vigorously. Then checked herself. "I know the Gipsy Kings," she offered.

Milan snorted. "I will bring you listen some good Rómska music."

Joan felt uneasy. Was she jealous? Milan was her only friend in Slovakia, but already she could see that he and Adriana swam in the same current, while she only floated by on a boat with other adults, tourists in the land of the young.

She cleared her throat. Adriana and Milan turned to her.

"The lady at the front desk will give us a cot for you, Adriana, for tonight. Then the room is yours."

Milan was clearly impressed. "Pani must like you," he said. Adriana looked confused.

"I'll explain later. Let's take your things to the room. You must be hungry." Joan herself was starving.

Milan lingered. Adriana asked, "Do you want to get some lunch with us?"

Milan shook his head. "Sorry?" he asked somewhat shyly.

Joan knew he had no money. To save him embarrassment, she said, "Milan is busy this afternoon."

Adriana gave her quick smile that reminded Joan of her own mother's.

"Maybe later I can take you both out for supper," Adriana said. "To say thank you. For picking me up at the station and for helping me." She looked flooded with exhaustion. Her hair hung limp and her shoulders bowed in the ill-fitting blue suit, which appeared stiff enough that it could stand up on its own, even if Adriana were not inside it.

Pani Svatoplukova watched unsmiling as Adriana signed her name in the guest ledger. She peered into Adriana's face as though looking for something.

"Moja matka bola Slovenka," Adriana offered. My mother was Slovak. Pani looked taken aback, but a slight smile hovered around her lips.

"Hovoríte po slovensky?" she asked.

Adriana nodded. "Len málo," she demurred. Only a little. Pani's face shone. She waddled to the back office and emerged with clean bedding, which she thrust into Joan's arms, and a key. Joan gathered, from Adriana's nimble translation of Pani's effusive monologue, that the cot was in a closet in her room, which was locked because of thieves.

"Pani Wattersonova," said the old woman. So it was the Englishwoman's cot. Adriana looked confused. The older woman chattered away to her, explaining the situation. Joan gathered her young guest understood most but not all of what was being said, but Pani seemed happy just to talk at her. Adriana could at least nod in the right places and murmur agreement. The old woman pressed something into Adriana's hands. It looked like a dusty satchel and contained some ancient scented soap, and a small package of tissues. A welcome package such as Joan had not received upon arrival.

Adriana followed Joan to her room, Milan trailing behind and pulling the suitcase. He seemed put out, Joan thought, perhaps because he could not smooth Adriana's way with Pani Svatoplukova as he was accustomed to. Without his role, what was he? A scrawny Roma youth with nothing to offer a Canadian like Adriana. This is what Joan imagined him thinking as he pulled the suitcase behind him, forlorn as a shepherd who has lost his sheep.

Joan turned on the light to her room. The wall sconces flickered and one of them buzzed slightly. The space looked tired and shabby to Joan as Adriana surveyed it from inside her expensive suit. But she slipped off her shoes and flopped onto the divan.

"Can I have a nap before I do anything?" Adriana asked. She looked like an Asian Barbie in a business suit, Joan thought.

"Sure," Joan said, "but don't you want tea and a chance to freshen up?"

Adriana was already nodding off, so tired she didn't even take off her shoes.

Milan didn't know what to do with himself. He helped Joan spread a blanket over her guest, then put his hands in his pockets and hunched his shoulders toward his ears. "I will go now," he whispered.

Joan nodded. "I leave tomorrow early. If you are awake before the sun rises, please come to say goodbye to me."

Milan nodded, looking pleased. Joan realized Adriana hadn't tipped him before she nodded off. She rummaged in her purse and found nothing but small coins and koruna bills too big to part with. Eventually she came up with a Canadian five-dollar bill. She'd been saving it for her return to Canada, in case she needed to buy snacks at the airport in Toronto or Montreal. Adriana could pay her back later. She handed the cash to Milan.

"This is Canadian money. Can you change it?"

Milan looked at it doubtfully. Sir Wilfred Laurier stared back at him. "Who is this man?" he asked.

"It is a prime minister, from years ago. The leader of Canada," she said.

Milan stared at him. "It is pretty—blue. Not like American dollars. My mother likes blue colour."

Joan knew that he would give it to his mother, who would hide it somewhere she could look at it without her husband finding it. She pulled a few small coins from her purse. "Then give it to your mother. This is for you," she added, blushing at the smallness of the offering.

Milan put the coins in his pocket. "Thank you." Without looking at her, he opened the door to the room quietly and turned toward Joan, as though trying to decide what to say. Then he took a breath. "One day when I am first Rómsky Canada—prime minister? I remember. I remember you give me first Canada five dollars." Joan's eyes widened. For a moment Milan looked disturbingly serious, but then he bowed with grin and a flourish and closed the door behind him.

Joan flopped into a chair. Adriana snored slightly, a muted rumbling. The cot, it seemed, would not be needed that night. Joan had to pack, to get ready to leave this place for a new home and a new job. She felt an old anxiety begin to creep up her throat, but instead of pushing it away she let it come, breathing her way through it. Her heart beat in her ears and her face felt hot, but as she sat in the chair watching Adriana, she thought of Milan at the train station, the way his hands looked so limp and helpless though his face had been red with anger as he shared the butcher's treachery toward his family. Joan thought how much harder it was to be young, with dreams swirling though your blood, not able to find their way out.

It was strange to think that she was no longer a young person. When had she crossed that threshold, from the flowering garden into the street, still shaded and pleasant and lined with trees, that led eventually to the cemetery? She realized she walked alone through streets sparkling with lights and garbage, and the sounds of laughter. It comforted her to know there were others, but they were not people who knew or cared about her—those were very few. She would always be a stranger, even in the city of her own life.

CHAPTER 9

Joan bolted awake early the next morning to the sound of water running. She had slept through suppertime, through the night. Her heart sank. What time was it? And was Adriana the kind of person who spent an hour on her morning bathroom routine? It was still dark outside. Joan relaxed slightly and rummaged for her watch. Six o'clock. She was due at the school at eight, so she'd better make sure she was early. She hoped she could find her way back there—Milan would help, but she didn't want to wake him too early.

As if on cue, there was a quiet knock at the door. Milan, rubbing his eyes with the heel of his hand, mumbled, "Sorry. I know you are leave early and I want give you this." He handed her a rough drawing. "Mapa," he said, "do školy." It was a map to the school.

Joan was touched by his thoughtfulness. Adriana came out of the washroom wearing a white bathrobe and rubbing a strand of hair with a towel. Her cheeks were pink, and she seemed excited to be awake and alive.

"Good morning!" she squeaked. Milan blushed and Joan looked away, smiling.

"Good morning, Adriana," Joan said. "I am going to be leaving this morning for my new job, where I will have a room. So this place," she swept her arm wide, "this will be all yours."

"I am living here, in hotel," Milan said. "I am helping if you need me." Joan could see he would like to put his arm around Adriana to comfort her, but instead brushed her sleeve with his fingertips.

"I won't be far away," Joan said. "And Milan is a wonderful tour guide."

Milan looked grateful. Adriana gazed at him, as though seeing him anew.

"Perhaps he can show you the dining room. When it opens in an hour."

"That would be great." Adriana nodded vigorously. "That would be—perfect." Milan blushed again, so deeply his face looked almost angry.

Adriana peppered Milan with questions that he answered carefully, trying not to make any mistakes with his English. Joan scuttled back and forth, gathering her things and stuffing them in her suitcases. Really, she was only moving a kilometre or so, but it felt like the journey of a lifetime.

Milan and Adriana, now dressed in sweats and a T-shirt adorned with a Canadian flag, helped Joan take her suitcases to the street, although she could easily have done it by herself. Pani Svatoplukova was sleeping, so Milan scrawled a note for her, saying the keys had been turned over to Adriana. Joan passed them to her lightly, but it felt like a serious moment somehow. Adriana fumbled and tucked them into her bra. Milan turned away, delighted. Adriana was awkward enough that Joan couldn't help but worry about her, alone in Bratislava. But then, she had Milan.

They passed the dusty pile of shoes and emerged into the cool pre-dawn. In the east, a thin molten line scored the horizon separating dark from dark. Joan clutched the map in her hand, but she wouldn't need it. Somehow in the morning twilight she knew where she had to go. Milan shook her hand.

"Canadian," he said with mock seriousness. "You visit us."

Joan nodded. "We will have coffee and cake," she said, "when I get my first paycheque."

Adriana nodded, clasping Joan's hand in both of hers. She looked lost, her dark hair framing her pale face.

The suitcases rattled behind Joan over the cobblestones, the small one balanced precariously on top of the larger. Winding her way past familiar shops that gradually became less so, she stopped eventually outside the entryway to the school, the pale sign of the jet plane glowing slightly in the dark. A crisp breeze was beginning to stir, and Joan experienced a mixture of excitement and skittishness. It made her skin tingle, and she thought that what she felt must be akin to happiness.

A light was on in the Burnses' home. She knocked and waited. Eventually she heard the padding of slippers, and the old woman she had met there the other day opened the door a crack and peered at her. Joan put on a pleasant face and began to explain in English that she'd been told to come for eight and she was a bit early, when the woman turned away from the door, leaving the chain fastened across it, and called out in a tremulous voice.

"Robbie, ona je tu." The woman turned away and waddled past Robert Burns as he barged toward the door, clutching what looked like a large vase. He unfastened the chain and stepped aside to let Joan in. He was perspiring slightly, and she saw that the vase in his hands was actually a trophy.

"Please forgive Pani Marta," he said. "I asked her not to let anyone in the house, not anyone, when I am not here or am busy, and she takes her instructions very seriously. I will give you a key to the back door, which we do not keep chained when the gate is bolted. Please," he said, "Come in. I am helping my wife get ready for the day."

Peter was sitting in a high chair in the parlour, his face smeared with something that looked like pudding. Wasn't he too old to be eating baby food? Miša sat in an old manual wheelchair, her eyes closed. She opened one of them and smiled at Joan but said nothing. Burns had a small table set up next to her, bearing a steaming electric kettle and a jug of water. He poured the kettle and jug of water into the tall trophy. He was dampening his wife's hair by dipping a sponge into the trophy.

"Kamilka," Miša said, her voice reedy, eyes shut, "is good for hair." Joan's own eyes widened.

Burns rolled his. "She swears this trophy is the best thing to make the chamomile tea in. Maybe it's the copper. I don't know."

Joan wondered whether this would be part of her duties, and whether she should offer to step in to help for learning's sake. But Burns said, "I do this only every month or so. Your job will be to take my wife to sit in the sun for the morning and then wash it out for her before lunch."

The boy stared at Joan. Then he thrust a spoon full of goop toward her, as though expecting her to take it.

"Peter," Miša cautioned. Pani Marta clucked and grabbed the instrument from his hand. She began scraping food off his cheeks and spooning it into his mouth. Joan felt slightly queasy. It smelled sweet, like prunes mixed with rice cereal, or something equally horrifying.

Miša shrugged. "It is terrible, no? Breakfast is terrible."

Burns, running a comb through her damp hair, chortled. "Breakfast is the best meal of the day. But only if you can chew and swallow properly."

Miša dropped her chin.

So... Joan thought.

Miša finished the sentence for her. "Sometimes I can't.

So Pani Marta prepares breakfast gruel for me. With fruit, sometimes yogourt. Peter likes to eat what I eat."

Joan looked at Peter, who had two fists in the air, opening and closing his goop-covered hands.

"Twinkle, twinkle," Burns coaxed. Peter opened his mouth and shut it like a fish, but no words came out.

"Do you sing?" Miša asked. Her husband wiped her hair dry, strand by strand. The room was a rosy purple still but lightening every minute. Joan shook her head.

"Anyone can sing," Burns grumbled with a mock frown. "I sing very badly, but I sing. Pedro doesn't sing, because he doesn't talk yet, but he likes it if you do." Joan felt a moment's panic.

Miša opened her eyes and smiled. "Later," she said, closing them again. "There is time."

Burns sighed. More than tired, Joan could tell. He was harried.

"Time, yes. There is time. But not enough." He kissed her cheek. "I must go to school soon. Miša, we should shower." He bent to kiss his son, who turned his head away but put his arms around Burns's neck and didn't let go when he pulled away. Burns gently peeled the small fingers from his beard and put a stuffed toy caterpillar in Peter's hands.

"Pedro, Joan will play with you a bit later. She'll take Mama to the garden and play in the sun." It occurred to Joan that Burns might miss the sun himself, stuck in his dingy office smoking clove cigarettes. "Pani will help you take Miša and Peter outside," Burns said to Joan. "There is a fence around the back garden, so don't worry."

Joan's nerves jangled. What had she got herself into?

"You look...alone and palely loitering," Miša gently mocked her. "Like Keats's knight." Peter gazed at them with serious eyes. Miša crossed hers at the boy and stuck out her tongue. He busied himself with his caterpillar but stole a quick look at Joan, who also stuck her tongue out and made a face. Satisfied, Peter marched his toy across the high-chair tray.

After Pani Marta wiped his mouth, she motioned for Joan to take him from the chair. Joan lifted him out, awkwardly, because he was stiff as a board with his arms hanging limply by his side.

"Peter," Joan murmured, "It's okay."

Miša beamed. "Give him to me." Peter curled on his mother's lap, buried his face in her chest. She cradled him with some difficulty. "My boy." Miša pressed her nose into his hair. "You smell like elves and fairies." Then she released him to his father, who passed him to Pani Marta.

Burns showed Joan how to help his wife get ready for the day. Joan was tentative, unsure how not to hurt her.

"Don't be afraid," Miša warbled. "I am not glass."

Burns was gentle and sure of himself. He unbuttoned her top and removed it, then pulled off her pyjama bottoms.

Miša sat stark naked in the wheelchair. "Today I will wear a shower cap over my kamilka," she said. "Joan, please. It is in the shower." Joan reached for the flowered plastic bunch and fitted it over Miša's head, then awkwardly began to push strands of hair under it. Miša chortled and murmured something in Slovak to Burns, who smiled.

"You're doing fine, lassie," he told Joan, who was beginning to feel a familiar misery.

Burns helped Miša transfer to the shower chair, explaining to Joan how to do it and how to help his wife transfer back. "Miša will give you very good instructions," he said.

Miša was rail thin and shaky, but Joan could see the musculature of her arms and her shoulders, surprisingly broad now she was naked. She must at one time have been athletic.

"Thank you, Joan," Miša said, slightly winded. "My husband and I will shower now."

Burns, slightly embarrassed, nodded without looking at Joan. She nodded back and left them. Behind the bathroom door, she heard the water come on and hit the plastic shower doors, and the low murmuring of their voices, quiet laughter.

"I am sorry, Joan, but you must push."

Joan managed to get the wheelchair to the back step, but moving it over the threshold proved difficult. Pani hovered nearby, giving Joan directions in Slovak, which of course she did not understand.

Finally, she realized she could turn the wheelchair around and pull it backwards over the bump. Miša gave a small cheer.

"You have passed the examination!" she said.

Joan reddened. Of course Miša had done this hundreds of times before but had waited to see whether Joan could figure it out for herself. Or whether she would ask Miša for instructions, which had not, in the moment, occurred to Joan. Her blush deepened.

"Peter," Miša crooned. "Can you find a flower for your mama?" She repeated the request in Slovak.

The yard was sparse and Novembery, but Peter began to search. The sun, which had settled on every surface, was dimmed by a cloud and a sudden gust of wind. Miša shuddered, her hands clasped in her lap.

When the sun emerged, Miša's damp hair shone dark. Joan felt warm, but Miša shivered again, even though it was mild for an early November day and she wore several sweaters.

"Please ask Pani for a shawl," she said.

Pani prosím, dajte mi šálu. Joan repeated the words to herself as she walked up the path to the house. Pani, prosím. Please, missus.

Pani Marta took her time coming to the door. Joan looked back over the garden at Miša in her chair, murmuring to the boy, who seemed to ignore her but did not stray far from her. He was busy digging a hole in the dust with an old spoon. The sun was at about ten o'clock, and everything touched by it turned gold. Pani opened the door. She held a colourful shawl that looked to be of a Slovak folk pattern design.

"Je jej zima?" she asked, gripping her elbows and shivering to demonstrate. Joan nodded. Pani handed her the shawl, grabbing another small coat for Peter, pale blue with animal-shaped buttons, off a hook by the door. She thumped herself on the chest and mimed knitting.

"Ja." I. I made it.

Joan fingered the small sleeve. "Pekné," she ventured, one of the few words she knew. Pretty.

Pani covered her almost toothless smile with a gnarled hand. "Pekné, áno."

Joan put the shawl in Miša's hands. She peered at it, surprised, her mouth crooked.

"It is clothes from many years ago. I was a folk dancer."

Peter glanced up briefly, then continued his digging. What was he digging for, Joan wondered. He'd made quite a hole by now. There were other holes in the thin grass— moles, Joan guessed.

"Please, can you—" With a jerky movement, Miša crossed her arms with her hands touching her shoulders, to indicate she wanted the shawl around her. Joan folded the shawl in half diagonally, and Miša held it around her by grasping it in one hand. It needed a pin or brooch—even a clothes peg would work. Next time, Joan thought.

Looking drained, Miša closed her eyes once more. Joan wondered how she would help her get into bed. Perhaps Miša could transfer from the wheelchair to the bed herself, or maybe Burns... Joan looked up at his office. He stood with his back, pear-shaped and slightly feminine, to the window, phone receiver in one hand, gesturing casually with the other. Was he speaking Slovak? Maybe Swahili. It wouldn't surprise her somehow. He'd already turned out to be quite different than what she at first imagined. She pictured him blushing earlier as he prepared to shower with his wife.

The sun had disappeared once more. Now there were goosebumps on Peter's arm at his dimpled wrist. Joan picked up a stick and dragged it in a circle on the ground.

"What do you think of my circle, Peter?" Joan asked. "It's a cookie."

"Sušienka," Miša said. Peter came close to examine it.

"See, the stones are chocolate chips and the ants are raisins," Joan explained. Peter stared. He tugged at his mother's hand.

"Peter, you want sušienka? It cannot be true! You don't like biscuits. Not at all." He tugged her fingers again, harder this time, his eyebrows furrowed. Miša withdrew her hand gently. "We go home. Ideme domov. There are no biscuits outside. Only pictures."

Joan wheeled Miša, with Peter on her lap and clinging to her neck, to the door, and turned the wheelchair around, giving it a tug over the threshold. The ride must be harrowing for someone as frail as Miša, but she did not complain.

"Go, Peter," Miša whispered. "Pani Marta has sušienka." Peter slid off her lap and disappeared down the hall. Miša's eyes closed and she let her head slump forward.

Joan could not stop herself from worrying. As they made their way to the front room, she said, "Miša, we have tired you out."

"The price of beauty," Miša whispered hoarsely, with a regretful smile. She tipped her head and pointed with her eyes to a basin on a tall dresser. "Please," she said almost inaudibly. "Wash my hair."

Joan went into the bathroom to fetch warm water. The basin was heavy, decorated with Slovak folk art flowers on white porcelain, and contained a pitcher of the same pattern.

Miša closed her eyes as Joan placed the towel around her neck and sponged warm water onto her hair. Joan remembered the last time she had washed Edna's hair for her, in the nursing home, what seemed a lifetime ago. Edna's hair had still been partly dark, but for the most part wiry and grey. Miša's was thin and soft, and her neck so long and slender Joan wondered how it could bear the weight of her head.

Burns appeared magically, like the sun coming out. As though Joan were not there, he took Miša's hand. "I saw you sitting in the garden. You looked glorious." Miša gazed up at him with shiny eyes.

Joan excused herself awkwardly and went to find Peter. He was sitting on Pani Marta's lap, watching television while she shelled peas. Pani Marta motioned for Joan to sit next to them, setting the bowl of peas between them first. Joan was grateful to have something to do.

But after a few minutes, Burns called her name in a low voice. Joan leapt off the couch, the last few pea pods tumbling to the floor. Pani Marta clucked her tongue, but cheerfully, and Peter stared at her. She scooped up the scattered vegetables and hurried to the front room. Burns was folding Miša's shawl.

"She is sleeping," he said, his Scottish accent more pronounced than she remembered. "She says you did just fine. Thank you for helping Miša get outside. I wasn't sure whether to leave you so soon—not because I didn't think you capable but because I know what it feels like to be left to your own devices the first day on the job—but I had an important phone call."

Joan nodded, self conscious, and straightened the bottom of her T-shirt.

"While Miša is asleep, perhaps you can look after Peter while Pani Marta goes to the market? I am afraid he is a man of few words, but he plays Lego with a vengeance." Burns pulled a big tub covered with an old blanket from the corner. "I spread this blanket out first, and if all the Lego stays on it all you have to do to clean up is scoop it up and pour it into the tub." He shook his head admiringly. "My wife's wisdom. If it's not genius, it might as well be. She has lots of little tricks for making things easier. You'll see."

Burns clasped his hands in front of him "There is a lot to learn about caring for my wife," he said. "And a lot that she needs of you that is more interesting than what you have done so far. I hope you will be patient with us," he said, almost apologetically.

"It's not that I am not glad to have work," Joan said. "It's just—I feel so unprepared. And useless." Had that really come out of her mouth? It was exactly how she felt.

Burns looked relieved. "It's normal," he said. "That's how I felt when Miša was first diagnosed. And when I started this school. And when I became a father." He swept his arm aside, indicating everything. "I do not know if that's what life is like for everyone—but that's what my life is like."

Joan didn't know what he expected her to say, so she nodded.

"Pani Marta will go to the market now. Peter is happy watching telly, then Lego. Don't worry," he said, patting her on the shoulder. "You are doing just fine."

Joan looked down and shook her head. She didn't feel fine.

"Joan." Burns sounded stern, and she glanced up quickly.

His eyes crinkled. "Don't worry. It is not nuclear physics. The world will not end if you make a mistake."

The day passed like a slow-moving stream. While Pani Marta went to the market, Joan and Peter watched a TV program that appeared to be a rerun about the Chinese Moon Festival and featured a lion dance. Peter was frightened of the roaring beast moving wildly to an invisible drum, and pressed his face into Joan's arm. But later, while Joan read an old news magazine in the front room, Peter built a lion headdress out of Lego. It was astonishingly sophisticated for a boy of Peter's age, Joan thought. Red, blue, white, and black, with yellow eyes, a black pupil at the centre of each, and even the small curl of whiskers. How had he even known where to start?

Pani Marta returned with net bags full of rye bread and vegetables. Then she beckoned to Joan to follow her up the narrow staircase, hoisting herself hand over hand from step to step. At the top, there was a landing with a number of rooms off it. A small blue room with its blind drawn at the front of the house appeared to be Peter's. In the dark, Joan made out the shapes of a stuffed giraffe and a crib. Wasn't Peter, curled up at that moment with his mother in her bed, too old for a crib? Perhaps his father was trying to protect him from getting up in the middle of the night and wandering down the perilous set of stairs by himself. Or perhaps because Peter had not yet grown into language, Burns still thought of him as younger than he was. Joan brushed the thought away. She was not sure whether she had a right to worry about Peter yet.

Joan's room was square, with a sunken single bed covered in an old quilt and blankets. A small desk by a window facing the backyard, next to a chair with a woven jute seat and a large old dresser. There was no closet but there were hooks on the wall by the door, and a bookshelf, almost bare.

Pani Marta patted the pile of blankets on the bed.

"Zima," she said, hugging her arms before she closed the door on Joan. Cold is coming.

Joan sat and bounced the bed gently, listening to the springs squeak inside the mattress. She wished she could stay there forever. If only everything outside would disappear and she could hurtle through space in a ship that was only this room. She lay down quietly and closed her eyes. Below, Miša was resting too, the chamomile shining in her hair. Peter was napping, his head tucked into Miša's neck. Pani Marta was in the kitchen making soup with the vegetables she had bought at the market. The domestic tranquility lulled Joan to sleep.

Joan woke with a start and panicked, until she remembered she was not in Hungary in Tibor's flat. How long had she slept? She darted across the landing to the steep stairs.

Her large suitcase sat at the bottom of them like a monolith, and Peter crouched next to it, examining the flowery pattern of its heavy fabric. He traced it with a small chubby finger until she had almost reached him. Looking up as though he had been doing something he shouldn't, he turned quickly and trundled into the living room. Joan followed him to where his mother lay, quietly awake and staring at the ceiling.

Joan felt a hand on her shoulder and stiffened. Burns stood behind her, smiling at the sight of his wife and child. Peter silently toddled over to his father, ignoring Joan altogether.

"She is thinking," Burns said, nodding at Miša. "You missed lunch, but we have kept some warm for you. After you eat, Pani Marta will rest here for an hour or more." He waved his hand toward a tiny room off the kitchen—big enough only for a bed—before he disappeared into the school again.

Alone at the kitchen table, Joan gobbled down soup, salami, and bread. There was another bowl cooling on the counter, for Miša, Burns had told her.

When Joan brought it to the front of the house, she set it on a side table. Miša seemed to be asleep again. How many times during the day did she drift off, Joan wondered. Pani Marta appeared from the TV room, her face sagging, and settled Peter on the floor with his Lego. She put her hands together in prayer position but under one cheek, so Joan knew she meant she too would sleep, in the room no bigger than a confessional.

Joan turned back to Miša, whose eyes, serious and blue, were now open.

"I am famished," Miša said. "But I am too shaky today. Will you help me eat?" Joan took the bowl of soup in her hands. "You must put another pillow behind my head," said Miša, pointing with her eyes to a pillow on the chair across from her bed.

Joan did as she was instructed. A tea towel from the back of the same chair could be used to catch drips. Joan pulled the chair close to the head of the bed so she could put the spoon in Miša's mouth.

With the first spoonful of soup, Miša closed her eyes, contented. "Ah," she said, and nodded for another bite. The bits of soft vegetables she chewed slowly. Joan felt her shoulders begin to ache after a few minutes.

Miša ate most of the soup, but near the end began to cough, and seemed to be choking. Joan panicked. What should she do? Peter looked up at the sound of Miša gasping for air. Joan tried to roll Miša slightly onto her side and rub her back.

Miša shook her head. No.

Joan shrivelled. She had done the wrong thing.

Joan picked up a jar with a straw in it and put the end of

the straw in Miša's mouth. She sipped and gasped several times before turning her head away.

"Thank you," she said with a gasp.

Peter resumed playing. Joan sat back in the chair, relieved but miserable.

Miša lay back on the pillows, exhausted. And closed her eyes. "Eating is hard work," she said, smiling. "I don't like it. But I must," she said.

Joan leaned toward her. "I am sorry," she said, miserably.

Miša looked at her in surprise. "Joan! Don't worry. Be happy. Will you read to me now?"

Joan nodded.

"Emily Dickinson," Miša said.

Joan searched the bookshelf and eventually found a slim, very worn volume lying on top of several other books.

"My husband doesn't like poems. Though his name is Robbie Burns. I don't like Robbie Burns's poems. But I love my husband," Miša said, smiling.

Joan opened the book to where a colourful bookmark decorated with Slovak folk art held the page. It was a poem she was not familiar with. Emily Dickinson's poems always seemed to Joan a kind of alchemy that transformed words into something rare and crystalline, but she wasn't sure she understood what a lot of them meant. She read quickly, woodenly, but Miša did not comment on Joan's delivery. She smiled with her eyes closed.

"*Frigate* is a ship," Miša said, repeating a word from the poem, "but *courser*?"

Joan examined the word. "A horse," she said.

"Ah!" Miša exclaimed. "Please read again."

Joan did, more slowly this time, and once more after that, with Miša's bright eyes fixed upon her. It was, she realized, a poem about poetry, and how it could transport a person to another world, much more inexpensively than travel.

"Yes," Miša said. "Thank you." She turned her head and closed her eyes. Joan put the book back on the shelf.

She settled into a chair next to Peter, who was building what looked like a wall around his lion headdress. Could it be a cage? Joan wondered if Peter had ever seen a zoo. She had a feeling the Burns family did not venture far from home.

Pani Marta appeared in the doorway, rubbing her eyes. This was a sleepy house, Joan thought. Did Burns too nap in his chair in his dim office, clove cigarette smouldering in the ashtray?

"Môj dobrý chlapec," the old woman said in her gravelly voice. Come. Peter disappeared into the kitchen with Pani, and Joan was left with the Lego, wondering what to do. For some time, she listened to Miša breathing, a sweet whistling noise. In sleep she sounded like anyone else. Joan wondered if in her dreams, Miša's body still betrayed her or whether she was able to dance again to Slovak folk songs.

Burns appeared just after four, and Joan was free to return to her room. She took a *National Geographic* magazine from the basket downstairs with her. It was out of date, but that hardly mattered. So, she thought as she sat down at the desk, am I. She put her head on her arms.

Joan woke in darkness to the sound of Burns putting Peter to bed. Through the door she could hear his muffled telling of Goldilocks and the Three Bears, in Slovak except for the protagonist's name.

When she wandered into the hall, Joan found her large suitcase outside her door where Burns must have left it. Downstairs, she saw Pani had placed a plate of food in the fridge, with "Jana" written on a slip of paper. Salad and sliced ham and bread. Joan ate quickly and silently in the kitchen, and returned soundlessly upstairs, just as Burns was emerging from Peter's room.

"You found supper?" he asked without preamble. She nodded, blushing, remembering the shower. "There is tea in the kitchen. Always on the back of the stove. Let this be your home," he said, as he trudged wearily downstairs.

Slovaks were known for their hospitality, but even so, this offer seemed more than generous. She was still an awkward stranger to Burns and his family, and yet they had opened not only their house but their lives to her. Perhaps they'd taken a gamble on her precisely because of her awkwardness, because they could see she was not a smooth talker or slick operator. And because, in Miša's situation, they needed someone. Anyone. Maybe they, like Joan, felt they had no choice.

Joan sat at her desk again and began to write in her journal. *Dear Ricky, A lot of things have changed in my life*. Joan imagined Ricky sitting at his kitchen table, his smooth brow slightly furrowed. Ricky had never left the province they'd both grown up in. She did not mention Tibor, which would only worry him to the point where his natural equanimity would be challenged, and she didn't want that. She wanted to imagine him peaceful, if mildly confused, and pleased for her.

I was ready for a fresh start. Joan swallowed. It wasn't exactly the truth, and she debated crossing it out, but she remembered the tingle of excitement she'd felt that morning, before this long day started. *I have a new job, a new home, and new people in my life*. Miša, Burns, Peter, and Pani Marta. Milan and Adriana—but she realized she didn't know what to call them. She had referred to the latter two as friends, but could she say it was true, in the privacy of her own heart? Joan decided she would call them that for lack of a better term, and in doing so made some kind of commitment to them, which both warmed her and made her uneasy. It had been a long time since she could say that she had friends other than Edna and Ricky.

Later, Joan lay in the dark thinking about Peter's astounding facility with Lego. Not yet four and weighing maybe thirty pounds, he had created something beyond her comprehension. And yet he was very much a little boy.

"Wow," she had said, as Peter lifted the lion's head toward her. "It is very scary. I am afraid!" She pretended to cover her mouth with her hands. "Eek!" she yelped. Peter chortled, a strange sound to Joan's ears. His mother had stirred then.

"Peter?" she had called weakly, from the edge of sleep.

Miša of the golden hair, who loved her husband and her son and Emily Dickinson. She was, Joan thought, as slender and worn as that very book of poems they had read from. The frugal chariot of Miša's body, the almost translucent pages of the book that contained her, would soon be unreadable. She was beginning to disintegrate, even under the touch of those to whom the poem of her life was dearest.

Joan woke the next morning knowing that she would not see the inside of a classroom. Teaching was the work she was familiar with, but it had been an ill-fitting glove. Still, she felt a pang for the loss of it, because she had enjoyed parts of the job, and she felt her parents' disappointment bearing down on her from across the ocean. But there was clearly enough to do in the house with Peter and Miša. As monotonous as it might seem, it didn't bother her the way she thought it would. Though adventure, uncomfortable and exciting, sometimes found her, Joan had never been one to seek it out.

When she came down to breakfast, Joan was embarrassed that she had almost missed another meal. Everyone was sitting around the square kitchen table eating porridge. Goldilocks, Joan thought.

Miša smiled and waved her spoon slightly erratically. "Here is Miss Lie-a-bed," she said. Joan shrank. "Wiser than all of us," Miša continued. "She has missed porridge."

Pani Marta, however, had set aside a bowl for Joan and, with considerable fanfare, brought it to her seat at the table. She motioned for Joan to sit. Miša groaned and laughed, a tinkling sound.

Burns regarded her kindly. "You are not late, don't worry. Your sense of timing is impeccable, actually. Otherwise we would need a pentagonal table." He put his hand over Miša's.

"You know how I hate pentagons," she said. "I prefer stars."

"That, "Burns said, "would be awkward. And expensive. Isn't that true, Joan?"

Joan, slightly bewildered, nodded, then shrugged. Peter regarded her morosely. She leaned toward him and made a terrible face, tongue lolling and eyes rolling. He grinned and hid his face in his father's shoulder, then peered at her with a shy smile.

"Pedro approves of you," Burns said. "And Pedro is boss."

Miša rapped the table with her spoon in agreement.

"Even if you were a horrible person, if Peter liked you, that would be enough," Burns said.

Miša laughed. "But you are not a horrible person," she said. "Not yet. We must see how long it takes. I do not know what made the last woman horrible. Maybe my commode, or maybe," she added, scrunching up her face, "my books."

Joan hadn't thought to wonder about the woman whose

place she had taken. Had she truly been horrible or had she left this job for another, better one? There was no indication of her anywhere in the room Joan occupied. She did not seem to be missed. Joan wondered if she would leave a mark on this family or whether she too would simply be one more stranger passing through, as though the house were a train station.

The week went by slowly, each day a variation on the same theme: meals, taking care of Peter, reading to Miša. Joan soon realized that she enjoyed most of all the times she was alone with her thoughts, when Miša was sleeping and Peter was busy with his Lego. She would sit and read a magazine, which tethered her to life in the West, with all its harsh glamour and excitement over nothing. And then she would sit quietly, bathed in the light from the window, watching the heads of the people passing by. There were many dour, unreadable faces, women with frosted hair and thick makeup, men with hard eyes, but also the heads of young people, some up-tilted with laughter, still joyous and open to the world. Joan thought about Milan and Adriana, who, if they passed this window, would walk with shoulders hunched, anxieties darkening their eyes. Their beauty was the effortless beauty of youth, but they were not without cares—the kind that bowed their backs but had not yet flattened their dreams. Joan realized her own dreamlessness was strange and almost otherworldly, but that it had preserved her somehow, as though she had been born to stand, like a deer fawn, moments after birth on wobbly legs, without having first learned to crawl.

CHAPTER 10
ADRIANA

Worried about Milan, I wasn't able to sleep very much last night. He is still in bed, curled in on himself like a baby deer, long knobbly brown knees pointing to his chest. Milan is tall and even in this position he seems to take up almost the length of the mattress. His eyelashes, long and dark, flutter against his cheek, but I hope he doesn't wake just yet. I like to watch him this way, peaceful and motionless for once. Milan is younger than me by two years. Two years is not so much, he tells me, but when I think of what has happened to me in the last two years of my life—the mental hospital, living on my own for the first time with Jazz, and going to university—eighteen seems like a lifetime ago.

And yet—Milan too has already lived an eventful life. When I told him about my depression and my time as a patient, he looked concerned for me but not alarmed. That was the first time he put his hand over mine. He kept it there as he told me about his cousin who had been stabbed to death over a minor debt when Milan was only ten years old, while his family lived in eastern Slovakia. His father, a self-trained mechanic, decided then that the family must leave their village. So he piled Milan and his brothers and sisters and Mária into their old Škoda. They made it to the outskirts of Bratislava before the car broke down for the final time.

Milan's father sold it to a garage for parts, and was compensated with cash and a ride for the family into the centre of town, where they paid for a room at the Svatopluk for the night. Mária took it upon herself to ask about the cleaning job advertised in the front window. And so there they stayed, in a set of two rooms. Mária collected her tips in a jar, but her pay was little more than the price of the rooms. Because Milan's father had not been able to find work, he started drinking his allowance from the government, and the small amounts of money their daughter sent from America and Milan's hustling were what kept the family in meagre groceries. Milan hadn't had a chance to go to high school, though his grades had been good enough. In fact, some boys from one of the local gymnáziums had beat Milan with their schoolbooks when they saw him speaking to tourists in the square, correcting information that the fake St. Francis of Assisi had given them.

"That is how they use their knowledge," he said, shaking his head and grinning. "To beat me and defend a liar saint."

I tried not to cry but couldn't help it. I sobbed over his hands, embarrassed and miserable. He brushed the hair from my neck and kissed my cheek. He looked surprised, and grateful, that I had been moved by his story.

"You are the first person I tell this to," he said. I nodded and impulsively lifted his fingers to my lips. He laughed. "In old Slovakia men kissed women's hands," he said, and he did mine. So I kissed him on the mouth. His body stiffened briefly with surprise, then I felt him relax and a long sigh escaped him, as though he'd been waiting just for this. Since then we have spent every moment together that Milan is not working.

Curled up in our bed, he is at peace, asleep. Naked beside him, I shiver and wrap the blanket around me. What am I doing? We've known one another a week. My teeth chatter so loudly I think he might wake. But he simply shifts and stretches, smiling in his sleep, his arm reaching over his head as though he is a swimmer doing the back crawl in a warm ocean, far from shore.

CHAPTER 11

On Saturday, Joan went early to the Hotel Svatopluk to visit
Adriana and Milan, and to bring Milan some money from
her first wages.

"We will pay you every Friday," Burns had said. "Cash."

Joan wondered if that was usual, but she was glad to have
it. Along the way she stopped at the market and bought
bread and cheese and tomatoes. From the butcher who'd
cheated Milan's family by selling them bad meat, she
bought a link of kielbasa. The man did not seem to register her, but handed her the sausage, took her money, and
handed her change from red, thick-fingered hands without
so much as a glance at Joan's face.

Pani Svatoplukova sat at the front desk of the hotel with
a ledger. She glanced as Joan entered the dim hall, then
waved her in without a word. Joan made her way to Adriana's room and knocked on the door. After a little while
with no answer, Joan decided she would go to the cafeteria
to see whether Adriana had gone for breakfast. But then
she heard a small voice inquire, "Who is it?"

Adriana opened the door wrapped in a blanket. Her hair
was staticky and her narrow shoulders were bare. She stood
in the door frame, without inviting Joan in, but clearly she
was glad to see her. "Will you wait for me? Outside. I—I
have to dress."

Joan nodded and retraced her steps down the dimly lit
hall. Pani Svatoplukova had disappeared into her back
room, where the ever-present television glowed like a blue

hearth. How did she manage to continue, day after day, Joan wondered. Her life seemed so dark and cramped. Joan realized that life at the Burnses' house was comparatively bright and warm and spacious.

Emerging into the crisp air, she took a deep breath. Saturday. She sat on the steps and hugged her knees, looking up at the bright, cloud-covered sky. Soon Adriana appeared and sat down beside her, pale and unfocused, as though she hadn't slept. Adriana didn't look at her, gazing instead down the cobblestone street, which soon disappeared behind a chalk-blue building of the same vintage as the Svatopluk.

"It was a strange week," Adriana said. "I wish I could have talked to you about it. But now it is over and you are here." She took a deep breath. "Milan is sleeping," she said. "He stays with me now. His father kicked him out. Isn't that awful? But it was because of me. His father called me a Canadian whore." Adriana covered her mouth with her hand. Joan wasn't sure whether she was trying not to laugh or cry.

"Adriana," Joan said quietly, shaking her head.

Adriana shook her head too. "What could I do? I wasn't going to let him sleep on the street."

Joan didn't know what to say. Adriana, barely past twenty, looked like a kid, and Milan...well, he was still a kid. Joan hoped he was at least eighteen.

"I'll be in Slovakia for a month," Adriana said. Joan could tell from Adriana's bleariness that she'd been thinking while Milan slept. "I'm going to visit the place my mother was born and meet her sister and find out more about her. I leave tomorrow. Milan is coming with me."

Joan's brain began to turn over. What about Milan's work? He was, at best, self-employed, so maybe it wasn't an issue, except if his mother counted on his earnings to feed the family. But now that he was out of their home, did they still depend on him?

"I want to find a way to bring him to Canada, because he can't stay here," Adriana continued. "There's nothing for him here. I'll marry him if I have to."

Joan gazed at her in disbelief. Adriana sounded staunch, but Joan could see she was quaking. Her hands shook, and her eyes were terrified, but her chin stuck out almost defiantly.

There were many things Joan could say to Adriana, some of which would cut her like glass, but that wasn't what Joan wanted or what the situation called for.

"Adriana—I don't know if there's another way. But maybe my boss—Burns—would know. Can I ask him for you?"

Adriana, relieved, exhaled a long, tremulous breath. "I would… That would be so… Thank you." Adriana looked as though she wanted to hug Joan, but instead, she wrapped her arms around her own shoulders, perhaps against the cold, but more likely against the future.

Brown hands appeared on Adriana's shoulders. She startled, and Joan looked up to see Milan, dressed in a button-down shirt and dress pants, kissing Adriana on the top of her head.

"Ahoj, Joan," he said.

Adriana leaned back against his knees, nervous but clearly happy. Milan, his restless energy having at last found a focus, gazed down at her, his face glowing like a polished shoe.

For a moment Joan thought of the black-and-white photo of her own parents before they married, tucked into her journal. So young, so happy, shielding their eyes as they stepped out of a dark entryway into the sunshine. Adriana might be older than Joan's mother was when she married, and perhaps older than when Gillian had Joan, her only child. How old, she wondered again, was Milan?

"It's so cold!" Adriana exclaimed, giddy with—what exactly?

Joan had so many questions, and she didn't want to leave them yet. "Can I invite you to go out for brunch?" she asked.

Adriana nodded vigorously. "I'm starving!" she declared, and jumped up.

Milan looked confused. "Brunch?" he asked.

Joan smiled. "It is breakfast and lunch together."

"Ah!" Milan said. "It must be good."

Joan nodded. "It is very good. Where is the best place to eat, Milan?"

"I think...Stará Tržnica. The Old Market Hall. There you can buy everything. And," he said, "you can try burčiak. Young wine! Yes. You must try, it is delicious."

Adriana clapped her hands, delighted. "I must change into something warmer. I'll bring your jacket, Milan!" She jumped up from where she sat and disappeared into the hotel. Milan gazed after her for a moment, then sat down next to Joan.

Joan pulled an envelope from her bag. "Here," she said. "It is to thank you for helping me find my job."

Milan took the envelope but did not open it. "Thank you," he said, smiling down at his hands. He looked well put-together. Only his shoes looked worn.

"How old are you, Milan?" Joan blurted.

"I am eighteen," he said. "Soon, next year, I am nineteen. I am old enough. I can drink alcohol. I can drive car. I can everything except go to school," he said bitterly.

Joan nodded. If Milan could have gone to high school, and then to university, his future would look so different than it did now. But then, he wouldn't have met Adriana.

Adriana returned with her hair pinned up and wearing the blue skirt she had on when she arrived in Bratislava, though instead of the ill-fitting blazer she wore a white sweater, a thin down jacket, and a scarf the colour of cornflowers. She looked lovely, Joan thought.

Joan realized her own sweater was baggy and dull, and her coat was one she'd brought from Canada four years ago. Milan, gazing at Adriana in undisguised adoration, ran a hand through his hair. Blushing, Adriana handed him his old jacket and a brilliant fuchsia scarf. Joan had never seen it before. Had Adriana given it to him? He looked, Joan thought, princely.

Adriana glanced at Joan. "Here," she said, and pulled a burgundy cotton scarf with sequins from her purse to give to Joan. "We must match." Then, more practically: "It will keep the wind off your neck."

Adriana was right of course. The scarf was as warm as it was pretty. It wasn't Joan's usual style, but she wrapped it around her. There was something festive about the idea of going out with Milan and Adriana on a crisp November morning to eat and drink together, and with the scarf she felt dressed for the occasion.

Buoyant, Milan ran down the steps and threw his hands in the air, dancing a few steps. Adriana laughed excitedly. Joan brightened, forgetting for a moment that the future was an unknown quantity.

Adriana shivered. "It's so cold," she said again, her voice a squeal of delight.

Milan threw his arm around her shoulders, then reached out to Joan, who was plodding slightly behind them, with his other hand.

"Come, Canadian. It's not far, just across the old town." Joan felt his arm across her shoulders. He was a head taller than Adriana and a head and a half above Joan, so his long arms reached comfortably in both directions. She felt a trickle of happiness as Adriana's peal of laughter vibrated through her. For once, Joan felt like she belonged to something.

After almost a kilometre, Milan halted in front of a shop window, and Adriana and Joan jolted to a stop too. Milan dipped his head toward the watch sales and repair store, where several expensive timepieces were displayed. He was not looking at the watches for sale but at the inner workings of an oversize model of a clock, its gears interlaced and turning.

"It is time," he said almost solemnly. "A time machine. Not for time travel. It is a machine that makes time."

Adriana gazed at a tiny watch face inside a heart-shaped locket on a fine chain. Joan peered at their reflections, a dark three-headed silhouette against the grey sky. If she had a machine that made time, what good would it do her? Winter was coming, perhaps she could stave off the cold for a while. Joan shivered, and Adriana, as if she could feel it through Milan's arm, shivered too.

"Brunch!" Milan declared, spinning them around to face the square. "Burčiak! Ideme."

People turned to look at them, some with curiosity, some staring as though they were freakish. Milan clearly didn't care. Adriana and Joan were tucked under his arms like baby birds, but Joan wondered if perhaps it was they who offered him protection.

The Old Market Hall bustled with vendors and customers, its tall windows standing above the stalls in glowing rectangles. Milan was clearly enlivened by the atmosphere. His arm fell from Joan's shoulders to point out traditional Slovak delicacies while he held Adriana at the waist with the other, leading them past baked goods, jellies and jams, root vegetables, and smoked meats. Joan and Adriana wanted to buy everything, but Milan, with a low and steady stream of commentary, steered them away from some of the vendors he thought were overpriced or offering poor-quality goods. When he stopped and pointed to a case of fried pastries with cheese, Joan took it as a resounding recommendation and bought enough for the three of them.

"Burčiak?" Adriana inquired mischievously.

Milan shook his head. "First we must eat. Then we buy burčiak from the—place of wine. You must have food in you before you drink, or you will be drunk as—" He pointed his chin at the Slovak men in the market's small beer garden, who were loud and hoarse and swaying.

Adriana laughed. "I know how to drink, Milan," she said, swinging her hair over her shoulder. Milan squeezed her waist. Joan turned away and bought three Americanos to go from a curly-haired barista in a black shirt, so handsome that Joan was taken aback.

They found seats around a small table where they could watch the market activity. There were strings of lights around some of the stalls, music playing in the distance, and throngs of people now that it was nearly ten in the morning. Milan's gaze flitted from one stall to another as he commented on the quality, price, and authenticity of the food. Adriana, listening with half an ear, seemed mesmerized by the people. She watched stylish couples with small children, old men and women bent double over their grocery carts, a trio of teenage girls at a stall that sold leather trinkets and wooden combs. Joan's eyes went from Milan to Adriana and back, each caught up in their own fascinations, occasionally talking over one another, and seemingly effortlessly intersecting at moments to point out something or someone of interest.

Milan had clearly given a lot of thought to what was successful at the market and watched keenly when new vendors and products made an appearance. It surprised Joan to learn he came here every Saturday morning, "to think," he said. It did not seem like the kind of place for deep thought— but if one was dreaming of becoming a vendor at the market, maybe. Joan knew he'd dreamt that for his mother, on a smaller scale, but what else did Milan wish?

"I want to buy a doll for my sister!" Adriana suddenly declared.

Milan considered, nodding. He pointed down the hall. "You can buy doll in traditional Slovak folk dress this way. It is same way as burčiak," he said, with some embarrassment. Perhaps, thought Joan, he did not want them to think he drank here often.

They wound their way through the crowd, Adriana holding Milan's hand, Joan holding Adriana's. Milan stopped before a small stall, where felt dolls dressed in Slovak folk costumes lined the table and hung above and beside it, framing the woman who stood in the shadows behind the table. Joan thought she might be the doll maker, her fingers rough from needle pricks as she picked up dolls to show them. Milan hung back, his hands in his pockets, while Adriana oohed and ahhed over the brightly coloured wares. Joan noticed the price, several hundred koruny, expensive in Slovak funds but a bargain for a handmade doll in Canadian dollars. Adriana selected one with long brown hair and a red, green, and pink shawl and matching skirt.

"She looks like my sister!" Adriana exclaimed.

Joan noticed one with black hair and a peacock-patterned vest and brilliant blue skirt. She also wore a cap with a peacock feather embroidered on it, reminding Joan of Edna. Joan held the doll toward the seller, along with a handful of koruny. The woman put it in a paper bag and handed it back to her with an ingratiating smile.

"I must give her a Slovak name," Adriana bubbled excitedly. "Gabriela, after your little sister," she said. Milan looked happy. "What will you call yours, Joan?" Adriana asked. She and Milan turned their dark eyes toward her. They did not know about Edna. They did not even know her name. Joan closed the drawstrings of her heart's purse, but she left it open, a little. She gave them Edna's Hungarian name.

"Orsolia," she said.

Just a couple stalls from the doll maker was a larger tent with tables and chairs and a counter in the back. A white picket fence enclosed the area. There was a line at the counter, but Milan pushed his way past and sat at one of the empty tables. A man behind the counter waved at him, and Milan, clearly pleased, waved back. The man, maybe forty, clean-shaven and dark complexioned, spoke a few words to two teenagers serving customers at the counter and approached Milan, wiping his hands on his apron. The young man and woman, who were handing out mugs of beer and bottles of wine as quickly as they took their customers' money, glanced Milan's way. Milan half-raised his hand—shyly, Joan thought. They nodded in his direction and continued working. Milan greeted the vendor with a handshake, and they held a quick, animated conversation in Romany. Adriana looked bewildered, but Joan listened hard to see whether she could distinguish other words in the stream of talk. She thought she heard the names of Slovak towns in the east. Prešov, Levoča, Košice. Perhaps they were sharing news of friends and family far away. Either way, they seemed glad to be in one another's company, and oblivious to Joan and Adriana.

Suddenly Milan seemed to remember he hadn't come alone. He introduced Adriana and Joan, and his Roma friend gave them a gracious half bow. Milan explained in Slovak that they had come to try burčiak, that Adriana was his best girl (which made her blush), and Joan was his good Canadian friend. And he introduced the vendor as Josef, who now grinned broadly, cocked his head, and tipped his cap. Then Josef brought a pitcher of orangey-gold liquid to their table, along with three glasses nested one inside the other that he carried upside down in one hand. Josef, Joan thought, was nothing like Tibor's father, though they shared the same name.

Milan poured Adriana and Joan each a glass, and clinked his to theirs enthusiastically.

"Nazdravie!" he said. Adriana, clearly thirsty, took a long swallow. Milan, grinning, put his hand on her glass to stop her. "Pozor, it is not juice!"

Joan sipped hers. It was cold and refreshing and *did* taste much like fermented juice, she thought, but a few sips filled her with a rosy warmth. She saw Adriana's cheeks grow pink and she knew hers were doing the same. Milan, who had only filled his glass half full, set the pitcher to his right.

"Just a taste," he said. "All else, I take home. To my mother."

After half a glass, Joan felt sleepy, but Adriana was enlivened and sparkling. Milan looked at her, eyes shining. He did not seem affected by the drink, except perhaps that his tone was more confidential than usual.

"Josef is entrepreneur," he said admiringly. "He started make wine to sell in his village. He one time came to Bratislava to sell wine at Saturday market. Then he bought flat here." Milan shook his head in wonder. "He is—unusual. I respect him very much. His children work for him." Milan nodded to the young people behind the counter, "And other Roma. But his children go to gymnázium and will to university. I am happy he is my friend. Some Roma think he is too—proud. But I think he is just enough proud."

Adriana reached for the pitcher. Milan pushed it away from her and fluttered his hand in the air. Josef waved back and sent his daughter to the table.

Milan began to chide Adriana. "Too much young wine for brunch, and you—"

"Will be drunk as punch!" Adriana quipped, and began to laugh uncontrollably. Josef's daughter, pitcher of water in hand, seemed familiar with the routine. She had a serious look, but a beautiful smile broke out on her face when Milan asked her how things were going at high school. She put down the pitcher of water and took the burčiak away.

Milan followed her with his eyes. "She wants study law!" he said.

Adriana, her cheeks still pink but her eyes slightly sleepy now, looked perturbed. "I want to decorate cakes," she said in a small voice. Joan looked at her in surprise. Milan too seemed taken aback. "I want to be a pastry chef," Adriana persisted. "I love beautiful things, and things you can eat."

Milan hugged her shoulders and looked over Joan's head at the rectangles of light that were windows. He breathed, "I want be engineer. I want build roads and bridges."

Adriana looked shocked. "My father is an engineer!"

"Yes," Milan said quietly. "You told me another day."

They both stopped talking for a moment, as though lost in thought. Joan sipped her water and cleared her throat.

"And you, Joan?" Milan asked. "What about you?"

Joan had been wondering the same thing. "I like to teach," she said. "But I don't know." How was a person to really know when they hadn't tried anything else? And who was to say there was anything she wanted to be? Except she *had* tried. She had been a failed bus driver, kitchen staff at a nursing home. Now she was a nanny and personal assistant to a woman who used a wheelchair. Joan realized with a kind of shame that she did not consider hers a real job, but a stop along the way to something else.

Milan pronounced loudly, as though to the whole world "Teach then. Until you know."

Joan smiled back at him and lifted her glass of water. "Nazdravie," she said, clinking his glass, and wondering if she would ever teach again.

A man with a violin and another with an accordion sat at a nearby table. After half a pitcher of burčiak, they began to play, music that was at once melancholic and buoyant. At least Joan could not decide what it was—it sounded both to her. Milan sat back in his chair and nodded his head in appreciation, until Josef came from behind the counter and gestured for Milan to join him. Milan jumped up and the two began to dance beside and around one another, their footwork slow and dramatic at first, until the music picked up speed. They became light and quick, clapping hands, slapping their chests and legs and clicking their fingers in the air at shoulder height. Joan and Adriana watched in astonishment. And then it was over as quickly as it had begun. Milan dropped back into his chair, panting and happy and slightly embarrassed.

Adriana beamed at him and gave him a hug.

Joan poured him a glass of water, which he downed immediately. "You are a very good dancer, Milan," she said.

He looked down at his feet, embarrassed. "I don't care about good, Joan," he said, almost too quietly to hear. "It is funny."

"You mean, dancing is fun?" Joan said, but Milan and Adriana were already headed to the counter to pay.

Josef, hands on hips, and grinning, waved Milan away, but Milan dug into his pockets and found the envelope Joan had given him. He pulled out some koruny.

"Josef's young wine is the best in Slovakia," Milan declared to Adriana and Joan.

Josef, puzzled, laughed a fine, bell-like laugh and clapped Milan on the arm.

"I have not tried all the young wines in Slovakia," Milan admitted to his Canadian friends. "But I know it is fact, because it is Josef's burčiak." Josef's daughter translated for him. With a sentimental look, he handed Milan a paper bag containing the remainder of the burčiak. Joan caught the word *tata* and imagined Josef saying, Give your father my regards. Milan, his happiness unfazed, shook Josef's hand.

CHAPTER 12

Milan is happy. He's been drinking young wine, of course, but it's like he's covered in gold. I've never seen him look this way, even when he smiles at me.

I feel bubbles of elation and a swooping feeling at the same time. I imagine Milan in Canada with me and wonder what there will be for him there that will make him feel this way? What will give him happiness and peace like drinking burčiak and dancing with a friend who knows his family?

I won't think about this now. I whirl around to face Milan.

"I want ice cream!" I declare.

He shakes his head as if waking from a nap, still golden. "Zmrzlina? It is cold outside!"

I announce, "I'll treat you both! It's my turn!"

Joan nods. "Canadians eat ice cream in every season, Milan," she explains.

He laughs. "Of course. So do Roma. But not when they feel cold."

I lift Milan's hand to my still-warm cheek. "I'm not cold! All that dancing."

Milan laughs again. "I danced, not you,"

"I know," I say, doing my best to bat my eyelashes.

Milan blushes deeply. "Okay. Zmrzlina. But we must also have káva. Too much young wine for brunch and...?" He looks at us both expectantly. This time it's Joan who continues his sentence.

"Not enough coffee before lunch and...?"

I struggle for a minute. "Ice cream will cure you, I have a hunch."

Joan smiles at me, but Milan looks confused.

"Hunch? Does it mean you are ill?" Milan asks with concern.

Joan shakes her head. "It means an idea," she says.

Milan looks bewildered.

I hunch my shoulders. "This also means hunch," I say.

Milan grins and throws up his hands in surrender. "English," he groans. "Ideme!"

We buy espresso from a little cart parked beside a piváreň. From inside, we hear loud voices and laughter and the sound of a passionate argument about a sports team or a rock band, I can't be sure which. We down our coffee, and immediately I feel the sobering effect. Milan leads us to an ice cream stand at the far end of the market. There are many people here now and the mood is festive, but Milan is settling into a warm calm. I can feel he is on the cusp of something, of deciding to leave. Maybe he dislikes a crowd, or maybe he's full of all the good things that've happened. I think it's the latter because when he joins the line at the ice cream stand, then turns around to beckon to Joan and me, he looks—relaxed. At home. I wish I had my camera to take his picture. I walk to him, reach out my hand to take his. His fingers are cool but his palm is warm and dry.

I buy tiny cones of zmrzlina flavoured with nuts and chocolate. It is the best ice cream I have ever tasted. We walk toward the market's exit, silently, reverently, licking our cones. We're finished before we reach the doors.

We walk slowly across the square, sated. Milan tells us about the first time he tasted zmrzlina.

"I was at summer karneval with my mother and father and Jana. I was five year old. Jana asked for zmrzlina. My father bought for us. I could not believe something was so good. I thought it must be same that angels eat. Then Jana wanted go on kolotoč—do you know it? With horse and animals going around? Yes, maybe merry-go-round—is nice English word. I wanted another zmrzlina, but Jana was tata's favourite. We went on kolotoč and Jana was ill. My mother and father took us home, and I did not have zmrzlina again till Bratislava." Milan smiles and shakes his head.

We stop in front of the watch repair shop again, the three of us reflected in the window, the fringes of our bright scarves floating away from our necks in the breeze. I survey the heart-shaped locket again, so small and dainty in the folds of display satin. The clock part is upside down, I notice, so that if a person wearing it around their neck were to turn it toward them to look at the time, it would be right-side up. Even this is beautiful to me, and it shocks me that I want this locket, because so rarely do I want to own something. But it's so small, so useful. I imagine the chain sliding into my hand and around my neck. I notice this time that it is old, that there's a little tarnish at the hinge, that it must have belonged to someone before it landed here. I feel a kind of curiosity, muted with sadness, about its former owner. Who would part with something so lovely unless they had no choice? And at that moment I remember I have something of Joan's, something her mother gave me to give her. Something I must not forget to do.

Milan takes a step back. "Thank you, time machine," he says, so fervently I at first think he is serious, "for making this beautiful morning for us."

It's almost noon. The other watches in the display tick dutifully away toward twelve. He bows low, and to my surprise, Joan follows suit. She grins, quick and sheepish. I thought her too serious to be silly.

I curtsy and say, "We three timekeepers salute you."

Milan grins. "This is the shop that tells me when is time to work and when is time to go home. It is my boss." But something tells me it is more to him than that. A place maybe where he pauses his frenetic, hungry life to dream of another future.

Back at the Svatopluk, Joan waves a few linked sausages toward us. "For your mother, Milan," she says.

Milan bows low and accepts them, wrapping them around his neck like a feather boa. When we head inside, the woman at the front desk is bending down behind the counter. When she straightens and sees us, she smiles uncertainly at me. I still don't know her name. Milan explains we will be leaving in the morning for a trip to the east. She nods her head warily. I tell her I'd like to keep the room for another two weeks, till we return, and then another week after that, until I return to Canada. She softens and accepts the fistful of koruny I hand her. We do not negotiate a better rate, but she slips a handful of one-hundred-koruna bills back to me, under the glass barrier. Thank you, Mrs.... Milan is not listening, but whistling and heading for the corridor. Please call me Alica, she says.

Milan dances a little as we head for our room, each of us swinging a net bag of food, delicacies and necessities we picked up at the market. When he passes his parents' room, he dips his head toward the door but does not stop. I scurry to keep up with him. When we reach our room, he opens the door, then turns and scoops me up in his arms. I giggle and struggle, but he doesn't put me down till he reaches the bed. Then we curl up together there, his head on my lap, the linked sausage still wrapped around his neck, and Milan falls asleep, his lips pressed to my hand. I cannot move, so I take a smoked oštiepok cheese from one of the net bags and nibble the end of it. It was my mother's favourite, the food she missed most when she came to Canada. I told this to Milan, and he insisted I buy it in memory of her. I always wondered what it tasted like.

"It is like the sound of sheep bells in mountain air, when the wood fire burns," he told me. I stroke his black hair and imagine him as a shepherd, his flock spread out peaceably below him in a mountain field. Shepherd Milan smokes a long pipe and gazes down at his charges, a faraway look in his eyes, until he falls asleep to the sound of crickets. Only then, when I see him asleep in my own imagination, do I too fall asleep in our bed in the Svatopluk.

CHAPTER 13

That afternoon, when Joan returned to the Burnses' home, she found Robbie in the back garden. He had a pair of shears in his hands and was snipping at the straggly bushes that lined the fence. Miša must be sleeping inside, Joan thought. Peter played with a toy dump truck at his father's feet. He looked up at Joan briefly, then ignored her.

Burns straightened, wiping sweat from his brow with the back of one gloved hand. He gave her a cheery wave but was clearly winded from his work. Joan walked up to inspect the bush.

"Gooseberry," said Burns. He pointed to another. "Black currant."

After that cursory explanation, he seemed ready to continue with his work, but Joan, determined to get it out of the way before her courage failed, asked, "I wonder if I can talk to you about something."

Burns straightened again. He smiled, but his eyes looked concerned. "Should I smoke?" he asked.

Joan realized this was his way of asking if it was a serious matter. She shook her head, then shrugged. It was serious to her, but for him it was merely a matter of information.

Burns took off his gloves and pulled a clove cigarette from his pocket. He indicated a bench by the wall that Joan should sit on. He sat downwind, so the smoke would not bother her.

Joan hadn't given a lot of thought about how to tell the story of Adriana and Milan. "I have a young Canadian friend here. She has a young man friend who is Roma. She wants to bring him to Canada." Burns nodded, his eyes darkening. "Do you know the best way? Will they have to marry?" Joan blurted. There, it was out of her.

Burns looked kind. "I think there are other ways," he said carefully. "He could go as a visitor and apply to emigrate. Depending on circumstances, he might be able to apply to become a refugee, but it is not easy, even though Roma face a lot of problems here."

Joan wondered how Milan would feel about being a refugee. She had the feeling Burns knew more about the matter he was not saying, just as she had not wanted to divulge the whole story.

"I helped someone go to America before," he added. "She also considered Canada. I learned a lot."

With his back to Joan, Burns squinted up at the tree in the neighbouring yard. Its leaves had mostly yellowed.

"Of course he might go to Canada as a student. But if he has no means..." Burns shrugged and turned back to the bushes, but his shoulders sagged slightly when he picked up the shears again, as though they were suddenly heavier than before. "There is also fatherhood. If your friend was pregnant with his child..."

Joan was taken aback, then felt an urge to laugh hysterically. The terror that suggestion would strike in her mother's unmotherly heart, not to mention Adriana's father's.

Joan spent the rest of the day in her room. She investigated the books on her bookshelf, which were not poetry but reference books. There was a Slovak-English dictionary, which Joan thought would come in handy, what appeared to be a Slovak Bible and a guidebook of the old Czechoslovakia in halting and sometimes indecipherable English. It was full of grainy black-and-white photos from the Communist era: stark-looking state buildings, a May Day parade with sombre military and flag-waving crowds; but also buildings from the sixties or seventies, which were then, she supposed, cutting edge—a shopping centre, a theatre; people walking in a tree-lined park; and the ubiquitous folk dancers shot from below, their arms outstretched above their heads, reaching upward to a towering statue of Lenin.

Fascinated by the old photos and unwieldy translation, Joan read about Bratislava, the Dunaj, and the Market Hall where she'd spent the morning with Milan and Adriana. The school was located not far from there, and the guidebook contained a map of the Staré Město—Bratislava's old town centre—plus a dot, unlabelled, which Joan determined was the school's location. It must have been made recently, she thought, because although the book was old, the ink seemed quite fresh. She turned to the front inside cover to look for the publication date and discovered a name in faded ink written by hand: *Elaine Watterson, Svatopluk Hotel, 1985.* This book had belonged to the Englishwoman Milan had spoken of, who had lived in Joan's former room at the Hotel Svatopluk. What was it doing here?

Joan came downstairs around suppertime, guidebook in hand. Burns and Peter were nowhere to be seen and Miša's bed was empty. In the kitchen a note on the table read, *We have gone for fried cheese and chips. Please eat anything. Miša says, please eat everything. Cheers!* Joan felt a wisp of loneliness. She opened the fridge door and found some pickled herring and a tomato, which she sliced onto a couple slabs of bread. She also chopped up raw onion and heated soup left over from the day before. There, she thought. That is a respectable Slovak meal.

Afterward, Joan went out into the street. It wasn't dark but soon would be. She walked quickly past the twinkling shop lights to the café on the corner. A bunch of children, too young to drink, were indulging in coffee and rectangular slices of torte, feeding the jukebox with koruny. Their voices were loud, their laughter, even the boys', high-pitched and giggly. They must have been barely teenagers, if that— maybe they were eleven or twelve. Joan ordered a small fruit tart and a slim slice of what appeared to be cheesecake, as well as an espresso. It had begun, she decided, as a day for indulgences and would end the same way.

She sat near the front window, where she could watch the street. There were women and children loaded with bags and packages, and men headed to or from the piváreň. Joan wondered how much beer Slovak men drank each year. She imagined huge vats of alcohol the size of industrial oil tanks dotting the landscape and men climbing the winding staircases to drink from them. Women drank too, but they did not frequent the dark pivárne, which seemed to be the usual destination for men after a long day of work. Then there were the hotel bars, the beer gardens, and the railway cafeterias, the grocery store shelves lined with slivovica, marhuľovica, and borovička. Alcohol was everywhere and flowed as freely as a second river through the Slovak capital.

And now that it was late fall, burčiak added to the stream of drink. Joan thought about the morning's adventure and how it felt to be happy and in the company of people she cared about. Burčiak, if she was honest, had been like the blood of that happiness. The whole morning had been bright around the edges, and young wine had gilded the memory of it.

As Joan gazed out the darkening window, she saw Burns pushing Miša's wheelchair slowly over the cobblestones. Peter sat on Miša's lap, clinging to her neck like a baby monkey, her arms around him. Burns was smiling and chatting to Miša, who was clearly at the end of her energy but looked happy. The ride must have been bumpy, as Miša's hair bounced from time to time and Peter clung to her neck as though for dear life.

Behind Joan, the young people had grown quiet. They were suddenly on all sides of her, seemingly oblivious to her presence, watching the small family wobble past. A young boy snickered and pointed while a girl, sombre-faced, said nothing. Perhaps they were not accustomed to seeing a person in a wheelchair traversing their streets. Joan had certainly not seen another family like the Burnses. She stood up in the middle of the group of youngsters and pushed her way to the door. A bell tinkled as she opened it into the street.

Joan did not have to hurry to catch up to Burns, his shoulders straining to push the chair the last hundred metres home. With the eyes of the young people in the café burning into her back, she strode up beside Miša's chair and asked, "Can I help?" Burns did not seem surprised to see her.

"If you could carry Peter, that would make my job easier." He halted. Peter's grip would be hard to pry loose.

Joan tickled him lightly under the arms and he squealed, letting go. "Come on, monkey," she said. With effort she lifted Peter, and although he stiffened, he did not resist. Miša closed her eyes, weary but good-natured.

Joan realized she had never carried a child in her arms before Peter. He usually smelled sweet, but his clothing had picked up the scent of frying. He placed his chin on her shoulder, and she imagined him staring back into the twilight at the young people spying from the café window. It was as though she, Burns, and Miša were all stepping toward the future, while Peter could not help but look back into the gathering dusk.

CHAPTER 14

Early Sunday morning at the train station, Joan stood on the platform waiting for Adriana and Milan. She saw them coming from the opposite end, Adriana pulling her suitcase behind her, and Milan loping beside her. When they came closer, Joan could see Adriana's face was pinched with worry, though Milan was clearly excited.

"We go east!" he said without preamble. "My family is from Levoča." He waved his hand. "But we will go to Prešov. Adriana's mother lived there." Adriana nodded nervously. "There are also many Roma there." It seemed to Joan the pinch of Adriana's face tightened.

Milan went to buy soft drinks from the cafeteria for the journey. Adriana plopped herself onto a bench beside Joan.

"My mother didn't like Roma," she said.

Joan remembered Adriana's mother's long, light-brown hair and her own pinched mouth. The woman had always looked as though she was on the verge of rage, Joan thought.

"I expect her family is no different," Adriana said. "I told my aunt I am coming with my boyfriend. She said she would be glad to meet him. She must think he is Canadian."

Joan remembered her own mother's bitterness at the fact her husband, Joan's father, had not told his parents she was Chinese before she came to meet them. Joan had always had the impression her mother had never forgiven her father, and this had blighted their marriage.

"Tell them," Joan said. The urgency of her own words surprised her. Adriana shrugged half-heartedly. "He won't forgive you if you don't."

Adriana gazed at her, startled. "I will call them when we stop. Yes, I should prepare them, for Milan's sake. If they only let us sleep in the shed, that's fine."

Joan told Adriana what Burns had said about her options for bringing Milan to Canada. He could come as a visitor, possibly as a refugee. She could marry him or get pregnant with his child. Joan recited these options hurriedly, mechanically, as though doing her duty. They mostly sounded preposterous, but she had told Adriana she would get information and she had. Adriana put her face in her hands.

"I think he could come as a visitor first," Joan ventured. "Maybe you can decide after that what you will do?"

Adriana shook her head. She's barely twenty, Joan thought.

"Where will Milan get the money for the plane fare?" Adriana asked, despairing.

Joan had no idea. She had no secret stash of cash herself. She didn't even know how she'd return to Canada, if she had to. Her parents would probably help, but she didn't want to depend on that. She couldn't really see herself in Canada anyway. What would she be going back to? There was no job she could get in Canada that was better than she could find here. There was Ricky—but Ricky was a friend, not a destination, not a home. At least Ricky had a little business doing home repairs and yardwork. Joan had nothing but a suitcase.

Adriana pulled something from her pocket. It was wrapped in wax paper and inside a plastic bag.

"I forgot I had this," she said. "Your mother gave it to me for you when I left."

There was a chain hanging out of it. Adriana pulled on the chain and the wrappings fell away, revealing a gleaming pocket watch. It had belonged to Gillian's father, Joan's

Chinese grandfather, and she remembered it as his prized possession. It was almost a hundred years old. It had passed to him from his own father, before Joan's grandfather had fled China. He had given it to Gillian when her mother died, the same day it stopped working.

Joan stared at the watch. Adriana thrust it at her. It swung back and forth, as though to hypnotize them both. Joan held out her hand, and Adriana let the watch settle on her palm, the chain slithering in a pile on top of it.

"Thank you," Joan said, putting it in her purse. She wondered why her mother would give Adriana the watch, why she wouldn't simply wait for Joan to return to Canada? It had been an act of trust on Gillian's part, to ask Adriana to deliver it. Perhaps it had been a test.

Milan returned, four different-coloured bottles of soda in hand. He set them on the bench beside Adriana, who tried to smile at him. Joan felt a surge of affection and worry for him, he who had smoothed her way into Bratislava.

It was time to go, she thought. Weakness swept over Joan, rooting her to the spot. With the openness of youth, Milan and Adriana had shared more of themselves with her than she would have thought possible in so short a time. It felt like she was losing family.

"When will you be back?" Joan asked.

Adriana, looking equally bereft, held out her hand to Joan. "Two weeks," she said.

Milan, still buoyed by excitement, must have felt the anxiety in the air between them. "Joan," he said. "We are happy." He squeezed Adriana's shoulder. Comforted, she lay her head against him. "This is not bad thing. It is good. Don't worry. Don't be afraid."

And Joan surrendered to a memory of Edna's voice, not the thin rasp of her later years but earlier, when it was still clear and commanding. Be kind. Finish what you start. Don't be afraid.

Joan smiled weakly at the young couple. And nodded. Milan and Adriana smiled back at her, dark eyes shining. They were so like one another that although their ancestors had parted ways long ago, walking in opposite directions from the root of the tree that sheltered them both, they seemed kindred.

Joan walked to the end of the platform, glancing back only when she was ready to leave. Adriana and Milan huddled together, their black hair touching.

She thought they might be counting what money they had, or talking about the future. She waved them goodbye, but they did not look up.

That day Joan wrote a letter to Madame B., her old boss at the language school in Budapest.

It was a very formal but contrite letter, and it pained Joan to write it. She had once considered Madame B. something like a friend, until she realized, when Joan decided to flee Budapest, that Madame B. simply regarded her as a delinquent employee who had left her boss in the lurch.

The letter contained her mailing address at Burns's school, where she said she was the director's assistant. It was not a lie, but it felt like one. She wanted desperately to ask Madame not to tell Tibor where she was staying, but she knew saying so would arouse Madame's suspicion. After some deliberation, Joan wrote, *I ask that you allow my address and employment situation to remain confidential. I will pass along my contact information to the few people I wish to have it.* Madame had thought she was leaving Budapest because of a boyfriend, and she would be happy if Madame continued to think whatever she liked, but Joan still felt the need to apologize for her hasty departure.

She also finished her journal entry to Ricky. A subtle shadow crept over the paper. There were things she did not want to divulge, even to herself, and others she did not feel at liberty to say. What if her journal fell into someone else's hands? *Bratislava, the capital of Slovakia, is on the same river as Budapest was, the River Danube*. That fact seemed important to mention, even though no one else would know why. Because it was the river that connected her to her past, to Edna, even though it also connected her to Tibor.

Joan wrote about the Burns family, and about Adriana and Milan, about their sojourn into eastern Slovakia to meet Adriana's relatives. She imagined Adriana and Milan were on a perilous mission, that they would have their hearts rent, but that it was still important for them to go. She did not write this, only a little about the life Roma in Slovakia faced. There were not many Roma in Bratislava, she realized, but in the east, where Adriana and Milan were headed, there were whole villages. She did not know much about these settlements, but suspected they were not paradises. Otherwise why would Milan's family come to Bratislava to live in a tiny apartment in a hotel, to be cheated by the market butcher and beaten by Roma-hating strangers for sport?

Joan wished she could hear Ricky's voice. It was quiet and comforting and Nova Scotian. She wished she could sit next to him on a bench, the way Adriana and Milan had at the train station, their heads together. But there was something completely outlandish about that thought that made her suppress a giggle. They had so little in common, really. But they'd had Edna, and somehow that was enough.

CHAPTER 15

"Read to me," Miša demanded hoarsely, as she lay in bed after lunch one day. Peter was making a new creation out of Lego and Pani was napping. "I want beautiful words."

Joan looked through the poetry books on the shelf. "What would you like me to read?" she asked.

Miša closed her eyes. "You choose," she said, barely audible.

Joan looked at the narrow spines of the poetry books. She recognized some of the names, but not all. Auden. Eliot. Rich. That one looked newer. Joan pulled it from the shelf and turned the front cover to see whether Elaine Watterson's name was inscribed there. She found something else.

To Janka, it read. *From your friend, Pani Profesorka.* Did every book in the Burnses' household belong to someone else? Joan felt she was seeing parts of lives, things she didn't understand.

Joan read to Miša until she fell asleep. The words felt dense, rich, and serious. Joan didn't notice at first that Miša was snoring. What was this poem about? A diver exploring a shipwreck, yes, but what did it stand for? Joan held her breath momentarily. Miša had fallen asleep, despite her eagerness to be read to. Was Joan one of those mute beings described in the poem, living under the surface of things? Or was she the one who descends into the wreck? There was much she felt she had forgotten.

The reason she had come to Europe was to honour Edna, she'd thought. But then she stayed. She'd hoped she might find something of Edna in Tibor, but she had not. She would not find her here either, even though the Danube, the Dunaj, wandered by too on its way to the sea. Perhaps it was not Edna, after all, she was looking for. What was she doing here then?

Joan stopped reading. She knew the poem was not about her, that it was about something else, but she felt it connecting dots in her mind that she hadn't been aware of—a constellation of the disparate stars of her own undiscovered longings.

Miša's breathing was slightly laboured. Perhaps she had a cold, Joan thought. The air had been chilly last night and stayed so throughout the day. There would soon be frost. Joan took a crocheted afghan from the end of the bed and spread it over Miša, who opened her eyes sleepily. Peter toddled over with a Lego construction that resembled a Portuguese man-of-war, or a Chinese dumpling, in its rippling, organic form. It was clearly a kind of ship though—a small, helmeted man and yellow-haired woman, each staring ahead and smiling fixedly, steered it from an open cockpit.

Peter held it up to his mother.

"Look, Joan," she cried hoarsely. "It is Robbie and me in a spaceship!" She brushed the hair from Peter's eyes and cooed, "Krásne!" Beautiful!

Joan couldn't help but wonder if it were indeed Peter's parents in the spaceship: where was he? Tethered, perhaps, and floating, on a solitary spacewalk, or on his own small world, like St. Exupery's little prince, waiting to be discovered. But in Peter's creation, he was absent, except as the hand that steered them through the murky living room, where evening shadow had begun to fall like fine volcanic ash over everything.

It happened the next day that the mystery of the books that did not belong to the Burnses but nevertheless filled their bookshelves was resolved. Joan wasn't even thinking about it as she pulled the well-worn Emily Dickinson from the shelf. Miša's favourite. Peter played near the bed, and when Joan picked him up and placed him close to his mother, he curled up beside her, gazing at Joan with his thumb in his mouth and serious eyes.

"Today, read me something that is not about death," Miša said, smiling wearily. Her face was pale and translucent as spiderweb. Joan thumbed the Dickinson poems, wondering if there were any. "No, not Emily today," Miša said. "Mrs. Watterson and I shared many things, but she was so vážna."

Joan glanced up. Miša's eyebrows drew together into a serious look.

Ah, Joan nodded. Vážna. "I stayed in the room at the Hotel Svatopluk where Mrs. Watterson used to live. Were these her books?"

Miša's eyes opened wide. "Is it possible?" she cried. "Mrs. Watterson was my English teacher! She taught a little bit at the school, but in the afternoon she would come and read and talk with me. I learned very much from her." Miša looked up at the ceiling. "When she died I knew she would go to her God. I wished he would send me a second Mrs. Watterson. He did not. But she left her books, and you are here." Miša's voice was kind. "Mrs. Watterson taught Jana also. Jana was a young woman who worked here before you, until..." Her voice trailed off. "It was some time ago," she said flatly. "Then another woman came and went. Pani Marta has been here since then, since Peter was still a baby. She is his Slovak babka."

At that moment Pani Marta came to take Peter to watch television as she shelled peas. She placed a withered hand on Joan's arm. "Je unavená," she said. She is tired.

Joan nodded. Miša rolled her eyes.

"I am not too tired for poems," she said.

Joan knew, however, that Miša would likely fall asleep when she began to read. She pulled a book of nursery rhymes from the shelf. Some were familiar from her childhood but there were many she did not know. "Baa Baa Black Sheep" and "Hickory Dickory Dock" seemed to have rhythms too lively for her purpose. "Mary Had a Little Lamb" was a better choice.

She cleared her throat and began to read.

Miša, her eyes closed, said, "Will you sing it?"

Joan, self-conscious, began again. Her voice felt rusty from disuse, but Miša didn't seem to notice. She tapped the bed with her slim hand for a moment, in time to Joan's quiet rendition. Joan hoped no one in the school on the other side of the wall could hear her. She finished the song, which had more verses than she remembered, under cover of the sound from the television. Why does the lamb love Mary so? The teacher's answer to the children was, of course, that Mary loved the lamb. It seemed a circular argument, but perhaps that was how love worked. Joan did not feel she had any expertise in the matter.

Miša's hand had fallen open on the sheet and her light snores sounded more like sighs. Joan had to admit the nursery rhyme was not exactly scintillating, but she had also sung it slowly, to give it the effect of a lullaby. She had hoped Miša would fall asleep, so she could have some time to sit and think.

Joan closed the book. It was square, with a picture of a round clock with a human face on the front, a mouse perched on one ornate large hand like a bird, the clock looking at it surprised, almost cross-eyed. Due to its vintage, she suspected it came from Mrs. Watterson's own childhood, maybe from the thirties or forties. She opened the front cover. Inside it, in blue ink, were the words *To Janka and her little Peter. From the ancient library of Elaine Watterson, 2003.*

Joan stared at the words for a moment, then closed the book. Peter and Pani Marta were in the television room, Peter no doubt beside her on the sunken sofa, twirling a pea pod absently in his tiny hands. His hair was black, his eyes as dark as Milan's. Not like his red-haired father and blond mother at all.

Joan went to the kitchen, book in hand. For lunch, she'd offered to make spaghetti sauce. It was Burns's birthday.

"I am forty. God preserve me," he had muttered, throwing his hands in the air. Pani had made a beautiful if rustic torta, iced in white with fruit decorating the top. When Joan offered spaghetti bolognese for supper, Miša had cried out with delight, and Burns, with mock formality, had pushed away from the table and offered to shake her hand. Pani was a wonderful cook, but her fare was simple and Slovak. She was from the countryside, and bolognese sauce was not part of her daily repertoire.

Joan browned the ground beef Pani had bought from the market with money Joan had given her.

"Drahé," Pani had reprimanded, clucking her tongue and rubbing her thumb and forefinger together. Yes, it was expensive, but it was a special occasion. Spaghetti was what Joan always had on her birthday, in honour of the fact that her mother had been picking tomatoes to make a bolognese sauce when her water broke and Joan was born, three and a half decades before.

The question of Peter's parentage was none of her business, Joan knew, but as she washed vegetables for the bolognese, it nagged her nonetheless. She felt the same uneasiness that had come upon her when her parents announced their divorce, and again when Edna's secret—her long-ago rape at the hands of her soon-to-be father-in-law and the child that resulted—had come to light. It was as though, Joan felt, she were waiting to be struck by lightning. But really, the lightning had struck already.

Garlic, onions, tomatoes, mushrooms, peppers. Pani kept her knives sharp, so it took no time at all to dice the vegetables and add them to the stockpot.

Burns had declared his undying love for spaghetti sauce and asked that extra be made to freeze. "If it were to rain bolognese for forty days and nights, one for each year of my life, I would make sure to set out every barrel and bucket in my possession to capture it," he had declared.

Miša nodded. "During the first great flood," she said, "my husband didn't care to save the animals. He wanted to fill the ark with food only." Burns looked at her with affection. "But only Noah's promise that some animals would later be eaten convinced him."

Burns shook his head in mock dismay. "And she," he declared, pointing to Miša with his thumb, "wanted to save only books and flowers."

Peter had looked from Miša to Burns, uncomprehending. When they joked with one another in English, they occupied a private world both foreign and adult. Peter busied himself mashing peas into his high-chair tray.

"And Peter," Miša said, smiling at her son. "If Peter was Noah, all the Lego would be saved."

Joan added oregano, basil, and bay leaves, then stirred in tomato paste. She wished she had a can of stewed tomatoes to add, but instead she added a bit of tomato juice that was already in the fridge. She needed to stir to keep the sauce from sticking to the bottom of the pot and could not let herself be distracted. If Peter was not Miša and Burns's biological child, then who was Jana? Had she been taught by Mrs. Watterson as well? The worlds Joan occupied connected through the dead Englishwoman but did not intersect. At least, so it seemed. As she tried to push it from her mind, she had an inkling that the connections would be revealed one day. Recalling the Adrienne Rich poem, Joan's gut told her that there was a secret constellation waiting to be uncovered.

She turned the stove down and left the bolognese to bubble quietly, then sat at the kitchen table, book in hand. There were drawings with each of the nursery rhymes, some of them in colour. These were originally watercolours and were reproduced in a dull matte. She flipped through the book and turned to the back inside cover. On a blank page, inscribed in pencil, was a rhyme Joan had never heard before. It began,

> *My Mother said that I never should*
> *Play with the Gypsies in the wood.*

Joan stared at the words. What would Milan think of it? The rest of the verse was about the narrator's father and mother scolding her, indeed actually lying to and threatening her, to no avail. The lure of Sally, a Roma girl with a tambourine, of the green grass and the dark wood, proved irresistible. In the end, the narrator, with no ship to cross the sea, bought a white horse and left forever.

> *I upped on his back and was off in a crack,*
> *Sally, tell my mother I shall never come back.*

Spellbound, Joan reread the rhyme. She wondered if Mrs. Watterson had added it to the back of the book, and what it had meant to her—or whether it was Jana who had added the rhyme.

Peter wandered into the kitchen. He reached for Joan's hand and led her to the TV room, where Pani Marta had fallen asleep knitting. The television flickered with static. Peter pointed to the screen, then sat on the couch next to the old woman, her head tipped sideways on her shoulder, snoring. Joan changed the channel to one playing a concert. A choir of men, their voices rugged and booming, sang a Slovak folk song. There was something melancholic about the performance, even solemn, but at the same time wild and earthy and heart-rending. She could not, of course, understand it, but hummed the melody under her breath, so that she could ask Miša about it later.

Peter, mesmerized, did not notice when Joan left to stir the sauce. The sound of the deep male voices followed her to the kitchen. Joan wondered what Peter would sound like if he talked. His parents accepted his silence so completely. Would Miša and Burns even recognize him if one day he were to speak?

Joan returned the book of nursery rhymes to its place on the shelf near Miša's bed. She was still asleep. Was it possible she was sleeping more and eating even less than usual?

"My throat. Difficult," Miša had told Joan that morning, then smiled, shaking her head at a peeled, thinly sliced apple. At least the bolognese would go down easy, Joan thought.

The television fell silent. Joan went to see if Peter had turned it off. He was sitting at Pani's feet, playing with a Lego horse that had a double row of Lego people on its back, making it look like a Viking ship with legs. In the sweet voice of childhood, he hummed a wandering melody that was part ABCs and part something else. The television was staticky again but without sound. Joan held her breath for a moment and turned back to the main room before he saw her.

So, little Peter knew how to hum a tune. His small voice followed her down the hall, becoming a muffled sweetness. Miša was awake and staring at the ceiling. She turned her head toward Joan with a broad grin.

"So, my little merman is singing. What do you think?" Her eyes glistened.

Joan felt like crying too, but instead she busied herself tidying the bookshelf. "He sounds... It's beautiful," she said. She turned finally and sat on a stool beside Miša, who was straining to hear her son.

Miša whispered, "Jana used to sing to him. She who... was before Pani Marta...she was very..." Joan looked down at her hands. "Jana liked to sing," Miša said, and that was all.

At supper, there was silence for the first few minutes while everyone sampled Joan's bolognese. Burns ate a whole plate quickly before declaring it "just fine—very fine indeed," and helped himself to another. Peter sucked the sauce off single strands of spaghetti before slurping them, his delicate fingers orange and sticky. Miša closed her eyes appreciatively as Burns spooned sauce into her mouth between bites of his own. Sometimes Miša fed herself, but, it seemed to Joan, that was more and more rare.

"It's like..." Miša crooned. "It's just like being in America!"

Burns's eyes crinkled. "You don't mean Italy, dear?" he asked.

"No," she insisted. "It is like spaghetti we had when I went to America with my dance troupe."

"That was fifteen years ago, Miška! You still remember the taste?"

"Yes, and the wine. The wine was terrible. I have never since had such awful wine." She smiled at Joan. "My grammar is excellent, is it not? Like your bolognese."

Joan felt uncomfortably pleased that her cooking had passed the test. She blushed and squirmed slightly. Even Pani nodded her head approvingly.

"Ako v reštaurácii," she said. Like the restaurant.

After supper, Joan offered to do the dishes. Burns usually did them, but it was his birthday.

"I'll dry," he said, "after I put Miša to bed and have a cigarette."

Joan was left in the kitchen with a mess of plates, cutlery, and wineglasses, and a couple of pots. She hated the way the soapy water turned orange from the sauce, but she would endure it for the sake of saving Burns from it. As she contemplated washing the pasta pot, Burns passed her on his way out the back door. When he hit the cool air and lit up a smoke, Joan heard him sigh. He leaned against the door frame, looking up at the deepening sky.

Joan wondered what to do about the left over sauce. Burns had said freeze it, but in what? She went to the back door and knocked on the door frame. Burns turned his head, lionesque against the dusk. It almost seemed indecent to interrupt his peace.

"Well, I am not sure what one uses to freeze things in small portions," he said. "I would like Miša to be able to eat some every day, since she likes it, and God knows there is not much in the food department that agrees with her."

Joan thought for a moment. "Perhaps a muffin tin?"

Burns stubbed his cigarette out in a potted plant. "Brilliant," he said. "That will work nicely." He straightened. "Joan, you are hiding your talents. What else can you cook?"

Joan blushed. "Just that," she said. "Only bolognese."

Burns looked taken aback, then laughed heartily. "But you are honest. An honest cook. That is your talent, I would say," he said as he stubbed out the cigarette and brushed past her to return to Miša's bedside. Joan wondered if she would forever associate the scent of cloves with this kind half-Scotsman. She gazed up at the stars for a moment, and they twinkled down at her like eyes crinkled with laughter.

Joan was filling the muffin tin with bolognese when she heard Burns joking with Miša over what she'd said.

"An honest, one-trick cook is better than a red seal chef who's a crook," Burns offered. Miša murmured something and Burns laughed softly, then their voices sank too low to hear.

Joan climbed the stairs to her room. Pani had stayed late to put Peter to bed. Joan waved at him from the hall, but he only stared back, and she shut the door to her room. She turned on the little glass lamp on her desk. It made her think of a much larger but similarly shaped lighthouse lamp she had seen in a museum in Halifax. The single burning glass eye that had once winked out into the night, warning ships of the danger of return, guiding them home.

There are many reasons a person leaves a place. As many as there are people and as many as there are places. Joan had left her home without a backward glance, but lately, she found, she was looking over her shoulder a lot.

CHAPTER 16

Adriana and Milan had been gone a week. They would soon return and then—what? Where would they find the money to get Milan to Canada? It felt like something heavy in Joan's pocket, but another worry preoccupied her. What would become of Miša, who appeared to be weakening? She seemed to have caught a chill overnight, and though she was only congested for a day, she hadn't gotten out of bed since.

Miša had been happily eating bolognese for three days before she fell ill. Pani made chicken soup and poured spoonfuls of broth past Miša's dry lips. She made appreciative noises, but, exhausted by the effort of eating, her head soon fell back on the pillow, and she slept after every meal. Peter played near her bed and every so often he would look up at her asleep as if to make sure she was still there. He did not climb up to cuddle with her, and Miša did not request it.

Burns ate his meals at Miša's bedside, gently encouraging her to drink, to eat just a mouthful. He bent to hear Miša's voice as it faded at the end of each breath. The second day, Joan heard him in the kitchen, making coffee, after an almost inaudible conversation with his wife. He had spent the night on the couch in the main room beside her, and Joan doubted he had slept. When the coffee grinder stopped, Joan heard him gasp, as though at the end of a sob. Joan was looking through the bookshelf for something to read to Miša, something comforting that was not barbed and dangerous.

Miša either had not heard her husband gasp or pretended not to. "Read me Emily," she said.

Joan flipped through the pages and was relieved to find what she was looking for, a poem she had glossed over in high school. "This one is about hope."

"Yes, that one," Miša murmured.

Joan paced herself over the singsong length of the short poem, wishing she could stretch it out.

When she had finished reading it twice, Miša turned her head and gazed at Joan. "Is it really so? Hope does not want anything from us?"

Joan, bewildered, shrugged.

"My honest cook," Miša said, hoarse with fatigue. She turned her head away, toward the window where the slatted blind was drawn almost to the sill. The slits glowed like bones in an X-ray. "I do not know either."

Peter showed off his latest Lego creation, a mask-like fish head that he held up in front of his own face.

Miša turned her head and seemed genuinely surprised. "Peter, what have you made?" she whispered.

He stood silently a moment, then thrust the fish head toward her. "Ryba," he said.

Miša's tired eyes crinkled but she did not remark on her son's first spoken word to her, except to say, "Veľmi dobrá ryba, chlapče môj." Very good fish, my boy.

The next day was Saturday. Remembrance Day had come and gone in Canada and Joan thought it time to call her mother. But first she was going to wander the city, maybe to end up at the Café Eureka again. She tried not to think about why it drew her, but she hoped the professor would be there.

Bratislava was grey and crisp and cool, and felt different now that there was a hint of frost in the air. Less on display, as though the real Bratislava was tucked indoors, behind the formal yet grimy facades and dark windows.

Joan made her way in the direction of the Eureka, coming upon the bookstore first. She decided to pick up a magazine to go with her espresso. The image of the Roma man with the books spread between his hands like an accordion was gone, replaced by a blond woman with remarkably white teeth and a white fur collar, books scattered beside her in the air, stars and sparkles denoting Christmas magic.

Joan climbed the stairs to the bookshop. It was busier than it had been on her first visit, and she had to wait in line at the counter while the same young man who had served her before patiently explained to an old man who was hard of hearing that the shop no longer sold postage stamps. The clerk's equanimity seemed unflappable, even though there was a loud clot of teenagers at the back of the store and a lengthening line of unsmiling customers.

To pass the time in line, Joan looked at the items under the glass counter. There were a number of English-language magazines, British and American, some she did not recognize. There were also playing cards, postcards, and expensive-looking pen sets in slim boxes. She had not thought to look for an Agatha Christie in the English book section. There was, she realized, enough going on in her own life and those of the people around her that was mysterious and anxiety-provoking, that she didn't need more in a novel.

When Joan got to the front of the line, the cashier looked at her, bored and expectant.

"I would like six postcards, please," she said. Instead of reading, she would write. She pointed to a string of four cards of Slovak folk dancers, then chose one with a Slovak castle in the snow and one of the Dunaj in summer, sparkling in the sun, behind a couple in shorts and sunglasses, heads tilted back and laughing. Both were images of a Slovakia she did not know, one formal and fairy-tale beautiful, the other carefree and warm. She had barely walked a couple kilometres in Bratislava, but to her, the city felt almost gothic in its dinginess.

Joan was relieved to emerge from the bookstore into the November air. People trickled past her on the sidewalk. She felt as though she were swimming against a current, though clearly there were also people overtaking and passing her from behind. It was rare for Joan to choose a destination purely because she wanted to go there, for her own pleasure, or at least for her own reasons. And what were those reasons? She wasn't sure, or perhaps she simply did not want to admit them to herself. The barista's kindness, and the professor with the furrowed brow, who reminded her of her father. Her own loneliness.

The Eureka was exactly where it had been before. Happiness and relief startled her. When she opened the door under its red-and-white-striped awning to the dim interior, however, there was a different barista at the counter and a few young people who looked like university students huddled over books. The professor with the laptop was nowhere to be seen. Deflated, almost stricken, Joan put her things down at the same table she'd sat at before. She did not look at the bulletin board behind her except to note that it seemed to be covered in a fresh round of job posters, but took out a pen and her postcards. The pictures on them now seemed to her remote and meaningless and foreign, although of course it was she who was the foreigner here.

Joan ordered espresso, and the barista handed it to her silently. She returned to her seat. No package of biscuits today. She turned over the four postcards of folk dancers, joined together with a serrated line between them. The back was blank except for four little boxes that indicated where postage stamps should go, and a line dividing the space for the address from the space for the message. The cards formed a single long narrow page divided by a black line.

It reminded Joan of something—a building she had once seen on a cliff outside Halifax. A bunker, her father had called it, though it simply looked like a concrete tower to her. She was also reminded of Chinese towers she'd only seen in a book, tall buildings with small windows that people of means in the south built for their families to take refuge from bandits. Diaolou. A memory of her mother's father pointing to a black-and-white photo in a book stood out from the hazy reaches of her childhood. Diaolou, he said, explaining that his wife's great-grandfather, a successful merchant, had built one and had hidden his family in it from the Japanese during the war. Joan remembered her grandmother sitting erect and proud on the couch as her husband talked, eyes shining in the dim light from the sheer-shrouded living room windows of Joan's childhood home.

Joan drew faces in the boxes meant for postage stamps. Her mother and father, Adriana and Milan, Burns and Miša and Peter. She drew herself in the last box. She was alone, so she drew Edna beside her in a cap with a long peacock feather that waved out the window.

Dear Ricky, Joan wrote at the top of the first postcard. Then she doodled some ornate decoration along the serrated lines between the postcards that now also denoted the demarcation between stories of the tower. What was there to say? It was as though Ricky, patient and smiling pleasantly, sat across from her. *Miša is starting to fail. She barely eats and can't sit up. Adriana and Milan have gone east to where Adriana's mother's family lives. Adriana wants to bring Milan to Canada, but I don't know how she will manage.*

Joan twirled the pen in her fingers. *Peter said his first word the other day*. The thoughts that came to Joan were disjointed and went nowhere. Even though it was only for her, part of her journal, Joan wished for more substance. More story.

I feel alone, she wrote. Joan regarded the words on the back of the postcard warily. *I feel like I don't know what I'm doing*. She pressed hard on the pen because she felt like crying. *I feel afraid because I am alone and I don't know what I'm doing or why I am doing it and I don't know what comes next. I'm afraid Miša will die and then what will become of Peter and Burns, and what will become of my job? I'm afraid Milan will not make it to Canada, and if he does, what will he do and how will Mária and the children eat? I'm afraid Adriana is more fragile than she seems, and I don't know how she will bear it if she fails Milan. And if she doesn't fail, I'm afraid she is not strong enough for him to hinge his life to. I'm afraid Tibor will come to Bratislava to look for me*. Her handwriting had turned into a shaky scrawl.

There. It was out of her. Joan stared at the words. She resisted the urge to crumple the postcards into a ball. She stared at the smiling faces in the diaolou windows. The postcards had formed a tower of protection for the people she cared about, but fear crept in anyway.

Joan tucked the postcards away in her bag and looked around. No one was looking at her. The students seemed to be taking a break from their studies. Though hushed, they laughed and chatted over cups of espresso and bottles of beer. The professor had appeared, on his laptop in the back corner of the café, his brow furrowed over a spreadsheet of the café's inventory or some minutiae of Slovak art history, or perhaps a letter of recommendation for a middle-of-the-road student. The barista who had served Joan on her first visit was tying a clean apron on behind the counter. She smiled at Joan and nodded. How long had she been there, while Joan was lost in her own world? It occurred to Joan that though the barista's thin shoulders seemed bowed with fatigue, her eyes, bright and curious, may have seen more than Joan wished.

Trembling slightly, she approached the counter. The young woman's face flickered shyly. Before Joan could say anything, she spoke.

"Thank you for the Canadian coin you left last time."

Joan was taken aback. The young woman remembered her?

"I—my boyfriend collects coins. He did not have a Canadian dollar and was glad to have it."

Joan smiled uncertainly and peered into the barista's face. She had a sharp nose and high forehead and looked a little like a bird—shrewd, intelligent.

As though remembering herself, the young woman asked, "Will there be anything else?"

Joan shook her head and dropped a few small coins in the pretty cracked teacup that served as a tip jar. The professor looked up and spoke to the barista quietly in Slovak. The young woman nodded.

"I am to remind you that we will be closed on November 17, Struggle for Freedom and Democracy Day." The professor also smiled, and Joan felt warmed to her core.

Still, when she left the café, it was a relief to be outside again, away from the almost intolerable kindness of the professor's eyes. Joan made her way to the telephone centre and had the operator dial for her. The sound of the phone connecting reminded Joan of the beeping of a heart monitor.

"Hello?" her mother answered.

"Hi, Mum."

"Joan! So glad to hear your voice!" Her mother was breathless as usual. She sounded happy, which put Joan on alert. "What have you been up to? How is your job?" Gillian asked.

"It's good, Ma," Joan said.

"How are your students? Do you have many classes?" It seemed so long ago that Joan had thought she would be teaching.

"I...My work is more for my director and his family...not so much teaching," she said.

"Oh! Well, I imagine a director of a school has a lot for you to do in the office. Guess what?"

"Ma, what?" Joan was thankful not to have to explain herself further.

Gillian took a breath. "David Song and I have been... dating, as you know. And we've even talked about marriage."

Joan's throat constricted. Her mother had been seeing Adriana's dad for—how long? A couple months? "That's... Ma, that's...soon." She wondered what her father thought, or if he knew.

"Joan," Gillian commanded. Joan was silent. "Neither of us is young. We are heading for sixty. We both know what we want."

What did her mother want? Joan never really knew. It seemed to change depending on who her mother was seeing at the time.

Gillian continued. "We are compatible. We have a lot of fun together. We spend all our free time together and with Adriana's younger sister, Beth, who could really use a mother figure in her life."

Joan swallowed.

"But most of all, we are comfortable together. It probably comes from having similar backgrounds. We both have Chinese parents and know what it's like to grow up in a country that in some ways has kept us on the outskirts."

It was the most thoughtful Joan had heard her mother be. She felt almost teary.

But Gillian continued, "I think there is something to be said for the fact that we are both Chinese. There is a certain unspoken understanding there. A lot of base-level understanding that you don't get with—other men."

Non-Chinese men, she must mean. Like Joan's father, for instance? Where did that leave him? And where did that leave her?

"How is Adriana doing?" Gillian clearly felt the subject of her and David Song's compatibility had been satisfactorily dealt with. "I don't think David has heard from her since her first couple days in Bratislava."

Joan sensed a degree of nervousness in her mother's voice. Was it because Adriana had had some objection to her, or was she genuinely concerned about the young woman's well-being?

"She... I think she's okay, Ma. She's on a trip east now. To meet her mother's family." After a pause for Gillian to absorb this news, Joan added, "She gave me the watch—grandfather's pocket watch. Thank you." Joan heard Gillian exhale quietly.

"Good," she said. "I wanted you to have it now, because. Well. We don't know what the future holds. It seemed like time."

Joan knew this was the barest of explanations, that her mother had other reasons, but it didn't matter to her now. She could feel the pressure of the future building up like water behind a dam.

"And you—are you okay?" Gillian sounded as though she genuinely wanted to know, like she was actually listening for an answer.

Joan nodded. "I'm okay, Ma," she said, relieved that it was true. But the question seemed to reopen in her the same pocket of vulnerability she'd just uncovered at the Café Eureka. She was fine—a fine that was delicately resting on the flutter of Miša's breath, on Peter's dark eyes, on Milan and Adriana and Tibor's whereabouts. She hadn't thought about Tibor for a little while, but she recognized now that his absence was one of the points on which her own equanimity depended. It was as though she were walking on bridges anchored to various peaks and crags. As long as none of them gave, she was fine. If any of them failed, she would surely fall, as long and as far as this netless world would permit her.

CHAPTER 17

Joan opened her eyes and stared at the ceiling. Monday again. The days went by so quickly, but she found herself spent by the end of each one. Looking after Peter and Miša, and trading off chores with Pani—it all seemed to happen in a continuous parade of busyness. She wondered how Burns managed the weekends with his family without Joan or Pani Marta, when he must be tired too. And how Miša, who had spent much of the week in bed now, kept her kindness. Though tired, she managed not to be cross and impatient when Joan clumsily dropped the (thankfully empty) bedpan and it clattered to the floor. Miša was too weak to get to the commode these days.

"Peter, Joan is too noisy," she said hoarsely. "Will you take her outside to play?" Peter dutifully led Joan out to the back garden. She sat in an old chair on a chill November afternoon while Peter, dressed in a small quilted jacket and hat with earflaps, dug holes in the ground.

Often though, while Pani Marta and Peter watched television, Joan would help Miša with something. In the past, she had taken dictation from Miša in English about the day's chores and the shopping, which Miša also translated into Slovak, spelling the words slowly so Joan could catch them.

"I am your teacher," Miša had said, smiling. "One day maybe you can write a letter in Slovak. Pani Marta helps me write to my mother." Miša's eyes were bright. "My mother is old, and her mind is—old." Joan bent close to Miša's mouth to catch her words. "My mother does not remember that I am ill and cannot travel. She does not remember I have a son. It is a long time since I have seen her." Miša swallowed and turned her head toward the window. "Please open it," she said. Usually Miša wanted the blind closed because the light was too strong, but that day she was not concerned. The morning was cloudy but bright. Miša turned her head back toward Joan, her eyes closed, lashes damp and dark.

But today Miša seemed to have forgotten letters and shopping lists. "Tell me about your family," she whispered.

Joan sat down, surprised. Miša had often peppered her with questions about Canada and her hometown, about what she liked to read and the music she listened to and her favourite artists, the kind of work she had done, what her favourite subjects were in school, and her favourite foods, animals, places, any number of things, but Miša had never gotten very personal. Until now.

Joan took a breath and dutifully began the story the way her parents always told it—how they'd met in London's Hyde Park while listening to Chinese Maoist students shout through a bullhorn. How when her father came to visit her mother in Canada, Gillian's mother had tried to frighten David away with Chinese food, and how he had instead won her heart by enthusiastically devouring everything from succulent chicken's feet to the eyeballs of the steamed fish. How when Gillian's mother realized her daughter was pregnant, she was determined to save face by staging a mock wedding with a substitute groom. Miša's eyes sparkled. Joan had to admit, the stories her parents had honed over the years were good ones, although her retelling of them now felt tired and dusty.

"And you, Joan?" Miša asked. Her hair fanned out against the pillow. Joan imagined her floating in a river like the

Lady of Shalott. "Your parents are funny. I think your story must too be interesting."

Joan shook her head. "No," she said, "I don't have a story." She knew as soon as she said it that Miša would object. But Miša only raised an eyebrow, amused.

"You don't want to tell me?"

"No, it isn't that." She took a breath and tried to remember. Then there was Edna. None of her parents' stories featured the woman who was her dearest friend as a lonely child and who practically brought her up.

Joan talked about Edna's kitchen, her poppyseed cake and other Hungarian delicacies, how she went to church wearing a peacock feather in her hat, had a number of admiring suitors, none of whom she ever married. How Joan had travelled to Hungary to remember her. She left out many pertinent details—the way her small arms ached when Edna squeezed her in a hug, how dazzled Edna was by Ricky's smile, Edna's rape and her son and how Joan had delivered the news to Edna's estranged husband.

It didn't matter though. Miša gazed at her with some amusement. "And what about you, Joan?"

"I loved Edna," she said simply. "She was my best friend." It was hard even to think about her own story as separate from what Edna meant to her.

Miša closed her eyes. "When I was nineteen," she said, her voice straining to be heard against the silence of her body, "I met Robbie. I was a folk dancer. He, a student. He went to New York with me, my dance troupe. I knew he loved me. In New York, something was wrong with me—my left foot could not move properly. I told no one—not Robbie, no one. But I fell in rehearsal, and for one minute I couldn't get up. Afterward, I sat in the hotel when my troupe danced. Robbie bought me coffee and wine and stayed with me while I cried." She opened her eyes, bright, Joan thought, as the Danube in sunlight. "That was the end of my one life, the beginning of this one."

Joan imagined Miša's slight frame racked with sobs, and a younger version of Robbie, curly-haired and stocky, his arm around her shoulders. She thought of how she had left Tibor on the floor in his flat, bleary-eyed and stinking. That was not a story she wanted to tell.

"I came to Hungary to say goodbye to my friend Edna. She is dead," Joan said flatly. "I came to Bratislava because here there is the same river—the same river as in Budapest. Edna's ashes are in the Dunaj, and I don't want to say goodbye to her yet."

Miša gazed at her, with understanding but also pity. Was it pity for the loss of her friend, or for Joan's admittance that she wasn't ready to let go of Edna—or was it for something else? Some flaw or deficit? When Joan next looked at Miša, it seemed that Edna's dark eyes gazed out at her.

Often Miša would ask Joan about English words, while Joan helped her dress or undress, and in between sips of the sweet black tea Miša favoured, even now that she barely ate anything. Although Miša was bedridden, Burns insisted that she wear something clean every day, even if it was just another nightdress.

On Tuesday, as Joan pulled yesterday's nightgown over her head, Miša asked, "How do you say, a story about a person who has died, in the newspaper. It tells about their family and their life?"

Joan ventured, "An obituary?"

Her nightgown removed, Miša lay naked under a blanket except for her panties. Joan piled a comforter on top of her. She would worry about the rest later.

"Ah," Miša said, "Obituary. In Slovak, nekrolog. Please. Open the Slovak Bible. There is an obituary for Elaine Watterson. From the English newspaper."

Joan's heart beat fast. The Bible had a soft brown leather cover and onion-skin paper pages. The newsprint obituary fell out of its pages and fluttered to the floor. As Joan bent to pick it up, she kept her eyes on the small grainy photograph of an old woman, thin and plainly coiffed.

> *WATTERSON, Elaine. It is with sadness that Elaine Watterson's friends announce her passing on July 13th, 2003.*

Just two years ago, Joan thought.

> *Born in England in 1927, Elaine lived in Slovakia for the past twenty years and had no known living relatives. She taught English grammar and conversation at various language schools, culminating with the English Language Tourism College in Bratislava, where she will be deeply missed by students and colleagues.*

Miša nodded. "It doesn't say very interesting things. It doesn't tell any stories." s

Joan nodded her agreement.

"Robbie had to hurry. There was little time, or all the students would talk," Miša said. "Also, the newspaper had deadline." Miša smiled and turned her head toward Joan, her voice fading. "Dead-line. For a nekrolog. That is funny, no?"

Joan smiled uncertainly.

"Tomorrow we must write my nekrolog."

Joan gazed at her, uncomprehending.

Miša stared back, her eyes deep and radiant. "Don't worry, Joan. I want to tell stories. I don't want to hurry."

The next day, Joan made her way downstairs for breakfast. She could see Burns hovering in the doorway of the main room. As she reached the bottom of the stairs, she saw there were people attending to Miša, a man with a stethoscope around his neck, and a smaller woman, pulling off disposable blue gloves.

Burns turned to Joan, worry written across his face. "She couldn't breathe well last night. This morning she was gasping for air." Burns was pale and unshaven, and sickly looking himself. "They're going to take her into the hospital. She might need antibiotics. She might need—"

Burns broke off as the male paramedic spoke to him. "Joan, I am going to the hospital with Miša. The school will run without me, but will you and Pani Marta look after Peter while I am gone, over lunch also? It will mean extra hours. I will pay you, of course."

He was watching Miša being lifted into a stretcher. She had an oxygen mask over her face and looked tiny and pale, all her limbs collapsing inwards as they lifted her, using the bedsheet as a kind of sling.

Joan nodded. "Of course," she said.

Burns turned quickly and, without thinking, gave her a fierce hug. Startled and panicked by the reminder of Tibor's hands on her, she froze. Burns, though caught up in his own worry, realized he had transgressed somehow.

"Joan, I am sorry. Forgive me. I didn't mean to offend you." He looked genuinely distressed.

Joan felt her anxiety easing. "It's alright," she said. "I— it's alright."

Burns preceded the stretcher out of the house. A small group of students had gathered at the ambulance parked so close to their school. They were mostly girls with long, lustrous hair, as young as Adriana and Milan. Burns spoke to them sternly, and with sheepish looks they hurried away, disappearing into the school's entrance. Joan, standing in the doorway, felt them milling on the other side of the wall, wondering in whispers about what had happened to Pan Burns's wife.

Joan couldn't see her face, but imagined Miša, eyes closed, smiling painfully at no one under her mask.

Pani Marta had kept Peter occupied with television and the last of the birthday cake for breakfast. When Joan appeared in the doorway of the TV room, Pani Marta motioned for her to sit down next to Peter. Her wrinkled face looked worried but she glanced down at Peter's head and put her finger to her lips. She then mimed putting the basket over her arm, which meant she was going to market. She patted Joan's cheek.

For twenty more minutes, Peter watched TV, Joan stock-still beside him, almost afraid to move. Then, when his show was finished, he took the Lego fish head in both hands and headed toward the main room to play. Joan followed him to the doorway. Peter could see that Miša's bed was empty, as well as her wheelchair. He sat down in the doorway with his fish head and didn't move.

"Peter," she said. He didn't look at her. "Your mama is sick. She went to the doctor today. The doctor will give her medicine so she feels better," Joan said hopefully.

Peter stood up and turned to look at her disdainfully, his eyes glowing in his small face. As though he understood her. He turned his back on her.

He knows, Joan thought. Even though he doesn't know much English, he knows I am making up a story to appease him, that I don't know anything. Joan gazed down at Peter, who had gone to stand at the front window. He was a tiny form silhouetted against the light. Joan wanted to clutch him to her, but she knew he would resist. He didn't trust her fully now.

"Peter," she commanded. He half turned to look at her. Joan stuck out her tongue and made an awful face. Peter sat down on the floor and began to play with the Lego. Joan sat down across from him, wanting to atone for her sin. "Your mum can't breathe, Peter. She is at the hospital." He looked up at her briefly, then returned to his work. "Maybe you can make something that will make her happy." Peter gazed at Joan. She felt he was considering her suggestion. "Maybe a butterfly. Or a flower. Motýľ. Kvetina."

But Joan was sure Peter would have his own ideas.

When Pani Marta returned from the market, she brought the usual vegetables, along with an animal's leg. A lamb perhaps? It looked horrific. She had a cup of tea and went to rest in front of the television. Joan offered to look after Peter, but he snuggled close to Pani on the sofa. Pani shrugged and waved her away. Joan, at a loss, went into Miša's room. She could tidy, and change the sheets. She noticed the pillow had a damp spot, that there was blood on it. Had Miša coughed it up? Joan panicked. Had Burns seen it? Had the paramedics? She would mention it as soon as she heard from Burns.

Joan stripped the sheets and fetched new ones from a tall wardrobe in the corner. In one of the drawers below the main section there were rubber gloves, masks, and gauze. The masks might come in handy if Miša had a respiratory infection. Joan opened the very bottom drawer of the wardrobe. In it were photos, black-and-white mostly. There were snapshots of folk dancers, with careful handwriting on the back. *New York, 1991. Paris, 1990.* No names, but a young blond woman, wearing bright lipsticked lips and full makeup, featured in many of them. Even then, Joan thought, Miša was slender as a wisp, more ballerina than folk dancer.

She found a headshot of a young red-haired man, his lips pressed to Miša's radiant cheek. Burns, clearly smitten. And there was Miša with a cane, next to an older woman, also with a cane, who was leaning toward her. On the back were the names Elaine and Miša. Elaine, Joan thought. Mrs. Watterson. She peered at the old woman's face. It was thin and sharp, but her eyes were kind. Her grey hair waved about her face in a short, no-nonsense style, but she was dressed smartly in what was clearly an expensive coat. And then there was a photo that made Joan stop breathing.

It was a dark-haired girl, maybe sixteen or at most seventeen, a colourful blanket wrapped around her shoulders and a baby in her arms. Joan turned it over. On the back in blue ink: *To Pani Watterson. From your Jenny H. and little Peter.*

A dark-haired girl with serious eyes. The blanket looked familiar—she'd seen an identical one in Milan's family's apartment, wrapped around his little sister, Gabriela, the one who was ill and couldn't eat. And the face of the young woman in the photo was like Gabriela's—flushed cheeks and lips, her hair thick and dark, her forehead broad, her chin pointed. A heart-shaped face. Milan's sister Jana been a student here and was now a travel agent in America who called herself Jenny. Joan let the photo drop from her fingers. Peter was Milan's nephew.

Joan's heart beat uncontrollably, like a bird in a snare.

And Milan—he must surely know that his older sister had had a child and that his own nephew was being raised by the Burnses. Or was it possible he knew nothing about it? He had said nothing to her. Just as the Burnses had said nothing.

Just as she had said nothing to Burns or to Milan or even Miša about her own life. About Edna and Tibor and how she really came to be in Bratislava. Just as Edna had hidden her child from Joan. Secrets were a part of life. Their existence did not mean that everything was hidden. But Joan could not help but think that what people kept to themselves said more about what cut to their hearts. It was true, at least, of her.

Milan and Adriana would return soon. Joan would have to decide how much to say. But first, of course, she would have to talk to Burns. But how, with Miša so sick? If Milan knew—was it possible? Joan didn't think so. His family was the most important thing to him in this world and he'd never shown even the slightest impulse to find out more about the Burnses and their child. It was quite possible Jana had kept it from him. Milan had, after all, only been a child when Jana would have been pregnant—and in many a Catholic household, Joan figured, to have a child out of wedlock would be considered a family shame. But maybe there was more. Jana had set her sights on going to the US, and likely bringing a baby was not part of her plans. Or perhaps her American boyfriend had objected?

If Milan didn't know— Joan covered her mouth with her hand. Didn't Milan, who wanted to move to Canada, have the right to know his nephew had been living only a stroll away from the Hotel Svatopluk? Joan thought so, but who was she to say? What if letting Milan know his sister's secret changed everything? Would that make her responsible for irrevocably altering the course of his life?

Joan's brain hummed with anxiety. This was intolerable. This was the kind of situation that in the past would have led her to consume a whole package of cough drops. But instead, she focused on breathing, the way a therapist would tell her to do, and counted. One, two, three... She was not responsible for anyone's happiness except her own... Four, five, six... Miša and Burns loved Peter... Seven, eight, nine... Milan knowing the truth wouldn't change the fact that Peter was growing up safe and healthy. Ten. It might not be her place to tell Milan—or it might. She didn't have to decide right now.

Peter wandered into the room. He looked lost, clutching the Lego fish head for comfort. He didn't look Joan in the eye, but she could tell he wanted to be close to someone. Joan took a book of fairy tales from the shelf and scooped Peter into her arms. He did not resist as she carried him to the chair where she usually sat to watch him play with his Lego. Joan quickly ran through the inventory of fairy tales she remembered. Were there any that didn't involve scaring the living daylights out of a small boy?

She opened the book to the Grimm tale of the fisherman and his wife. Peter pointed to the drawing of a fish head peering out of the sea. This was the tale of a fisherman whose greedy wife wants more and more from the enchanted prince in fish form. The fisherman asks on her behalf that she live in a lovely cottage, then a castle, and finally that she become king, emperor, pope, and God himself. It is the last wish that sees them back where they began—living in a pigsty by the sea.

Joan did not want to read Peter such a moralistic tale, one that ended with disappointment.

"Once upon a time," she began, but from there the tale diverged. In Joan's story, the talking fish was a woman who had been under the spell of a malevolent wizard and given birth to a child. She attempted to steal away with her baby in a rowboat, wearing the only thing of value she had in the world, her silver-and-gold wedding dress. But the wizard, waking to find her gone, transformed her into a fish and set the wind to blow the baby in the rowboat far away. The mother-fish swam after him in desperation, a thousand kilometres to another land, where a fisherman found the boy and hauled him ashore. The fisherman noticed the big fish glinting beside the boat and thought it a good omen that the baby had brought such a big fish to him.

"I will catch it and the whole village will feast in celebration of our new son!" he said.

The mother-fish knew she would have to come up with a plan to get her son back, and in the meantime, she wanted to ensure he was safe and comfortable.

When the fisherman caught her in his net, instead of thrashing, she looked at him with her enormous eyes and said, "Fisherman, I am a woman enchanted into this form by a wizard. Do not hurt me. I will bless you many times if you let me go."

The fisherman thought about this and said, "What will you give me?" The fish, who had nothing to give except her silver and gold scales, said she would give him one. He was well pleased and with it bought a lovely cottage for his family. As time passed, the fish allowed herself to be caught again and again in the fisherman's net. And to give up more and more of her scales, which caused her great pain. In the end she swam very slowly, and the fisherman caught her one last time.

"Fish, you have no more scales to give me. It is time we eat you." The fish had no strength to struggle. She allowed herself to be hauled ashore, hoping to see her son one last time.

Now her son was a young man, and he pitied the poor fish. "Father, this fish is not fit to eat. Look, it has lost all its scales."

When his father told him the secrets of his wealth, and how it was of no more use to them but was fine to eat, the young man was aghast. He knew how to handle his father. "I will not eat it but I will feed it to our animals," he said. "Let me take it to them." The father grumbled but he had to agree. The fish did look awful.

The young man gently tended to the creature. His mother-fish was so happy. The young man brought her bread crumbs every day and spoke to her kindly. She did not tell him she was his mother. Every day she grew stronger. But it was not her scales that grew back. She grew human arms and legs, and the young man kept this secret from his father. One day, the fish had fully transformed into a woman dressed in a petticoat, except that she had the head of a fish.

"Who are you?" the young man asked.

"I cannot tell you until you kiss me," she said.

Reluctantly the young man kissed the fish head and immediately her hair sprouted gold and silver from her head and her face transformed into that of a woman old enough to be his mother.

"My child," she said. "You have proven yourself kind and smart. Now show me that you can face the truth." She told him about his parentage, and he wept but agreed to set out with her in the rowboat he had been found in to face the wizard, his father.

Joan looked down at Peter, who was snoring slightly in the crook of her arm, clutching the fish head. When had he had fallen asleep, Joan wondered. She had been so engrossed in her own tale that she'd forgotten all about him. Joan shifted slightly and Peter jerked, his eyes flickering open. He lay still in her arms, gazing unseeing at Joan's face. Still dreaming, she thought.

She was content to sit there as long he wanted. But Pani Marta waddled into the room and picked Peter up.

"Obed," she commanded. Lunch. Joan trailed after them, pulled, as if in their wake, by the sight of Peter's small brown hand curled around Pani's shoulder.

That afternoon Peter began to climb the steps to his room by himself. It meant he was tired and wanted to nap in his own bed, a rare but welcome occurrence. Joan moved to follow him when he handed her the Lego fish head, and Pani waved her on. She clearly did not want to climb the steps herself, and made the sign of the cross as if to bless their ascent of a perilous mountain.

When Peter reached the top of the stairs, he went straight to his room and looked at Joan to be lifted into his crib. He was getting a bit big for a crib, she thought, even though he was still small for his age. Joan lifted him in and he immediately lay down on his stomach with his thumb in his mouth. She placed the fish head beside him. Unlike most of his Lego creations, this was one he showed no signs of abandoning.

Joan watched Peter's eyes flutter closed. She felt a tug on her heart at the sight of his small brown legs, poised to kick like a swimmer's. He was diving into a secret ocean where neither she nor anyone else could follow.

As Peter slept, Joan wrote her father a letter.

Dear Dad, she began, sitting at her small desk in her bedroom. *I don't know if Mum told you I am in Bratislava now. I work for a family that owns a language school.* There, Joan thought, relieved. That is true. *I am doing fine.* She chewed the end of her pen. What else? *I have spoken to Mum on the phone a couple times, but you were away and it's very expensive to call, so I am writing to you instead.* She hoped he would understand. Her father was easily hurt, despite his gruff, pipe-smoking exterior. She knew it to be a shell that he had developed around a tender and idealistic core against life's disappointments, his own daughter being one.

Joan longed to ask how much he knew about the other David, Adriana's father. Whether he realized her mother and the other David were so close to hinging their lives together. Her father had his own girlfriend—Gloria someone, herself a Polish transplant to Halifax, and a nurse—but Joan couldn't help but think that her father would be a little bit troubled by her mother wanting to get married again.

Instead, Joan told him about Adriana. *Do you remember Adriana, the Songs' girl? Chinese dad and Caucasian mother? She is here in Slovakia too. She came to meet her relatives on her mother's side. Her mother died when she was a kid.* For some reason Joan felt the need to establish some sympathy for Adriana. She is here to explore her roots, Joan thought about writing, but decided against it. She wants to know where her mother came from. *I think I might like to do that one day. Go to China and see where Grandma and Grandad Wong were born.*

Joan had not known she was going to write that. The idea had come to her in the classroom on her last day of teaching in Budapest and had been hovering in the back of her head ever since. Would her dad wonder why she didn't want to know more about her English ancestry too? The truth was, Joan only felt English by accident. Her father, a super-fan of Chairman Mao since his teenage years and an ardent supporter of a strong China, almost seemed more Chinese than her mother. She hoped he would understand.

How are you? Perhaps she should have started with that question. *I hope your trip to Mexico went well.* What else was there to say? She'd barely spoken to her parents the last year she was home—the last year of their marriage—simply because it seemed they didn't know what to say to one another. *How's Gloria?* she asked, because it seemed like the polite thing to do.

Joan realized that although she thought of her father fondly, they were practically strangers to one another. Her mother infuriated her, but they at least talked. Whereas she and her dad—it had been a long time since they'd had a conversation that hadn't led to whether she should go back to school or why she couldn't keep a job. His worry and exasperation made her feel tongue-tied and small. She didn't think she wanted to go back to school, and she didn't know why she couldn't keep a job—but she felt like she'd done okay since the nursing home.

I like my job. It keeps me busy and is helping me develop a new skill set. Those were words straight off a handout she'd grabbed at an employment centre once. New skill set? If she didn't elaborate, she knew her dad wouldn't ask. She was learning how to empty a bed pan, wipe a little boy's nose, and do her own detective work by snooping through her employer's books and photos. Here she would have to fudge a bit. *Office management. Tourism and hospitality. Group facilitation.* Joan felt miserable. Maybe she could scratch that line altogether. *I am learning flexibility, time management, and organizational skills.* It wasn't totally untrue. It would have to do.

Joan felt herself weakening. One day, she would like to tell her father the whole story. Starting with Edna's story, which, strangely enough, felt like the beginning of Joan's own story. Had her mother told him? Edna had shared the truth with Gillian many years before she told Joan, who had been at that time plodding as reluctantly through childhood as a soldier must through mud.

Joan would sit across from her father in his study and he would chew on his pipe and they would both drink whisky.

And she would tell the story of how much Edna had meant to her, of how, somehow, Edna's story had become her own because Joan's story was full of childhood loneliness, small humiliations, and painful ephemera that made it hard to recall. She would speak like a river flowed, from that trauma of Edna's that was not just Tibor's conception, but her conception too, of the fears and pleasures and boredoms and disappointments of her own small life, to the very end. And what was the end? Joan in Slovakia, looking after a woman fading before her eyes, a woman with a child who was also the child of another?

Joan finished the letter with some touristy information about Bratislava that would interest her father. He liked architecture and history and culture. He was, after all, an educated man. And, as though it was an afterthought, she asked if any mail had come for her. She had given her father's address to the Budapest language school as her home address, the one to which they could forward her mail. She'd been afraid her mother would open her mail, and she'd also wanted to be clear in her own mind that the house her mother lived in, in which Joan had grown up, was no longer her home.

Joan was expecting a letter soon from Madame B. with her termination papers. She wanted to be sure that chapter of her life was closed and that she had been honorably discharged. It mattered to her that Madame thought well of her. Despite the way Joan had left her employ, she had considered Madame her only real friend in Budapest—after almost four years in the city. Joan felt a pang of grief when she thought of the cold formality with which Madame had let her go, but perhaps she too had felt a stab of pain—the pain of losing a reliable employee, to be sure, but also that of saying goodbye to someone she cared for.

Joan took the letter to the post office. Before she posted it, she asked for the Burnses' mail. There were a few envelopes addressed to Burns at the school, a slim piece of mail for Miša, and one for her. Joan looked at it in surprise. It was an envelope addressed to her in her mother's handwriting. Inside was an airmail envelope addressed to Joan at her father's house, in blue ink and the standard penmanship of a Hungarian teacher. It was from Madame. A sticky note on the outside read, *I picked up your father's mail and this had come for you! Call me soon.* Joan was thankful her mother hadn't seen fit to open her mail too.

Crestfallen, Joan realized her letter to Madame B. was pointless, as she would not have received it before she sent this letter to Joan's father's house. Joan mailed her short letter to her father and put the mail for the Burnses in her shoulder bag, then made her way to a bench at the edge of the square.

Madame B.'s envelope held a couple of folded papers, forms that that had been filled out on a typewriter. There was her record from teaching for several years at Madame B.'s school. Where the form asked the reason for the termination of her employment, Madame had written *quit* in Hungarian and English and remarked that appropriate notice had not been given, but that Joan had been an adequate and reliable teacher. Adequate. Joan's throat ached. But there was something else, a handwritten note.

Dear Joan, I trust you are well. I am sorry for the delay in sending your papers. I hope you have settled in your new home. I will send this to the only address I have for you—in Canada. Things are very busy at the school. As you know, you left us during the most demanding season of the year. (Joan shrank. Madame did not mince words.) *I am sorry to say I have some sad news to share. Tibor Szabo, our mutual friend, has died.*

He fell into the river last Saturday evening. The police have not said whether it was an accident.

Joan stared at the prim blue handwriting. She could see Tibor on the bridge, hazy and drunk, talking to Edna, whose ashes he had scattered from the same point. Leaning to peer into the dark water, leaning too far and stumbling, falling, clumsily, heavily, into the river, which folded him into itself.

It was not long after you left. He missed you I think.

Joan could not read more. With trembling fingers she thrust the letter and the forms back into the envelope. Her letter to her father forgotten, shoulders bent, she rose. The church stood across the glowing sea of cobblestones. Joan could see the fake St. Francis, arms upraised, beckoning to the pigeons. She turned and headed home.

Peter was still sleeping. Pani was sitting in the TV room. She looked up at Joan and her face wrinkled with concern.

"Chorá?" she asked, and put a palm to her stomach and the back of her hand to her forehead.

"Áno," Joan said, not looking at her. She pointed upstairs and mimed sleep. Pani waved her away. Joan saw the old woman clutch the rosary beads in her pocket and knew she was being prayed for, along with Miša.

Joan went straight to bed, curled into herself with the covers cocooned around her. Her head felt hot but she shook with cold as though she were nothing more substantial than a leaf.

Over and over in her mind, Tibor fell into the dark water. A paunchy, balding man with yellowing eyeballs and fingernails, whose remaining hair wisped around his head like laurel. Slightly unkempt appearance, at the border of shabby respectability. One black shoe coming off as he fell. He folded into the water like paper tucked into an envelope, disappearing, the shoe bobbing upside down, bumping against a bridge pier among the foam and fallen leaves.

Joan did not get out of bed until the next day. At some point, Burns had come home and Pani had left. Joan knew she looked terrible, but Burns did too. He was unshaven, and his eyelids were swollen as though he'd been crying. Peter was sitting in his high chair eating porridge, his shiny, black-haired head bent over his bowl.

"Good morning," Joan croaked. Peter looked up, a spoon in his raised hand.

Burns nodded weakly. "Are you feeling better?" he asked, in a voice that sounded as if it had been unused for years.

Pani must have told him she was sick.

"No," said Joan. "I feel terrible."

Burns nodded, looking down at his bowl. "Miša is not well. She may not come home."

Joan stared at the table. Her thoughts were crowded inside the black box of her mind. "I am sorry," she said simply. The weight of the air on her head and shoulders was intolerable. She felt it was all she could do not to go upstairs and lie down again.

"I am taking Peter to the hospital with me," Burns said. "Miša asked me to bring him. Will you come too? There will be times I want you to take him out of the room. I gave Pani Marta the day off because she was here until late last night."

Joan knew she was not in any condition to look after a child. If Peter brought his Lego and she could sit and stare into space, maybe. "I am not very well, but I will come," she said.

"Good," Burns said flatly. He continued to eat his porridge. Joan wasn't hungry but drank a hot cup of tea with a cube of sugar, then went upstairs to get dressed. In the shower she imagined Miša's tiny form, an oxygen mask half obscuring her face, the bloated corpse of a man floating in the dark river. They had nothing to do with one another, their paths only happening to intersect at this juncture in the diorama of Joan's imagination. She knew, however, these visions were now coupled like prisoners in leg irons, and would shuffle after one another in an endless parade.

The hospital was a no-nonsense pale brick building in the suburbs. Burns had driven them there in the family van. Joan sat beside him in the passenger seat. Peter sat in a car seat in the back, so quiet that Joan kept looking over her shoulder to make sure he was still there.

They signed in at the hospital's front entrance, and Burns led the way down a dark hallway to an elevator. Before they got on, a Roma woman, seemingly of middle age and clutching a baby swaddled in a ragged blanket, exited, followed by a man and a young girl who was holding on to his finger. They looked sombre, but the woman's sequined top was a blaze of red and green and orange. The little girl gazed up at Peter, tucked against his father's shoulder, and pointed, while Peter buried his face in Burns's neck. The Roma man pulled the girl after him and the elevator doors closed. Joan could hear the little girl screeching something, followed by the muffled clunking of the elevator as it made its way upward.

Burns looked wholly demoralized. In the elevator he seemed to have somehow shrunk, his robust energy dwindled. Even Peter looked big against his father's shoulder. Burns tried to smile at Joan, but when the elevator stopped, his face more naturally assumed a position of resignation and terror.

He handed Peter to Joan. The boy clung briefly to his father's neck but seemed to understand that his cooperation was required, and quickly buried his face in Joan's shoulder.

"Wait here, please," Burns said. He started down the hall and went through the second door on the left. There was a large potted plant and a pale red vinyl-covered chair in the small landing on the other side of the hall, along with a supply cart and a large window alcove.

Joan sat on the chair with Peter on her lap. He gazed over her shoulder at a large, faded reproduction of an Impressionist painting. The original colours must have been off because the overall cast of the picture was a dull red and blue, a horrifying landscape to Joan's eyes. Peter reached out to touch the frame. A nurse in a stiff white cap appeared, perhaps to take the cart away, and she clucked her tongue in disapproval.

Joan put her hand protectively on Peter's back as he turned his head toward the nurse, staring at her. The nurse smoothed her skirt with her hands and busied herself rearranging the syringes, gauze, and gloves on the cart, smiling from time to time in Peter's direction.

"Váš chlapec?" she asked Joan, politely if briskly.

Joan knew she was asking if Peter was her son. "Nie, Michaely Burnsovej," she said.

The nurse peered at Peter so intently that he turned his face away. "Ah," was all she said as she backed the cart into the hall in the direction Burns had taken, the clip of her heels echoing off the waxed tiles.

Burns appeared not long after, exhausted but slightly more cheerful, Joan thought. He motioned for Peter to come to him, and Joan set the boy on the floor so he could toddle over to his father. Burns scooped him up.

"Please give us ten minutes. You could—there's a cafeteria in the basement," he said, and then they were gone.

Joan bought an espresso from a tired-looking woman in a dirty apron and sat under the bare fluorescent lights of the basement cafeteria. There was a Roma family huddled near the back of the room, the children sharing a package of potato chips and the adults drinking from tiny espresso cups. Other women also had coffee cups, and a man sitting alone, a stethoscope around his neck, was wolfing down a hot meal near the front of the cafeteria. Positioned somewhere between them, Joan wondered if she looked out of place.

The nurse who had asked Joan if Peter was her son entered the cafeteria and grabbed a tray, choosing yogourt and coffee, and an expensive package of nuts. She glanced Joan's way and gave a perfunctory nod as she sat down with another nurse, then said something to her colleagues. They turned to stare at Joan.

"Cigánsky chlapec," she heard the nurse say.

Another shook her head. "Nie je Cigánka," she said. She is not a Gypsy.

Joan stared back at them until they turned away from her—but she felt the eyes of the Roma family on her too. Miserable and self-conscious, she left for the elevator without looking back.

Joan returned to Miša's floor to wait for Burns and Peter. It was a relief to sit there in the red vinyl chair, having to face no one. Joan realized she was vibrating slightly, thrumming with anxiety. Tibor's face, eyes closed in a drunken stupor, rose unbidden in front of her. She closed her own eyes, hoping to shut him out, but he was still there, his face swollen and bristly, because of course in death he had not shaved.

Burns came to fetch her. Peter was not with him. Joan stood up quickly, on alert for a disaster.

"Peter is with his mother," Burns said. "She wants you to come see her."

Burns was brusque with emotion. Joan followed him down the hall. Miša's room was to the left, a white, sunlit space with a couple of beds. Miša was the sole occupant, however. Peter was asleep beside her on the hospital bed, her arm curved around him, so slender it could be a bone. Miša wasn't wearing her oxygen mask, but didn't seem to have any trouble breathing, perhaps because she barely was. Joan sat in a chair near the head of the bed where she could look out the window into the white sky.

Miša fluttered her fingers against Peter's back by way of greeting. "Hello, Joan," she whispered. Her voice was almost inaudible. Joan leaned closer. "I am coming home. But it is too hard."

Burns had left the room. He knew perhaps that they would have this conversation.

"I want you to look after Peter and Robbie."

Joan stared at Miša. She knew what the ill woman was asking.

Miša looked down at her son. "He will not remember me," she said, her voice cracking. She turned her head to the window, her cheekbone glowing in the light.

Joan wanted to touch her face, as a mother would, but she knew it was impossible. As her caregiver, Joan had touched Miša's body in many intimate ways—but never with affection. Joan stood, one hand on the railing of the hospital bed, the other on Peter's back, her wrist resting against Miša's.

Burns re-entered the room, his face ashen. Joan stepped out of the way so he could gently lift Peter to his shoulder. The boy woke only briefly, nestling into his father's neck. He must be very tired, Joan thought. Suddenly she was hit with it herself—the weight. Tibor on the bottom of the river, his shirt and coat floating and rippling up, his body resting heavy among the stones. It was as though it were Joan who lay there, her blouse and skirt suspended and swaying in the current.

CHAPTER 18

Miša came home the next day, again by ambulance. It was understood she had come home to die. It was Friday, a day Pani Marta usually cooked extra food for the weekend. Her old face was wet with tears when she appeared at the front door, but she wiped them away with her scarf and, red-eyed, went to work in the kitchen, preparing a big pot of soup with the hope Miša would eat.

Joan felt like a ghost, drifting through the house, trailing after Peter as he went from television to Lego to his parents to the kitchen. If he understood what was happening, he did not show it, except for a restlessness and lack of focus that was uncharacteristic for him. When he went to his father, where he sat near Miša's bedside, Burns picked him up absently, and when Peter pulled his beard he did not seem to notice. Peter slid soundlessly off his father's lap and returned to playing. Joan felt sorry for him, but, lost in her own fog, it was all she could do to follow him around.

Later, Pani Marta brought a bowl of soup to Burns on a tray with a white lacy napkin and a silver soup spoon. Miša had no energy to turn her face away, but when Burns lifted the spoon to her mouth, she did not eat. Soup dribbled down her chin onto the pillow. Pani turned away and put her fist to her mouth. Burns wiped the mess and ate the soup himself, mechanically, with dim eyes. Miša tried to say something, but no one could understand her.

When she slept, Burns slept too, on the couch. Joan kept Peter from the front room. He watched endless television, curled like a cat on the seat next to her, till he too nodded off. She covered him with a crocheted afghan that Pani Marta had made. Joan went to the kitchen to see whether the old woman needed help. Pani Marta sat at the table peeling potatoes. The leg of lamb she had brought from the market the other day was roasting in the oven. Joan did not know who would eat this meal but she picked up a potato and began to peel it with a paring knife. Marta smiled at her through tears and patted her hand.

Later, Joan wandered into the hall. Peter was still asleep, she noted as she drifted past. In the front room, Burns still slept also, but Miša's eyes were open, staring at the ceiling. Joan swallowed. Miša blinked, and Joan, relieved, grasped her hand. Miša squeezed it feebly.

"Shall I read to you?" Joan asked.

Miša's lips looked dry at the corners. "Emily," she mouthed.

Joan nodded and opened the slim volume to a poem she knew from her own childhood. It was not about death, she thought, and the finale was glorious. It was about a bird with a velvet head and frightened eyes. At the end there was a silver sea and butterflies that leapt from the banks of the river of Noon into the ocean of sky, without a splash. Joan gasped. It was more beautiful than she remembered.

Miša was illuminated, her eyes golden, unseeing, Joan thought. Or rather, they looked inward, at some landscape inaccessible to anyone else. But Joan was lifted for a moment from her misery, imagining the same winged divers in a river of sunlight that Miša surely saw in her reverie. And so, although they did not speak, it was as though Miša and Joan stood side by side on a riverbank, basking in a summer day that would never end.

That evening, Burns put Peter to bed early. The child was exhausted, Joan thought, from his own frenetic pacing, back and forth from one room to another, trying to escape the doomy mood of the house. Joan too was exhausted from trailing after him. Pani had gone home after supper, saying she would return in the morning, but Burns had waved her away.

No. Rest, he said in Slovak. Pani had begun to protest, but he insisted. We will be fine, he said.

Joan, for the second time during her stay at the Burnses', washed the dishes. One was a roasting pan full of drippings.

"Leave it," Burns said from the doorway, startling Joan. "This weekend you will have off, as usual. Thank you for helping us today," he said wearily. His eyes were grey, hazy. Joan shook her head. "We have plenty of food to eat, thanks to Pani Marta. Peter and I will spend the weekend at home with Miša. There is no need for you to exhaust yourself further. I will need you during the week. Take Saturday and rest Sunday, like the Christians do."

Joan felt torn but relieved. Perhaps Adriana and Milan were back from the east. She was anxious to see them, a feeling that was composed at least in part of worry over how Milan had been received by Adriana's family. But there was something else. Since the news of Tibor's death, it was as though she'd been adrift, without shelter from her torment, and the Burnses' home could no longer be a refuge for her. Miša's impending loss, expected though it was, felt like a bomb ready to detonate.

Joan went to bed that night, steeling herself in a way she hadn't been able to before Edna's death, which had come suddenly and swiftly like a bird of prey. This time, there was a slow progression, a conveyor belt that would dump her and Pani Marta and the Burnses over the edge into...what? Joan didn't know, but she was tensed for a fall.

That night she dreamed her arms and shoulders ached as she trailed after Peter from room to room in a house she knew was his but that had many more hallways than she remembered. He carried his fish head with him, but now it was a real fish head, gold and silver with tendrils floating from it. At the same time it was a helmet of sorts, one that could protect him. He wandered from room to room, looking for his mother. At the end of a hallway, they came to a dark cove where water lapped gently at the pebbled shore. Peter turned to look at Joan as though to ask what to do. She could not answer. Behind him, washed up like a beached shark, Tibor's bloated corpse shone whitely in the dark, the toes of one shoeless foot curled under like a baby's.

Joan awoke, gasping for breath. The moonlight made a cold white shadow on the floor of her room. She sat up, her heart beating faster than a deer's.

Tibor, in death, would not leave her alone. It was not that he harried or accosted her. It was simply his presence, his corpse's persistent insertion into her thoughts and dreams, that was as unavoidable as if it were pursuing her. And like a hunted deer, she knew no escape route, although instinct told her she would eventually have to turn and embrace the corpse if she wanted to free herself of it.

Saturday morning Joan woke late and soundlessly descended the stairs. There was murmuring from the front room, Burns speaking to Peter in low tones while Miša's ragged breaths scored the air. Joan glided by the doorway without stopping so as not to disturb them. She went out the back door into the yard and headed for the gate. There was frost on the grass, each blade outlined in hoar and stiff as a bristle brush. Joan knew her shoes left a wake of silver imprints, irreparably bending the leaves in her path. She did not look back on the damage but closed the door of the gate behind her and headed into the alley.

It led to a side street that ran perpendicular to the main

road and the square. Some cobblestones in the shadows were still frost-covered, others glistened in the sun. Joan was careful not to slip. She headed to the grocery for rolls and jam and soft white cheese, the cheapest breakfast she could buy, and she bought enough for Milan and Adriana also. Food was a gift she could give without embarrassment, and that would disappear into their stomachs, leaving only a pleasant satiety.

At the Hotel Svatopluk, the lobby was, as usual, dimly lit. The pile of shoes, dusted in white powder that today reminded Joan of the morning frost, rested beside the desk. Pani Svato-plukova looked at her with disdain and slight perturbation. Was the woman worried about her trustworthiness?

"Milan a Adriana?" Joan asked, and was waved onward with barely a nod. Now that Joan no longer paid for a room, she supposed she was a nonentity. That suited her fine.

She headed down the hall to the room she once occupied, which had been Elaine Watterson's some time before her. Now it belonged to Adriana and Milan, and then? To no one. To strangers who would know nothing about any of them. Something then would have come to an end.

Joan knocked on the door, and it creaked open. She was surprised Adriana had left it unlocked, but inside she caught the sound of argument, taut hushed voices. Adriana: urgent, borderline hysterical. Milan: subdued, resigned. And another voice. Whose? Joan pushed the door open a little further, revealing Milan's mother, slightly bent and wearing old clothes as though for cleaning. She offered a brown hand, creased like a map of a river, in a gesture that made it clear she was reasoning with him.

Milan's right eyelid was purple and swollen shut, a cut above it bandaged with a white cloth wrapped around his head. His right arm was also bandaged, and his right pant leg was slit to the knee, exposing a swollen calf, bruises mottling the skin in almost iridescent colours. He looked dejected and depleted, slumping forward, while the two women tried to convince him of something he was in no position to refuse. And yet he shook his head slowly in response to their urgings.

"Nie," he replied, "žiadna polícia." No police.

Joan stood in the doorway. She opened her mouth, but no sound came out. Milan noticed her and lifted his hand in greeting. Adriana, startled, gasped when she saw Joan. She did not bother with hellos.

"Milan was attacked by skinheads on the train," she said. "We went to the hospital in Košice. They were rude, practically vicious." Her voice trembled with indignation. "There was a room full of Roma there. Filthy, not enough beds. So we came home."

Joan recalled the Roma family she had seen at the hospital, huddled at the back of the cafeteria. So that's how it was.

Joan put the bag of food on the table. Milan's mother, Mária, glanced gratefully in her direction and dabbed at her son's forehead with the corner of a cloth. He winced but didn't move his head. Joan wondered anxiously whether his neck was sore, whether he had had a proper physical examination.

"Mamo, na," he protested. Mária held out a couple of white pills and a can of orange soda. He opened his mouth with difficulty, and she placed the painkillers on his tongue, then the straw between his lips. He held it with his left hand, which Joan noticed was bruised at the knuckles. He would not be able to work, Joan realized. He could barely move without pain.

Adriana, tense and insistent, spoke to Milan in a low stream. Joan didn't know if he was listening, but she was.

"The people that did this to you cannot be allowed to get

away with it. It was brutal. There were five of them, I have a description. I wrote it down while we were in the ambulance. They were white, one had a tattoo of an ornate cross on his neck, one had letters on his knuckles. The girl with the dog was younger, her hair was dyed blond but her eyes were dark, almost violet. We should tell the police everything. I have the time, the train number, the station we had just passed, everything."

Milan was too tired and hurting to be angry. "You have nothing," he said simply. "The police do nothing for Roma."

Adriana drew herself up straight, her thin shoulders trembling.

"I am a Canadian citizen. If they do not listen to you, they will to me. And if not, I will go to the embassy."

Milan looked alarmed. "No," he said.

Joan imagined Adriana and a dilapidated Milan approaching the Canadian embassy. Two exhausted, wounded children. The idea was preposterous, but so was every other possibility.

"I wish I could put you in a suitcase and ship you to Canada," Joan blurted.

Adriana and Milan looked at her strangely. Joan reddened. Mária, who had not understood, continued to tend to Milan's wounds. Joan realized too late that she might not know of Milan's hopes to go to Canada and was relieved to see her words had not slipped into his mother's consciousness.

Adriana's mind was clearly skipping around something. Milan, troubled, looked at Joan with concern. Joan thought it best to let them talk. She turned away and gestured at the bag of food to Mária.

"Bread, cheese," Joan said. "Raňajky." Breakfast. She remembered Milan's younger sister, Gabriela, the girl with the fever, who Peter's mother Jana so closely resembled.

Mária had the same broad forehead and Roman nose. Joan wasn't hungry. She hoped Gabriela and the children would eat more, if there was more to go around. Mária looked in the bag and tried to smile. She said something Joan couldn't catch and left with the bag in hand.

"We should go to the police. And if they don't act, we ask them for the paperwork," Adriana insisted. "Document everything."

Milan shook his head slowly. "Police no give Roma paperwork. When butcher cheated us, we went to police. They did nothing. They gave us nothing. We waited, five hours, for nothing." He wasn't angry, just matter-of-fact. "This time will be worse. They will keep me, ask questions. They will say I was fighting."

Adriana looked fearful. Joan felt Milan's weariness come over her. Life was so heavy when nothing a person did mattered. Every movement a burden, like walking through quicksand. Tibor's river-swollen body, in a black coffin. His friends—the pallbearers, not young themselves—must have struggled down the church steps to heave him into the back of the hearse, only to bury him under the ground for worms to feast on.

"Don't worry," Milan said, his eyes closed against the pain. "Let us go to Canada. I will study there."

Adriana shook her head and looked down at her hands. "It's not so easy, Milan," she said. "You must have money."

Milan nodded. "I know," he said, and looked away. His eyes were red-rimmed, but not from crying. Joan thought he might have a fever. His forehead looked pale and clammy.

The door creaked open, and Mária reappeared with a steaming pot of soup and the plastic bag Joan had given her over the crook of her arm. She pulled soup mugs out of the bag and scooped the fragrant broth. Chicken soup filled with onions and garlic. Joan marvelled at the scent. Was chicken soup a universal balm? Her Chinese grandmother had made it often, and Edna too.

Mária pressed a spoonful against Milan's lips. He closed his eyes and swallowed with difficulty. He did not open them again until she was finished. He hobbled to the bed to lie down, Adriana supporting him on one side and Joan on the other. He groaned and shivered slightly, then seemed to settle into sleep.

Mária and Adriana whispered together in Slovak as they ate their soup, trying, no doubt, to think through the situation. Mostly, Mária listened, and Adriana, overexcited and full of fear, spoke too quickly for Joan to catch more than a few words. Hospital, police, skinheads. Joan watched Milan as he slept, his dark, damp hair plastered to his forehead. He needed a doctor, she realized.

"Adriana." Joan put her hand out to quiet the younger woman. "I think Milan may have an infection."

Adriana leapt up and Mária rose more slowly.

Joan pressed the back of her hand to Milan's forehead. "He is too hot. We should call an ambulance."

Mária looked pale. She gently massaged her son's temples.

"Yes," Adriana agreed breathlessly. "I will ask Pani at reception to call for us." She hurriedly left the room.

Mária stroked Milan's hair. He groaned in his sleep. She bent to kiss his forehead, trying to look brave. She asked Joan a question. It had the word *domov*, home, in it and Burns. Joan nodded.

Mária hesitated. "Žena," she said, and mimed using a wheelchair. Is the wife well?

"Nie," Joan said, and shook her head.

Mária looked worried. "Malý chlapec?" she asked, holding

her hand above the ground at Peter's height. "Ako sa má?"

"Good, dobre," Joan said, nodding again. The little boy is fine.

"Zdravý?"

"Yes, healthy."

"Šťastný je?" Joan nodded and, to her surprise, felt tears forming behind her eyes. Yes, he is happy.

He likes Lego, she told Mária, in her rudimentary Slovak. He makes things. He is an artist. Young, yes, but very good.

"Ahhh," Mária said, nodding happily.

Adriana hurried into the room. "They are coming," she said. "I will gather his things."

Mária poured some soup into a glass jar she'd brought with her, thrusting it into Joan's hands along with the plastic bag of remaining rolls. Joan knew Mária had to stay at home with the children. Her life was mostly contained within the walls of the hotel.

Joan wished she could say something to reassure her that Milan would be okay. But Mária melted away before the ambulance arrived.

Adriana looked terrified. "I didn't tell them he was Roma."

They woke Milan, who, weak and pale, looked in that moment almost as thin as Miša. His cheekbones and forehead glowed with perspiration. Adriana spoke to him in low tones, in Slovak.

"You need medicine," she said. "We will go to the hospital and this time we will make sure you get it."

The paramedics came down the hall, the stretcher rattling. Adriana went out to meet them. When they entered the room after her, Joan had a flashback to the scene at the Burnses place, of Miša being taken to hospital. A similar big, blue-uniformed male paramedic and a shorter, slimly built young man attended to Milan, who was only half conscious. The paramedics took his vitals, asking short, sharp questions of Adriana. She gave one-word answers in return. Joan could not tell if they knew Milan was Roma, whether they knew he had been at a hospital before. Please, please, please, she pleaded silently. They lifted him onto the stretcher and he groaned.

Adriana's face stretched painfully as she led the way back down the hall. Doors cracked open, and sometimes a face appeared, but no one inquired. Mária's door stayed firmly shut, and children's high-pitched voices covered the sound of the stretcher. Did Milan's father know what had happened, Joan wondered.

Pani Svatoplukova regarded Milan on the stretcher with a severe look that was either judgmental or concerned. The bigger paramedic stumbled slightly in the dim light. A shoe had strayed from the pile by the reception desk. He muttered a curse word and shone his flashlight on the shoes.

"Pozor," he told the other paramedic, kicking the shoe out of the way. Joan, following behind, watched the younger paramedic as he glanced at the shoe pile, faintly white in the dark due to the powder sprinkled on it, and wrinkled his nose.

Something gave way in Joan's chest. She felt a wave of anguish, of humiliation and regret. That pile of discarded footwear, a reminder of the Hungarian memorial to the slaughtered Jews who'd left their boots and shoes on the riverbank before they were shot to death at the edge of the Danube. How afraid had they been of the black water facing them, cold as stone? Tibor, in death, had joined them, his compatriots now, at the bottom of the river—his black coat, waving like the wings of a stingray, seemed to beckon from its depths. She'd had a chance to beat him with her fists, to accuse and cry and scream as he lay dazed on the floor, but she had not. She had walked away, her coldness an armour to cover her fear and disgust—but also a weapon that penetrated his heart.

Joan stumbled out of the hotel and into the light. The paramedics loaded Milan into the back of the ambulance, and Adriana, pale and dishevelled, hovered behind them. Joan wanted to turn and walk away. She did not have the heart for any more. But Adriana's face, so stark against her black hair, turned toward Joan, eyes beseeching. She needed someone, anyone, for comfort, and Joan was the closest thing to family she had at hand.

For the second time in a matter of days, Joan went to the hospital. Milan was taken into the emergency room, where it was discovered he did not have his identity card with him. After several hours, during which a nurse and ward clerk debated what to do, a doctor gave him a cursory inspection, ordered antibiotics and an IV, and Milan remained parked on a stretcher in the hallway, outside a room with four beds overflowing with visitors. He slept feverishly, Adriana beside him on a folding chair, dabbing his forehead with a damp cloth.

Joan sat on the floor, leaning against the wall, as there was no other chair. Adriana's hair was limp and dull under the fluorescent lights.

"I'll get coffee," Joan offered. Adriana nodded, and Joan headed toward the cafeteria.

She dreaded going in. It felt like revisiting the scene of a crime in which she had been a victim. It was almost the same as it had been on her previous visit—there was a huddle of three women, nurses perhaps, near the food counter and a Roma family at the back of the room—a bleak-eyed man, a weary-looking woman wiping the chins of two young children.

Joan turned her back to them and took a tray, which she filled with two cups of coffee, chunks of rye bread, and two bowls of goulash, for herself and Adriana. She paid the dour *pani* at the cash register, then sat down at one of the tables in the middle of the room. She ate quickly, without looking up, soaking bits of bread in the goulash and spooning them into her mouth. She would take the coffee and food for Adriana back to the hallway. Joan stood up. A small Roma girl stood in front of her, clutching a soft doll with long yellow braids. Staring at her. Joan nodded weakly. The girl regarded her blankly, then thrust the doll in her direction. Joan didn't know what to do, so she took the doll.

"Tvoja bábika?" she asked. Your baby?

The girl pointed to a bandage on the doll's arm, then began to walk away. Joan held the doll, her mouth open. Had the girl mistaken her for a nurse? What was she supposed to do with it?

The girl sat down with the Roma family, who stared at Joan, their dark eyes unreadable. The girl had her back to her. Joan sat the doll in the chair next to her and put Adriana's bowl of goulash in front of it. She raised her hand briefly to the Roma family. The mother's haggard face broke into a smile, and she dipped her head in acknowledgement. Joan felt suddenly relieved, calmer. Leaving the goulash with the doll, she set off with coffees for Adriana and herself.

When Joan returned, Adriana was engaged in an animated conversation with a nurse. Adriana's pale face was strained, her dark eyes darting. Frightened, Joan thought. The nurse was nodding, but Joan could see she was merely waiting for the young woman to finish. When Adriana's fevered speech came to a halt, she coughed into her sleeve. The nurse, in what Joan supposed was meant to be a reasonable tone, began to explain something about nemocničná politika.

Adriana shrieked, "I don't care about hospital policy!" She began to cry and fumbled in her purse for her Canadian passport, which she held up like a shield, but the nurse would not be moved. Joan put the coffees down on the floor. She took a pen and notebook out of her purse and began to write a note. The nurse looked at her and walked away without a word.

"Joan, what are you doing? I was trying to get that nurse to move Milan into a room somewhere."

Joan closed the notebook. "I am taking notes. Date, time. Do you know the nurse's name?"

"Why? Joan, why are you doing this?" Adriana sounded close to hysteria.

"Adriana. It is wrong how Milan is being treated. Don't worry, just do what you need to do. But now you must go eat. The cafeteria has goulash. I will sit with Milan. He looks better, don't you think?" Joan made it into a question, so it wasn't a lie. Adriana searched Milan's face and held her breath for a moment. She nodded, stood weakly, and Joan handed her the coffee. Her hands closed around it as though for warmth as she headed down the hall.

Joan sat down on the chair. Milan's eyes were closed but his eyelids flickered.

"Milan," Joan said in a low voice. He turned away. "Milan," Joan persisted. He opened his eyes slightly. "You are in a hospital. Adriana is at the cafeteria." He turned his face toward her. "You are going to be okay," she added hopefully.

Milan squeezed his eyes shut and groaned softly. "Don't tell my father," he said.

Joan wondered if Mária had already done so. "I won't," she agreed.

Milan turned his face to the wall. "I cannot go to Canada."

"What?" Joan asked.

"Canada. I haven't money. I cannot leave my mother."

Joan said nothing.

"What will I do? I cannot go to school or work. I will be tourist. Adriana will be tired of me," he said, turning his eyes to the ceiling.

Joan took his hand. "Don't worry now, Milan. You must feel better. Then you can decide."

Milan closed his eyes and said nothing.

A man in a white lab coat with a stethoscope approached. After a curt greeting he began to take Milan's vitals. Joan stood up and pushed the chair out of the way. He began to say something to Joan in Slovak but she shook her head.

"Nehovorím po slovensky."

He looked at her sharply. "English?" he asked.

Joan nodded.

"His fever has abated," he said with a British accent. "He needs to go home, before he catches something worse."

Joan nodded.

"Where are you from?" the man asked.

"Canada," Joan said.

"I hear it is beautiful. I love to ski," he added, appraising her. Joan felt her cheeks redden.

The man asked Milan for his name and what day it was.

Milan kept his eyes closed and swallowed. "I am Milan."

"Ah. That is my name also," the man said, with a hint of a smile.

"Are you a doctor?" Joan asked, her voice squeaky.

"Yes," the man said, then corrected himself. "A doctor in training."

He looked old for a medical student, Joan thought. But how was she to know, really?

"He is Roma?" the man asked, without looking at her.

Yes, Joan nodded, but he did not see her nod.

"Skinheads did this?"

"Yes," Joan said.

"He is lucky," the man who called himself Milan said, and shook his head. "I love Slovensko, but we are not kind to Roma. Especially now we are cruel capitalists." The last two words were pronounced with sarcastic relish. "How do you know him?"

Joan shook her head and sat down in the chair again. She didn't have to answer his questions. He examined Milan's soiled dressings, took his pulse and blood pressure, then turned to Joan.

"He will not die, your friend. But he might if he stays here. Bratislava is more dangerous for Roma than you might imagine."

Joan put a hand on Milan's arm. The student doctor gave a curt nod and walked away without a word of farewell.

Joan stared after him. Had he meant to be helpful? Or threatening? She watched him disappear down the hall, nodding casually to other hospital staff as he passed them, hands tucked in the pockets of his white lab coat. Joan wrote the name Milan among her notes. She wondered if it was his real name. She doubted it.

Adriana appeared beside her. She put her hand to Milan's head and looked relieved. "I think the fever has broken," she said.

"I think we should take him home."

Adriana looked up, startled. "Don't they have to discharge him?"

Joan shrugged. "I don't know how it works. We can ask."

"Do you really think he is ready?" Adriana asked, her eyes filling with tears.

Joan nodded. "It might be worse if he stays here."

Adriana bent close to Milan's pale forehead and whispered

in his ear. He stirred and turned his head toward her, a smile cracking his dry white lips.

Joan went to the cafeteria to give them some privacy and to fetch a cup of water and a napkin to wipe his mouth. The Roma family and the doll, along with the bowl of goulash, had disappeared, but a knot of nurses peered at her as she entered. Were they the same nurses who had been there earlier? Maybe even the same ones who had been there the other day, who had commented to one another that she was not a Gypsy? Joan, a spark of anger leaping in her throat, felt like shouting at them to stop staring at her, to mind their own business. Instead, she turned her back to them.

When Joan returned to the corridor, Milan was sitting painfully on the edge of the bed. Adriana was feeding him his mother's soup. Joan pulled a shirt from the bundle of clothes on the bed beside Milan. There was blood on the sleeve, but she did not remark on it. Adriana helped Milan put his good arm into the left sleeve first. He winced when he lifted his arm, and she didn't try to help him with his right arm, instead draping the shirt over his right shoulder. The hospital staff had cut his jeans to get them off, but, thankfully, Mária had included some sweatpants in the bag along with the food. Draping a sheet over his thighs, Adriana began to work the sweatpants over his feet and calves. In order for him to get them on completely, he would have to stand. Joan grasped him by the left elbow while Adriana shimmied the sweatpants up to his waist. They hung off him from his hip bones and reached only to the middle of his calves but stayed up. He looked down at them.

"These are my father's sports pants," Milan said.

"Your mother sent them," Joan said.

Milan slowly shook his head. "He hates me," Milan said, quiet and despairing.

Joan and Adriana took Milan by his elbows and started down the hall. No one gave them a second glance. The two women at reception ignored them. Adriana remembered she would need to call a taxi, and spoke to one of them, who, without looking up or commenting, dialled the number. Joan was resigned to the curt, unsmiling nature of Slovak service, but she felt Adriana begin to unravel. Joan knew she was worried, hungry, exhausted, and at the end of her rope, but she needed Adriana to get Milan home.

"Ďakujem," Joan said loudly to the woman who had called the taxi. The woman ignored her.

Milan and Adriana sat down in a vinyl love seat. Joan put her hand on Adriana's shoulder.

"Why did she have to be so rude?" Adriana asked, her voice trembling with emotion. Joan squeezed her shoulder. She realized they'd probably been mistaken for sisters, or mother and daughter. The situation was awkward, but Joan felt Adriana needed propping up. The younger woman had travelled across the globe after spending time in a mental hospital, fallen in love with someone whose fragile place in this world had become starkly obvious. The three of them sat in deflated silence, waiting for the cab.

The driver helped Milan get into the front seat, where there was more room for his legs. He was stocky, dark-haired, and spoke with a Hungarian accent. And though he'd been visibly surprised when Joan greeted him with the Hungarian "Szia" before giving the address to the hotel, he only nodded and smiled. Milan slumped against the door. The driver looked at him with sympathy.

"Your friend," he said in English, glancing at Joan in the rear-view mirror. "He is okay?"

Joan nodded, even as she realized she didn't know. Adriana wept silently, her hand compulsively rubbing Milan's shoulder from the seat behind him. Joan shook her head.

The driver turned on the radio to a local pop station. It was terrible music, Joan thought, gritting her teeth. But he did not turn it up too loud. He asked Milan in Slovak if he liked the band. Milan shook his head. The driver laughed and switched to a CD. Joan recognized the first line of the first track as a Slovak folk song, a lullaby—čierne oči, choďte spať. Dark eyes, go to sleep.

"The favourite of my brother's little girl," the driver said. He first began to hum along, and then to sing, in a particularly fine baritone.

Joan thought how strange it was to be travelling in a cab driven by a Hungarian man singing a Slovak lullaby in a voice that sounded as though it had been trained for the opera, along with a pair of young lovers, a weeping Canadian girl and an injured Roma boy. It seemed to her, as they pulled onto the cobblestones of Old Bratislava, that there was something particularly twenty-first century about it, an experience that perhaps no previous generation could have had. And at the same time, it was an ancient story about strangers and travellers and lovers, a slight variation on themes humans had always claimed as their own.

CHAPTER 19
ADRIANA

On the drive home, Milan's body aches quietly. Sitting behind him, I can feel the pulse of hurt and heat. He slumps in the front passenger seat until we reach the Hotel Svatopluk. The driver is burly and helps Milan out slowly. Milan leans on him, slipping out of the circle of my arm around his shoulders. I wait till Milan is out of the car and then fling open the door, anxious to be beside him, and cling to his arm as he climbs the stairs, panicking that he will collapse on the stone step. Oh, Milan. Forgive me.

Joan holds on to my free elbow as though she thinks I will fall. I feel like I *am* falling into a familiar dark place I fear. I fear it like some people fear air travel or swimming. My throat constricts, and bubbles of panic rise and burst, rise and burst behind my eyeballs.

Joan is not like her mother at all. Gillian flutters like a butterfly. Joan is quiet and solid. Thank God. We drag ourselves up the steps like we're staggering from a life raft up a beach to safety.

Milan and I wait inside the door while Joan pays the driver.

"Here is my card," I hear him say in English, "in case you need a taxi again."

Milan leans heavily on my shoulder, panting from the exertion of climbing the steps. Pani Alica comes out of the back office where a TV is on. She calls out to me, but I only wave to her, too upset to speak. She waddles after us. It's the first time I've seen her out from behind the desk and only now do I realize how short the woman is, and that she has a prosthetic lower left leg.

She waves an envelope in one hand. "Od policie!" she calls, crackling with concern. I snatch the letter from her. For a moment, she stands looking after us, then I hear her creak her way across the floor to her place behind the desk.

A door cracks open as we pass. Someone knows we are back. It is infuriating. As we pass Milan's family's door, I hear the usual sounds of life—children's voices, dishes being washed, and the smell of cigarette smoke creeping under the door.

My heart aches. This is what Milan left behind to be with me, for what? To be thrashed by racists, who wouldn't stop when I pleaded in Slovak, only when I screamed at them in English? To be barely tolerated by my blood relatives, who I imagine now had also balked at my slanted eyes and black hair. I should have known. My mother's people. I should have realized.

When we reach the room, Milan falls, groaning, into bed. I rush to plug the kettle in and mutter under my breath, "Mária will know we are back."

Joan nods. We both know such news cannot escape Milan's mother for long.

I leave the envelope on the bedside table while I hurry to make tea. Feeling frantic is easier than feeling fear.

Milan appears to be in almost as bad shape as before he went to the hospital, but his breathing is quiet and regular. I try to calm myself. He's alive, I chant inside my head. Alive, alive. With half-open eyes Milan sips spoonfuls of tea and sugar from my hand, but he's too tired to speak. After a while he sinks backward into the pillow. I stare at him, as though it will help keep him alive, the spoon shaking in my hand.

"Adriana." Joan puts her hand on my shoulder. "Adriana, have tea."

I take the cup she offers. It is warm and I am trembling with cold.

She hands me the envelope. "It's for Milan," she says.

I examine the return address and the official police crest and rip open the envelope.

"Adriana, I don't think…"

I scan the delicate paper. "There was a witness on the train, when Milan was beaten. A Slovak man who reported it to the police. He found Milan's identity card. They want him to come to the station."

"There's no way he can travel right now," Joan says.

"Of course not," I snap. "They want him to report to the station in Košice. But…"

Joan shakes her head.

There is a knock on the door. I jump. It might be Mária, but I am afraid. It is Joan who opens the door to Milan's mother, bearing a vacuum flask and a small, stoppered glass bottle.

"Polievka a medicína." Soup, and a strange-smelling home remedy. I hug Mária hard. The lines on her face seem to have deepened since that morning, but it might only be the light.

A stream of imperfect Slovak pours from me, about what had happened at the hospital, and that her son's fever has broken and we decided to come home. She nods, smiling, and tears stream down her face. How to comfort a mother who knows she cannot protect her child? From illness, racists, poverty, hunger, hopelessness, and the myriad small and casual offenses, dismissals, and disappointments of this life, which in the case of a young Roma man like Milan, are a constant trickle that would wear a person to the bone by her age? I cannot help it. I cry in her arms. We cannot comfort each other.

CHAPTER 20

"You need to sleep," Joan told Adriana. Listless and sodden with tears, Adriana lay down on the couch and closed her eyes. Mária was pouring soup from the flask.

"Jana," she said, handing Joan a cupful. Joan shook her head and patted her stomach.

Mária put the steaming cup on a bedside table near Milan's head. "Jeho najlepšie jedlo," she said quietly. His best dish.

Joan nodded helplessly, remembering how Milan had said the same about cream of wheat and palacinky.

The scent of broth seemed to stir Milan. His eyes barely opened, but he craned his neck toward the steaming cup. Mária sat beside him and stroked his hair and murmured to him, spooning broth into his mouth. The scene reminded Joan of a Rembrandt painting. She wished she had a camera, but she knew that even then she would not be able to capture it. It was one of those kindled moments that either quickly faded to ash or blazed into something else. Lost, either way, except to the imagination.

Milan kept his eyes closed, as if it helped against the pain. When he was finished the soup, he relaxed into his pillow and slept again, the sound of his breathing mingling with Adriana's.

Mária looked at Joan shyly. "Dve deti," she said. Two children.

Joan had to admit they looked it. But she also knew that at their age Mária had children of her own, and Joan herself had realized her life would not be what she had been led to imagine. She might be witnessing Adriana and Milan's crash into the first, cold wall of adulthood. She hoped not. They were already more worldly and weary and wounded than she would have hoped for them.

Joan wondered if Adriana had told Milan about her stay in the mental hospital. It seemed likely they had shared everything, but she doubted Mária knew. The way Mária looked at Adriana, with a mixture of meek adoration and expectation, Joan knew she thought of her as a protector— or even saviour—of her son. Maybe she hoped Adriana would take him to Canada and his life would take on the Western golden sheen that burnished her imagination.

Joan and Mária sat silently, thinking about the future. It was their first time, for all intents and purposes, being alone together. Between them in the silence was the Burns family—Robbie and Miša and Peter. They were almost a physical presence in the room. Maria would know from Milan that Joan worked for the Burnses, of course. Joan imagined Mária straining to find a way to ask about Peter. What would become of him when Miša slipped the net of this life and disappeared into the ocean that reclaims us all? Joan wanted to reassure Mária that all the adults who surrounded Peter would fill any gaps, but she knew the truth was that Robbie would be demolished by his wife's death, Pani Marta was old and gnarled as a tree root with arthritis, and Joan herself—adrift on a sea of guilt and grief and regret—feared the loss of Miša as a wave that could sink her. If she were Peter's only life raft, she would be a sorry and precarious one.

Mária held her son's hand and massaged the point where thumb joined forefinger. Joan had a hazy memory of her mother's mother doing the same thing to her when she was ill. Or *was* it a memory? It could be she had simply superimposed her grandmother and herself onto the present scene.

Mária turned to her. She was tired, and her eyes glistened. "Pani Burnsova—zomrie?"

Joan strained to hear.

"Zomrie?" Mária asked again, more loudly.

Joan did not know if it was her place tell Mária that Miša would die. She shook her head and looked down. "Neviem."

Milan opened his eyes with some difficulty. "Mamo," he said. "Aj nezomrie."

Joan realized Milan had heard his mother ask, "Will she die?" and thought she was asking about himself.

Mária hugged her son's head fiercely with both hands. "Nie, nie," she said.

Milan blinked. He looked as though he were surfacing from underwater. Adriana stirred but did not wake up.

"Mamo," Milan said. He and Mária carried on a hushed conversation as she began to tend his wounds. He winced frequently as she applied her home remedy, but there was something urgent he wanted to tell her, Joan could tell. Mária tried to hush him, but he did not stop talking until he was finished. Whatever he told her left him lying spent against his pillow, and Mária looking contented and peaceful.

Something had been settled then. Joan felt the weight of recent events tugging her downward. She felt she could sleep for a long time. Tomorrow, Sunday, they would rest, and Monday she would return to the Burnses' house, a house filled with grief, for the impending death of Miša. It was a heavy house, but Joan was heavy herself. It was where, for now, she belonged. She envisioned Peter standing in the hallway clutching the Lego fish head to his chest, absorbing the darkness around him, and she knew that for his sake and for her own, she needed to be there to open the curtains.

CHAPTER 21

Adriana was supposed to return to Canada in a week. It probably wasn't enough time for Milan to obtain a passport, and he had no money for a plane ticket. Adriana said she could borrow the money from her father, but Milan adamantly refused.

"I must stay and wait to be more healthy," he insisted. "Later I will come." Adriana looked desperate. Milan wiped the hair from her face. "I must have my identity card," he said. "There is not time for all. Don't worry, later I will join you in Canada."

Adriana, pale and stricken, insisted. "At least we must go to the police station to get your card back."

Milan shrugged and winced.

Surely they could not go by train, Joan thought, after what had happened. She pulled the taxi driver's card from her pocket and handed it to Adriana. "Take this cab to Košice tomorrow. I will pay for it."

Adriana looked uncomprehendingly at the card. Milan's face was a blank mask.

"Milan, you helped me find my job," said Joan. "This is how I can say thank you." He smiled painfully, then looked away.

That was the night before. This morning, the sun streamed in the window, through the ancient sheers. Joan imagined Edna peering at her from outside, her hands cupped against the dusty pane. Mrs. Watterson, and then Joan's own grandmother, looking severe and primly clutching her handbag in front of her, hovered behind Edna. They were hazy, outlined with a lambent glow. Joan squinted and all three dissolved into sunlight.

She showered and dressed in the bathroom. When she emerged, Adriana was sitting up on the sofa, her hair sleep-tousled.

"I must go to the Burnses' house," Joan said, in a low voice. "They need me at work."

Adriana nodded, her mind far away, absorbed in thought. Joan felt deflated. Alone. She closed the door soundlessly behind her.

The Burnses' home, far from being dark, was bustling when she arrived. Pani Marta was there to greet her at the door. She smiled and frowned and squeezed Joan's hand, then pulled her toward the sitting room. A nurse tended to Miša while chatting, bright and incessant, to Burns. Miša's eyes were closed, and her ragged breaths too far apart.

Burns sat with Peter on his lap, next to Miša's hospital bed, a Slovak storybook spread before them. Peter, in a tentative voice, was sounding out words slowly but steadily. Joan was astounded. How had he learned to read? Peter had silently gobbled up the storybooks Joan read to him while he sat in her lap. Had he been learning all along?

Burns, looking haggard, nevertheless beamed with pride. "Our wandering friend has returned," he said.

Peter stared up at her, his dark eyes wary. She had not been there through the weekend, and with a pang she realized that Peter perhaps had never considered her as anything but outside the small circle he could depend on, the circle that included only his father and mother and Pani Marta.

Joan sat down across the room on the same stiff sofa she'd occupied on her first visit to meet Miša. Now she surveyed the room through different eyes. Joan knew the time had passed for goodbyes. Could Miša hear them? Or had she already slipped too far away from the shores of this life? Joan had the stark realization that she'd declared her allegiance by spending the day with Adriana and Milan—that Burns had even made sure of it by insisting she take the day off. He looked up from the children's book at her, his eyes dark and glittering. He was with his son but he was also walking the dim path with Miša until her last breath unfurled.

Joan felt herself a container for all the sadness in the room, even though her eyes were dry. Mutely, she smiled at Burns and Peter.

The nurse turned to Burns and spoke in a low voice. He closed the book and, without a word, lifted Peter into Pani's arms. Joan stood up.

"I will be alone with my wife now," he said.

Joan trailed soundlessly after Pani and Peter, as though caught in their wake. Pani turned into the television room, Peter on her shoulder, and began to sob quietly. Joan felt Peter's dark eyes on her as she continued past them to the kitchen.

There was a pile of dishes with a pot turned upside down on top. Joan emptied the sink and filled it with hot soapy water. She washed everything, and then she heard a sorrowful wail from the front room. Burns. Hands trembling, she took the pot and dried it, and put it on the kitchen table. She continued with bowls and cutlery. The murmur of the television continued in the background. Pani would be saying the rosary.

Joan could not leave the kitchen. She polished the counters jerkily, wiping her eyes with the back of her hand, but they remained dry. She put the dishes away and looked in the fridge. She stared at the small sliver of cake left over from Burns's birthday.

There was also a ragged leg bone from the lamb Pani Marta had bought at market. Joan, who had learned the basics of making soup by watching the older woman cook, placed it in a stockpot to boil, and then took all the vegetables from the crisper—onions, carrots, potatoes, celery, and a couple of withered apples. She washed them and began to chop them. It might not be up to Pani Marta's standards, but she would do her best. There were no more wails from the front room, and no sign of Pani Marta or Peter.

Joan finished chopping a small mountain of vegetables. She washed her hands and checked the lamb bone. It was boiling quietly, the broth a grey colour with a dirty-looking foam around the edges of the pot that she would later skim off.

Joan sat down at the table again and put her head on her hands. She would rest, just for a moment.

Sometime later, she lifted her head to the sight of Pani Marta's back to her, busy at the stove.

"Ona už nie je," Pani Marta said without turning. She is no more. The old woman made the sign of the cross and continued stirring. "Peter spi." He sleeps.

Joan made her way to the TV room. Peter was curled on the couch, breathing softly, his thumb in his mouth. She sat beside him without touching him.

The front room was quiet. Had the nurse left? Joan wondered if Burns was alone with Miša's body, and whether she or Pani Marta should go to him. But then she noted the familiar smell of clove cigarettes drifting from the back door. He must have passed her, sleeping with a pile of chopped vegetables in front of her on the kitchen table.

Joan spread a blanket lightly over Peter, then slipped past Pani Marta in the kitchen and opened the screen door without a sound. Burns was sitting on the bottom step, his forehead in one hand and a cigarette in the other. Joan sat on the top step and said nothing.

"She asked about you," Burns said.

Joan's heart sank.

"She wanted to know if you would take her books. The poetry. And if you don't wish to have them, to donate them to the library."

Joan nodded mutely. It was bright and frost was in the air. Burns turned to look at her, and she could see that he had been crying.

"I am so sorry...for your loss," Joan said.

Burns turned back to the bright sunlight. "As am I, lass," he said.

Very early the next morning Joan woke to music. She peered out the window into the dark and saw a small procession in the back lane. People leaning into one another, laughing, cursing and stumbling, made their way through the dark, following a small group of musicians. The music, a swirl of violin and accordion, sounded Romani to Joan. It appeared to be a wedding party and, sure enough, the procession was soon followed by the sound of hooves. A tall white horse with two dark figures on its back came into view. The couple on the white horse slumped forward, as though drunk or asleep. Joan imagined they carried a secret, curled in the woman's womb like a green bud, waiting to unfurl. When they had passed, a gust of wind swept down the lane behind them, scattering dead leaves in their wake.

Joan crept downstairs in her bathrobe to make a cup of tea. The house was quiet, and Miša's body lay wrapped in a sheet and covered with a blanket in the front room. The scent of clove cigarettes drifted from the back door. Joan felt a slight panic, trapped between a dead body and a grieving man. She was reminded of Tibor, and the intolerableness of the situation drove her to hold her breath and soundlessly climb the stairs back to her room.

Peter was standing in his doorway, clutching his Lego fish head, which was wrapped in a small blanket. Joan hesitated for a moment at her own bedroom door. How had he got out of his crib? She realized he was big enough now to clamber over its sides.

"Čierne oči, choďte spať," Joan whispered to him. "Go to sleep, Peter." She gave him a gentle push into his bedroom and closed the door, then entered her own room and did the same.

Joan sat on her bed trembling. Tibor's face and the dark bulk of his shoulders loomed over her. His eyes were closed, and he was clearly dead, but she was afraid. She moved to the desk and began to draw a picture in her journal, of Tibor in death, his face bloated, eyes closed, one shoe on and one floating above him. It did not look like Tibor, but Joan knew it was him, and that was what mattered.

Realizing time had escaped her, and it was late morning, she hurried downstairs, past the body in the front room to the kitchen where Pani was feeding Peter in his high chair. They stared at her, their expressions unreadable. There was no scent of clove cigarettes from the back door. Joan felt as though she wanted to run out that door and never return. She saw Burns trudging slowly up the walk from the back gate.

He was deep in thought, preoccupied. Joan sat down at the kitchen table. Pani Marta, with concern in her eyes, pushed a bowl of porridge toward Joan across the table.

Burns entered the house and sat down at the table across from her, in front of his own half-eaten bowl of porridge. "There's horse shit in the lane," he croaked.

Pani Marta looked up, eyes wide. She did not know English, but the word *shit*, Joan imagined, she recognized from movies. It was not like Burns to be vulgar.

Joan said in a wobbly voice, "There was a wedding."

Burns nodded slowly. "That would explain it," he said, fingering his spoon.

They ate in silence, until Pani cleaned off Peter's face and lifted him from his chair. She then took him by his hand to the television room, glancing back at Burns and Joan with a worried expression.

After he finished his breakfast, Burns put the spoon down. "Joan," he said. "Will you help me wash her body?"

Joan's mouth fell open.

"Miša has no other friends," he said sadly. "She didn't want strangers touching her. She asked me—to ask you to help."

Joan again felt the urge to run. But instead she nodded mutely. In life, Miša had not asked much of her. She could at least do this.

Burns carefully rolled the wool blanket from the body of his wife as though not to disturb her. He hesitated briefly, then peeled back the sheet. There was Miša, as though asleep, but slacker, or sunken—something Joan didn't quite know how to describe. Miša's face did not look the same. This was almost a relief to Joan.

Miša was wearing a nightdress and slippers. Living, she would have complained of the cold, but in death, the chill preserved her. Burns tenderly rolled the nightdress above his wife's knees. Joan wasn't sure where to look. Miša wore a diaper of late, but it seemed the nurse had removed it and replaced it with a pair of Miša's pink bikini briefs.

Her breasts were small triangles. Burns gently turned the body of his wife and slid the nightdress off her shoulder and over her head, then down the other arm.

Miša looked so tiny, her bones like flutes, but her shoulders broader than one would expect. From transferring to and from and wheeling her chair and from holding Peter in times past, Joan supposed. And from her days as a dancer. As though her past resided there across her shoulder blades, not as a burden but perhaps as strength.

Joan took a sponge from the basin of water Burns had placed at Miša's feet and began to wash them. Her small toenails painted coral pink. Miša's legs had been shaved by the nurse or someone else before she died, and they were smooth as a baby. Burns washed the other leg, humming under his breath.

She was not sure what would happen when they reached the bikini briefs. Burns ignored them and continued wiping Miša's hip bones which jutted out above the tops of them, so Joan, relieved, did the same. She wiped the torso, under and over the breast and each arm to the armpit. Burns also turned his wife so Joan could wash her back. They worked swiftly and quietly. Even though Miša's body was dead weight and neither of them presumably had washed a body before, it seemed easy, almost effortless, Joan thought. Was it because they were used to helping wash Miša when she was alive?

"There," Burns said. "I will wash her face and dress her myself. Thank you." He turned his back to Joan.

She felt bereft somehow. She knew he had to have the last moments with Miša, but she felt the need to say a proper goodbye.

"Wait," she said. Burns turned to look at her. "We should rinse her hair with chamomile." And sit her in the sunshine, Joan thought.

Burns's eyes widened. She could see the grief in them now.

"May I?" Joan asked. Burns nodded. He took the copper trophy down from the mantle and went to make chamomile tea.

Joan was left alone with Miša's body. She went to the bureau for a clean sheet to spread over her charge and remembered the photos in the bottom drawer. Without thinking, Joan took the photo of Jana and Peter out and left it lying on the side table, and the one of Miša and Elaine Watterson, leaning over their canes and grinning. She found another close-up of a very small baby with big, serious black eyes. It was Peter, no doubt about it, in whose arms she did not know, but she placed the photo in Miša's hand and crossed her arms over the sheet, across her chest.

When Burns returned from the kitchen with the tea, he set it down on the side table.

"I found these photos," Joan said, trembling. "This one of Peter. I hope you don't mind."

Burns touched the photo in his wife's hands and smiled sadly. "Yes, that's Pedro."

Joan wet Miša's hair and rubbed the chamomile into it with a small towel. Burns sat down heavily beside her in a wooden chair that creaked under his weight, and picked up the photos from the side table.

"I have not seen these before," he said. "Where did you find them?"

Joan pointed to the bottom drawer. "There are more."

Burns gazed at the photo of his wife and Mrs. Watterson. "She loved that old Englishwoman. Elaine Watterson." He looked puzzled and shook his head. "She was very prim and proper around me, but they had fun. They called themselves Cane and Able. The forgotten daughters of Adam and Eve."

Joan squeezed golden chamomile tea from the ends of Miša's hair. Wet, it looked darker than it had before, but surely when it dried there would be hints of gold. She wished she had been able to do this for Miša before she died.

Burns had fallen silent, staring at the photo of Jana holding Peter. The muscles of his face seemed to stand out under his skin.

Joan deliberated a moment and said, "I know Peter's uncle. He is Jana's younger brother."

Red-faced, Burns stared at her, then looked down. His eyes burned.

"Milan is young, poor. Racists attacked him on the train and he is hurt."

Burns's hands trembled. He looked up with a pained expression.

Joan was struck with an idea, one that was terrible to mention given the timing, but she forged ahead anyway. "He has a Canadian girlfriend, my friend, Adriana. If you pay for Milan's flight to go to Canada with her, he will have a better life there than any he could have here."

Burns was dumbstruck. Joan could see clouds and other forms pass quickly over his face. She imagined his thoughts as heavy and swift as freight trains thundering through him.

"He has no one to help him," she said. "Jana lives in America, but her husband wastes their money drinking." Joan was surprised to hear the bitterness in her own voice.

Burns stood up and turned his back on her. "I must smoke," he said, and left the room.

Joan slumped in her chair. What had she done? Trembling, she wrung the small towel back into the copper trophy, and tears welled with no escape route. Cruel, cruel, she thought. She had been so cruel to put this request to a grieving man. But it was as if she couldn't help herself.

Joan sat beside Miša's body, a faint perfume of cloves drifting in from the back of the house. She tucked the photo of Jana and Peter into her pocket, so Burns would not have to see it again.

Joan had been Miša's only friend, Burns had said. And Miša had been her friend also, though Joan hadn't really thought of her that way. She had been both taskmaster and task, the employer and content of the job. And a life that, like a slim branch, had turned slowly into a piece of driftwood on the shores of this world.

Miša's hair, though dark and damp around her pale face, glinted gold in the morning sun. There was something formal and elegiac about the moment. But Miša was already gone. Joan had the strange feeling of a crisp absence, as though Miša had risen from her body and slipped away in the dark to follow the drunken revellers of last night's wedding party.

Goodbye, Joan said silently. You wsere a good friend. A good mother and a good wife. It was all she could think of. What passed through her in response like a night train was the tail end of the rhyme handwritten in the back of Peter's book.

Sally, tell my mother I shall never come back.

Joan found Pani asleep in the television room with Peter, her arm around his shoulders as he stared intently at a toothpaste commercial on the screen. When Joan entered, he turned his head to stare at her just as intently. She held out her arms ,and he got up and toddled over. When she picked him up, he buried his face in her neck, the way he did with his parents. He was sleepy, she realized. It was almost lunchtime, but she decided to carry him up to his crib for an hour's nap.

Peter was already limp with sleep when she placed him on his mattress and covered him with a blanket. He looked, as sleeping children tend to, angelic. She surrounded him with his stuffed toys. The Lego fish head she had left on the couch beside Pani Marta. It was too awkward to carry both him and his creation, now, she thought, that he was almost four years old.

Joan went back downstairs. Miša's death changed everything. The way she felt about this house, for example. It was as if it had lost its hearth, its centre. Miša's life had been at the heart of everything. Now they were like acquaintances, or even strangers, Joan thought. Like people in different sleeping compartments of a train.

Peter upstairs in his bed. Pani in the TV room. Miša sleeping now forever in the front room. Only Burns and Joan were awake, the scent of his clove cigarettes drifting through the cracks in the back door frame. It was too cold now to leave just the screen door closed. Joan shivered. Time to do more dishes. She put on Pani Marta's apron, smaller than the one Burns wore that hung next to it.

She began with a tub of hot soapy water and an empty dish drainer. Soon it would get messy, but with the work not yet begun, she could imagine the outcome—a pile of clean white dishes, the sink rinsed and scrubbed. The nursing home where Edna had lived, Joan thought, dipping the first few mugs in the water, had large stainless-steel sinks and an industrial dishwasher. She swirled a dishcloth around inside a mug. When Joan was young, Edna had always used a scrub brush and bleach to make sure they sparkled, but here there was no brush, only a bottle brush for wine bottles. Joan began to cry soundlessly.

She saw Tibor falling into the Danube, his trench coat billowing behind him, the heavy, solitary splash as he hit the water. Jana in bare feet, wrapped in a blanket, cradling baby Peter in her arms. Edna, sitting in her wheelchair while Joan washed her hair, massaging shampoo into her old friend's scalp in rhythm to Edna's crooning of an old Hungarian melody, one that made Joan think of wind and bells and the keening of sea birds and women who watched the sea for loved ones who would never return. She wiped her eyes with her forearm. The back door opened and Burns, coughing, entered. She heard a kitchen chair scraping the floor and Burns sit down heavily.

Joan wiped her hands on the apron, dried them with a tea towel, then turned toward the table and sat down too.

"Forgive me," she said, not looking at him. "I didn't meant to be cruel."

Burns said gruffly, "Dinna matter." He poured himself a cold cup of tea from the pot on the table into a mug Joan hadn't yet washed. They sat in silence for a moment. Joan felt crestfallen. He would never trust her again.

"This Milan—your friend." He squinted painfully. "Peter's uncle."

Joan nodded without looking up.

"What kind of man is he?"

Milan was a man, of course, but in her mind still a boy.

"He is...brave. He is honest. And he is kind." He is without options, in an untenable and dangerous situation, Joan thought.

"Does he have skills? Any education?"

"He speaks quite a lot of English. He did not have the chance to finish school," she said.

Burns grimaced. "Like his sister. She was very bright. She was one of our top students. Then she got pregnant. Probably on a class trip to Budapest."

Joan looked up, her cheeks flushing.

"The father was a Roma man. One night and she didn't want anything more to do with him. She told her parents and her father kicked her out. He blamed her, but I think he just didn't want another mouth to feed."

Joan opened her mouth—to agree or protest, she wasn't sure. It was likely true Milan's father didn't want another hungry belly in his cramped apartment—he and Mária couldn't afford to feed the ones they had already. Jana would have known that too.

Burns continued. "We let her stay with us. Miša was beginning to need help. It worked out nicely," he said flatly. "Elaine Watterson was the one who suggested it. She was the one who had convinced us to forgo Jana's tuition from the beginning, otherwise the girl could never have attended college. And Elaine was the one who thought, when Jana was trying to decide what to do about the baby, that Miša and I might like to adopt."

Joan pictured the four of them. Miša, bright-eyed, and Burns, wanting a child of their own. Elaine Watterson, brow furrowed with concern for the situation the silent, morose Jana found herself in. There would have been no question in the Englishwoman's mind that the girl, for whom marriage to the father of her child (already receding into the dim light of the past) was not an option, must need help fixing the problem.

Joan knew, as Jana herself must have, that the young woman's place in college depended on those three adults. Joan imagined Jana longing for an escape route from what motherhood promised, from Slovakia, and from this kitchen.

What about Mária and her husband? Had they been a part of the conversation at this same table? Joan doubted it. She felt the hollow darkness that must have filled Jana's throat. Jana did not want her parents there. It was enough that her mother had, behind her father's back, handed her a blanket and some gold earrings. As if she might change her mind and marry the man who was really just another nameless Roma boy from Hungary who she'd met on a school trip and who she'd never see again.

Burns was gazing down at his hands, creasing and uncreasing the placemat in front of him. "She loved him," he said, and Joan felt confused. "Miša loved Peter the moment she laid eyes on him. I knew we had no choice. I loved him too. But not like her. I think I loved him because she was so in love with him."

Joan shivered.

Burns looked at her squarely. "He is my son. I would kill anyone who tried to hurt him." He was trembling, and seemed somehow smaller. "I am afraid, Joan. I am afraid that my boy will suffer the same fate in this city as every other Roma boy I have met."

Joan knew what he meant. That he would be dismissed, shunned, mocked, threatened, brutalized. Just like Milan.

"This city that I love, that has been my home since I was still a boy—this city will not love my son."

Joan nodded. She knew it was true.

"Before Miša died, she made me promise something."

Joan had a presentiment. She looked at the clock on the wall above Burns's head. By lunchtime, Peter would be awake.

"She made me promise I would sell the school and take Peter to Scotland."

Joan nodded, but she was looking at the clock. How much time did she have?

"What I will do in Scotland, I don't know. But she asked me… She told me I should ask you to come with us."

Joan felt a wisp of desperation. Half an hour, tops. She held up her hand to stop him. "Burns."

But he did not stop. "I would marry you, of course. Peter needs a mother, and I—" Burns did not finish the thought. His offer struck Joan as old-fashioned, preposterous.

Joan held her breath for a moment. "No."

He looked deflated, vanquished by sadness. She pitied him, the way she had pitied Tibor. She was not afraid of him, but she didn't trust his judgment because he couldn't see that what he was asking of her would make her pity him. And because she couldn't trust his judgment, she knew she would leave, and that it would be today, before Peter woke.

Then he said something she wasn't expecting. "If you will marry me I will pay for Peter's uncle—your Romani friend—to go to Canada."

Joan opened her mouth, then closed it. She felt her pity turn to anger in her throat. His offer of a bride price was, to her ears, the same as a bribe. The idea sickened her.

Burns knew immediately he had gone too far. He put his head in his hands. "Forgive me," he muttered. "I am so tired."

But Joan stared at him icily. Without a word, she left the kitchen, heading upstairs to gather her things.

She would miss the room, she thought, as she stuffed her few clothes back in the suitcase. The old sunken bed and its handmade quilt, the portrait Pani Marta had made out of her own hair. The books. She took from the shelf the English–Slovak dictionary and the book of nursery rhymes with the hand-scrawled verse in the back. She left the dictionary but took the book of nursery rhymes and put it in her bag. Miša had wanted her to have the poetry, or to donate it, but Miša had also used her dying breath to try to orchestrate a future for her husband and son. Joan could not, would not blame her though. She wasn't the one who asked Burns to barter Milan's airfare for her future. *Sally, tell my mother I shall never come back.*

There was the big suitcase and the small one. She could balance one on top of the other, but not down the stairs. She took the big suitcase downstairs first, its wheels bumping from step to step. Pani Marta and Burns would know from the sound she was leaving, but it didn't matter now. Flushed from the exertion, she headed back upstairs to fetch the small suitcase.

Peter was standing in the doorway of his room, holding a doll's hand in his own. Joan felt a small gust of tears pass over her face and wiped them away with the back of her hand. She reached out her hand for him, but he did not come to her. Then she made a face at him, sticking out her tongue and rolling her eyes, but still he did not move. She grabbed the handle of the small suitcase and began to drag it downstairs.

Burns appeared at the bottom of the stairwell. Joan stopped. He looked pale, thick, and dishevelled.

"Please. Please reconsider," he said quietly. "We need you."

Joan continued downstairs. "Peter is awake," she said, pointing over her shoulder with her chin. Burns did not move. Joan felt fury rising in her. "Your son climbed out of his crib. You should make sure he doesn't fall down the stairs."

Burns's face was already drained of colour. He grabbed the banister and pushed past her, up the stairs.

That was the last she'd see of him, Joan figured. She was sad not to say goodbye to Pani Marta, but it couldn't be helped. She perched the small suitcase on top of the larger one and pushed it over the threshold, down the two stone steps, and out onto the cobblestone street.

CHAPTER 22

There was nowhere for Joan to go but the Hotel Svatopluk. On the way she stopped at the post office to pick up any mail that had come for her. There were three envelopes, one each from her mother and father, one in handwriting she did not recognize, and a postcard. From Ricky. Her heart crumpled a little. All the people she had in Canada. She tucked them in her bag.

It had been two days—surely Milan and Adriana had gone to the police station to retrieve Milan's identity card and would be back by now. But when Joan got to the hotel, Pani Svatoplukova shook her head.

"Nie sú doma," she said, her arms crossed. Not at home.

"Mária?" Joan asked.

"Mária upratuje," the woman said.

Joan felt desperate. "Nerozumiem," she replied. I don't understand.

Pani Svatoplokova sighed and began to mime sweeping with a broom and polishing the counter with an invisible rag. Mária was cleaning. Joan knew if she waited long enough, Mária, with her headscarf and rags, would appear.

"Môžem ja?" she said, sitting down on one of the dingy chairs in the hallway. Pani Svatoplukova was cross, Joan could tell, but she turned her head away.

The multitude of shoes still sat in their pile beside the reception counter. Where had they come from, Joan wondered, as she had many times before. They bore the usual sprinkling of white powder, like a dusting of light snow.

Perhaps they had belonged to Elaine Watterson, although there were children's shoes as well as women's in the pile. It just seemed to Joan that Mrs. Watterson's hand was everywhere, in everything.

Mária appeared a few minutes later, wiping her forehead with one gloved hand and holding a bucket in the other. Pani barked something at her, and she put the bucket down to greet Joan. With bright eyes, Mária held out her arms to Joan and wrapped her in a hug. Joan, suddenly incredibly tired, hugged her back weakly. They both, it seemed, needed comforting.

Joan pointed to her suitcases, and Mária motioned for her to bring them down the hall.

"Milan a Adriana," she said, swishing her arms. "Šli na policajnú stanicu." Police station. Joan nodded.

Mária had the key to Adriana and Milan's rooms, of course, since she was responsible for cleaning.

"Shhh," she put her fingers to her lips. Don't tell Front Desk Pani.

She let Joan into the room that had once been Elaine Watterson's, and where her young friends now lived—but Joan felt the dead woman's presence there like a heavy caul upon her head. She knew she wouldn't be able to stay long. A plan was formulating in her mind. She would sell her grandfather's pocket watch to the watch repair store on the square near the old town market to buy Milan passage to Canada, and she would head off again to find herself a job as a teacher, maybe in a small town or maybe farther afield—Joan didn't dare to think at the moment where.

Mária was dusting the sheers.

"Čaj?" Joan asked. Mária turned with a surprised look on her face. Did she think Joan was asking her to make tea? Joan blushed and got up and went to the kettle. And pretended to pour. "Chcete?" Do you want some?

Mária nodded, and kept dusting.

Joan made tea and patted the seat next to her on the sofa. "Prosím."

Mária put the duster away in her apron pocket and took off her gloves. Her hands were brown but surprisingly smooth, unlike her weathered face, and she wore a gold wedding band and another ring with a black stone in it— onyx maybe.

Joan handed her a delicate teacup with two cubes of sugar on the saucer. "Tvoja," she said. Yours.

"Ahhh," Mária said, settling back into the sofa.

They drank their tea in silence, watching the afternoon sun through the sheers.

Joan pulled the mail she had retrieved the post office from her bag. The postcard from Ricky she left on her lap, but the two envelopes from her parents and the mystery envelope were not for Mária's eyes. Joan tucked them in the voluminous pocket of her sweater. As she did so, she felt the pocket watch that Adriana had given her. And there was something else...the photo of Jana and Peter. Would it be cruel to Mária to give her the photo? Joan decided it was less cruel than not giving it to her.

"Tvoja," Joan said, handing it to her.

Mária gazed at the photo and her eyes melted into tears. "Moja," she said, pointing to Jana, and then to Peter. Mine. And she pressed the photo to her heart.

Ricky's postcard showed a Nova Scotia flag waving in the sunshine next to a motel sign. The Happy Holiday Inn, the sign read. She couldn't help but smile. A freebie Ricky probably picked up while he was doing work in exchange for a cord of firewood (in years past, it might have been for a bag of weed). Joan turned the card over, then glanced at Mária, who was lost in her own reverie, her cheeks still shining with tears.

Hi Joan. I got your address from your mother. Sorry I haven't written before now. Joan flushed, knowing she hadn't written to him at all except in her journals. *I've been working a lot on the north shore. I miss you. Your friend, Ricky.* That was all. Something stabbed at Joan's heart. Ricky was kind, good-natured, and dependable, and most importantly, beloved of Edna, but between them was a gulf bigger than the Atlantic Ocean, Joan thought.

She felt a familiar feeling. Stark and vulnerable: it was loneliness. But she had always been alone—first as an only child among adults, and then among her schoolmates, and finally as an adult who somehow had not yet found her place. She felt stripped down again—of home and family and friends. It was uncomfortable at times, but she was used to it. Loneliness somehow seemed to fit her, like the handle of a tool, sharp and awkward, that she had neverthe-less worn by long use to the shape of her own hand.

Something brushed her fingers and she startled. It was Mária's hand on hers. Mária gazed at her sympathetically.

"Chlapec?" she asked. Was it a boy that caused her heartache?

Disoriented, Joan shook her head, then shrugged. Mária was older than Joan by a matter of a year or two. And yet she must think of Joan—childless, husbandless, and bound to no one—as a girl, not a woman.

Mária had been no more than a girl when she'd had her own children, Jana and then Milan. She may have already been worn down by the time the younger four or five sibl-ings came along. Now her face seemed held together by the web of lines that mapped it. And yet there was something in her that burned with a fiery youthfulness Joan did not possess and never had—a hungry curiosity and ravenous desire for connection that, while damped down under daily cares and duties, nevertheless lit her from the inside like a lamp.

Mária fingered the postcard, her eyebrows knitted with puzzlement. "To nie je Kanada," she said. It's not Canada.

Joan was about to protest when she realized Mária meant the flag. "Nové Škótsko," Joan explained.

Mária's eyes lit up. "Home," she said, pleased to be able to share a word in English.

"Áno," Joan said. Yes. But it did not feel right somehow. The word *home* no longer fit.

Joan felt a wave of questions well up in Mária, ones they didn't have the common words for and ones that, even if they did, would have been too sensitive. Joan was relieved to have the barrier of language between them.

Mária looked down at the postcard. "Moja Janka," she said. "Amerika. Prečo? Nerozumiem." Mária could not understand what had driven her daughter to America with a man she did not love, away from her own child. Joan gathered this from the hurt bewilderment in Mária's eyes. She turned to Joan and lightly poked her finger in Joan's breastbone. "Ty? Prečo Slovensko?" she asked earnestly.

Joan recalled Tibor looming over her and his sour breath on her neck. She saw Edna's letter in her hands, the crisp hundred-dollar bills, and the entreaty that she go to Hungary to deliver the letter to Josef that would beg his forgiveness. This letter, Joan realized, had also been Edna's way of pushing her away, away from a stalled life and into the future. Joan saw Edna smiling down at her, so many years ago in the Jamiesons' kitchen, thrusting poppyseed cake in front of her. Eat, Edna's eyes had said. And she saw the dark-haired toddler Tibor had been, standing in his crib, watching his mother leave her home more than a lifetime ago, never to return.

Why had she come? She didn't know. Except that Edna had tried to bring together the people from her two lives. Edna, who had had her future thrust upon her, wanted to be the architect of something better. And Joan, who had been gently and sometimes violently swept along in the wake of so many other people's lives, had allowed Edna to have the final word in the conversation between them. She knew her love for Edna was the driver of so many of her decisions, but she had obeyed that impulse blindly and, looking back, almost automatically, as though she were a cog in Edna's machine. It was as if Joan had chosen to follow the path Edna set out for her to avoid having to decide for herself. The thought had never occurred to her before, and it flooded her with shame.

Joan put her hand over Mária's. It was too hard to say in Slovak, and too hard to say in general. "Neviem," she said, shaking her head. I don't know.

They sat silently. Then Mária stood up, and Joan, overwhelmed, closed her eyes.

Mária took her bucket and rags and closed the door quietly behind her.

But Joan did not sleep. She felt like an elephant shot by a stun gun must feel. She could not move. Alone in the safety of the apartment, a wave of anger and sadness welled up in her chest, and all she had lost crashed down like a wave upon the beach of herself. Miša and Tibor, Burns and Peter and Pani Marta, and Edna. All of them gone from her life as though they were no more than smoke. She clenched her fists and rubbed the backs of them against her eyes.

But there were still the letters from her parents, bulging from her pockets. Her mother's seemed the most urgent somehow. Inside was a pair of fine wool socks and a letter in Gillian's round, girlish script. *We are getting married!* Joan stared at the blue ink. *December 24. Come home!* The rest of the letter described wedding preparations, dresses, flowers, et cetera, but Joan could not absorb the details. There were ten fifty-dollar bills enclosed. Not enough for a ticket, but her mother had probably figured it would be a help.

Joan's father's letter was short and bittersweet. *Your mother is getting married. Please use the enclosed money order to buy a ticket home. The wedding is on the 24th of December. I miss you*, he'd scrawled on a piece of scrap paper. Her father would go to the wedding, of course. Her parents had split amicably, and he'd had a girlfriend or two, but his letter said nothing about his latest, Gloria.

Joan fingered the money order, which was generous and more than enough for a return ticket. Her father, unlike her mother, had thought ahead to the fact that Joan would likely return to Europe, to her life and job, after the dust of the wedding had cleared.

But, of course, he did not know that there was no life or job for her to return to. She stuffed the envelopes again with their respective contents. The third envelope was small and light and, Joan assumed, was the wedding invitation. She did not, at the moment, feel like opening it, so she put it with the other two in her suitcase and pushed it under the bed.

Joan lay awake on the divan when she heard a key in the lock and the sound of Milan and Adriana coming in the door. Neither of them seemed surprised she was there. Milan lay himself on the bed without greeting Joan, and within seconds his breathing was rhythmic and peaceful. Adriana flopped down in a chair, dropping some papers on the table and her head into her hands. Joan got up and made tea. When she handed Adriana the cup, Adriana held up Milan's ID card for her to see.

"We got it," she said. "But not without an interrogation. At least this time there is a report. I have a copy." She pointed to the few papers stapled together on the table.

The news to Joan was a sprig of hope. Perhaps Milan could get a passport now?

"Your taxi driver—" Adriana said, shaking her head in disbelief. Joan was alarmed. What had he done? "He wouldn't accept payment. He said we must take him for espresso one day instead." Adriana laid the money Joan had given her for the taxi on the table, then drank her cup to the bottom. "I'm going to lie down now," was all she said when Joan offered her a second cup. She moved to the divan and, like Milan, fell asleep almost immediately.

Joan sat down at the table. She thought about the money her parents had sent. In Canada, she at least had family, and she also had Ricky. But she realized the people she cared about and who cared for her were not magnets but the opposite. No. She would not go back. Not even for her mother's wedding.

Somehow she had to find her own way now. It was as if her life depended on it. She had felt an inkling of this before—when she'd sought out a job as an elementary school bus driver, even though that had ended so terribly and caused her to retreat. But she also knew—had known since her flare of anger at Robbie's bribe—that something had changed. Joan knew there were things in her that had never seen daylight, that needed expression, and the only way to express them was to live a life of her own making.

Without Milan's help, Joan wasn't sure where to look for an English teaching job in Bratislava, but she figured the university would be a good place to start. There might be a job board, and there would definitely be students who spoke English. She would call the Hungarian taxi driver, if she could find the card she'd given Adriana.

Joan shifted the papers Adriana had placed on the table. The driver's card was there under the pile of koruny he had not accepted to take Milan and Adriana to Košice. She glanced for a moment at the police report and recognized Milan's name and the word *Roma*. Farther down the report she saw "Cigán"—a pejorative she would not have expected to see in a police report. She did not read further because she did not understand enough Slovak.

The taxi driver's business card was black with Slovak and Hungarian flags crossed on the front over a yellow taxicab. On the back was the name "T. Balla" and the phrase Friendship Taxicab Service was printed in English, Slovak, and Hungarian.

Joan left the apartment with the business card in hand. The hallways were dim as usual, and none of the doors opened a crack when she passed.

At the front desk, Pani turned her back when she saw Joan, who felt a streak of dislike and impatience.

"Pani, prosím?" she asked, and thrust the business card toward Pani Svatoplukova, pointing toward the phone number. The woman turned around. She had been crying. Joan softened, but Pani immediately assumed a cross face and thrust the phone toward her. Joan thanked her and dialled the number for the taxi. After a couple rings, the driver answered in Slovak.

"Szia," Joan replied, "can I please have a taxi to Hotel Svatopluk?"

"Of course," he said. "I will be there soon."

Ten minutes later, he arrived. She noticed an ornament swinging from the rear-view mirror—two pompoms on a string, in the colours of the Hungarian and Slovak flags.

The driver smiled. "Where to, madam?" he asked.

Joan got in the front seat. "I want to find a job. Can you take me to where there is a job board for English teachers. Maybe the university?"

The driver frowned. "It is late, the job centre will not be open." He brightened. "I can take you to café where are advertisements for jobs."

"How far is it?" she asked.

"Not far," he replied. "But it is not safe to walk there in the dark."

They headed in the direction of the square.

"Thank you for what you did for my friends," Joan said.

"Which friends?" He seemed genuinely surprised.

"My young friends who stay at Hotel Svatopluk. You dropped them off not long before I called you."

He shook his head and shrugged.

"You drove them to a police station in the east."

He smiled and said, "I too had business in Košice." He turned the radio up. Tinny pop music filled the car.

They arrived at Café Eureka in less than ten minutes. Joan stared at the awning and the open sign, the cursive letters traced by small blinking red lights. How strange that he had brought her to this café, the only one in Bratislava that she knew well. She'd tried to move forward and now it felt she was turning in circles. Until Joan realized the café was something she'd sought out herself, that she had found on her own. Though she was not given to superstition, it felt like a sign that the driver had brought her to Café Eureka, a sign that she was on the right path somehow, a path of her own choosing. That she was ready to step out of the slipstream of other people's lives and make one of her own.

"My friend owns Café Eureka," the driver said as he pulled up to the entry. "He is professor at the university. Musicology." It must be the same man, Joan thought, the man who reminded her of her father, who'd sat frowning over his laptop the last time she had been at the café, and who looked at her in a way that made her feel seen. She felt a bright streak of recognition run through her.

The café was lit up, and through the windows Joan could see a lot of young Slovaks studying texts, debating, and a few working on laptops. Several older men sat among them, drinking from tea glasses and tiny espresso cups. In the daytime the Eureka had been dim and nondescript. Now at night it seemed as though it had come into its own. It certainly looked like a university hangout, she thought, and a little anxiety crept up her throat. But Joan, swallowing the feeling, determined this was a good thing for her and her future. It had to be.

The driver opened her door for her as she dug in her purse for koruny.

"It's okay," he said. "Pay me inside. I also will have coffee."

Joan felt a mix of dismay and relief—relief that she wouldn't have to walk inside alone but unsure of the driver's intentions. Did he think her easy pickings, a woman over thirty, alone and looking for work in a strange city? But she had managed to deal with Tibor and with Burns. She could deal with this.

When they entered, the barista at the counter looked up at them. Joan was disappointed to see it wasn't the young woman who had served her before. The barista waved and called out a cheery "Szia, Tibor."

Joan froze. Tibor was a common Hungarian name, she told herself. It was nothing. Even if it was a dead man's name.

Tibor approached the counter, ordering espresso for himself and for Joan, and laughing and joking in Hungarian. The barista indicated Joan with his eyes.

"She is a Canadian teacher looking for a job," Tibor said in English.

"Ah," said the barista, and smiled at her. "Kanaďanka." He turned away from the counter a moment, returning with a small scoop of vanilla ice cream. Joan nodded, and he plopped it on top of the expresso. "Nie Café Americano. Café Canada!"

Tibor and the barista laughed heartily. Joan, not knowing how to react, paid and looked around for a place to sit.

Tibor motioned to the empty table by the door, the same table Joan had chosen when she'd first visited.

"No one sits here at night. It is too cold," he said. "But it is private. Wait here." Tibor nodded encouragingly. His teeth were slightly coffee-stained. She did not think he smoked because he did not have the telltale stain on his fingers. For some reason, this mattered to Joan.

Tibor went to the back of the café, where a young woman wearing headphones sat working on her laptop. She removed the headphones and nodded to Tibor, who Joan could see was asking the young woman to join them. She indicated she would come when she was finished. Tibor nodded.

When Tibor returned, he sat down and stirred his espresso with a tiny spoon. "That is Ania. She knows everything about everything." He flashed a grin.

Joan looked over at the girl. Her shoulders were slightly hunched under a drab sweatshirt and her dull brown hair dangled on either side of her head.

"How do you know her?" Joan asked.

"I know many students," he said. "Many Hungarian students call on me when they want a taxi. There are many of us in this country." Then, almost with apology, Tibor said, "Her mother is Hungarian. Her father, my friend, owns this café."

Joan stared at the young woman's bowed shoulders. She felt something—could it be envy? Ania, whose father the professor so reminded Joan of her own that they could be sisters.

"Ania lived abroad for a few years. Her English is very good," Tibor said. "She will know something about English teaching, I think. But if she does not, she will know who to talk to."

Joan nodded. There were students of a variety of nationalities and ethnicities in the café. Slovaks, dark-skinned Africans, a couple of East Asians, and a young man in the corner with dark curly hair, softly singing a Hungarian folk song as he strummed a guitar.

Tibor downed the coffee in one gulp and wiped his mouth with a paper napkin, peering at Joan's face, her almond eyes. "Ania's boyfriend is from China. Very smart. He is good at physics—first in his class at the university."

Joan was curious about why a Chinese student would choose to study in Slovakia, but then, she too had ended up here without really meaning to. It almost took her breath away, how random it all seemed, though if she traced a line backward through time and space, there were, of course, causes and effects all along the line that had landed her in Bratislava.

Across the room Ania took off her headphones and closed her laptop. One of the Asian guys a few seats away immediately closed his laptop too and came over to her table, where they spoke briefly before heading to where Joan and Tibor sat. Tibor pulled two chairs from a stack in the corner near them and beckoned for Ania and the young man to sit.

He extended his hand to them both. "Ania, Boris, meet Joan," he said.

Joan recognized Ania as the woman who had served her at the Eureka on her earlier visits. Ania recognized Joan too, and a gasp escaped her. She put her hand out to Joan.

"We meet again!" she said, and then, as though remembering herself, she adopted a more aloof look. Joan felt a whiff of disappointment. Nevertheless, she shook the students' hands—Ania's, tentative and bony, and Boris's, which tugged her hand lightly up and down in a single shake.

Boris seemed like a strange name for a Chinese person, but then if he had come to Canada as a student, he probably would have chosen Brent or Brad instead. The pair looked very serious and Ania, almost severe. But Tibor's face was shiny and tender, indulgent even.

"Please explain what you want," he said, gesturing to Joan.

"I am an English language teacher, and I need a job," she began. Promoting herself felt foreign, but necessity made it easier to ignore the discomfort. "I do not have a university degree. But I have several years' experience." She thought for a moment, and added, "I do not want to teach children."

Ania finally smiled and nodded slightly. "It is difficult to get an English teaching job now without a university degree," she said, in the high-pitched nasal tone that reminded Joan of someone else. Who? It was, she realized, the voice of Madame B. in Budapest. "Do you specialize in anything?"

Joan considered. She was a specialist in nothing—espresso drinking maybe, and drifting.

"I have taught business English," she said. "I do not consider it a specialty of mine though, no," she added miserably. The business terms had sometimes bewildered her and she had to do a lot of preparation every time she taught vocabulary.

Boris spoke to Ania in Slovak. Tibor nodded and shrugged.

"Are you willing to go overseas?" Boris asked in crisp English.

Joan nodded, her face growing hot. The same idea had been sprouting even before she'd first come to Bratislava, but she'd barely dared to think it. "I would like to go to China," she blurted.

Boris turned to Ania, then to Joan, and grinned for the first time. "Please teach us something—so we might be able to give you a good recommendation," he said.

Joan thought for a moment. "What would you like to learn?"

Ania laughed, a high tinkling sound, and Boris smirked. "You Americans, you like freedom, but you like other people to think for you."

Joan shrugged. She was used to this kind of response. "I am Canadian though. What about a song?" She thought back to her last class in Budapest and the way she'd left. If a million dollars landed in her lap, what would she do now?

"A Christmas song?" Boris asked tentatively. Ania gasped and tittered, and Boris reddened.

Joan thought of the Christmas songs she knew. None of them struck her as the type of song that would recommend her as an English teacher to non-children in particular. Of other songs she knew very few lyrics. She began to panic a little, but then it came to her. Joni Mitchell's song about a river to skate away on.

It was one her high school English teacher, an old hippy who'd sported long hair and a beard, had given his class to learn. A quintessential Canadian song, he had called it.

"I am going to teach you a quintessential Canadian song," she told them, and explained what quintessential meant. Ania and Boris scribbled the word in the notebooks whipped from their backpacks. She could see that Ania's was full of all manner of things—phone numbers, quotations, statistics, abstract doodles. Boris's looked to be mathematical equations and small landscapes. They did not look like they were of local places. Perhaps he missed China.

"I know the lyrics," Joan admitted, "but don't know how to sing it."

Tibor, who had been looking on attentively, exclaimed, "Moment." He waved the guitar player in the corner over. The young man got off his stool and ambled toward them. Ania blushed and stared at her notebook while Boris's face turned stony and pale. The musician shook Tibor's hand easily.

"Ahoj, Anička" he said.

Joan could see that at one time he and Ania must have been a couple and that Boris also knew this. Whether Tibor did or not, Joan couldn't tell.

"This is Antal, Joan."

Antal extended his hand amiably. He was the Eastern European version of the boys she'd had secret crushes on in high school—talented, good-looking, and effortlessly charming—but there was also something absent about him, as though he did not contain all the ingredients that made up other people. Angst, for example. And insecurity.

"Do you know this song about a river, by Joan Mitchell?" Tibor asked.

Joni, Joan thought but did not correct him.

"I can play it," Antal said agreeably. He reminded her of Ricky.

Antal began to play, and Joan could see they were waiting for her to begin. She cleared her throat and hummed a few bars, then began to recite the lyrics to the song she had learned by heart in high school. It was a song of escape— escape from the trappings of Christmas, but also from a heart's disappointment.

Tibor began to sing along. Other café patrons turned their heads to listen, and Joan was dumbfounded. Not only was his voice as fine as any she had ever heard, but he remembered the lines she'd just recited. She realized she should keep reciting the lyrics and that he would follow her, singing, as if in the wake of the words she spoke.

Somehow it worked. Ania and Boris furiously scribbled the lyrics in their notebooks, looking up from time to time to watch Tibor and Antal. At the end of the song, Ania gave Tibor her lyrics and he sang the entire song again. Ania and Boris were mesmerized. By the end of the second performance they looked like beach stones that a wave had washed over—sparkling and new, and as young as they actually were.

Antal extended a hand for Tibor to shake. Boris also solemnly offered his hand and Antal shook it, then ambled back to the stool in the corner he'd originally occupied.

Tibor was perspiring slightly. He wiped his forehead with his napkin.

Joan nodded. "That was... It was great," she said, adding, "Joni Mitchell would be proud."

Boris leaned forward. "That song is a story. A love story. It is beautiful."

Ania nodded. "It's sad," she said. "But it is true."

Joan resorted to a foolproof method to keep the conversation going. "Tell me more about that, Ania. Why do you say it is sad and true?"

Ania looked slightly cross—or fierce. "It is sad because she remembers someone she lost and it was her fault and he was good. It is true because—I mean, it is real. It feels real. It feels like life."

Boris nodded dreamily. Behind his glasses, Joan saw a river reflecting the sunset, winding through a winter landscape. He leaned forward. He might be a whiz at physics, Joan thought, but he was also an earnest romantic.

"It is strange. She left someone. She feels sad and she thinks she made a mistake. But she does not apologize and ask him to be her—her boyfriend—again. Instead she wants to skate away, fly away." Boris looked puzzled. "Why? I wonder why she wants to fly away?"

Joan felt a dash of affection for him. He truly wanted to know.

Ania spoke up. "That is life too. The river flows in only one direction."

Boris was not satisfied. "The river is frozen. It is possible to skate both ways."

Ania shook her head. "Only on the top," she said.

"On the surface," Joan rephrased.

Ania blushed. "Of course," she said. "My English. Only on the surface. Below, the water runs always in the same direction."

Boris said nothing. Ania gently shoved his shoulder.

"Boris," she said. "It is physics. You are good at physics, no?" She was clearly fond of him, but it struck Joan that perhaps it was nothing more than friendship.

Joan folded her hands on the table. They looked at her expectantly.

"You are both very good students," she said. They looked pleased, and Ania tipped her head back and laughed, exposing a smooth white throat against which a gold chain lay. Boris looked at her, then looked down at his hands and smiled.

"It was good, your lesson," Tibor said, and Ania and Boris nodded vigorously.

"Was it a quintessential Canadian English lesson?" Ania asked in her high-pitched voice.

Joan smiled and shrugged.

Boris placed the tips of his fingers and thumbs together and said with mock seriousness. "It was a quintessential Canadian lesson about physics and romance."

Ania laughed.

"Romantic physics," Boris added, wiggling his eyebrows in an exaggerated fashion.

Ania snorted and blushed. "Not physical romance."

Boris looked sheepish, but put his arm around Ania's back and she did not resist. His hand rested lightly on her shoulder. His fingers were long and brown, and Joan could see from the musculature of his hand that he was either an athlete or had done physical work. Neither he nor Ania were what she had at first thought.

Tibor gazed affectionately at them, his eyes glistening slightly. These young people were more to him than customers, they were dear to him, Joan realized. She wondered if Adriana and Milan had reminded him of them in some way.

"Excuse me," he said, getting up. He gestured toward the back of the café where the restrooms were. Joan noticed that the professor, Ania's father, had appeared and was sitting in his usual seat with his laptop. When Tibor reached him, they greeted one another with a kiss on each cheek. The professor looked over, and Ania waved at her father, whose expression softened. Joan felt a pang of longing.

Ania and Boris were conferring quietly in Slovak. They seemed to be considering whether to tell her something. Boris pulled a coin from his pocket. It was a Canadian loonie. Could it be the one Joan had given Ania? He spun it without fanfare and watched it settle on the table. Tails. Finally Ania nodded and Boris leaned in toward the table.

"My father owns a language school outside of Guangzhou," he said.

Joan startled. Guangzhou was the biggest Chinese city close to where her mother's family's village was located. She remembered her grandmother saying it was a hundred and fifty kilometres from Guangzhou. A hundred and fifty kilometres—less than the distance between Bratislava and Budapest.

Boris and Ania seemed to be waiting for Joan to say something. Joan wasn't sure what, but it was as if a door had been left open a crack.

"Is he—your father, does he need teachers?" She felt right away that this might have been the wrong thing to say, but Boris and Ania looked at one another.

"If you like, I will ask him if he needs a teacher. Even though you did not study at a university, there is a chance," Boris said. "Every term—how do you say—teachers come, teachers leave."

"Turnover," Ania said confidently. "Like here, in café. It is business."

Joan was stunned. But maybe Boris's offer was not so unusual, even to a stranger, if that stranger was presentable and spoke English. She had known Madame B. to visit youth hostel cafés in Budapest and ask random travellers if they were interested in a term's work, inviting them to come for an interview. Some did, and a handful were hired over the four years Joan had been there.

"I will tell my father you speak quintessential Canadian English and you are a good teacher. Also, you are not Chinese, but you look like..." His voice trailed away.

"My mother is Chinese Canadian," Joan said. Boris and Ania, surprised, exchanged glances. "My father is English."

Boris nodded. "It's good. It will be interesting for my father." He blushed. "Chinese people prefer not-Chinese teachers. They think they are more Western. But my father is a proud Chinese."

"And a good Communist Party member," Ania joked.

Boris ducked his head and shushed her.

Ania rolled her eyes. "Boris, don't worry. This is not America."

Boris blushed. "And you, Joan," he said. "You are not like Americans."

She wondered if he meant she wasn't like the loud-voiced, shaggy-haired youths she had seen on the street, who travelled Europe with stuffed backpacks, who always had money for bread, cheese, and wine, and a quick week-end trip to hike in the Tatras, who frequented the clubs and taverns.

"Canadians are more...they are a little bit like us."

It was Joan's turn to blush. She knew it meant he was comfortable with what she had to offer and who she was. For Joan, accustomed to feeling awkward in almost every social situation, it was a high compliment.

Nevertheless, it seemed—strange. As though a sparkling set of doors had opened before her, and what she'd thought to be a cupboard was actually a doorway to another world. One she'd been aware of for a long time but still seemed almost too far away to be real or to venture to on her own. Again, it was as though luck was with her, ushering her toward the future. But she realized that this time she was not being pulled in someone else's wake; she was taking advantage of a half-magical current, yes, but she was swimming with it, in a direction that felt right.

"I would like that," Joan said. "Thank you." She pulled a curriculum vitae from her purse. "Please take this for your father." It was, she realized yet again, alarmingly short and lacking.

Boris and Ania bent their heads together over it. Ania wriggled in her seat. "You taught in Hungary?"

Joan nodded.

"And you worked with old people!" Ania exclaimed. "I want to be a doctor for old people. My grandparents took care of me when I was a child. It was my happiest time." She looked pensive, remembering.

Boris nodded. "My grandparents also. It means you have patience and kindness if you cared for old people."

Joan nodded uncertainly. She had cared for one old person, Edna. But she had loved Edna, and that hadn't required any special skill.

Boris bent almost double over the table to tell Joan, "The school maybe pays your airplane ticket."

Ania bent close too and said confidentially, "It is not good if many people know this. Because many people will want to…to have friendship with Boris only to have a free ticket."

Boris nodded. His shoulders bowed, and he pushed his glasses up the bridge of his nose.

Tibor sat back down at the table, startling the three of them. "Such serious faces!" he said, smiling broadly.

Boris's eyeglasses flashed, and Joan realized the glare from the overhead lights was overwhelming her ability to process anything more.

"Are you tired?" Tibor asked.

Joan nodded. As she stood up, she realized she didn't have a phone number to give Boris. But Boris handed her a card and scribbled his own name and phone number on the back of it.

"Call me after one week," he said. "I will speak with my father."

After enthusiastic handshakes, Joan followed Tibor from the café. On the way back to the hotel, she sat next to him in the front seat. He turned the Slovak pop station on at a low volume. She felt he wanted to ask what had transpired while he was away from the table—but as he was a taxi driver, professional discretion perhaps made it seem impolite for him to ask where money and business were concerned.

Instead, he told her a story about himself.

"I come from a small village in Hungary. People called me the Boy with the Big Voice. I studied opera in Budapest on scholarship. But then my father fell ill. I went back to my village to take care for him. I lost my scholarship."

Joan felt a swoop of disappointment in the pit of her stomach for him, but he shook his head.

"I am not sure if opera singer or taxi driver is better," he said, his teeth glinting in the dark. "I meet many interesting people in my taxi." He flicked a glance to the rear-view mirror. "Boris came from China and didn't know anyone, and no Slovak. Ania is part of student government. She called me and we went to meet him at the airport. Now we are friends." Tibor shrugged. "Ania likes to help people. She helped me to have a concert at the university. Boris is very smart. People think he is only very smart, but he is many things. He likes poems. He plays..." Tibor searched for the word in vain. "with...as Robin Hood?" he asked.

Joan thought a moment. "Archery?" she asked.

He furrowed his brow. Joan mimed plucking a bow, sending an imaginary arrow sailing across the square, and Tibor laughed and nodded.

He also collects coins, she thought. They were almost back to the Hotel Svatopluk, so she dug in her purse for koruny. Tibor was about to wave her away, but Joan touched his sleeve.

"Tibor," she said, "you must live too. This is business." He looked hurt. "You have helped me a great deal tonight. You helped my friends," Joan continued. "I consider you my friend too."

He smiled broadly, clearly delighted.

"Friends treat each other fairly." She pressed the koruny into his hand. "I appreciate your help. You are a good man."

His eyes welled and Joan was alarmed.

"I am not so good," he said. "But I try. You don't know me," he said, shaking his head and wiping his eyes. "But I am your friend too."

Joan stood on the steps of the hotel as Tibor drove away, his tail lights bouncing over the cobblestones. She wanted to clear her head before she went inside. Adriana and Milan were probably up now, making plans, trying to solve problems. Joan felt as though something heavy had drained away from her, and yet her head was still a tangle. It was unfamiliar to feel so light and still have so many questions. Questions that hung inside her like balloons, suspended high above her heart, tethered to it only by the thinnest of strings.

Milan and Adriana were sitting with their heads close together, bent over the coffee table. They were studying the police report and scribbling notes on a pad of paper. Milan looked a little lacklustre and said nothing when Joan first entered the room, but raised a hand slowly in greeting. His shoulder clearly bothered him.

Adriana was agitated. "Look, Joan," she said without any preamble. "The police report is ridiculous. It uses the pejorative Cigán in several places, it mentions Milan made his initial report without any identifying papers even though we returned to the police station because his ID card was turned in by a witness to the original attack! And it says it's unclear who started the 'fight'—even though the police admitted that the man who turned in Milan's ID described an attack on Milan. I don't understand how they could even write this. It sounds like—Kafka."

Joan sat down. She hesitated a moment. "It might help your case that it shows police bias if you want to claim refugee status in Canada, Milan." Joan turned toward him. He shook his head slowly but said nothing.

Adriana was back to rereading the police report. "The man who turned in Milan's ID is a doctor," she said.

Milan roused himself enough to say, "They do not believe doctor. Of course, they do not believe me. I am only stupid Cigán."

Adriana's face turned pale. "Milan," she began.

But Milan had come to the end of something. "It's no good, Adja," he said. "I cannot go to Canada."

The papers rattled in Adriana's hands.

"I have police report, yes. But it is not good thing. What will Canadian officials say? A stupid Cigán who had fight with some good Slovak youth. Maybe they think I am criminal."

Adriana sat up. "But Milan, look…" she began.

"No, Adriana. I have not money for ticket to Canada. If you ask your father for money, I will leave and you will not see me more."

It was more than Joan had heard Milan say since he'd been beaten. He pressed his shoulders against the back of the couch and turned his head away, closing his eyes.

Adriana stood. Her shoulders bowed, but her eyes were wild with pain.

Joan stood too, alarmed. She wanted to reach her arms around Adriana's frail shoulders.

Adriana stepped away from her. "I'm going out," she said.

Joan followed her to the door. "It's dark," she said, and pressed Tibor's business card into the young woman's hand. "Please be careful."

Adriana closed the door between them.

Milan's eyes remained closed. Joan sat down again. She thought of the money her parents had sent her, tucked away in her suitcase.

Milan put his hands to his face. "I have ETA," he said. Electronic Travel Authorization. Burns had told her about them. Slovak residents needed them for travel to Canada under ninety days in length. "I have passport."

Joan stared at him.

"I wrote for it before...before we...before our trip to East. I want to surprise Adriana. Now I don't want her know I have it. She must go to Canada. I must stay here."

Joan could feel that Milan had steeled himself against despair. That he had thought about his family and his pride and his love for Adriana, and all had figured into his decision. He had reached the bottom depths and decided he could survive there, that he must, for the good of all three. Joan had a vision of him, hiding among the rocks on the ocean floor, Adriana in a bright submersible floating above him like the sun.

Joan stood up and retrieved the money her parents had sent her from her suitcase, along with the small unopened envelope, then sat next to Milan on the couch. She put the ten fifty-dollar bills and money order on the coffee table.

"Milan," she said. "I am going to China. To teach English."

He gazed at the money, then at her, then looked down. "Congratulations," he said. "You will again be profesorka." He looked up again and leaned back, squinting at her in pain, but offering his bandaged hand to shake hers.

"My airfare will be paid," Joan continued.

Milan nodded toward the money on the table. "I see," he said. "You have much luck."

Joan shook her head. "The language school will pay for my flight," she said. She hoped it were true, but she was going ahead with her plan regardless. "This money is from my parents."

Milan looked at her and then the money and said quietly, "You are lucky two times."

Joan could see Milan would need it spelled out for him.

"My mother is marrying Adriana's father," Joan said. "When Adriana goes back to Canada, they will surprise her. I am supposed to come also, to buy a ticket to fly back with Adriana in a few days."

Milan nodded, but his eyes looked slightly fogged, as though the thoughts in his mind were steaming up his brain from inside as he tried to understand what she was telling him.

"I am not going, Milan. I am not going to Canada."

He opened his eyes wide.

"I want to give you this money. I want you to fly to Canada with Adriana."

Milan looked at her and closed his eyes again, and shook his head. But Joan pushed ahead.

"Adriana is my sister now," she said simply. "I can give her this money and tell her my plan. But I am giving it to you. You can choose."

Milan opened his eyes.

"There is enough money here to give some to your mother to start her cooking business again. There is enough money for you to fly to Canada. And if you wish, there may be enough to visit your sister in America."

Milan looked bewildered and hurt. He shook his head. "I cannot take this money," he said.

"Then I will give it to your father," Joan blurted, then felt herself flush. Where had that thought come from?

Milan stared at her, incredulous.

Joan pushed ahead. "Oh, I would rather give it to your mother. But if I do, she will give it to your father anyway."

"Why do you do this?" he asked her. There was indignation, even rage, in him.

"Milan," she said. "Do you remember it was Elaine Watterson who helped your sister get a place at the tourism English school?"

Milan glared at her. "My sister was excellent student."

Joan nodded. "Your sister was very good. A top student. But she would not have gone to college if not for Mrs. Watterson."

Milan nodded stonily, looking at his hands. "It was not fair," he said.

"No, it was not." Joan agreed. "Just as it is not fair that I have money and you have not. It is not money I earned. It is not fair that you were beaten on a train and the police did nothing. It is not fair that your sister's husband drinks her money and she has nothing left to send you. And it is not fair that your sister had to leave her child behind when she went to America."

Milan slowly lifted his head to look at her.

"Yes, your sister had a child. Her little boy lives with Robbie Burns. He doesn't know, of course. Burns is the only father he knows."

Joan could see this information was too much, but she had to continue. "Milan," she said. "Burns loves your sister's boy. Peter is his name. Burns is a good father. Miša, his wife, was a good mother—but she died two days ago. It was Mrs. Watterson who arranged for your sister to give them the child to raise as their own."

He looked up at her, his forehead furrowed. She could see he didn't understand, and Joan realized she didn't either—not Elaine Watterson's conviction that her interference was best for Jana and Peter, nor Joan's own decision to offer this money in a way Milan couldn't refuse. Her proposal, like Burns's offer of marriage in exchange for Milan's airfare, was an outrageous manipulation, she realized. Joan began to crumble, but caught herself.

"I want to give you this money because you are my friend, and I want to help you. And because I don't want this money." She paused. "If I keep this money, it means I must go back to Canada, and I don't want to."

That was the bottom line, Joan realized, as soon as the words spilled from her.

"I would like you to go to Canada with Adriana, and to be closer to your sister in America. But I don't want to choose your life," she said. "I am not Elaine Watterson. I want you to choose."

Milan was silent for a full minute. Joan was finished speaking, so she sat back with her hands in her lap. If Milan did not take the money, she would make sure his mother got it. It was simple for her now.

Milan did not look at her. He reached a hand for the bills and, folding them between his fingers, he tucked them into a pocket without discernible emotion. Then he lay down on the couch, his eyes open, unblinking.

Joan lay down on the cot without even taking off her coat. After a while, Milan rose stiffly from the couch and left without a word. Joan slept then, leaden and dreamless. When she woke, it was still dark. She saw Adriana asleep on the bed, but Milan was not with her. The money order was also gone. Joan was relieved she had remembered to sign the back of it.

She got up and made tea. Adriana would awaken soon, and Joan would have to face her. Adriana, her soon-to-be sister, who was quick and high-strung and, Joan knew, prone to despair. She would have to tell Adriana what had transpired for Milan to leave in the middle of the night. In the dark, Joan stirred a sugar cube into one of Elaine Watterson's fine china cups and felt the warmth leave her skin and her fingers. Her teeth began to chatter. Maybe it didn't matter what she did or didn't do, it occurred to her. Someone would always be caught up in the wake of her actions or refusal to act.

Joan heard Adriana stir. In the dark, the young woman turned onto her back—Joan could see her eyes glinting in the shadows. Adriana turned her head to look at the couch, which was empty, then away.

Joan sat in the dark a long time, thinking. Though the east began to glow like molten iron, the sky remained grey and dull and heavy. It felt like snow. It was light out before she realized that Adriana wasn't going to get up. Joan made toast, the scent of butter wafting from it as she placed it next to Adriana's head. Then Joan made toast for herself, ate it, and made another cup of tea. She sat down to wait.

The wedding invitation envelope, its edges still crisp and bright, shone on the coffee table. Joan took a sip of tea and opened it. Embossed in gold on the cover were two ornate letters, D and G, their curlicues intertwined. It was written in a stranger's blocky hand.

Dear Joan, it read. *I wanted to thank you for taking care of Adriana. I was worried about her, but so thankful she had you to help her. I hope you will both come home safely, and I look very forward to meeting you again. Gillian wanted Adriana to be surprised about the wedding but I am not sure it is a good idea. If you feel the same, please feel free to tell her. Warmly, David.*

Joan stared at the words.

Her mother, far away across the Atlantic in Nova Scotia, would have her head full of the wedding, Joan knew. She would have chosen a dress, and she'd be busying herself with ordering flowers and arranging catering. It was just the kind of thing her mother loved. So many years ago, when Joan was but a seed growing in her mother's womb, Gillian's disastrous first wedding had been dictated by Joan's grandmother, who was trying to save face, while Joan's father, David, was a thousand miles away across the ocean in England.

Joan knew the story well, repeated many times by her own mother and father when she was young: how Grandma Wong had organized a Chinese feast, half catered from a local restaurant and half potluck, had chosen a young schoolmate of Gillian's as the groom's stand-in, how they had scrubbed the old schoolhouse where the wedding was to be held until its uneven hardwood floors gleamed, and Gillian had succumbed to exhaustion. How Gillian had lain in bed for days drinking her mother's beef tea, until the day arrived when she was strong enough to be made up like a Chinese doll in a traditional red-and-gold wedding outfit. How, as she stood resigned at the front of the schoolhouse, Joan's father, David, who everyone had been told had a broken leg and could not come to Canada for his own wedding, leaped up the schoolhouse steps in time to see Gillian "married" to a Chinese Canadian youth in his stead. And how Gillian had fainted on the schoolhouse floor and woken, a married woman, in that same bed in her parents' home.

Joan's parents always laughed when they told the story, but she knew their relief was a product of the light load time can make of a burden, even one originally dark and ponderous. Joan imagined their wedding her own way, and it had come to represent in her mind a foreshadowing of her parents' unsatisfactory and ultimately doomed marriage. She knew Gillian would have determined things would be different this time, with Adriana's father, now that she was in control of the affair. It would be a celebration to wipe away the memory of that first wedding to an absent fiancé.

Joan noted how ironic it was that her mother was marrying a Chinese man, and this time she would have a white wedding, a Western wedding, at a hotel, no doubt, with a North American–style buffet and no trace of the red-and-gold banners Grandma Wong had sewn with auspicious but failed blessings for the happiness, longevity, and fertility of Gillian's first marriage. Joan drew a sharp, cool breath and exhaled with relief that she would not be there.

CHAPTER 23
ADRIANA

There's a knock at the door. I shift in bed but I know it is not Milan because I can hear his footsteps inside me when he is approaching, as though he has bells on his feet. I won't get up until he comes back.

Joan opens the door. Whoever is there says something Joan does not understand.

"Mária, Nerozumiem," Joan says, ushering Milan's mother into the room. Mária begins to cry. I sit up in the darkness.

"Where is Milan?" Mária asks in frantic Slovak. Joan turns the wall sconces on, then dims them.

"Mária, what is wrong?" I call out in Slovak. Joan will not understand us, but maybe that is better for now.

Mária sits on the couch and puts her face in her hands, sobbing that her husband has fallen and cannot get up. He had been drinking, but it is more than that, Mária thinks. He was in pain, she says, when she tried to help him sit up and now refuses to let her touch him.

Mária stands up. She must get back to him.

I stand also. "Mária, let me call an ambulance."

Mária shakes her head. "No. My husband is afraid of hospital."

My hands feel cold and shaky. "Mária, let me help you." Mária shakes her head and disappears out the door.

I sit on the edge of the bed and wail a deep, painful, hopeless sound such as I have never made before. Joan comes to sit next to me. She puts her arm around me and massages my hand. Between sobs, I share what Mária has just told me.

I imagine her bombarding me with comforting words. It will be alright. You'll be fine. Milan is fine. You did your best. Don't worry, it will be okay. Joan is awkward and clunky, but she is all I have right now and my heart is bottomless. She is with me in this and I am grateful.

Joan caresses my hair, which is damp on the ends from crying. The tears have finally subsided and I've been hiccuping, enough to make myself laugh between sobs. I lean my head on her shoulder and she looks down at her lap. Then, as though she has been debating a long time about whether to tell me, she says, "My mother and your dad are getting married."

I sit bolt upright.

"It's sudden, I know," Joan says, examining her fingers. "It was supposed to be a surprise, but your dad thought you should know. And I agree."

I think I see a tear run down her cheek, but in the dim light, it is hard to say. It occurs to me that Gillian thought it would be easier to hide her and my father's plans from me if I were out of the country. A lump in my throat—outrage? But this was my father's doing too. And I have to admit that I am glad I'm not there to witness the flurry of activity that is certainly underway.

Having emptied myself of the most pressing pain, I decide to shed my secrets too. I speak into the shadows, knowing Joan is listening.

"Before we went to see my mother's village near Prešov, I called my aunt and told her that Milan is Roma. She didn't say anything for a moment, and then—'We welcome you, niece, and this Roma boy, if he is clean and honest, can stay in the garden house in our backyard.' I was going to say that we would both stay in the garden house in that case when the phone clicked and the operator said I needed to insert more koruny to continue the call. I decided to let the call end. I did not tell Milan. I decided I'd have to greet my aunt in such a way that she'd know where my allegiance lay."

I feel the story unravelling. It needs to come out and Joan needs to hear it.

"Milan was excited about the trip. Why had I mentioned it? But it was too late. My aunt was expecting me. I couldn't back out.

"The train trip was uneventful, the house easy to find. But when my aunt Livia opened the door, even before we knocked, I knew immediately I'd made a mistake. Her face was impassive, her eyes a steely blue-grey. She managed a half smile and an ingratiating welcome, not acknowledging Milan at all. He played it cool, but I knew he was bewildered and hurt. We walked through the house to the kitchen, where lemonade from a big jug had already been poured into glasses on the table.

"After, Livia showed us the backyard and the garden house where Milan was to sleep. I had planned for this.

"'Oooh, it is lovely! And spacious. We will be very happy to stay here,' I said, plumping my bag on the floor at the foot of the single cot. It was actually quite musty and dark, but I didn't care. I would rather a thousand times be there with Milan than in the house with my iceberg of an aunt.

"Milan seemed to have no idea. He was relieved to lie down on the cot. 'I must rest,' he said. 'You must have time with your aunt.'

"'No, no, no,' I said. But my aunt was waiting at the door of the garden house for me to return to the kitchen with her. We walked up the path, me following her, stiff-backed in her housedress. Suddenly, she stopped and pointed at a chrysanthemum, its yellow-orange petals glowing.

"'Your mother's favourite flower,' she said, smiling back at me what seemed like her first genuine smile, tentative and sad. I felt something glacial move in me, a warming I hadn't expected.

"My aunt and I sat at the kitchen table and talked a long time. I told her about my father and sister, Beth, and my stay in the mental hospital. I was surprised to hear myself saying the words, but my aunt simply nodded, her expression of shrewd-but-kind interest unchanging. She told me about her divorce from a stolid bookkeeper who drank too much and finally pinched one too many koruny from the till of his best client, the local grocer. And she told me about her children: the apple of her eye, oldest daughter Karolína, who had gone to university the year before, in Prague; her son, Vladomír, who was a carpenter; and her youngest daughter, Saskia, who had got pregnant and married at sixteen, and lived an hour away. I did not ask about my mother, nor did she, though my aunt had not seen her alive since her wedding.

"I had thought somehow there would be a house full of people, but there was only my aunt. I estimated she was older than my mother by ten years. She was middle-aged, but her stiff formality and greying hair, wavy like my mother's but shorter, made me think of a much older woman. Everything in the house seemed dated and faded. It had been a long time since a child had played there.

"And strangely, as soon as that thought crossed my mind, there was a knock at the back kitchen door. Livia looked startled—obviously she hadn't been expecting anyone. But whoever it was came straight into the house, and Livia seemed to melt in her chair when a cheery 'Ahoj, Mama,' followed by a small child's voice singing 'Ahoj! Ahoj!' punctuated the air. I gathered it was Saskia, and that the small blond boy who tumbled ahead of her was her child. Livia bent over in her chair and opened her arms to the boy.

"'Moje srdce,' she murmured. My heart, my heart. Saskia looked at me, curiously.

"'This is your cousin, Adriana,' Livia said. Saskia's eyes opened wide.

"'From Canada?'

"Livia nodded. Saskia seemed suddenly slightly aloof, but I knew it was a cover for her confusion and insecurity. When I smiled and put my hand out, she held my fingers briefly.

"It was clear Saskia did not visit often and that Livia was preoccupied with them. She began pulling plates of cling-wrapped food out of the fridge, salads and rolls and cheese and sausage and fish that she excitedly exclaimed she would fry for the boy. I realized she had probably prepared the food for me and Milan, but I was glad of the distraction so I would not have to make conversation with Saskia. I cleared my throat and yawned delicately, and Livia looked up from her grandson, as if surprised to see me sitting there.

"'May I take a plate to the garden house for Milan? I need a rest and he will be hungry now.'

"'Of course, of course!' Livia said. She pulled a serving platter from a cupboard in the kitchen and began to pile food on it haphazardly. She also took a jug of water from the fridge.

"'Please,' she said. I apologized to Saskia and the little boy, who by now was staring at me with sleepy blue eyes.

"'Excuse me,' I said. I left it to Livia to explain why I was headed to the garden house instead of upstairs.

"I reached the door of the garden house before I realized I had forgotten my purse in the kitchen. It contained my passport and all the money Milan and I had for the trip. Panicking, I ran back to the house. Though it was a cool

November day, my aunt had opened the screen door for me and forgotten to close the inside door, so I heard Saskia's voice pitched high with disbelief.

"'Cigán?' Saskia asked, her Slovak an outraged snort. 'But why?'

"I stopped short at the screen door.

"Livia shushed her and murmured, 'She would not have chosen so poorly if not for the fact that she is sick in the head.'

"I opened the screen door, and they turned to me with guilty eyes. I said nothing but took the purse from the back of the chair where I had been sitting and left.

"Milan was snoring in the cot. I perched on the dusty lawn chair and nibbled the plate of food in the dark. When he awoke, Milan arched his skinny body, arms thrown back over his head. I went to nestle against him and fed him cheese and sausage and the white rolls. We drank copiously, the whole jug of water, which had never tasted so good.

"Later, with the evening darkening around me, I brought the platter and jug back to the kitchen and left them on the doorstep. Through the window, I saw Livia and Saskia speaking quietly at the kitchen table, the tousled head of Saskia's boy in his mother's lap, a small plump arm outstretched.

"Early the next morning, I roused Milan from his sleep. He needed to pee badly, so I showed him the spot in back of the garden house where I'd crouched, shivering in the night. He stood facing away from me, and I heard a stream of urine hit the ground.

"'We must leave,' I said. 'Before my aunt wakes up. I don't want to say goodbye to her. I don't want to see her face.'

"Milan said nothing, but gathered his things. The platter and jug were still on the step. Bitterly, I placed several hundred koruny on the platter and set the jug on top of it.

"Milan shook his head. 'She is your family. Do not insult her this way.' I glared at him. He slowly folded the koruny bills and placed them in my jacket pocket. I turned away.

"'Ideme,' I said.

"We walked through the town to the train station, but neither of us was ready to return to Bratislava. The air was bright and crisp. We hitchhiked into the Tatras and sat on the side of the mountain, then walked to an off-season resort, where they let us sleep on the floor of the dining room the first night, then offered us a week's work of cleaning for bed, meals, and cash. Milan jumped at the chance. I wasn't much good at cleaning, but soon they had me on the phone with some Americans living in Prague who hoped to book a ski vacation. I clung to the phone while Milan whistled cheerfully.

"On Struggle for Freedom and Democracy Day, we and the few other staff had a holiday. The manager and his wife cooked a huge meal, and we ate and drank to the students who had died in 1939 during an uprising against the Nazis, and fifty years later, the demonstrations that led to the Velvet Revolution and fall of the Communists in Czechoslovakia. We were all happy to have a day to idle and listen to music. Though he drank only a little, and waited till after the clock struck twelve, Milan leapt off the couch and danced to the clapping and whistling of the others. He was as happy and free as I have seen him. I forgot my aunt and my cousin and my worries, and we slept that night as peacefully as children in the arms of their mothers.

"At the end of the week the manager drove us all the way back to Prešov, treating us to a hotel meal and beer. He drove off after kissing my hand and clapping Milan on the back while handing him a fistful of koruny.

"'I never saw a man work like you, and Roma to boot!' If Milan was offended he didn't show it.

"Milan put the money in his shoe. He was quiet on the train, pensive, and I wondered if he was thinking maybe he should have stayed. The work was hard but the mountain air was fresh. We passed through Levoča, the town he'd come from, and he hadn't expressed interest in stopping to see his remaining family there. I wondered if he was embarrassed to meet them empty-handed, as his plan was to give the money he'd earned to his mother. Or whether he was reluctant to explain the rift with his father. I like to think Milan wanted to save me from the many questions.

"Then skinheads, walking slowly up the aisle of the train and peering into each compartment, found us. With rising panic I told them in a shrill Slovak that the seats were taken, but they sat down beside us, coolly. Milan slumped in his seat, resigned. By accident, his foot brushed the knapsack of one of the intruders. For this they beat him quickly and brutally, while I screamed at them in English to stop. Milan's shoe came off. A few passengers hurried by our compartment but did not interfere. When the train stopped in the next small town, the skinheads sauntered off with Milan's money while he lay bleeding on the floor of the compartment."

My story is finished. I am shaking, as I had on the train home. But even before that, I'd started shaking—when I first heard my aunt and Saskia's ignorant words, when I first arrived in this country, when my father brought me to the mental hospital. I've been shaking like an aspen leaf for almost as long as I can remember. Joan, beside me, holds my shoulders. Hush, she says. Hush. Hush.

I hear bells inside me, from far away. I lift my damp face to the slate-grey early morning light, listening. Milan is coming.

After a few minutes, the door creaks open. Milan, looking haggard and pale, stops a few steps into the room. Joan and

I sit bolt upright on the bed. Perhaps he'd hoped to return before we woke. He eases himself onto the couch. For a moment he says nothing, his face a mask of exhaustion and pain. Joan gets up to make him a cup of tea, but I don't move.

"I saw Peter," he says. Joan lets a spoon clatter to the floor.

Peter? Confused, I lean toward him.

Milan nods. "My sister's boy." He begins to speak in Slovak, explaining to me how Peter had been conceived and how he'd come to live with the Burnses. Then, in English, Milan continues. "I stood at the door. I told the Scotsman, I am Jana Holubova's brother. I want see her boy. Peter."

And then I am shocked into remembering. "Milan, your father fell. He hurt himself."

Milan looks startled.

"You must go to him. Your mother says he needs to go to the hospital, but he won't."

Milan stands slowly, painfully, and pulls a photo from his jacket, letting it settle on the coffee table. Joan stares at it without touching it. I pick it up—a photo of a small baby with dark hair.

"Burns gave me. I tried pay him money, to buy my sister's son again."

Joan looks at Milan in disbelief. I tremble. Milan gently pulls the photo from my hand and returns it to his pocket.

"He said no. I must not ask him again, but I can visit Peter if I want." Milan shakes his head as he opens the door to the hall. "I must go to my father," he says.

I follow him with my eyes. Joan sits back in a chair and closes hers. It is a reversal of sorts of the myth, the damning tale, that Gypsies kidnap the children of good white folk.

Peter, Joan says, is not a lost or stolen boy, but was taken in by parents who love him. Nevertheless, there is another family—a Romani grandmother and uncle—that longs for him and grieves him, his loss echoing in the silence around his name. In the dark, Joan recites a nursery rhyme I have never heard, as magical as money, and as full of loss as life and love. *Sally, tell my mother I shall never come back.*

CHAPTER 24

Milan returned late in the afternoon. Joan turned from the window when she heard him come in. She watched as he flopped onto the bed Adriana had vacated for the shower, and said nothing. Joan's anxiety, which had thrummed through her, settled to a low hum. She felt inhabited by tears that she could not release, as though she were locked with them in a dreary dance. When Adriana emerged from the bathroom wrapped in a towel, her hair damp and black, she went straight to the bed and wrapped her body around Milan's back.

Joan felt she must leave them alone. She closed the apartment door behind her. She traversed the dimly lit hall, past Milan's family's door, behind which it was unusually quiet, past Pani asleep in front of her television in the back room, and past the pile of white powdered shoes, out into the grey light. Snow was definitely coming.

It had been some time since she'd walked without aim or purpose. Joan set out in the general direction of the square. Would she see the fake St. Francis, she wondered, with the air so cold and the tourists few and far between? She crossed the street to pass by Robbie Burns's Tourism English School, keeping an eye out for anyone standing in the windows of the school or house. It seemed deserted. Joan had a wild thought that Burns had fled with Peter to Scotland, abandoning the buildings. But the faint scent of cloves hung in the air, so Joan hurried past without stopping.

Once out of sight of the school, she slowed down. It was almost too much to wonder what Milan's father and Mária had done. Had Milan convinced them to go to the hospital? What would be done for him there if they had? A thin rivulet of despair ran through her. Perhaps nothing.

The square was empty but for a few pigeons, perhaps because the sky was threatening to open. But music leaked from the cathedral, sombre choir and organ music—a funeral service or some other sober affair was happening inside. She wandered past, kicking a large pebble that skittered across the cobblestones, sending a pigeon into the air. Elation, tinged only slightly with remorse, rose in her chest. She was free in this space between the impassive sky and the stones beneath her. Joan took a sharp breath in and exhaled, heat turning the sadness around her to steam as it hit the frosty air.

She had an urge to run across the cobblestones, but she feared she would trip. Instead she put her arms out and turned languid circles. Who was there to care what she did? The first flake fluttered against her cheek, melted.

Joan stopped to watch a carriage drawn by four black horses, black plumes fastened to their heads, clatter onto the square from the nearby roadway and pull up in front of the cathedral. They paused behind an idling black hearse that she had not noticed before. The horses' breath was white and their sides heaved slightly as they waited. Soon the main doors of the cathedral opened and the pallbearers appeared carrying a black-draped coffin. They loaded it into the waiting hearse while a young family, dressed in black, climbed into the carriage. Mourners poured out behind them like black beetles. The cemetery would be near, Joan thought, as the funeral procession trailed after the carriage on foot.

She was tempted to follow, never having seen a Slovak funeral. But she let the procession trail away in the distance as the snow began in earnest, heavy wet flakes that stuck to the ground where they fell. The cathedral door was ajar, so she went to sit in a pew and wait it out. It occurred to Joan that Miša might have a funeral, and she would not be there.

The church was dimly lit by wall sconces, as in the hallway at the Hotel Svatopluk. The stained glass burned richly in red and blue and green. Joan sat near the back, not wanting to interfere with the devotions of the pure of heart. A woman entered and sat ahead of Joan, bowing her head. She prayed hurriedly, fervently, Joan thought, her forehead resting on the back of the pew in front of her. Then she rose to go, crossing herself and dropping to one knee before she turned to leave.

It was Mária. Joan could see her face was streaked with tears as she hurried past. Mária stopped at the locked fund box and folded a couple of bills to deposit there. She turned once more and crossed herself before leaving the cathedral.

Joan followed Mária out the door. Mária had crossed to the closest street bordering the square. The children waited there in a huddle for her. Together, they disappeared down a side street. Joan did not pursue them.

The snow was falling steadily now. Joan decided to head back to the hotel, but to stop en route for pastries to bring back to Adriana and Milan. She was feeling celebratory. Life was hard, but she knew what she was to do, and for the moment, she was free.

Joan entered the cake shop she had sometimes frequented when she lived with the Burnses. It was almost empty, except for an old man slowly stirring his espresso with a tiny spoon. Joan ordered a box of cakes and sat down near the window with her own small cup to watch the street. A few people passed, pulling their coats tight. Fashionable women without hats. A threesome of rosy-cheeked youth, laughing and shouting to a young couple they knew on the other side of the street as they passed. The boy ducked his head to evade a snowball one of the three lobbed at him, while the young girl who clung to his hand with hers smiled stiffly. Something told Joan that they had a secret. Perhaps they were engaged and had not yet announced it. Perhaps she was pregnant and afraid. So many things were unknowable, and some unimaginable, in other people's lives.

She had chosen two each of poppyseed cake and marble cake, plus a half-dozen tarts and something that looked like a rectangle of cheesecake for herself. Everything was good, she wasn't worried about that. Joan wondered instead whether Milan and Adriana would have talked things out, how Mária's husband was faring, and even how Burns and Peter were coping. She imagined Peter wandering around his mother's empty room, unable to fathom his loss.

Joan savoured the cheesecake. Could it be the best thing she'd ever tasted, the tiny espresso the very blackest and best? The bell on the door tinkled and she heard a familiar laugh, both high and throaty. It was Ania from the Café Eureka. Joan turned around to greet her. She was with someone, not Boris, but a young man Joan recognized. It was the clerk from the bookstore.

Adriana turned her head quickly before Ania could see her, her heart beating fast. Ania ordered some cakes and the young man paid, taking the box under his arm. Ania, sparkling and excitable, looked much more attractive than she had in the Café Eureka, bowed under the burden of her studies. As Ania turned away from the counter, Joan put her head down and pretended to be absorbed by the dregs of her espresso.

"Joan?" Ania asked.

Joan lifted her head and allowed herself to look surprised. The young man set the box of cakes on a table. Ania, flushing, sat down in the chair opposite Joan.

"Please don't tell Boris," she said. "This is my brother, Marek. We bought cakes for Boris's birthday. If you come again to the Café Eureka tonight, please do not tell him!"

Joan felt her shoulders relax. It was, she knew, unlikely she would get to the Eureka before Boris's birthday. "No, I won't tell him. I won't spill the beans." Ania looked confused, but Marek smiled broadly.

"American idiom," he said in clear, clipped English. "It means, I won't tell the secret."

Ania laughed with relief. "Joan is Canadian. She taught us 'quintessential.'" Now Marek looked confused. Ania laughed again and hugged her brother's shoulders. Joan could see the family resemblance in their high cheekbones and long noses, though Marek was blond and Ania's hair was curly and brown.

They spoke for a little while about the birthday plans for Boris.

"He misses his family," Ania said, wistfully. "Tibor says he take us to čínska reštaurácie across town tonight. But Boris says, is not real Chinese food. He has—depression." Ania crumpled and straightened a paper napkin.

Joan nodded. She too felt the sudden emptiness, which was not the absence of parents or friends but her own absence in the familiar places she had once called home.

"If only I could cook, I would make him something Chinese," Joan said. Ania brightened. "But I can't, I'm sorry," Joan said with real regret. "Besides, my friends have a family emergency and I must go back to them."

Ania pressed Joan's hand. "It is okay. Boris is wonderful cook. He will make Chinese food for us, and we will bring cakes and much drink. If we went to restaurant, Tibor wanted invite you—but I think you are...occupied."

Joan nodded. "Wait though. Let me write something to Boris. To wish him a happy birthday." Joan took a pen from her purse and eased a paper doily from under the little vase with fake flowers on the marble table. She felt the eyes of the girl behind the counter regarding her severely, but she didn't care. Joan chewed the end of the pen. What to say? She settled on the song "Happy birthday to you, happy birthday to you, happy birthday, dear Boris, happy birthday to you." Joan drew some music notes around the edges and signed it with the Chinese name her grandfather had given her more than thirty years ago.

Ania gazed at the characters, delighted. "What does it mean?" she asked.

Joan blushed. "It is my name. It means 'pure character.'"

Ania and Marek smiled. Joan, self-conscious now, said her goodbyes and left the cake shop, the bell on the door and Ania's laughter tinkling behind her.

At the hotel, Pani Svatoplukova was no longer asleep, and instead of looking cross she seemed relieved to see Joan, which was a great surprise. She knew the Pani had a soft spot for Adriana and her efforts to speak in Slovak, so Joan thought she would try.

"Pani...?" She opened the box of cakes to offer the old woman one.

But Pani waved it away. She spoke a hoarse stream of Slovak at Joan, who picked up only a little. Something about Mária, and about Milan, and about the hospital.

Joan looked apologetic and shook her head. Pani tried again briefly.

"Mária nie je doma. Gabriela je sama." She pointed down the hall, looking worried. Joan nodded, understanding half the words, but not their import, and hurried to knock on Mária's door. But before she reached it, she noticed a small figure at the end of the corridor, pushing a mop back and forth with some difficulty. It was Gabriela.

"Mária? Tvoja mama?" Joan asked.

The girl shook her head, and tears began to slip down her cheeks. Joan was worried now too. Had Mária and the children returned and left again, or made their way to the hospital? If Mária had left with the younger children and told Gabriela to do her chores, she must have anticipated being away for some time.

"Come for tea," Joan said. Gabriela shook her head, tears in her eyes, then turned her back and continued mopping.

The room was empty, no Milan or Adriana. No Mária. Joan put the box of cakes on the table and sat down. Helpless.

Soon they would be back, she reassured herself. Joan lay down on the couch, heavy-headed, and fell asleep. She dreamed of darkness, of water swirling around her, of Tibor plunging heavily from the surface above toward her as she lay immobile on her bed at the Burnses' home. At the last moment, she rolled aside and woke, half hanging off the couch. Her heart beat quickly. Darkness was falling in the outside world, and her stomach rumbled with a long, low sound like thunder.

Joan lay there for a moment, gathering herself. She was still alone. Where could they be? She decided to try Mária's door, to see if Gabriela was there, but there was no answer.

Joan returned to Adriana and Milan's room. She would wait a while longer, then she would call Tibor the taxi driver to take her to the hospital. Tibor knew so much about all of them and their business already that she would not hesitate to call him. Perhaps that was what it meant to be a taxi driver—to be a keeper of secrets and runner between lives.

The door opened a crack. Joan sat up, alert and silent. A small figure stood silhouetted against the light from the hall. It was Gabriela, who looked so much like Jana, the mother of Peter. She was shivering though she was wrapped in a blanket. Joan beckoned for her to sit down, which she did. Joan made her a cup of tea.

"Thank you," the girl said in a bell-like voice. Joan was surprised. She hadn't been sure the child knew how to speak English, though she'd seemed to understand Joan earlier in the hall.

"My name is Joan. You are Milan's sister." The girl nodded. "What is your name?" Joan asked, though she knew the answer.

"My name is Gabriela."

Joan opened the box of cakes. "Please have some, Gabriela."

This time, the girl did not hesitate. She was clearly hungry.

"Your mother and father. Are they at the hospital?" Gabriela nodded. "And the other children?" She nodded again, tears streaming down her cheeks. Joan wished she could put her arm around the girl's shoulders, but she felt awkward.

Joan thought for a moment. "I think Milan and Adriana will come home soon," she said. Gabriela looked up and nodded, wiping her cheeks. "Will you help me prepare a party for them?" Joan tried.

Gabriela nodded again with a small smile.

Joan set Gabriela to shining the teapot and organizing the glass cups and sugar and jam, as well as slicing a lemon. Joan washed the cups in the bathroom and looked at herself in the mirror. She noticed a couple of strands of grey in her hair, and they shocked her. She was not yet thirty-six, and her mother's hair was jet black still. Soon, she thought, she would look not like her mother's sister but her mother's mother. The idea made her giggle, and she put her hand over her mouth. She did not want to alarm Gabriela.

But when she emerged from the bathroom, Gabriela was gone. The door was open. Joan hurried down the hall and knocked on Mária's door. Nothing. She continued to the front desk, and there was the girl, standing on tiptoe at the counter, speaking with Pani Svatoplukova. She had brought the woman a piece of poppyseed cake. When Gabriela saw Joan, her face fell. Joan, however, nodded approvingly. Pani Svatoplukova patted her hand and smiled at Joan.

"Dobré dievča," the woman said. Good girl.

"Gabriela," Joan said, "it was kind of you to bring cake to the lady."

Gabriela looked uncertain. Joan nodded again. She turned to go back to the room.

"Počkajte!" Pani Svatoplukova said. Wait. She waddled into the back room where the TV was on and came back with a photo. It was the photo of Peter that Burns had given Milan. It must have slipped from Milan's pocket.

Pani handed it to Joan and nodded. Gabriela followed the photo with her eyes until Joan tucked it into a pocket. Pani put a couple of candies, wrapped in shiny red foil, into Gabriela's hand, along with something wrapped in a cloth bag.

"Dobré dievča."

Back in the apartment, they continued their party preparations. Gabriela arranged the sliced lemon on a plate, then sat back, looking lost.

"What did the pani give you?" Joan asked. Gabriela opened the cloth bag and pulled out a pair of shoes, still dusty with powder, although the woman had evidently tried to wipe them clean.

"They are very nice, very good shoes," Joan ventured. Gabriela nodded.

Joan remembered the book of nursery rhymes she had taken from the Burnses' home. She dug it out of her bag and handed it to Gabriela, saying, in what she hoped was an encouraging voice, "Nursery rhymes. They might be a bit young for you, but I love the illustrations." The girl sat and stared at the cover for a long time, almost unblinking. "Poézia," Joan said. Poems.

Gabriela turned the pages slowly, scrutinizing the pictures and silently sounding out the words. "Čo je to?" Gabriela pointed to the picture of the baby lamb who followed Mary to school.

"That is a lamb," Joan said.

Gabriela's brow wrinkled. Joan wondered if it was possible she had never seen a picture of a lamb before. She had to admit this one was cartoonish. Puffed up like a little cloud, it didn't look like a real lamb. Joan thought a moment, then bleated. Gabriela put her hand over her mouth and giggled. She was only about nine years old, Joan thought.

Day slid into evening, and Joan continued to worry. She turned up the dim wall sconces. Gabriela lay on the couch and stared at the ceiling. Joan went to her suitcase and found the doll she'd bought at the market. Orsolia. She hesitated for a moment, then took it to the girl, who tucked it under her arm. Joan covered them both with a blanket.

There was a commotion in the hall, and the apartment door swung open, admitting Milan and Adriana, Mária, and the rest of her children. Gabriela sat up on the couch and Mária moved toward her. Gabriela slouched as though waiting for a slap, but Mária hugged her hard and kissed her hair.

"Your papa will be okay," she said in Slovak. Gabriela burst into tears.

Milan and Adriana looked tired but happy. Their hands were full of bags of food. They spread them on the table, opening packages for the younger children and slicing bread and cheese and sausage. Joan made another pot of tea and lemonade for the children using lemon slices and sugar cubes. Mária was talking excitedly, and Adriana and Milan responded in Slovak. Joan knew she would have to wait to find out what had happened. Used to travelling in the foreign waters of languages she barely understood, she busied herself serving the children lemonade and wiping their mouths.

After they ate, the children piled onto the couch with Gabriela to look at the book of nursery rhymes. Clutching the doll close to her chest, she read them slowly and clearly in English, then explained in Romany what she had recited. Occasionally Gabriela would look up from the book to ask Joan what a word or phrase meant. Owl? Pussycat? Pumpkin eater? London Bridge? Joan would either use sound effects or pantomime to explain. From the sly smile Gabriela wore, it was clear to Joan that the girl was asking simply to see how she would demonstrate the word. The children wriggled and squealed, their noses runny and their cheeks rosy with excitement. Joan, relieved, felt a glow of warmth come over her.

Mária, Milan, and Adriana spoke till the children began to curl around Gabriela and close their eyes. Adriana stood up and said something to Mária, who put her hands on her shoulders and kissed her forehead. Gabriela collected the children and ushered them out the door, waving the book of nursery rhymes like a flag. Joan nodded to her—yes, she should take the book. It really belonged to Peter, the girl's nephew, not to Joan. One day Gabriela might have the chance to meet him and return it. Gabriela didn't even ask about the doll. It was clear she'd claimed Orsolia as her own.

Mária followed Gabriela soon after. But first she held Milan's face and kissed him tenderly on both cheeks. She did the same to Adriana, and then, to Joan's surprise, to Joan. Mária said something indecipherable and made the sign of the cross. She took a bag with a loaf of bread and some cheese and sausage and closed the door behind her.

Milan and Adriana fell on the couch together. Joan sat on one of Elaine Watterson's chairs and waited. Milan began to speak.

"My father is okay. No bones broken," he said. "When he was finished being drunk, he felt stupid to be at hospital with only bruises. In a room with Roma he met some friend who was very sick. My father lost his pride." Adriana squeezed his fingers. "He swept the floor. He fixed a hospital bed. My father is very good mechanic," Milan said proudly. "The nurse saw that he cleaned and fixed things. She scolded him and told the doctor. When my father left the hospital, the doctor said wait. A director came to talk to him. My father thought he had made problems for himself, but the director asked him if he wanted work. My father said yes. The director said, 'When you feel better, come talk to me.'"

Milan shook his head in disbelief. "My father did not work for five years. Now he goes to hospital drunk and comes home with job! My mother says it is a miracle." He grinned. "She prayed for him to be well, not to have a job. But maybe it helped that I gave Canadian dollars to the hospital so my father would have a bed."

Adriana shook her head in disbelief. Joan's mouth hung open.

"Yes," said Milan, reddening. "You said I must choose my life, Joan. I have chosen." Adriana stroked his hand. He pulled an airplane ticket from his pocket. "I go to Canada with Adriana."

Joan felt a huge swath of relief, as though someone had come along with a scythe and cleared the tall weeds blocking her view.

"My mother has a little money to start a business. She is thinking about what to do." Milan blinked. "Money," he said, and shook his head in wonder. "With money you can do anything!"

Adriana shook her head. "Money didn't stop me from being depressed and from ending up in the hospital." So she *had* told him.

Milan put his arm around her shoulders. "I know. I know money is not happiness." he said. "But when you haven't money you also can't be happy. It is like water. One must drink it to stay alive, but then too much and it can make someone sick or drown," he said. The thought did not seem to dampen his mood.

Milan jumped up. "We must have music!" He clicked his fingers and turned on the ancient clock radio that inhabited the table by the bed. The sound was thin and jangling, but notes like those played by the Roma musicians in the market tumbled from it. Milan took a few dramatic steps, then began to dance, Adriana clapping to keep the beat. He pulled her to her feet and she danced too, pretending to swirl a long skirt and fan her blushing cheeks. Milan took the fuchsia scarf Adriana had given him and tied it around his hips, pretending to belly dance, his hand cocked provocatively behind his head. Adriana giggled and handed him another scarf, which he used as a veil.

Milan danced for a little while and then flopped onto the chesterfield beside Adriana. Joan poured him a glass of lemonade, which he downed gratefully. Then, planting a damp kiss on Adriana's lips, and with effort, he stretched out to remove his shoes. He lifted his long-socked feet onto the table and wiggled them. "I am too hot. I must smell as footballer."

Adriana kissed his ear. "You will be fine after a shower. And we will sprinkle powder in your shoes. No one needs to know you are a belly dancer."

Joan remembered the shoes Pani Svatoplukova gave Gabriela. They troubled her, though she wasn't sure why. "Milan, Pani at the front desk gave Gabriela some shoes. I think they were from the pile in the corner."

Milan's eyes widened, then darkened.

"They were a gift," Joan said.

Milan looked incredulous.

Adriana cleared her throat. "Pani Alica has kept those shoes for forty years," she said. So, Joan thought. Pani Svatoplukova has a real name. "They belonged to her and her daughter, whose name was Gabriela too. Pani lost part of her leg in the fire that destroyed the house they lived in. The entryway was stone and the shoes were untouched by the flames, but Gabriela perished. It was Pani Alica's ex-husband who set the fire. He showed up drunk in the middle of the night and threw a Molotov cocktail through the window."

Stunned, Joan slumped in her chair. Milan stood up and moved toward the door.

"Milan," Adriana said quietly. "Don't." He stopped. "They are shoes. Gabriela doesn't know any differently. Alica only told me the story because I asked her. In forty years, no one had asked her about those shoes."

Joan turned away from them. While they talked into the night, she lay down on the cot and fell asleep. In her dream, Gabriela, wearing the powdery shoes, was sailing in a boat with the owl and the pussycat—then Joan was Gabriela and Pani was at her desk with a birthday cake decorated with one candle lit like a sparkler. It sizzled and sputtered and she gave it to Gabriela-Joan, who stood in the prow of the boat and held it aloft. The owl and the pussycat had become Adriana and Milan and the scene shifted and they were all in the apartment, and the cake had become enormous, enough to share with the whole population of the Hotel Svatopluk, the people behind closed doors who Joan never saw. Milan invited them in and they were ghosts, wearing the white powdered shoes from beside Pani's desk. They were cheerful and drifted around like snow in a snow globe.

Joan woke in the middle of the night to Milan and Adriana breathing softly in one another's arms. She was filled with a sense of peace she hadn't felt since before Edna had died, before she had moved to the nursing home, when she lived in a small apartment with a kitchen window that looked out over Halifax Harbour.

"It is like the sea!" Edna had exclaimed, and she was right, it *was* like the sea, was in fact part of the sea, the Atlantic Ocean. She and Joan sat and gazed out at the water, the silver glow on the surface from the mid-afternoon sun, and dreamed separately of the past and the future. Somehow Joan had believed Edna would live there forever, that the shadow that had begun to fall on Edna's mind would forever be held at bay. But of course this could not be, and many shadows, some mountainously slow and some fleet as deer, had passed over the surface of Joan's life since that time. Joan had not known before that this was what a life was made of. Shadows and light, surface and depth—they needed one another as a mother needs her child and a child their mother.

As she drifted back to sleep she imagined China spread below her like a carpet. Orange trees and pagodas. She knew this was not China, but a curtain behind which the real China lay in all its complicated, overpopulated beauty and ugliness. She imagined putting on a mask, a Chinese lion's head like the one Peter had made several Lego creations ago, and stepping into a strange world of polluted, socialist grey, where brilliant red and gold laundry hung from apartment towers, and police stations and subway trains sported ads for teeth whitening, luxury cars, and the Communist Party of China. Her Chinese family were faceless to her, small and drab, but she tried to follow them through the wide boulevards filled with people and the narrow streets. She did not know if her vision reflected the truth, and she hoped somehow the mask would protect her. But it had not protected Peter. Creating it had absorbed him for a while, and he had carried it around like a talisman, but in the end it was only a toy. Joan knew that where money and luck ended, she only had herself—her wits, her skills, and her stubborn persistence—to depend on. And yet there was something else she could not name that buoyed up the world and the creatures in it. What was it? It had different faces—imagination and memory, hope and love. Perhaps it was the same thing Mária prayed to. Joan felt it to be part of her the way her own hands were attached at her wrists, but she did not know what to call it.

CHAPTER 25

It was a frosty evening, and garish wreaths, which had begun to appear on the lampposts of Old Town Bratislava, glittered in the dusk. Joan waited for the call to go through, then pulled her mitten back onto the hand that held the receiver, her breath against it white and otherworldly.

"Ahoj?" Joan recognized Boris's voice.

"Hello? It's Joan, the Canadian English teacher."

Boris paused and put his hand over the receiver to muffle his comment to whoever was with him in the room.

"Ahoj, Joan," Boris said. "Ania would like to say hi."

Ania's nasal "Hello!" came over the receiver and Joan felt relieved. Ania was upbeat, clearly excited. "We have found you a river to skate away on," she said, and laughed. "Happy Christmas to you!" And before Joan could respond, she'd passed the phone back to Boris.

"My father would like you to start teaching the winter term, January," Boris said. "He had an American teacher, but that teacher cannot come. So he is very happy you are available."

Joan exhaled.

"He will pay for your flight if you will sign a two-year contract."

Two years? Joan swallowed. It was a big commitment to a school she did not know, but it was Boris's father's school. It was near Guangzhou and her grandfather's village, and that was the only place she wanted to go now anyway. Joan's fingertips began to tingle.

"Okay," she said. "Thank you. Can I ask…" But there were so many things she wanted to know that she didn't know where to begin.

"Don't worry," Boris said, "be happy."

"With a little help from your friends," Ania chimed in in the background. They laughed at their own corniness. "Have Tibor drive you to the Eureka tomorrow night," Ania said. "We will celebrate."

Outside the phone booth, Joan looked up at the cloud-covered dark. The crisp and brilliant moon was up there somewhere, and so was the pale wintery sun, and the needle-like stars. But all she could see was a metal frame in the shape of an angel, wrapped with white and silver tinsel. It blew a trumpet as it flew, announcing the Good News to the people of Slovakia in their sleep. It was not for Joan's news or Milan's that the angel blew its trumpet. The news that excited and perturbed her was her secret, but she still shared the spirit of that solitary being, poised against the frosty cloudscape, silent and triumphant, bearing glad tidings to the world. Joan held out her arms and turned a full circle as she looked up at the sky. Out of the darkness, small flakes, sharp and cold, like messages from the future, landed on her cheeks.

Joan called Tibor the next day. She was glad to get out of the apartment because Adriana and Milan were busy preparing to leave for Canada. They disagreed over small things, but Joan knew it was simply nerves on both sides. Milan was in particular concerned about his clothes, and Adriana kept trying to reassure him.

"Milan," she said, "it doesn't matter. If you don't like what you are wearing we can find you new clothes in Canada. It is less expensive there!"

"I won't meet your father wearing rags, like a poor Gypsy," he said.

She rolled her eyes but was clearly hurt. But when he pulled a new pair of Levis and a blue bomber jacket out of hiding, her eyes widened.

"You look fabulous!" she said. He put a pair of sunglasses from his pocket to hide his eyes, but he couldn't mask his elation.

As she stood on the steps of the Hotel Svatopluk waiting for Tibor, Joan thought about her own appearance. She looked plain and uninteresting, she knew, but maybe now that she was about to start teaching in China she should think about ways to look more professional. Maybe lipstick? But if she wore lipstick, wouldn't she have to do other things she knew nothing about? Could one wear lipstick without worrying about the rest of her face? Joan honestly didn't know. Her forehead crinkled.

Tibor arrived and rolled down the window, calling to her. "Miss Joan. I am here."

She climbed into the passenger seat. Tibor was chewing gum, and the scent of mint filled the car. As he pulled away across the cobblestones, the ornament on his windshield mirror bounced.

"Eureka?" he asked cheerily. Joan nodded.

They drove without speaking, their silence covered by the radio's insistent tinniness. Tibor cracked his gum.

"Good news?" he finally asked.

She nodded, smiled, but did not offer more.

Inside the café, Ania and Boris sat with their heads together. They looked up at the same time, brimming with excitement, pushing back a chair each for Joan and Tibor.

"This time we buy coffee," Ania said, and went to the counter. Boris pushed some papers toward Joan. They were typewritten with an old-fashioned typewriter. Joan could see it was a form to apply for a visa; there was also a letter of invitation, printed on what looked to be a modern ink jet.

"You must bring these to the embassy," said Boris. "My father made sure they will expect you."

Tibor sat back in his chair, smiling broadly. Joan surveyed the papers and shook her head.

Boris looked alarmed. "What?" he asked, as Ania sat down with the espressos. "Is something wrong?"

Joan shook her head again. How could she explain it? It was as if, magically, the path had opened up before her, yet again, without her doing anything in particular to create it or deserve it. How could she explain to these young people that her life was not like theirs, or what they had been led to believe theirs would be? That she was a leaf, a feather, usually caught in the swirling dust in someone's wake?

But Joan knew she wanted this. She'd dreamed of going to her grandparents' old family home with a bag of oranges in hand and knocking on the door. And perhaps this vision of herself, one of very few Joan had ever had in her life, was guiding her now, pulling her out of the slipstream she hadn't even realized she was caught in.

Joan realized they were waiting for her. "No, it is fine. It is just hard to believe—that it's happening so soon."

Boris's brow furrowed. "Too soon?" he asked.

"No," Joan said, and smiled.

His thin shoulders relaxed. Joan thought for a moment of Harold, the young Chinese man who stood in for Joan's father at his own wedding. Her mother had laughed when describing him. But Joan knew Boris was smart and helpful and perhaps carried a weight on his shoulders she knew nothing about.

"No, it isn't too soon," Joan said. "Thank you for your help. I—I am surprised. That it is happening at all."

Boris grinned. Ania piped up, "It was your name. Your Chinese name, pure character, that made Mr. Leung decide."

Boris blushed and looked down at his hands, sheepish. "My father is old-fashioned. He believes names are destiny."

Tibor stirred sugar into his coffee, saying little, while the two students chattered about the place where Joan would teach. It was a small city, in southeastern China. Joan would fly to Hong Kong and then on to Guangzhou, and from there she would take the train and bus. Not to worry, there would be many people who wanted to prac-tise their English and who would help her. Joan nodded. In Hungary she'd had Tibor; in Slovakia, Milan. And in China, there would be others. People were, she realized, generally helpful, hospitable—and the hunger for English was insatiable.

Tibor stood up slowly. "I am afraid I must go. Joan, if you would like me to drive you back to Hotel Svatopluk, I can, or you can call another taxi." Ania and Boris looked surprised.

Joan stood up and swept the papers into her arms. "I must go also," she said. "My roommates are going to Canada tomorrow."

"Of course you must go," exclaimed Ania.

Boris added, "Please contact me before you go to China. I would like to tell you something more about my home city, and the school. And to say goodbye."

Ania tousled Boris's hair and he bobbed his head away from her. "From both of us," she said.

Joan was lost in thought as Tibor drove. Two years. It'd been some time since she'd been able to say what her life would hold beyond tomorrow.

Tibor turned on the radio, in a buoyant mood. "You will be a teacher. In China! It is exciting, no?"

Joan nodded, tingling with the thought. Tibor happily accompanied the Slovak pop star on the radio, all the way to the hotel.

Joan put koruny in the cup holder, including a tip she would normally have considered extravagant. It was Christmas, after all. And Tibor had helped her so much.

He did not refuse it but shook Joan's hand.

"Thank you," he said. "May God bless you. Please call me when you need to go to the airport."

Joan dipped her head and took her hand back. "Tomorrow," was all she could muster. She did not explain that the ride was for Milan and Adriana. The speed of the current had momentarily taken her breath away.

As soon as Joan entered the room, Adriana bombarded her.

"Joan, I am glad you are back. I've been frantically trying to think what to bring home for your mother and my father as a gift. I can buy them some liquor at the airport, I suppose I'll do that, but I'd rather give them something more special."

Joan thought for a moment, then shrugged. Milan would be enough of a gift. It occurred to her that Adriana was getting her revenge for their parents' surprise marriage, even though Joan was sure Adriana wasn't thinking about that at all.

Adriana didn't look at her. "You aren't coming back for the wedding." It wasn't a question.

"No," said Joan. "No, I have a contract to teach in China in January."

Adriana looked startled. "I love my father," she said.

Joan nodded. "I love my mother too, Adriana," she said.

"I hope you don't mind that I won't be there."

Adriana nodded. Her hair fell around her face. "When we went to visit my mother's family in the East," she said, "I thought I would learn things about her that would make me feel closer to her. But all I really learned was that she had wanted to leave the country, and when she met my father he was her ticket out. She might have loved him but she was also very...pragmatic. Is your mother pragmatic?"

Joan smiled. "My mum tends to be a strange mix of pragmatism, romanticism, calculation, and impulsiveness. I don't suppose that helps."

Adriana shook her head.

"My mother loves your dad. She has no reason to marry him otherwise. She is comfortable, she still works, she has a house. She is not marrying your dad because of money."

"No." Adriana said in a small voice. "I know."

They sat in silence.

"If you were to bring back a wedding present—for our parents—could it be from both of us?" Joan asked. Adriana's eyes widened. "Could it be something a little unusual?"

Joan wasn't sure what she was proposing yet. Her mind kept coming back to Peter's Lego dragon and fish head, and his spaceship. Could she possibly ask Burns to let Peter make something for her mother and Adriana's father as a gift? Of course she could, she realized. She would simply have to talk to Burns. It was only a matter of her own willingness. And why, otherwise, would she want to talk to Burns now, after what he had proposed to her? She felt a wistful tug, like a small hand, trying to get her attention.

But regardless of her feelings, something Peter made was the most meaningful wedding present she could think to give the couple, who wanted for nothing. It would tell the story she could not tell, of what she had been doing in

Slovakia, caring for a child who she had, in the end, abandoned but who Milan had insisted was family. And because Milan was their family now, so was Peter.

Whatever Peter made would be extraordinary, otherworldly, and would carry a seed of significance apparent to no one—not to Joan, nor to Peter himself. She knew her mother would be confused, but even if he did not understand, Adriana's father, an engineer, might appreciate the skill of a not yet four-year-old prodigy who could build such complex and beautiful structures out of plastic blocks.

Adriana was busy thinking her own thoughts. "My father always said that the best present is the presence of the ones you love. Corny," she said, shaking her head and smiling. "That's my dad." Adriana put her hand on Joan's. "He would love to have you there."

Joan shook her head. "I'm sorry I won't be," she said. But it gave her an idea.

Tibor drove Adriana and Milan to the airport the next morning, and Joan accompanied them to say her final farewell. Milan and Adriana had bid a tearful goodbye to Mária and her husband and the children. Milan was still bruised from his injuries, so his younger sisters and brothers were shy about hugging him. Instead, they held hands and, led by Gabriela, lined up for him and Adriana to kiss them. Milan's father shook Milan's hand. Milan, a head taller, put his hand around his father's back and kissed him on the cheek. The older man reddened, but straightened. His eyes had a distant look, as though he remembered something he had long forgotten. He even nodded to Adriana with a gruff "dovidenia"—until we see each other again. Adriana's head bobbed but she was too shy to address him. Instead, she tickled Milan's younger siblings and thrust candies into their hands.

Milan had hugged his mother gingerly. She held his face gently in both hands and bent it toward her, kissing him on both cheeks. Her eyes were full of happiness and tears. She turned to Adriana and pressed a pair of gold earrings into her hands, and kissed her on the forehead. Joan knew then that Mária had realized her son and Adriana would marry one day, and she would not be there to witness it.

When the cab pulled away from the Hotel Svatopluk, Milan gazed back through the rear window for a second or two. It had, after all, been his home for a good number of years. Joan had watched him say goodbye to the women in the kitchen. His friend among them, Lenka, wept copiously, pushing a Christmas loaf into his hands. Pani Alica at the front desk simply nodded and said a curt goodbye—and then frowned and stated that Gabriela would miss him. Now, behind him, Mária stood tearfully waving next to his father—his hand also raised in farewell—looking worn and bent even though her eyes glowed. Milan turned away, putting on his sunglasses although the day was overcast.

Joan, in the front seat, turned too to the road ahead. It was a long way to the airport. Milan and Adriana looked out the windows, pointing out the landmarks they passed, chattering over one another in their excitement. Tibor turned the radio on low, but then he began to speak quietly and deliberately to Joan.

"I am going to meet someone at the airport too," he said. Milan and Adriana in the back seat were absorbed in their conversation.

"Who will you meet, Tibor?" Joan asked.

He stared straight ahead with a small smile. "My daughter," he said.

"I didn't know you had a daughter," Joan said. "Where is she coming from?"

Tibor gripped the wheel a little harder. "Canada," he said. "Toronto. I will meet her for the first time. She is twenty-two years old."

Joan imagined the reunion of a father and daughter who'd never met. Like Peter and the man that Jana had known briefly when she was only seventeen.

"Her mother and I met not a year before she was born. She was an opera student. Very talented. She went home to Canada and I did not know she would have a baby. I sang and drank and sang and I did not think about her. Then two years ago, she wrote to me a letter. She was sick—cancer, she told me—and she was dying. And we have a daughter." Tibor shook his head and wiped his eyes. "She did not sing. After she had the baby. She was busy working. She was poor. And I did not know. And now she is dead."

It was an old story, an ancient one, and yet, for Tibor, Joan could see, it was as delicate and freshly redolent of grief as a blossom in spring.

"My daughter wants to see me now. She was angry before. Why I did not try to find her mother. Why I did not see that there was no news of her. Why I did not try." He shook his head, his eyes wide. "The truth is hard. I forgot her mother. She was not my great love. She was just one girl. I did not think about her. And I must tell my daughter the truth."

Tibor gripped the steering wheel. "I went to give my confession at the church. The priest was not helpful. I went home. I told to myself, I will try to help people. Young people like my daughter. Like her mother was. I will try." He lifted one hand from the steering wheel and made a gesture of—surrender? "I try." At a red light Tibor turned to her and spoke in a low voice. "Thank you for letting me help you."

Joan nodded. She felt there was an alcove inside her, where Tibor had placed a lantern. Where, she wondered, do such thoughts come from?

At the airport, Tibor shook hands with Milan and Adriana and wished them well. They thanked him profusely, grateful for his kindness. Tibor said he would be back, for Joan to wait. She nodded, though she had an inkling this would not be the case. When he saw his daughter, she thought, he would forget. Joan watched his thick back disappear into the crowd.

She sat down beside Adriana and Milan. Adriana had her suitcase and Milan carried a large duffle bag. He looked stiff and nervous in his new clothes, and he kept his sunglasses on the top of his head, lowering them over his eyes once in a while, perhaps when he didn't want anyone to read his expression. Adriana was nervous too, her thin hair framing tired eyes and a faltering smile.

In the distance, Joan noticed a man pulling a large suitcase in one hand and holding the hand of a very small boy, who toddled beside him, with the other. She turned her attention to Milan.

"My Roma friend," she began. He sat up, alert and confused. Joan had never addressed him this way before. "I will not be able to come to Canada with you, but I wanted to make sure I had a wedding gift both for my mother and Adriana's father, and for the two of you."

Milan waved his hand. "Joan. My ticket was your gift."

Adriana, leaning on her elbows over her knees, nodded vigorously in agreement. "Besides, Joan, we can't carry anything else. We already have too much."

"Don't worry then," Joan said. "My gift is quite small and light." She took a long envelope from her bag and gave it to Adriana. She had not sealed it, intending for her two young friends to see it before they presented it to her mother and Adriana's father.

Inside was a string of four postcards with Slovak folk dancers on the front and a diaolou Joan had drawn in the back. This diaolou was similar to the one she had drawn in the Café Eureka, but contained small portraits of her mother and Adriana's dad at the bottom, kissing; Adriana and Milan, their cheeks pressed against one another; Joan and Edna, waving; and at the top, Robbie and Peter, hanging a banner out the window that had the Chinese symbol for double happiness. And instead of a list of fears, it contained the names of the people in their windows, in English, Chinese, Roma, Slovak, and Hungarian. Joan and Edna were also Jana and Orsolia, and Joan's Chinese name, "pure character," was inscribed like graffiti beneath the window they hung out of.

Peter was Pedro and Robbie was Burns. Milan's last name, Holub, was represented by a pigeon flying past. He wore a T-shirt that sported the phrase "I heart Adja," and Adriana wore a T-shirt with the words "Addy and Milan 4ever."

Next to the names of Joan's and Adriana's respective parents, Gillian and David, there was room to inscribe their Chinese names. While drawing, Joan had realized with shame that she did not know her mother's Chinese name, but she'd done her best. In the picture, Mária and her husband and children stood on the grass waving up to the people in the diaolou.

Adriana and Milan looked back to Joan. Milan seemed perplexed, but Adriana, Joan thought, understood. They kissed her on both cheeks and Adriana tucked the envelope into her purse.

Robbie Burns stopped a few feet from the three of them, with Peter, solemn and clutching his latest Lego creation to his chest as he hung on to his father by a finger.

Burns was pale and his hair and beard looked slightly neglected, but his eyes crinkled kindly.

"Hello," he said. Joan nodded. Milan leapt to his feet, his face burning with anger. Burns seemed preoccupied with the floor at his feet.

Milan gazed at Peter, who looked solemnly up at him. Burns bent down and spoke gently to his son, who took a step forward and offered the Lego bird's head to Milan. It was a glorious thing, with feathers of flame. Joan wondered where Peter had seen such a bird. She imagined Miša reading to him from a book of ancient stories, and Peter, filing away in his memory the illustration of a majestic creature, wings spread in fire.

"Peter, this is your uncle Milan," Joan said.

Burns nodded. Joan felt troubled. She had not been thinking properly when she'd asked if Peter could make a Lego sculpture as a wedding gift.

"I'm afraid Milan cannot take this beautiful phoenix to Canada," she apologized to Peter. "Look—he has a big bag already and the Lego will not fit." Joan's heart swooped with disappointment and shame. A phoenix symbolized rebirth out of the eternal fire, life and destruction bound to each other like a mother to her child. It was, Joan thought, a message of hope, one she harboured for her own mother and David's marriage, for Milan and Adriana, for Mária, and indeed for herself. But now it would sit on a shelf gathering dust or be dismantled by Peter's small and restless hands.

Milan, beginning to protest, squatted to Peter's height. Adriana, clearly bewildered, put her hand on his arm. Milan turned to her.

"This is my sister Jana's child," he said. He spoke to Peter quietly in Slovak and in Roma. Adriana, strung tight with anxiety, put her hands over her face.

"You will not need to carry anything more," Burns said. "Joan asked us for this gift and we would carry it to China if necessary," he said, reddening. "But we are going to Canada also, for a holiday."

Milan's eyes opened wide. Joan too was shocked. When she'd telephoned Burns the night before, he hadn't mentioned it.

"Prosím?"

"Hello, Burns. This is Joan."

Hesitation. "Forgive me," Burns said.

Joan was prepared for this. "I forgive you for offering to bribe me to marry you. You were tired and full of grief. In Miša's honour and for Peter's sake, I forgive you."

Burns exhaled. "Thank you," he said. Humbly, miserably, Joan thought. He was, after all, alone now.

"Peter's uncle Milan is travelling to Canada tomorrow."

"Oh—so soon…" There were both torment and relief in his voice.

"Can Peter make something beautiful, a Lego sculpture, for Milan to take with him? It will be a wedding present for Milan to give my mother and the father of Adriana, Milan's girlfriend. But it will also be something to remind Milan of his nephew. Because Milan will live in Canada now." The ask came out of Joan in a hurried stream, confusing, she thought, and ridiculous, but she did not care.

Momentary silence. "Of course," said Robbie. "What time does their plane leave?"

Robbie stood, solid but apologetic, his hand cupped around his son's chin. "It is right that Peter know you," Robbie told Milan. "When you came to me to take him back, I was afraid. After Misa's death, I thought I should take him away, right away. To Scotland." Milan turned pale. "Then Joan told me you were going to Canada. But I knew things were not right. Peter has no brothers and sisters. He has only me. But now he also has you."

Milan knelt in front of Peter, who stepped back toward the only father he'd ever known. Milan, undaunted, and inspired by some strange impulse, dropped to his hands and barked and panted, like a dog. Adriana put her hand over her mouth, beginning to laugh and cry at the same time.

Joan flooded with relief. She bent toward Peter. "Your uncle Milan is really just a friendly puppy," she said. "Dobrý pes."

Joan reached out to pat Milan on the head. Peter looked shy but delighted, and put the phoenix head on the ground in front of Milan. Milan pretended to sniff it and even pushed it with his nose.

"Dobrý vták," he said in a scratchy voice, then pretended to howl. Peter put his fist to his mouth and giggled. Then peals of laughter escaped toward the high ceiling. A few passersby turned to look but kept walking.

Burns smiled with a tinge of sadness. Perhaps he was thinking of all the time and affection he and Miša had invested in their young son, and how his wife would have loved to hear the sound. Joan held out her hand to Burns, a symbol of forgiveness and comfort. She too had never heard Peter laugh like that before. Feelings of happiness and regret for the past and the future cascaded in her like rivulets trickling to the sea. They found paths she did not know were there.

Milan pushed his head under Peter's hand. Peter stroked his black hair, and Milan, puppy-like, panted with his tongue out. Then he got to his feet.

"Now I am not a puppy. I am Uncle Milan," he said in Slovak. He tousled Peter's hair briefly. The little boy gazed at him, his face turned upward in wonder. Of course Peter knew Milan was not a dog, but in the way of children, and indeed all people who hope, he was still able to entertain an opposing belief.

Adriana's cheeks were damp and her eyes were red. She bent toward Peter, offering him a candy from her pocket. He looked up at Burns, who nodded. Joan noticed the candy was wrapped in red foil, like the ones Pani Alica had given Gabriela. It was almost Christmas, after all. Joan had nothing to offer Peter but the amusement of her usual angry faces. Then she remembered the photo in her pocket, the one Pani Alica had scooped off the floor of the Hotel Svatopluk, of Peter as a baby. She wondered if he had ever seen it. She pulled it out and handed it to him.

"It's you," she told him. He looked at it for a moment and took it in his small hand, then gave it to Burns to hold. Burns nodded his thanks, eyes shining.

It was time for the travellers to make their way through security, and time for Joan to say goodbye.

Milan and Adriana stood and gave Joan a hug together, their cheeks pressed to hers. Burns had brought his camera and took a photo of them, and then Joan took a photo of all the travellers together, Peter standing on Burns's shoes, clutching his father's finger in one hand, but glancing up at Milan's face. Then Burns took one of Joan squatting beside Peter, her eyebrows drawn and tongue sticking out while he smiled at the camera. Strangely, when the bulb flashed, Joan felt something catch, as though a part of herself had been suspended in time, like an insect in a drop of sap that would over centuries harden into amber.

The group disappeared though security, Adriana turning one last time to wave at Joan over her shoulder. Then Joan was alone in the bustling airport, surrounded by strangers.

She wandered to the windows before which the planes parked, and gazed out at the huge expanse of runways and field. The day was overcast, but the brightness of the cloud-covered sky dazzled her eyes. They would fly to London and then to Halifax. Her mother and Adriana's father would no doubt greet them. Joan had sent a letter in the envelope with the diaolou for Adriana to give to Gillian. Joan knew her mother's heart would sink with disappointment that Joan was not with them, and that Adriana's father wouldn't know how to comfort her, but that couldn't be helped. She had her own path to follow, one that unfurled across a strange landscape through which she didn't yet know the way.

Joan waited a long time in the airport, but Tibor did not come. She thought his daughter must have arrived and, as she knew would happen, in his happiness, he had forgotten Joan. She didn't care. Hours later, she bought a bus ticket to the centre of town. She would go back to the Hotel Svatopluk, but she would not stay in Elaine Watterson's old room any longer. She would take her bags and she would find a room where she could watch the river. Before she left Bratislava, she needed to make her peace with it. She needed to step out of the river, to shake its water from her like feathers.

Joan sat on the bus and gazed out the window at the city, which had never been hers, or Edna's. A city of strangers, some of whom had found one another and become a family. A container in which to transmute grief-filled and bitter stories into beautiful ones. It struck her that a river always divides something from itself, the way the Milky Way kept two mythical Chinese lovers from one another, even as it unites. The Dunaj connected her to Edna but kept her from herself. She would shake its water like dust from her feet and make her way alone to her grandfather's house, carrying a bag of oranges. She would knock until whoever was inside opened the door and invited her in. And when she left she was determined to go—emptied of stories and empty-handed—ready to receive into her arms whatever life in its boundlessness next thrust toward her.

The fields of dead grass and kilometres of road began to give way to the city itself. Joan closed her eyes and leaned back in her seat, preparing to enter its heart for the last time.

ACKNOWLEDGEMENTS

Many thanks to Leigh Nash of Invisible Publishing for believing in this novel, even in its initial, most troubled and imperfect state; to Stephanie Domet for agreeing to be my editor, which also always means to be my encourager, enforcer, and eraser of anxiety—she has been essential to making this book better; to Paul St. Clair, to whom I was referred by Romani Canadian novelist, linguist and activist Ronald Lee (1934–2020). Paul helped me understand the issues for Roma in Slovakia and newcomer Roma to Canada. Thanks to Magdaléna Sládková and Dominika Sládková Paštéková, who did the first check of the use of Slovak language in my text; to Jen Schwartz, my sensitivity reader for the character of Miša and disability; and to Dr. Petra Gelbart, my sensitivity reader for the Roma characters and context. Petra's help was also critical to correcting the Slovak language in a later draft, adding Romani language where needed, deciding on appropriate Roma character names, and correcting details in many other areas. Thanks to Dr. Cynthia Levine-Rasky, author of *Writing the Roma: Histories, Policies, and Communities in Canada* (Fernwood Publishing, 2016) for her scholarship and for connecting me to Petra. Thanks to Arts Nova Scotia for the Arts Equity grant in 2020 to hire Petra and Jen and to incorporate their invaluable feedback into my manuscript. If, however, there are errors of language or anything else, they are my own.

Also partly funded by a grant from Arts Nova Scotia in 2016, I researched and wrote a good chunk of the first draft of the novel for three months in Toronto. I found Svinia in *Black and White: Slovak Roma and Their Neighbours* by David Z. Scheffel (University of Toronto Press, 2005) at the Toronto Public Library. It provided illuminating background information about the lives of Roma in Eastern Slovakia. Thanks to Jamie Kwan, who rented me her Toronto bungalow's basement cheaply, and to my family in Ontario, especially Aunt Winnie, for keeping me company and feeding me often.

Thanks to the Writers' Federation of Nova Scotia for their advice and support, and for connecting me to Ella Dodson for legal advice on my publishing contract (thanks, Ella!).

Thanks to all those whose lives, joys, suffering, and celebration have inspired this story, its themes, and characters.

A special thanks to the friends I made in Nitra, Slovakia, three decades ago as an English conversation teacher. Because of you, my summer in your country was full of beauty and magic, before almost a decade of mistakes and misery. Though we have lost touch, that year stands out in my life like a ruby on a ring.